ON A WING AND A PRAYER

Ward Tuchman now understood Stallart's admonishment to "stay cold." He felt frightened and very alone, but stored his emotions in a corner of his mind that remained disconnected from his actions. Most of his body moved automatically, executing remembered instruction as his mind feverishly planned ahead. The world seemed to move in slow motion as he shifted slightly.

He didn't have long to wait for the Wing troops. A squad of armored figures bounded into the edge of his augmented sight. The first four positioned themselves in a lazy W formation, moving closer as they flickered from cover to cover at the top of the hill. A fifth, armed with a multiport HE rocket launcher, trailed the others.

Ward grimaced. He hadn't expected a whole squad and he didn't really have the ordnance for a protracted fight. Ward realized at that moment he was truly on his own.

He looked back and cursed. In his zeal for ambush, he'd forgotten to plan a line of retreat. He didn't see so much as a blade of grass behind him for a full ten meters. A large oak beckoned temptingly to him from that distance, but it seemed to be a football field away.

Ward looked back at the Wing troops. The point troop pulled an emissions scanner from an equipment belt and began playing it back and forth over the twelve-o'clock sector. Ward knew that eventually the point guard would aim the box in his direction and he would be well and truly screwed.

BEN OHLANDER

ENEMY OF MY ENEMY

DAVID DRAKE

TERRA NOVA

ENEMY OF MY ENEMY

This is a work of fiction. All the characters and events portrayed in this book are fictional, and any resemblance to real people or incidents is purely coincidental.

A Baen Books Original

Baen Publishing Enterprises
P.O. Box 1403
Riverdale, NY 10471

ISBN: 0-671-87692-9

Cover art by Paul Alexander

First printing, November 1995

Distributed by Simon & Schuster
1230 Avenue of the Americas
New York, NY 10020

Typeset by Windhaven Press, Auburn, NH
Printed in the United States of America

DEDICATED TO

Robert Heinlein,
whose *Starship Troopers*
were there first

and, of course,
to Elizabeth,
for everything.

Chapter 1

Ward Tuchman stepped down off the transport carrier, careful not to let his day bag hit the compressor assemblies on the craft's stubby wings. He used his right hand to shade his eyes from Alpha Centauri A's bright light while he squinted across the dusty landing field for his escort.

"I thought my guards were supposed to meet me here?" he yelled at the driver.

"I dunno, Mr. Tuchman," the retainer called out, trying to be heard over the spinning compressors, "they just told me to go and get you."

"Bastards," Ward said petulantly. "You'd think they'd have the common decency not to keep me waiting." His eyes had adjusted sufficiently for him to move off the landing circle. "I suppose you'd better get back to work. Give me a couple of minutes to get clear."

"Not even a 'thank you'," the retainer grumbled as he closed the hauler's canopy. The plastic opaqued almost immediately as the polarizer damped the hot sun.

Ward grabbed his bag and jogged clear. Even that little bit of effort made him sweat profusely in the late summer heat. The ground-effect vehicle's compressors cycled up, pushing air underneath the stubby wings to create a boundary layer. The car lifted up, turning as it rose before accelerating away.

Ward waited a few minutes, fanning himself and

regretting he hadn't brought sunglasses, until he finally saw a transport tug break from the distant camping grounds and glide towards him. Ward shook his head. "A lousy tractor? How dare they! Where's the damn carriage?" But he started walking towards the vehicle.

He'd closed to within a few dozen meters when he saw the muzzles of automatic flechette guns peeking from beneath piled sacking beside the driver. That set him back. By custom, auto-guns were supposed to remain within the Assembly's bivouac sites. People crowded too close together at the inter-clan gatherings to permit area-of-effect weapons.

"What the hell's with the guns?" Ward yelled as soon as they came within voice range.

The guards looked at each other, then at Ward.

"We're s'posed to take you to Tim," the driver said. "He told us to bring heaters."

His partner nodded once in silent agreement.

Ward climbed up into the bed. The guards seemed tense and alert, far more so than an Assembly usually called for. Some of their tension communicated itself to him. He started to get jittery.

"What's goin' on?" he demanded.

The driver, Emilio, turned his head.

"It's bad, Master Ward," he said. "Your father wanted you down here. Tim'll give you the scoop."

The driver flicked his control yoke, spinning the air-cushioned vehicle and flinging dust over Ward. He sighed and scratched his tousled brown hair. He was grimy enough from the morning's cattle count without adding that.

They rode to the encampment in silence, passing between the tents and plastic temporary shelters that lined the black silicate road. It seemed to Ward that an extraordinary number of sentries patrolled the fringes between the campsites. His own guards appeared to grow more tense as they got into the more crowded areas. The driver reached down and shifted his autogun closer to his feet. The tiny gesture spoke volumes to Ward. Assemblies called for caution and wariness, but this paranoia seemed a bit much.

Ward jumped out of the transport tractor the moment it stopped and headed for his father's headquarters shelter. The temporary building, painted bright Tuchman red, gold, and blue, stood isolated in the middle of the compound. He pulled the door open and saw only spoon-shaped temporary shelter sections stacked on the floor. He looked around in confusion.

"Ward! Over here," a voice called from his left. He turned his head and saw Tim waving to him from another nearby shelter. He walked over to his father's secretary, glancing back and forth in confusion.

"What's goin' on?" he asked. "Where's Dad's stuff?"

"Come inside, I'll tell you," Tim replied.

Ward followed him inside and waited for the door to close.

He saw all of his father's usual setup, the portable computers and communications array, humming quietly in what was supposed to be a supply shelter.

"Is there a reason why this stuff is over here and not in the HQ dome?" he asked.

"Yeah, it's called security," Tim answered.

"Tim, this cloak-and-dagger routine is a lot of fun," Ward said with heavy sarcasm, "but I got packed off to the north forty, remember? I've still got cows to count."

Tim frowned. "You'd have been able to come with us if you hadn't gotten caught screwing off. Again."

Ward opened his mouth to retort. Tim cut him off.

"Save it for another time. We got trouble."

Ward wasn't willing to let it go so easily.

"What, did someone steal some of your precious grain?"

"No," Tim replied coldly, "two of our people got thrashed by a gang of Wing retainers."

Ward sobered. "What happened?"

Tim scanned a printout on the camp desk. "Erlich and Corinne were down on Vendors' Row. Wing called them out. Erlich tried to back down, but Corinne wouldn't have it."

Ward shook his head. "She's tough."

"She *was* tough," Tim corrected. "She's in the dispensary now. Got some of her teeth kicked in. Erlich's better, but he's going to look like a raccoon for a while."

"What was Wing's excuse?" Ward asked.

Tim shrugged. "Corinne's story is garbled. She says they didn't do anything and were set upon without provocation."

Ward looked skeptical. "I'm young, but not stupid. *Nobody* is that innocent."

Tim scratched his jaw. "She said that after she was down and they started kicking her, the leader kept repeating 'This is for the *Conveyor*'."

"Wing's missing starship?" Ward asked. "That was lost six weeks ago. What took them so long?"

"Beats me," Tim answered, "but it appears from what happened to Corinne that we are going to be blamed."

Ward glanced out of the temporary shelter's open door and up at the cloudless, too-blue sky. "I don't get it."

"It gets better," Tim continued. "They've called a dozen of our people out already. The dueling grounds have already been used, and it isn't even the third day yet."

Ward rubbed his forehead. "Well, there are always dust-ups here at Assembly," he said. "You watch your back, stay in the public areas, and keep your eyes open." He let a bit of ire show through. "I just got carted in by two grunts with the most ostentatiously hidden weapons I've ever seen. That seems a bit much given that we've had two people, and only two, get whipped."

Tim looked defensive. "I thought a discreet show of force would ensure your protection."

Ward made a rude noise. "There was nothing discreet about that. They did everything except hang a damn flag on the side of the wagon."

"Spare me the sarcasm, will you?" Tim replied. "The tension down in the Fair is thick enough to be sliced and served on toast. Hell, we've had more fights in two days than we did all last year."

Ward contemplated his chewed fingernails. "Well, that seems a little unusual, but I don't think that justifies the siege mentality. What's Dad think?"

"He's playing it as business as usual," Tim answered dryly.

"I take it you don't approve," Ward said.

"I think Wing really got its nose pulled out of joint this time. They've been bitchin' and stormin' to anyone who'll give 'em the time of day. Your dad's worried, but doesn't want to piss off the Council by starting something here."

Ward looked disgusted. "So you sent the thug brothers to bring me in, carrying flechette guns. What were you thinking?"

Tim shrugged. "Not my department. I just do paperwork."

"Nice cop-out," Ward replied. He could tell Tim wasn't the least bit happy about being called on the carpet.

Tim looked down at the thick stacks of printouts perched precariously on the camp desk. "Did you bring the cattle projections?"

"Nice subject change," Ward answered. "I left them behind when I got the word to come here. Doing a census on cattle is sooo much fun." He looked exasperated. "I'd like to know how Dad gets out of filling out forms."

Tim sat on the camp stool behind the desk. "Your dad is the Clan Chief. You are a Clan Chief wannabe. There is a vast gulf between the two."

"So I've been told. What is it I'm supposed to do here?"

Tim tapped his watch. "Your father wants you to join him at the Clan Assembly at one o'clock. He wants you to observe crisis management in action."

"Great," Ward said, "that gives me about an hour to see the Fair."

"I don't think that's a very good idea," Tim answered. "It's not safe right now. It would be better for you to stay here and help me with these papers." He tapped the thick stack meaningfully.

Ward leaned against the door and sighed. "Can't we put this off?" He looked back at the secretary, trying to draw him towards the shelter's open door and the summer day beyond.

Tim picked a sheaf of printouts up from the pile. "These are the crop projections for the coming harvest. They, together with the livestock census you conveniently forgot to bring, are what Benno is going to base next year's provisions on. Your father needs them before Assembly ends to arrange next year's contracts."

Ward looked bored.

"Look," Tim said, the slightest irritation in his voice, "your father's been on my case about having you learn this. Taking heat from Benno is no fun."

"Tell me about it," Ward replied dryly.

Tim tried again. "Your father's worried the Wings're going to storm off and abandon the Assembly *before* he makes his corn deals. So we do a week's work today so he can get that done before we go back to LaPort."

"Is the situation that serious?" Ward asked.

"Haven't you been listening?" Tim answered, exasperated. "Your dad's even had Alma and Stallart draw up an emergency evac plan in case it all falls apart here and we have to bug out." He looked across at Ward.

"I'm going to check out the situation for myself," Ward replied, squaring his shoulders.

"That would be a bad idea," Tim argued.

Ward turned to gather his possessions. "You guys are always telling me not to take things on faith. I'm going to walk around the Fair a bit and check things out." He winked at Tim. "You know, shop the competition."

Tim realized he fought for a lost cause. "Remember, this is New Hope, not Earth," he chided as Ward took a laser from beside the pile and buckled it on. "Wear your sun-jacket and watch out for Wing."

"Thanks, mom," Ward said.

Tim didn't look impressed. "Hardly," he said as Ward walked out. He frowned and turned his attention back to the rows of numbers and yield estimates. "Lazy bastard just wants to go play," he muttered.

Ward breathed a sigh of relief as soon as he stepped outside, picking up the scents of a warm summer. "Too damn hot to stay in that plastic bubble," he murmured to himself.

He glanced around the hilltop camp, attempting to judge the tenor of the day for himself. Everything seemed in order. The temporary shelters had been neatly arranged in family clusters circling the Clan Chief's own camp dwellings. Pallets for the spoon-shaped shelter sections lay stacked nearby. The chief of the Tuchmans prized an orderly camp, even though he tended to be sloppy in his own habits.

Ward crossed the center of the camp, passing beneath the belt of Terran pines that provided comfort and shade for the clan. Local muta-forms clustered around the base of the pines. A few tendrils groped upward like ivy as the local flora modified its genetic structure to exploit the climbing opportunity.

Ward didn't understand the finer details of New Hope botany. He'd been told that Benno's pet scientists had discovered that local plants retained obsolete snippets of DNA and simply readapted them as circumstances changed. They'd proven so successful at modifying themselves to survive that they had no impetus to evolve into higher life forms. Genetic samples of the entire range of New Hope's flora showed a variation of less than one-hundredth of one percent. Ward had heard it said that by Earth standards, almost all the local plants were genetically the same species, even though the physical forms assumed myriad variations.

He used to think that the local muta-forms didn't have a prayer against the Terran imports. He'd since realized that the locals' flexibility made them almost indestructible. Poison them, stomp them, burn them for two generations, and the offspring would be tough, stomp-proof, and fire resistant. It made Terran kudzu look tame.

"I wonder what the human equivalent would be," he mused. "The ultimate survivor." The idea made him maudlin. He shook his head as he turned away from the hill crest and towards the fun of the Fair.

He smiled and nodded to many of the clanspeople he passed on his way to the vending booths. Most folks seemed to be in a hurry, either to get down to the kiosks and entertainers or to place shopping bags inside shelters before scurrying back. Life in LaPort, Clan Tuchman's seat, usually remained slow and staid. The clan's awakening from torpor at Assembly time never failed to amuse him.

Many of the clanspeople he waved to called him by name. Singers and dancers performed to musicians' songs, while other buskers in Tuchman red-blue-gold tuned their instruments or performed street magic. A smith traded lies and lines with a client while etching the plastic and aluminum stock of an expensive laser hunting rifle, Children played in the narrow dirt streets of the camps while their caretakers laughed and soaked up the sun. Ward smiled. Everything seemed as it should be, a fact Ward would report to his father.

He turned towards the Fair itself and passed alongside

the air-cushioned ground skimmers and ground-effect flyers that made up the bulk of New Hope's commercial transport. He came around the side of the wagon park and frowned as he saw the thug brothers standing by the doors to the portable stables. One stood smoking and offering helpful advice while the other pulled and tugged at his gun's jammed bolt. Ward shook his head in exasperation and walked quickly over to them.

"Emilio, Mort! Do you guys *have* to stand out in the open with those things?" he said as he pointed to the auto-guns.

"Damn thing's stuck," Emilio informed him. "The plastic pipe we're using to make shell casings keeps sticking between the loading gate and the ejection port."

The second guard gave the bolt a savage tug.

"These new ten-millimeter jobs are shit," Mort said. "I want my old twelve-gauge back."

Ward didn't care for the criticism.

"If the supply of number twelve pipe hadn't dried up, you'd still have it," Ward answered. "What we do have is mounds of ten mil cluttering up the place."

"At least there ain't no shortage of flechettes," the first guard offered.

"That's 'cause there ain't nothing cheaper than converting a nail stamping press," the second retorted sourly. "Benno's nuthin' if not cheap."

Ward made a face. "Are you going to do something about the weapon, or stand out here and bitch all day?"

Mort made a face, then set the gun down butt first. He put the toe of his boot on the bolt and used his weight to force the action.

The left-hand barrel slid back with a *Cha-chack* and a white plastic shell tumbled out of the ejection port. The right-hand barrel slid forward, its muzzle shroud peeking from the end of the barrel housing

"That was damn stupid!" Ward snapped. "The rocker arm won't take that kind of abuse."

"Naw," Emilo said, "pointing the gun at 'is face was dumb." He grinned and flicked the smoking butt into the grass. "Not that he could do much damage."

Mort grimaced at his partner. "Damn plastic guns," he grumbled. "Next thing you know we'll be making the barrels out of PVC pipe, too."

"Yeah," Emilio said, "I've seen the workshop where they turn these out. They don't call 'em *Tuch Specials* for nothin'."

"Look, the tube's clear," Ward snapped, "will you get those things out of sight?"

Emilio sketched a salute. "Who-oo, the cub's growing teeth," he said. "We'd better do as he says."

The guards turned away. Ward took that for victory and turned to continue towards the fair.

He clearly heard one of the guards say "spoiled brat" in a quiet, carrying voice. He considered ragging them out for disrespect, but couldn't figure out how to do it without seeming to be an asshole. He chose to pretend he hadn't heard and stumped away.

He headed for the Assembly in the shallow valley below. He whistled as he walked through the playing fields and porta-privies towards the road spur that connected the Tuchman encampment with the Fair portion of the Assembly. His boots crunched in the black silicate as he walked. Ward remembered working on the road, built by his father to cut down on erosion from the hilltop. It had been one his first "real" jobs—his official coming of age—when he'd been assigned the resources and the task of building the spur. It didn't seem like much now, but three years ago it had been a significant moment in his life. He saw a familiar face in the crowd at the Fair's edge, a young man trying unsuccessfully to blow on a penny whistle.

"Hey meester," Ward called out, "how much for your seester?"

Lupe Vargas whipped his head around and grinned.

"*Una precia buena,*" he retorted in an accent that was as faked as it was thick. "Very good price. She virgin, just like her mother."

Ward laughed. They traded hugs and back slaps.

"How've you been?" Ward asked, grinning at his friend.

Lupe shrugged and managed to produce a blatting sound from his whistle. "So, so," he replied, "I'm takin' the agribusiness courses Dad needs from the virtual university. He's tryin' to buy out that old Gibson place. It's eleven hundred hectares. Good land, but the claim is cloudy. You know how it goes."

Ward agreed with a shake of his head. "There've been so many fights and vendettas that it's almost impossible to sort out a deed. How'd that little fracas with Hsu go over that piece of ground over by Complein?"

"I wanted to thank you for speaking to your dad about that," Lupe replied. "You and I went to school together, but that don't cut no ice with most folks. You big clans don't usually help someone who ain't beholden." He shrugged. "Benno was cool about it. He backed my dad's play without any strings." Lupe smiled. "Big, bad Tuch lined up behind itty-bitty Vargas made the Hsu boys and girls negotiate. We worked out a deal."

"Speaking of deals," Ward said, "what do you know about this thing between us and Wing?"

Lupe refused to let his mood be affected by Ward's switch to politics. "Well, I heard it started out as a pushy-pushy thing," Lupe said. "You know, when somebody wants to piss on somebody else's turf without irritating the Council."

Ward nodded.

"Anyway," Lupe continued, "your girl stayed inside the lines. Wing wasn't having any of it. They jumped her. I heard she's a cripple."

"Naw," Ward replied, " she just lost some teeth and pride. Dad may have to sit on her a while. If I were her,

I'd see a Law-Speaker and get a ruling about invoking the sections of the *code duello* relevant to disfiguring injury. I'd then call every one of the sonzabitches out, Assembly or no."

Lupe quietly agreed.

Ward looked around him, sizing up the atmosphere of the Fair. "Do you think it's tense down here?" he asked.

Lupe gave him a puzzled look. "No more so than usual." He paused. "Why do you ask?"

"Well," Ward said, "when I got here, everybody told me to stay out of the Fairgrounds. Too dangerous."

Lupe grinned. "Only for virgins."

Ward laughed. "I hope this doesn't screw up the Assembly."

"Well," Lupe answered cheerfully, "I don't know about that. We're only a single vote, so we don't count for much. Dad thinks that the Wing-Tuch rivalry is the best thing to happen to West Hills."

"How's that?" Ward asked.

"Simple," Lupe replied. "Mi padre thinks that everything is fine as long as you two never agree on anything." He punched Ward's shoulder before shadow-boxing in front of him. Ward put his fists up and mimed ducking and weaving. "I'd sure hate to see you guys lose your pathological rivalry."

"Thanks," Ward answered dryly.

"Speaking of rivalries," Lupe continued, "I hear Goldman is crowding your turf."

"Yeah," Ward answered, "trying to recover their place in the sun, I guess."

"I knew Goldman used to be *the* player hereabouts," Lupe said.

He and Ward stepped out of the way for a pushcart carrying goods to roll past them and up the spur towards the Tuchman camp. Ward used the break to walk forward. Lupe paced him while Ward warmed to his tale.

Ward stretched his shoulders. "Well, you know we took their Clansite last summer?"

"I heard about it third-hand," Lupe answered. "I was up dipping sheep and missed Assembly. How'd you get it from them, anyway?"

"Well," Ward said, rubbing his hands together, "me and some of dad's retainers slipped out one night and moved our boundary flags about twenty meters into Goldman turf. We had a great time sneaking around in the dark, moving border markers. I thought we were gonna start laughing and blow the whole thing!"

"Where were the Goldman guards?" Lupe said, laughing with his friend as they walked between the colorful, close-packed stalls.

"I haven't a clue," Ward answered. "Anyway, the next morning we'd faked outrage at the Goldies for movin' *our* flags, I stood there, my foot covering one of our old post holes, screaming at them for their duplicity."

Ward held his side as he tried to control his laughter. "Dad thought the whole thing was a riot. He called out the *whole damn Goldman clan*. Challenged 'em to a pitched battle, right then and there. His tongue was stuck so far in his cheek that it looked like he was chewing tobacco. I've never seen him trying so hard not to laugh."

Lupe grinned. "What'd they do?"

Ward shrugged his shoulders. "What could they do? The Council intervened, as expected, to keep the thing from turning into a Clan fight. We pretended to let them talk us into a ritual battle to settle the issue of whose honor had been violated. It was a sort of a 'king of the hill' fought in powered battle armor. Dad made the campsite the price of victory if we won."

Ward's cheerful mood evaporated. "You know the rest."

"Yeah," Lupe replied, "I was at Andrea's funeral. Was an airfoil in your retainer's face worth the campsite?"

Ward kicked at the dirt. "I don't know," he replied

honestly. "I asked my dad that. He told me: 'It is if you're Clan Tuchman'."

"Damn," Lupe replied, "that's cold. No wonder so many of the small fry are banding together. Goldman's been up to see my dad several times about organizing."

"I didn't know that," Ward answered.

"Yeah," Lupe affirmed, "th' Goldies put most of the indemnity your dad paid for Henno's broken back into the continental treasury to advance unification."

"Bastards," Ward said. "That money should have gone to his family; that's what the code says."

"Chaim Goldman's got some funny ideas about what's right," Lupe said. "Hell, I heard he even leaves flowers at Andrea's grave!"

"Yeah, I heard that too," Ward said tiredly, "and he came to the funeral and he offered to sponsor two orphans, and blah blah blah. All hail Saint Chaim."

Lupe looked upset. "He really does feel badly about it. He knows his people didn't check their suits. That combat ring-penetrator never should have been there."

"What are you, his cheering section?" Ward snapped.

"No," Lupe answered, affronted, "it just isn't as simple as you make it out."

"She wasn't your clan!" Ward snapped.

"That's true," Lupe admitted, "and she was barely one of yours. I'll bet you can't even tell me who her brother is."

Ward furrowed his brow. "Evan," he said firmly.

"Wrong," Lupe answered. "She had two sisters. I made passes at them both."

"What's your point?" Ward demanded.

"You barely knew her," Lupe pointed his finger at Ward to drive the point home, "so don't you think this big outrage scene is just a bit overdone?"

Ward realized he'd been boxed. "Damn you." He laughed.

"Yeah," Lupe said, for the moment Clan Vargas rather

than friend, "well, that little spat over pecking order nearly derailed the West Hills Assembly. You guys are the ones to blame for the Marshals watchin' over all of us." He grinned at Ward again. "You can't possibly mind if they keep a special eye on Clan Tuchman."

Ward smiled at the jab, letting Lupe lure him back into a good mood.

Lupe faked a punch. "Us small fry depend on the Assembly far too much to let you big fish screw it up, you know."

"Oh, how's that?" Ward answered.

"Well, in addition to the trade and public meetings . . ." Lupe's voice trailed away.

Ward glanced over at his friend and saw him openly staring at a woman who sashayed past them. She wore no bra, leaving her ample breasts to move freely as she walked. Lupe said something in Spanish.

"What the hell was that?" Ward asked as Lupe resumed his walk.

"That," Lupe replied, as though explaining the secret of the universe, "was a hooker."

"I figured that," Ward answered in exasperated tones. "What'd you say?"

"That, my friend, was a *piropo*." He laughed at Ward's blank stare. "It's a Latin tradition. They're fairly explicit remarks about a woman's, umm, assets. Usually borders on the obscene. Latinas expect it."

He shrugged his shoulders in the manner of a man performing an unpleasant public trust.

Ward wasn't buying it. "What about your sister? What would you do if someone said something like that to her?"

"I'd call 'em out," Lupe answered at once.

Ward pounced. "You just said Latin women expect it."

"Rosa isn't a woman, amigo," Lupe huffed, "she's my sister. That's different."

Ward didn't see the distinction, but let it go. "Anyway,"

he said as they walked on, "you were telling me what the benefits of the Assemblies are to the smaller clans."

"Sure," Lupe said, still looking over his shoulder at the departing prostitute. "How many other chances do we get to exchange genetic material with people outside our own clans? Cross-pollinatin' by itself is far too important to risk havin' the Assembly get torpedoed by nit-shit games."

Ward laughed. He noticed their seemingly aimless wander appeared to have acquired a sense of direction. "Where are we going?"

"Well, if you don't mind," Lupe answered, "I'm supposed to see a gun dealer to pick out a laser for my dad. Wanna go?"

Ward looked at his watch. "Do you know anything about lasers?"

"Yeah," Lupe replied, "the killin' stuff comes out the pointy end."

Ward sighed dramatically. "Okay, I'll tag along. I got about a half-hour."

Lupe grinned. "Got a date?"

"Nope," Ward replied, "I'm supposed to join my dad in the Assembly bowl around one o'clock."

Lupe lengthened his pace. Ward followed him to the area where small-time weapons dealers worked their trade, and waited while Lupe looked over the stock.

Lupe handed him a laser. "What do you think?"

"Looks pretty good," Ward said. "The focusing element can't be warped more than thirty degrees, the ruby is only in three pieces, and there's no pesky argon gas to align the beam." He turned the weapon over and used a stylus to open the battery well in the hand grip. "Just as I thought," he said, showing the corroded tube to Lupe. "There's been so much leakage from the power cell that the contacts have been etched. You won't get solid contact, even if you could get the gunk cleaned off the prongs." He handed it back. "I'll bet it shoots around corners really good. Unless it blows up in your hand."

"How do you know so much about these?" Lupe asked.

Ward shrugged. "I got grounded for joy-riding a ground-effect car last winter. Dad put me to work converting hand lasers into suit models. I learned a little about them."

Lupe made a face and dropped the gun back on the pile. "Okay, then, Einstein, you find me one."

Ward half-bowed, then looked at the pile of surplus weapons. Most were covered with a thin gray dust. He wiped his finger across one and turned towards the vendor. "You really aren't selling them like this, are you?" he asked, holding his finger up so the man could see it.

The dealer didn't look impressed. "That dirt is direct from Io. All these Mark III's came from the mining station there. They're registered for both excavation and self-defense."

"I see," said Ward. "Do you have any in usable condition?"

The weapons dealer waved his hand over the bin. "Search for yourself. Each pistol and battery pack is guaranteed to work as well as it does."

Ward and Lupe scrounged in the box for a bit, sneezing as they searched. They eventually collected three that seemed better than the rest.

"Which one should I get?" Lupe asked him as they laid them out.

"All of 'em," Ward answered.

Lupe held up a protesting hand. "Look, if I could afford three, I could afford an Execuline and skip this crap."

"You miss my point," Ward answered. "We'll break all three down and take the best from each. Ham-fisted as asteroid miners are, they can't have broken *every* piece."

He expertly tore down the first weapon, field-stripping it on the vendor's table. The man didn't seem amused, but didn't protest as he began handing parts to Lupe. "It's too bad you can't just get an Execuline," he said. "You only get three shots, but they are a lot lighter to carry. The pieces aren't overbuilt." He took a deep breath. "I could loan—"

Lupe cut him off with a raised hand. "Look, we may not be Tuchman or Dickerson, but we aren't charity cases, either."

Ward looked hurt.

Lupe tried to soften his rejection. "Besides, I *like* big, bulky guns. They're manly."

Ward let himself be mollified as he reassembled the composite weapon. "None of the painting lasers work on these. You can get another one cheap when you have this one tuned. I'd buy a new powercell if I were you. I'm sure these have all been recharged to death."

"Batteries," Lupe mused, "who'd have thought? I thought magic smoke made the boom-boom light come out the end."

Ward grimaced as he checked his watch. "Asshole. I think I'm going to have to go. I've got just enough time to get some lunch before I meet my dad." He looked martyred. "Another dreary Assembly. Damn, I hate them. I make it a point to arrive not one second early."

"Me, too," Lupe answered, "but I'm off the hook this time."

They exchanged a knowing look.

"Are you going to be around later?" Ward asked.

"Yeah," Lupe answered, "I'll leave a message with your sentries."

Ward walked away, leaving Lupe to argue out the details of the transaction with the arms dealer. He knew his friend wouldn't haggle and would willingly pay a ruinous price for the gun if Ward stood there. Lupe's pride would suffer a depleted credit chip before it would suffer Ward thinking him poor. Ward understood that Lupe's clan was neither destitute nor wealthy, but

Lupe judged his worth only in comparison to those who had more. Ward, born into a wealthy family, accepted money as a fact of life. He didn't know what he would do if the river of credit ever dried up.

His thoughts flitted from subject to subject as he stepped back into the Fair's main traffic flow. He lengthened his stride, trying to see as much as he could in his too brief free time. He liked Assemblies and their cheerful assault on the senses. The bright colors the West Hills clans displayed on their kiosks clashed with the equally bright colors worn by browsing clanpeople. Most of the clans weren't as self-sufficient as Tuchman and needed to buy outside. The fairs were one of the few sanctioned opportunities for folks to buy outside their own clan. Prices were usually a bit inflated, but that didn't stop lookers. Or buyers. The most expensive luxury items were those made on Terra. But there were buyers for them, too.

Ward paused by several fruit and vegetable stands, looking for a light lunch to fit his mood. He continued past an open-air bakery, the sharp smells of cinnamon and honeytree sap masking the earthy odors of the fair. His stomach growled a bit as he thought about biting into a buttery, spiced roll. He considered it, then shook his head. His last two meals had been bakers' products, and such things were noticed. The son of the Clan Chief had to maintain impartiality, even in his menu choices.

"No bread for lunch," he said to himself, "lest I slight the truck farmers."

He paused at a Tuchman booth, easily identifiable by the small red, blue, and gold boxes that held the produce selection. He sorted amongst the lettuce, squash, and local leafears offered. He hefted one head of lettuce, turned it over and examined the stalk for bugs or color enhancers. He saw none. It was good, fresh produce. Tuchman produce.

"May I help you?" came a voice over his shoulder.

Ward turned to face the stand's proprietor, a short, weatherbeaten-looking fellow in farmer's coveralls. Ward hefted the lettuce. The proprietor's face split into a lop-sided smile.

"Oh, Master Ward, I didn't see it was you. Shall I put that on your father's account?"

"Um, huh," Ward replied, already distracted by other sights. He walked a little further, nibbling the succulent lettuce leaves directly off the head.

He heard the sound of jump thrusters firing in the middle distance, beyond the tents that sprouted along the edge of the vending areas. Intrigued, he walked towards the noise. A linking machine clattered as it reloaded coil gun magazines, stacking the rings with their ferrous sabots in the magazine tubes. The *thuff! thuff!* of jump thrusters firing in short cycles to purge air from the fuel systems beat in time with his heart. The sounds of pending combat stirred his blood and drew him towards the field as a lodestone draws iron.

He passed through the last line of tents and saw a shallow depression about a hundred meters square. It had been chalked off into a quarter-sized dueling field. A smattering of people sat on the slope's edge and watched the combatants below. Ward walked up and sat beside a man his own age in Dawkins green. He appeared to be taking notes.

The Dawkins looked at Ward as he sat.

"Ho, Tuch!" the man said, greeting him formally.

Ward knew the courtesy wasn't really necessary, but he fed it back anyway.

"Ho, Dawkins!" he answered. They shook hands, completing the ritual.

"Why so serious?" Ward asked him. "We used to be allies, once upon a time."

"Clan policy is to step light around you and Wing," the man answered with a grunt, "so I step light."

"I see," answered Ward, who really didn't. "What are you doing down here?"

The Dawkins man held up his pad. "I got a cousin who's doin' her first fight tomorrow. I came down to see what her opponent might look like. Doesn't look like it's going to happen, though."

Ward looked down at the depression. "This is new."

"Yeah," the Dawkins man answered, "all the fill dirt for the Assembly bowl came out of here. Somebody decided to make it into a dueling ground."

"The fighting area can't be more than a hundred meters a side," Ward scoffed. "That's pretty small."

"Its almost ridiculous," the man confirmed with a tiny sneer, "but it's large enough for the quick and dirties."

"Damn, this is like pistols across a table," Ward said. "Who uses it?"

"Chumps, mostly," the man shrugged, "or greenhorns. Weak clans, with borrowed armor or lame gear." He pointed with his chin. "This one's a judicial fight. Something about a contract dispute or some similar grievance. It's several months old. I didn't hear the details." He looked back at the field and turned a page in his notebook. "We use it because deaths are rare here, mostly the result of stupidity and incompetence, rather than malice." He smiled. "Most of the disputes get settled quickly, without much shooting. The place is so small they often look more like schoolyard scuffles in armor than duels." He made a sweeping gesture. "This here's Dogpatch. It's a good place to get some experience before going up *there*, to Madison Square Garden." He pointed to the Assembly area's main dueling ground, the standard four-hundred-meter square.

Ward glanced at Dawkins. The man shaded his eyes with one hand while making notes with the other. It occurred to Ward that sitting up on the rise watching the newbies stumble through their paces would be a good way to kill time while eating his lunch.

Dawkins drew his attention to one small crew desperately trying to ready their principal's partially armored suit. The arms and legs were visibly too big for the tiny woman who paced along the edge of the field in her underwear. "Think they borrowed her suit?" Dawkins asked.

Ward looked at the naked exoskeleton, unprotected by any vestige of appliqué work. "Probably," he answered, "otherwise she wouldn't look so half-assed."

"Bare-assed is more like it," the Dawkins retorted. "At least she knows to strip before she armors up."

"She's braver than me," Ward said. "You can get a nasty burn in one of those. I wouldn't get into one without a layer of clothing." The Dawkins raised his eyebrows. "Look," Ward said, "I'd rather get the twitchies from having my sleeves brush the contact sensors than from a live current. Those old hard metal suits were *notorious* for electrocuting asteroid grubbers."

The Dawkins looked skeptical. "The shock hazard is overrated. It's usually the result of bonehead maintenance. Still, if it's a problem for you, why not just wear one of those new Terran bodysuits?"

Ward whistled. "Have you seen what one of those costs?"

The Dawkins man shrugged. "They are nonconducting."

They watched the service crew and made quiet jokes while the techs removed the arms and legs from the core of the suit. One ran a diagnostic computer linked to the air filtration system, the jump pack, and the batteries.

Dawkins made another note. "That should all have been done before they got here," he said disapprovingly.

Ward started to laugh quietly.

"What's funny?" Dawkins asked.

Ward only pointed with his finger.

The other two members of the girl's maintenance crew

used an unlinking tool to remove segmented rings from one arm. The rings, each about five millimeters wide, contained sensors, insulation, and armor and could be added or removed to accommodate the length of the wearer's arms, legs, and waist. It looked like an exploded goosenecked lamp.

Dawkins peered through his hand glasses. "I just hope they get the bars adjusted correctly. I don't see any calibrating equipment, and that girl's going to have a broken leg if exosupport slips. The rings won't hold her weight by themselves."

"I didn't know that," Ward replied. "It's not something I ever had to deal with."

"Yeah?" the man answered. "What do you use?"

"Higgins custom," Ward answered, "Mark IV."

"Oh, rich boy, huh?" the man replied without heat. "Well, the rest of us get by on partial personal body armor like that." He chewed his lip a moment. "We used to be allies once, so I'll tell you a secret. The bars on that kind of PBA are just like bones. You break 'em, especially the legs, and down your opponent comes."

One of the maintenance techs kicked the suit's coil gun as it leaned against a tree. The weapon slowly fell to one side and lay pointed at the crew. Ward shook his head and pointed. Dawkins nodded silently and exhaled. "Check me if I'm wrong, but is that coiler loaded?"

Dawkins peered at the weapon. "It sure is," he replied, "damn fools. It looks like they took the gun off the suit with a magazine still in it."

"I wish I had a camera," Ward mused. "This is a textbook case of what not to do."

He looked at Dawkins. "What color is the magazine?"

Dawkins zoomed the binocs. "Blue. Training rounds."

Ward relaxed a little. "Well, that's something anyway. I wouldn't be here if they were using green tabs."

Dawkins whistled. "Yeah. Can you imagine what kind

of damage they'd do if they were spraying combat loads around here?"

Ward laughed. "Maybe they're just exceptionally stupid. "I can't watch this anymore," he said. "Three-hundred seven-millimeter airfoils pointed right at them and they haven't a clue. All they need now is a live capacitor and a little bad luck."

Dawkins chuckled. "That's bad juju, depending on luck that way."

One of the techs casually picked the weapon up by the barrel's truncated metal coil and leaned it back against the tree. Ward and the Dawkins exchanged horrified glances.

The maintenance crew had shortened the woman's limbs to the right length and had adjusted her suit struts for her height. They hurriedly checked safety equipment, placing a blue occlusion shield over the lethal lasers, allowing only the target designator to fire.

"I guess it's a friendly fight," Ward said.

Dawkins made more notes. "They're taking some precautions, at least. Good. My fight tomorrow is staged to give Tina some experience. I wanted to make sure they'll be careful before I let her go in. I'll insist on a test fire before the fight, I think. God only knows what'll be in the repulsion coil otherwise."

Ward thought back to the dead Andrea. He nodded in sober agreement. "Are we gonna need to move back?" he asked. "I've heard stories about stray rounds, even plastic ones, taking out bystanders."

Dawkins grinned and got to his feet.

"Want some rabbit food?" Ward asked as he held out the badly depleted head of lettuce.

"Thanks," Dawkins said as he tore away several leaves.

They stood together and munched as the participants went through their final preparations. Ward's wrist alarm chimed just as they began to squat and stretch, testing their contact sensors and control software.

"Damn," he swore quietly, "I have to go."

"Too bad," Dawkins replied, "you're gonna miss the fun."

"Tell me about it," Ward answered with a grimace. "Great comic relief."

He raised his hand in farewell. "Just Day to you, Dawkins."

Dawkins returned the pleasantry as Ward gathered his things. "Just Day, Tuch."

Ward left for the Assembly at a fast walk. He had passed through two lines of storage tents and stepped across the ropes of a third when a hand snaked out of a hanging door and jerked him inside a storage dome. He frantically groped for his laser. A set of warm, soft lips pressed against his before a demanding tongue pushed against his teeth.

"Seladra," he said sometime later as they came up for air. His heart was still pounding and he was a bit out of breath from the deep kiss. "Seladra, that was stupid! I thought you were an enemy. I could've killed you."

"You could have tried, anyway," she replied impishly. "Anyway, you're Tuchman, I'm Wing, we're supposed to fight. Don'tcha remember your clan history?"

"Yeah, yeah," he replied. "I know. Me Capulet. You Montague."

She furrowed her brow. "Actually," she replied, "I think that's supposed to be the other way around, but I missed the Stallone retrospective."

He responded by pulling her close. She squirmed against him, faking resistance a moment before she settled in. He felt her lithe figure beneath her bodysuit as she pressed against him. "Look," he said, "I can't stay. I'm supposed to be at Assembly this afternoon. My dad thinks there's going to be a vote. I need to be there for it."

"Nothing's going to happen," she said. "This is going to be our only chance together . . . while everyone else is down at the Assembly arguin'." She slithered one hand between them and began to unbuckle his gun belt. "Bet I can think of something better than fightin'," she whispered archly.

"What if someone comes?" he asked with a glance at the thin cloth.

She lifted an eyebrow before she noticed he was serious. "Then we get caught," she replied matter-of-factly. She leaned back in his arms so he could see the swell of her small breasts. "My father cries 'rape,' yours cries 'entrapment,' and we all troop off to the dueling ground to settle it in blood."

She abruptly bent forward to nip his throat, just hard enough to hurt a little and leave a mark.

Ward winced.

"Cross-clan sex isn't a big deal most of the time, you know," she continued, "and is even encouraged somewhat amongst the retainers."

He grinned impishly, recalling Lupe's words. "I'm told it keeps the gene pool from getting stale. But that doesn't apply to us." He tried to pull away. She held him tighter. "Each of us is too important to our families," he said unhappily. "There's too much bad blood for either family to overlook a scandal."

She nodded soberly, then nipped at his neck again.

They both knew their families would have to save face if they were caught together. It bothered Ward a little, but only a little, that someone might possibly die. A friendly duel under those circumstances would be almost impossible. It bothered him even less when his gun belt fell to the straw and Seladra Wing's questing fingers went to work on his fly.

"I wouldn't worry about getting busted in here," she said sometime later as she pulled him to the straw-covered ground. "I know the owner."

He looked at his watch. "Okay," he said grinning, "Twenty minutes. Or so."

An hour later Ward stared at his reflection in Seladra's small signaling mirror. He looked a fright with his flushed face and mussed hair. Seladra still lazed on the cargo blanket they'd put down to protect them from the scratchy hay. She stretched, catlike, her small, high breasts jutting forward.

"Sure I can't talk you into another?" she asked.

Ward looked at her, tempted.

"Sorry," he said. "I've got to get to the gathering. I'm already late."

She faked a pout. "Just like a man. Eats and runs."

He smiled and turned back to the mirror, trying to fix his hair. He didn't want to wander in looking dishevelled, but the best he could do with his hair was comb it with his fingers. Blue eyes, just a little accusing, stared at him from the mirror. She caught him staring at himself. "You've got your father's good looks," she said as she rolled onto her stomach.

"Yeah? Thanks." Ward answered. "I never thought so."

She arched her back. Ward heard vertebrae pop and winced. "You and your dad are a lot alike," she said as she finished her stretch.

Ward looked at himself again. "Naw. We're opposites. He *likes* to work. I'm much more quiet and withdrawn."

"Quiet and withdrawn, huh?" Seladra said with a laugh. "The guy who seduced me sure as hell wasn't quiet or withdrawn."

Ward turned to face her, incredulity on his face. "Hey, hey, *hey*. For the record, missy, you seduced *me*!"

She got up on her knees and grabbed his belt. "Come here, boy. I'll show you seduction."

Benno Tuchman looked at his watch and scanned the front rank of his clan's seated contingent, looking for his son. "Damn it," he grumbled to himself, "he's late. Again." That small irritation joined the great big one caused by the man standing across the meadow to give him a pounding headache.

Efram Wing stood on the bench in front of the Wing assembly contingent and tried to wave them into silence. The Wing men and women wore their clan colors, blue and white, and by that at least were distinguishable from the clans on either side. Sub-clans within Wing wore their own variations on the basic colors to show their simultaneous clan loyalty and individuality. The component families did the same thing, resulting in a confusing welter of blue-white swatches, patterns, and base colors that made Wing distinctive. This was replicated by the other clans at Assembly, resulting in a hodgepodge of convergent colors.

Efram waved his arms vigorously, shouting for silence, and was being ignored. The clan was chattering amongst itself and cat-calling the Tuchmans, who sat scattered along the opposite slope.

The rivals faced each other across the shallow bottom of the crater-shaped Assembly bowl that nested within the larger valley. Lesser clans filled in the nether spaces between Wing and Tuchman. The bigger, more powerful clans used their muscle to laze over disproportionate areas, squeezing the lesser clans together. There would doubtless be some light dueling over the seating arrangements, but mostly between the small fry. They didn't have the deep pockets that Tuchman and Wing did, nor could they match the number of champions the big clans could. Here at Assembly, like everywhere else on New Hope, a clan either overcame or accommodated.

Representatives of each clan stood in the center of the bowl, each waiting to take their turn. A Council representative stood in the center. Her job ostensibly was to referee the meeting, to influence the agenda, and to advise the locals on Council decisions. She carried a sound-phone and yelled into the din every now and again as she tried to restore order.

She eventually grew tired of being ignored and took a whistle from her tunic pocket. She blew it directly into the sound-phone's pickup. The resulting feedback shrieked across the myriad conversations. Clan members across the amphitheater covered their ears and winced against the violent, electronically enhanced screech.

When she finally ran out of breath and took the whistle from her lips, there was silence in the bowl.

"Thank you," she said at last. "Now, as I recall, Efram Wing had the floor before we were so rudely interrupted."

She glared at Benno Tuchman, whose clan behind him had tried to shout down Efram during his last speech. That had inspired Wing to try and shout down Clan Tuchman. The descent into chaos, the third in as many hours, followed hard upon that. Benno, his back straight and his arms crossed, glared back at her, unrepentant.

Efram perched on his wobbly bench. "Now, as I was sayin'," he began, "and all the Wings of Skywing agree, that it's about damn time we did sometin' once and for all about the damn Earthers. The Ambassador, his nosey staff, they're *all* spies." He raised his fist dramatically and pointed one finger at Benno.

"You 'member what the Hegemony did at Jupiter. Opened it up for colonizin' right nice they did at first, gave us the red carpet. Then once we bled, and died, and built a world, they came back. No red carpet this time, just a boot. Five years to get the hell out." He tapped his foot on the ground for emphasis. "We came here." He paused a moment for breath and opened his arms as if to enfold them all. It looked to Benno like a practiced speech with prepared gestures.

"Now we done it again," Efram continued. "We built worlds, homes, here on New Hope. Out there as well." He gestured skywards with his chin. "Now they're back. You can bet why, too. New Hope is ready. We dug it up, terraformed what we needed to, started cities and industries." He made mincing gestures with his hands, starting to get caught up in his oratory and the emotion that powered it. "They'll be here soon, ready to build their little rabbit-warren Environments."

The way he said "En-VI-RO-ments" caused titters through the center section.

"And what'll become of us?"

He waited a second to let the grumbles build. "We get packed off to some other pesthole. Don't think for a moment that they aren't sizin' us up." His voice rose in pitch and volume as he warmed to his topic. "When you see an Earther, you see a spy! A spy! And likely as not settin' poison, provokin' us to fight amongst ourselves!"

He seemed to expect some kind of rousing cheer as he raised his fist to the sky. It didn't come. He seemed momentarily lost, then finished lamely: "Remember, I told ya so!"

He stepped off his bench with a flourish, ceding the floor.

The Wing Clan hooted and clapped in support of their man. The applause wasn't all it might have been. Efram wasn't terribly popular in many of the Wing sub-groups, and clan loyalty warred with personal animosity, but Wing subsided only when the Council referee raised her sound-phone threateningly.

Benno stepped forward when quiet had been restored. He lacked Efram's flashy tricks and so just stood, hip-shot, with his back to his own clan.

"Wing, as usual, has its head up its ass," he said in a conversational voice that carried across the now quiet bowl.

He held up one hand with the fingers extended and began ticking off points, pushing each finger down as he talked. Benno wasn't well educated, but he spoke clearly and well. When he was calm.

"First, the Hegemony ambassador has diplomatic credentials. If the Council pulls those, then the least the Hegemony'll do is cut us off. In case you haven't noticed, the Centauri colonies need Earth at the moment more than it needs us.

"Second, Efram here is panicked that the Hegemony is going to invade. Ignoring for the moment that an invasion across four light years is ludicrous on its face, what better way to piss off the Earth and maybe spark an invasion than by kicking out its ambassador? Typical Wing thinking.

"Three, Wing here keeps saying 'we were' like he was there and personally got his ass kicked off Io. He wasn't even a gleam in his mother's eye when that happened. So don't let him snow you about his tragedy."

Benno lowered his head to stare directly at Efram. "Unless you count the tragedy of his birth." He paused to see if Efram would make a move.

"Four. Wing asserts that the Hegemony reps here are at best spies, and at worst, provocateurs, spreading mischief and making us fight amongst ourselves."

He grinned. "Since when did we need help in fighting each other?"

He smiled broadly and raised his hand so all could see. The only finger that remained extended was the middle. Benno presented it to Efram. The assembled Clans burst into laughter. "Four reasons to remember: This is Wing talking. Consider the source."

He sat down.

The center clans hooted and laughed. They were long since used to the staple Assembly diet of Benno versus Wing. Efram was the new kid, and Benno could hear distant murmurs as the crowd subsided. He grinned. Speculation that he'd chewed Efram up and spat him out was running three to two for.

Benno considered Wing and Tuchman too finely matched to do anything more than snipe at each other on the Assembly grounds, though Dickerson was gaining enough strength to tilt the balance. Benno made a mental note to send Candace Dickerson an invitation to dinner.

Efram got up at the Council referee's nod. This time ignoring his bench, he spoke directly to the lesser clans.

"This threat 'tis real, for all that Tuchman's 'leader' wants ta' ignore it. And it's coming. Tuchman likes the way things are, split up, divided, so they can rule the roost, or at least their corner of it." Efram held out his hands in supplication to the middle clans as he mock pled. "We've got to unify, to get our shit together, so when the Hegemony comes we can stop 'em. We can resist 'em, but only if'n we form a unified front."

Benno stood up. His bass rumble, now raised, cut through Efram's reedy voice like a ring-penetrator through flesh. "If a unified front means Tuchman knuckling under to Wing, I'll see you in hell first!"

Benno opened his mouth to continue, but a voice rose out of the crowded smaller clans, cutting him off in turn.

"Yeah, that's a Tuchman for ya, pissin' and whinin' 'bout someone doin' to them what they been doin' to others."

Benno turned to face the heckler. The man stood up in the middle ground amongst the lesser clans, but could easily be a Wing plant.

"Your man, Wing?" Benno coolly asked Efram.

Efram spat on the ground. "I wouldn't dirty my feet on his hide, Tuchman!"

"I see." Benno's eyes narrowed and his lips thinned. "Come on down, shithead."

The heckler pushed his way through the seated clansmen. He wore the brown and gray of the Hardestys. His coveralls were mussed and dirty, and very out of place among the Assembly-goers wearing their best. He was clearly drunk. Benno checked the audience for other Hardestys and saw none.

"Which Hardesty are you?" Benno asked in a deceptively cool voice.

"Stewart," the man called out, drawing it out so it sounded like "STU-at," "and ah'm sick to death of you Tuchmans. Ya'll stand here tellin' us how much we need the Earth, how much we depend on the Earth ships. You bastids just don't wanna lose your precious Earth-built lux'ries." He spat on the ground.

Benno heard one of his clansmen behind him murmur softly to another, "Where'd this asshole come from?"

The other whispered back: "It's such a shame when cousins mate."

Benno tried hard to keep a straight face, but the corners of a smirk slipped through his careful mask.

Hardesty pressed on, his voice rough with bitterness. "You rich folks can afford Earth-made. The rest of us cain't." He paused a moment, swayed, then jabbed a finger at Benno. "If you gave a flyin' damn about the Centauri colonies, ya'll wouldn't be squeezin' the rest of us inta dirt. Folks like us, real people, can't afford Earth-made. It don't matter to us if the ships come or not!"

"Are you finished?" Benno asked.

His face was set and hard, his amusement lost. It wasn't just the accusations that bothered him, it was being taken to task by a third-rate hick like Hardesty.

"'Bout time somebody here stood up to you Tuchmans." Hardesty turned to face the middle ground. "No, I ain't finished," he declared. "I'm tired of being pushed around. You cain't just shut me up!"

"Wanna bet?" Benno answered.

Hardesty turned back to Benno, who moved forward to meet him, fists clenched. Stewart's eyes narrowed and he stepped into a fighting position, his hand traveling towards the obsolete revolver in his shoulder holster. Faster than a drunk should have been able to draw, he pulled his revolver out and shot at Benno Tuchman. The bullet spanged off of Benno's partial armor. Without thinking Benno drew his heavy Mark III.

A brilliant green beam lanced out of the hand-laser. The actual killing stream was a fraction of a millimeter lower and invisible to the naked eye. It sliced into Hardesty with a crackle and whiff of ozone, killing him instantly. Water surrounding the laser's impact absorbed the energy as heat and flashed into steam with a loud *pop*. The burst blew Hardesty's body backward.

"Dammit," Benno cried, turning back to his retainers. "It didn't penetrate my armor, but it damned well might have!"

No other Hardestys were present and no clan medic moved. Bystanders stayed well back from Benno's line of fire and watched impassively.

Efram turned towards Benno. The Tuchman leader stood, feet and legs poised and balanced, his laser held at shoulder level. Coolant gas vented like smoke from the tip of the exposed focusing element.

"Okay, Tuchman," Efram said, "you made your point. Are you gonna collect your pound of flesh?"

Benno turned towards Efram and said, "That'll get the bastard off my land." He shook his head and sighed as he holstered his pistol. The collective silence lasted a few more seconds, then, like the coming of a hard rain, everyone began to talk at once. The Council referee, by her appearance the most shaken, stared at the corpse. Those seated nearest to Stewart's body moved away and left it where it lay. The removal of Hardesty dead was a Hardesty problem. The District's Council would step in and fine the diminished clan for leaving the body as a public nuisance if they didn't take care of the corpse promptly.

Efram, one hand on his own laser, stabbed a finger at Benno. "We know how Tuchmans do things." He waved his hand towards Hardesty.

Benno, furious at the way Efram had set him up,

shouted across the open space between them, "Do you have a point, Wing, or are you trying to piss me off, too?"

The referee blew her whistle again, this time without amplifying it through the sound-phone. The crowd, for a change, quieted at once.

"The late Hardesty has raised a most excellent point, Tuchman," Efram continued, shifting gears.

He saw Benno's high color and the set of his jaw and figured the Tuchman leader would be easy to bait. He maneuvered to capture the high ground with cool language. "Where precisely do you obtain the funds for your Earth imports?"

"None of your damn business," Benno grumbled stonily.

Efram, his body tense, leaned towards Benno. "I would opine that it's Wing's money," he said in a voice so soft that Benno barely heard him.

Benno heard the heckler's voice behind him. "Opined? What the hell is opined?" There were soft chuckles all around. "What's he gibbering about?"

"Six weeks ago," pressed Efram, "a Wing ship coming from Earth, the *Stellar Conveyer*, radioed her arrival in the Centauri system. It went missing, hijacked." Efram's voice gathered strength and volume as he spoke. "Nine days ago Tuchman began installation of a gas separation plant. Expensive hardware, Benno, even more so when you consider that the *Conveyor* had a gas plant in her hold. Coincidence? Maybe, but I think not."

Benno looked so cool, butter wouldn't melt in his mouth.

"If you say so, Wing," he replied.

Efram pressed his case, playing to the audience. "In the time since the *Conveyer* vanished, Tuchman has placed orders for a lot of fripperies, imported a lot of nice things. How do you manage it, Benno? Are the Tuchmans doing that well?"

Benno shrugged. Efram waited a moment, let the silence build.

"You stole it Benno, you stole our ship."

He watched Benno's face redden and played his sudden advantage.

"Is that it, is that why you want Earth ships to come? So you can hide behind your vaunted honor, while plundering the rest of us?"

Benno's temper snapped.

"Bastard!" he roared. "We didn't take it! Accuse Tuchman again and I'll kill you!"

Efram, backed by three hundred armed clansmen, sneered. "Just like you did Hardesty, I'll bet. A cheap shot."

Benno went purple. He reached for his laser. His cousin, more alert than most, leapt to his feet and restrained him before he could get the weapon out. His hand over Benno's, he pressed close and hissed in the Clan Chief's ear, "No, not here! Kill him, you spark a war."

Benno tried to pull away.

"The Council wants peace," the man continued urgently. "They'll have your ass if you start it!"

Benno looked around and saw he was standing with his hand on his gun in front of the assembled West Hills clans. He glanced at Efram who looked pale, but ready. Both Wing and Tuchman were as taut as banjo strings. The referee clasped her sound-phone to her chest like a talisman. One move, any move, would start a bloodbath.

Benno pondered a moment, the heat slipping from him. He felt tired. "Okay," he said to his cousin, "I'm okay." He looked around again at the tense clans. "Let's go home. I've had enough." He turned towards his assembled clansmen, who began to break up and drift away.

"Has anybody seen my damn son?" he asked

plaintively as some of the clansmen shook their fists and shouted curses at Wing.

The Wing loyalists yelled and threatened in return. The moment for violence had passed, though, and it was just talk.

Efram relaxed and grinned. He raised his index finger to his lips, touched the tip with his tongue, and mimed toting up a score. "That's one for me," he said to himself.

Many of the clan members in the middle ground were looking over at Hardesty's smoking form. The soft susurrus made Efram smile again. The tide definitely flowed against Tuchman.

Benno allowed himself to be led away. "We lost that one, I think," he ruminated. "Damn, I let him get to me."

He let his cousin draw him towards the path that led to the upper part of the bowl and back to the Tuchman site. Word of the bad Assembly moved like the wind ahead of him. He felt the angry and speculative stares as he climbed the hill.

A few minutes later the Council referee and Hardesty were the last two in the assembly area. She unclipped her comm-link and began her report, bouncing it through a repeater to a satellite.

Benno, surrounded by clan loyalists, had almost crossed the trading grounds when he saw his son emerging from between two temporary shelters. He was busy tucking in his loose shirt when he saw his father. Benno had almost recovered his equanimity and managed a wan smile.

"Where have you been?" he asked Ward. "I needed you down there."

"Um," Ward shuffled a bit as he approached, a little evasion, "something came up. I had to deal with it."

"I see," said Benno.

Ward jumped to change the topic. "How'd it go?"

"Bad," responded Benno. "I let that rat-bastard Efram push me, and I lost it." He looked hard at Ward. "I needed you there, son, to keep me out of trouble."

Ward dropped his eyes. "Sorry Dad, I didn't know what was up."

Benno looked carefully at Ward. "I'm not in the mood for another drag out," he said tiredly, "so I'm going to ignore you being late. Okay?"

He clapped Ward on the back. The younger man winced and hissed. "You all right?" he asked.

"Sure, Dad," Ward answered, just a little too quickly.

"Got a set of stripes, did you?" Benno chuckled, male to male rather than father to son. "Well, you'd better get something on them before they fester. Then come help me get everyone packed. We'd better get out of here."

Chapter 2

Two days after the clan returned from Assembly, Ward opened his bedroom's plexiglass doors and padded out onto the balcony in his bare feet, the dew-covered tiles cold against his toes. He let the morning sun wash over his naked body, tipped his face back and felt the warmth wash the chill from his bones. He stretched his arms until the joints popped, hissing a little at the pain as the angry scratches on his back pulled.

"Damn, Sel marked me good," he grumbled.

He remembered how Benno had laughingly joked about Ward earning his "stripes." Little did he know. She'd clawed him deeply enough to draw blood. He hadn't taken care of them when he should have, and now a couple were infected. He gingerly reached his hand over his shoulder and felt the raised welts.

"Screwing her's more like war than love," he said to himself. "Great war, though."

He leaned on the balcony rail, carefully positioning his elbows to avoid the armor hooks and the weapon mount. "Damn, I can't wait to see her again," he mused, "it's been two whole days." He sighed at the unfairness of it all.

A tap on the door behind him roused him. He stepped quickly back into the room and scrambled into his robe as the door opened.

Stallart entered the room, his eyes flicking around the bedroom, searching for hidden danger. "Nice to see you're up," he said sarcastically.

Ward ignored the gibe. "What's up?"

"I was going to ask you that," Stallart replied. "Mona and I thought you'd be gone a week. We went camping. We came back to see cars and skimmers moving hither and yon."

"There were problems," Ward said.

"So I gather," Stallart replied dryly. "I came in and found your father closeted with the rest of his advisors." He gave Ward a long look. "Most of them, anyway."

Ward looked at his wall clock. "Shit," he swore, "I'm supposed to be down there."

Stallart grinned. "Me too. I learned a long time ago, however, to do a recon before exposing myself to danger." He scratched his neck. "It seemed like a prudent idea to get some information *before* I'm asked for an opinion."

He sat in Ward's only uncluttered chair and crossed his legs. "So, what happened?"

"It got out of hand," Ward answered. "Wing accused us of stealing a starship and I'm told Dad let his temper get the better of him."

"Told," Stallart said. "Weren't you there?"

"Um," Ward blushed, "I got sidetracked."

"I see. Well, go on."

Ward repeated the story of the altercation with Hardesty and Wing as he had heard it. Stallart often asked him to repeat or clarify details. "The leavetaking got nasty," Ward concluded. "Wing had their blood up. They thought they had us cold for raiding their ship."

He stopped and looked Stallart in the eye. "They didn't just dance around us, and they didn't seem to care about pissing off the Council by picking a fight."

"How bad was it?" Stallart asked.

Ward pursed his lips. "Three killed for us, two for them. We weren't ready for a free-for-all right then. The Law-Speakers are going to have a field day sorting out the weregeld."

"Well," Stallart commented pragmatically, "it could have been worse."

"You're right," Ward agreed. "It kills me to say this, but Dad kept his temper until the families were away. He didn't come unglued until we got back here." He rubbed the pine floor with his toe. "Then it got bad. I got both barrels."

Stallart tipped his head to one side. "I assume everybody else did too." He raised his hand before Ward could answer. "I've been there. Your dad has a gift for invective. Is there more?"

"Yeah," Ward continued, "the Hardestys did their best to stir up trouble. They laid 'ole Stewart on a board alongside the road. Under other circumstances, we'd have laughed. As it was . . ."

"It made things worse," Stallart said.

"Yeah," Ward agreed, "they put a sign over his head that said TUCHMAN JUSTICE. Gifford and his hotheads tore the thing down and set the body on fire. The small clans usually won't give Hardesty the time of day, but they did this time. We almost had a riot then and there." He took a pair of pants out of his wardrobe and began to slip them on. "Gifford shot a couple of Wings and a bystander, a Davies."

Stallart pressed his thumb and index finger together on the bridge of his nose, trying to stave off an incipient headache. "Peachy," he replied. "Did he kill anybody?"

"No," Ward answered, "we got lucky. But he shattered what good will we might have had." He bent to look for his shoes. "Right now no one is talking to us, not even our allies, until we pay up for the Davies kid."

Stallart puffed his cheeks out. "What's your dad been doing?"

Ward scrounged for a loafer that had slid under the king-sized bed. "Between strategy sessions, he's been ranting and raving." He snagged the errant shoe with his hand and sat on the edge of bed to slip the loafers on, sans socks. Stallart watched him silently as he went to his closet. The carousel slid silently outward as he opened the door. He began to hunt through the racks for a shirt.

"So far," Ward said, his voice muffled by the clothing, "the only visible sign has been a doubling of the patrols."

Ward saw no reason to tell Stallart he'd passed a part of the new patrol schedule on to Seladra. The last thing he wanted was for her to get captured crossing into Tuchman lands to get to the fort that served as their usual rendezvous.

He selected a shirt and let his robe drop to the floor. He was careful not to let Stallart see his back. "Dad's worried, though," Ward continued, "even though he'll die before he admits it."

"How's that?"

He tucked his shirt in and ran his fingers through his hair to comb it. He stretched again, more careful this time not to stress the scratches.

"Well," Ward answered, "he sent techs up yesterday to lubricate the railing's spindle mount. They had to chip the old paint away first." He raised his thumb and pointed towards the metal plates stacked discreetly by the French doors. "They also checked to make sure the balcony's armor plates fit the hooks."

"Well," Stallart said, "if it comes to that, we've the best house defenses this side of Foundation."

Ward thought about the locally quarried white fieldstone that formed the house's outer layer. Its large crystal structure would break down coherent laser energy through refraction and diffusion. The fieldstone was backed by an insulating gel with ablative and insulative properties. The innermost layer was a carbon-resin matrix that formed the last line of defense against penetration.

"Layered, flexible defense has always been a good selling point for homeowners here," Ward said with a grin.

Stallart didn't look amused. "The sarcasm and flip answers have to go, Ward. Someday you'll likely be head honcho around here, and you're gonna have to learn to lead. Sooner would be better than later."

Ward turned his back on Stallart. He stepped across the Earth-made imitation bearskin rug and ran his finger along the hologram tapestries of the Grand Canyon and Io's Gods' Tears formation.

"I know," he replied angrily, "but how do you expect me to learn that? You aren't teaching me to lead. I'm down there with you, Dad, and the rest. All of you pat me on the head and treat me like a little boy!"

"You are a little boy," Stallart said coldly. "You're a still damp twenty-two-year-old who wants to be treated as an equal by men twice your age. Or more." His voice softened. "If you want the respect of the people in that room, you're going to have to *earn* it. That means doin' what you're told, when you're told, and usually, how you're told. You'll be treated better *once* you've shown them, shown me, you deserve it. Any questions?"

Ward, still turned away, glanced at the small table by the clothes press. He saw the pictures of his mother, who had died nine years ago in a skimmer accident, and his father. Ward didn't think the pictures did either justice. They hadn't been stiff, formal people, the way they looked in the portrait. They just looked uncomfortable.

"I remember when Mom died," Ward said. "Dad came to my room the night of the funeral and told me to cry. Ordered me to, in fact." He brushed a speck of lint off the frame. "When I was done, he told me that was the last time I was allowed to cry about it. I didn't."

Ward looked at the much younger version of his father. His mother stood, beautiful and proud, her hand on his shoulder. "I hated him for that. He even took away my grief."

Stallart cleared his throat. "Grow up, Ward. Act like a man. And before you wallow too deep in self pity, your dad didn't allow himself even that much when your mom died."

Ward stood silently, his eye drawn to the wall display of his schoolboy trophies: ribbons for spelling, a skyball victory medal, and his wrestling and shooting awards. Next to the school mementos were his dueling trophies, tokens and armor chips taken from the three men and two women he'd bested.

"Do you remember Dania?" Ward asked Stallart.

The trainer looked puzzled. "The Luris girl? Yeah. Why?"

Ward turned to face him. "She was my first lay. We were both sixteen and hadn't a clue what we were doing." He shook his head sadly, tied to the bittersweet memory. "Three years later I killed her in a duel."

Stallart nodded. "Your dad assigned me to train you after that fiasco. You became my *special* project."

Ward squeezed his eyes shut. "She found I was seeing Christa behind her back and called me out. She wanted live rounds. I didn't want to hurt her. I liked her. I tried to brush her back during the fight. She jumped the wrong way and ran into my coil gun stream. She died instantly."

Stallart glanced at his watch. "Ancient history. So what?"

"I've built my rep as being the guy who iced his girlfriend. I worked hard to convince myself I was tough enough to not let feelings get in the way of what needed to be done." He took a deep breath. "It's a front. I'm not sure I really have what it takes."

Stallart blew out his breath, exasperated. "That's *it*?" He sounded incredulous. "Damn, boy, that's a long way to walk to find out the store's closed." He furrowed his brow as he composed his thoughts. "Your dad and the rest of us'll be assigning tasks commensurate with your abilities and your future. If we have to fight, you won't be leading troops or be in any pitched battles. You simply aren't ready." He half smiled. "Does that help?"

Ward looked relieved.

"Don't get too relaxed," Stallart chided. "You're not off the hook. Your job'll be to watch what we do, ask stupid questions, and learn how to fight the *next* war. Okay?"

A polite tap on the door distracted them before Ward could answer.

"Yes?" Ward called. Stallart wasn't sure if Ward answered him or the retainer. "Your father wants you downstairs in his study, ASAP," the valet called, his voice muffled by the wood and plastic door.

"Okay, okay," Ward called out, then said dryly, "His master's voice."

"I need to use your can," Stallart said. "It's probably going to be a long session."

Ward looked up at the wall clock and felt a sinking feeling gather in the pit of his stomach. He hoped he'd get free from his dad's pow-wow in time to make his planned lunch with Seladra near the old border fort. He sighed. It was hard enough to see Seladra under normal circumstances, but that would be nothing to trying to sneak time during a clan war. His sex life depended on peace.

No one knew of his trysts, so far as he could tell, and he was just as happy to keep it that way. He smiled ruefully. His father would have kittens by the litter if he knew Ward was exchanging bodily fluids with the enemy. Shakespeare would have been proud.

Stallart came out of the bathroom just as he stood and checked his clothing in the full-length mirror. He snapped on his gun belt after checking to ensure the laser's charge light glowed bright green, fully ready. He drew it and touched the diagnostics blister. He heard the cycling hum as it vented the lazing emitter, lenses, and focusing elements, and ran the power system. Three green flashes, fully operational. Stallart nodded approvingly as he reholstered the weapon.

They crossed the central hall towards the mansion's grand stair. Ward noted that while the materials had been placed to prepare the upstairs positions, nobody had actually begun to fortify just yet. That indicated to Ward that Benno didn't see an armed conflict as the only outcome. At least not yet.

"Is he trying to talk a solution?" Stallart asked. Ward bobbed his head.

"Wing's grown strident in its claims we took the ship. Dad surprised everyone, probably at Wing and certainly here, by wanting to talk." He motioned Stallart ahead. "That's fine by me, although a little out of character."

"Don't underestimate your father. He can be a crafty bastard when he puts his mind to it."

They went down the broad, reinforced central stair to the study. They passed the retainer guarding his father's study. The woman looked bored in her battle armor as she slouched against the wall. Her combat helmet lay overturned by her feet, ready to be snapped on and integrated on a moment's notice.

Despite the slouching, she seemed reasonably alert. Stallart looked her over, then opened the door, satisfied that her equipment appeared in order. Ward, standing behind Stallart, saw her roll her eyes.

Ward followed him into the gloomy study, where Benno stood in front of his desk. Most of the light strips were off. Behind him, embossed onto one wall of the study, was the current Tuchman family tree. It had begun as a simple graph and had long since developed into a confused and twining bramble as the clan's lineage had grown more complex. Benno, of course, loved it; it was his family.

Alma Reinquist, security chief and most senior of

Benno's non-family retainers, leaned over the desk. Ward remembered that when Benno had hired her, she'd asked him if he wanted a yes-girl to run his security. Benno had told her "no." She took him at his word and fought him on almost every issue. Benno had once said that she made him think things through. He'd also said a number of vile things to and about her.

At this moment they were arguing—again.

"Benno, for pity's sake," she asserted, "you have to keep the guards at their posts! At least until you get this thing resolved." Her voice had the carefully strained sound that suggested this was a rehash of earlier arguments and that she was getting exasperated.

"Damn it, Alma," rasped Benno, "*everyone* thinks Efram beat me at Assembly with his damn tricks." He turned and faced the room. "If it gets out that Benno Tuchman is hiding in his house, surrounded by guards, I'll be a laughingstock."

Alma placed her hands on the desk, palms down. "The guards give you early warning, better than the passives or the alarms." She paused to give her words weight. "Unless you plan to sleep in your armor, you'd best keep them. Otherwise, some Wing fanatic is going to slip in and put a powerknife in your heart."

"Give me a break, will ya'?" Benno snapped back. "This is Clan Tuchman, not some outback bush league like Dawkins or Hardesty. You want me, you have'ta cross my whole clan. Who's gonna be able to do that?"

"I could," Stallart mumbled quietly.

Alma turned. Ward thought she looked distinctly unimpressed with his comment. She continued, "Benno, you've built your reputation by fighting your own battles. That's part of the problem. Right now half the clans are convinced that Tuchman is pirating transports. The other half are convinced you're after them. What happens if somebody decides Benno Tuchman equals Clan Tuchman and tries to take you out?"

Benno opened his mouth to speak.

Stallart quickly cut him off. "I've been watchin' this thing," he said. "I'm still getting the full story, so I don't know what facts are going to inconveniently step on my theory." He took a deep breath. "Here's what I think so far. This isn't the usual pissing contest. The small fry are scampering for the woodwork and you've traded kills with Wing. And that's just foreplay." He ran his hand through his closely cropped hair. "I'll bet you've suddenly got unimpeded access to the Council."

Ward saw Alma nodding in agreement.

"There's three big clues that somethin's up," Stallart continued. "Shit, you've had every sign and portent except the Four Horsemen riding up and asking directions."

Alma gave him a grateful look before she waded back in. She took two quick steps towards Benno, around the desk.

"The planetary Council don't like to get involved at the district level," she said, her hand chopping the air. "Yet they told you Wing is seriously torqued about the *Conveyor*. Wing wants satisfaction, and they may not stay within the code duello, so *take some precautions*."

Benno set his jaw. Stallart and Ward exchanged glances. They knew Benno's reputation for stubbornness underestimated the reality.

"The day I can't take care of myself," the Clan Chief said slowly and evenly, "is the day they bury me. The guards go. End of discussion."

Alma sighed. "And the doubled patrols?"

Benno thought a moment, unwilling to be seen to bend even that much. "Okay," he said at last. "I can live with that."

Alma shook her head, clearly not satisfied. "Half a loaf is better than none, I suppose," she said tiredly, "so I'll take what I can get."

One of Benno's other advisors, Hardy, spoke up from

a corner chair. "Well, Ward's here. What does he think of all this?"

"Thanks a lot, asshole," Ward murmured as he gathered his thoughts. "Figures you'd be the first one to stick it to me."

"Um, I'm not sure I'm up on what's going on," he ventured lamely to the room.

He saw his father's disappointed expression and heard the *wehoosh* of an exasperated exhalation from somewhere in the gloom. The novelty of his father's disapproval had long since worn thin, but he was used to it. Taking heat from the hired help was another matter entirely.

"Umm, I think it's g-going to blow over," he offered.

Benno gave him a sharp look. "What makes you say that?"

Ward felt his collar growing tight. "Well, the halflife of these things is like, umm, three days, you know?"

Ward felt the advisors' silent eyes boring into him. He felt he'd stumbled from the fryer into the fire. "I shoulda' kept my damn mouth shut," he whispered to himself.

They all seemed to be waiting for him to continue. He saw no choice but to do so. "The big clans, us included, are too attached to making money for this to continue." He took a deep breath. No one had shot him down. Yet. "Our overhead is too high. We can't afford to keep farmers and workers patrolling. Neither can Wing." His confidence grew a bit. "Right now there's no trade or work getting done, and we have less than two weeks to plan for the harvest."

"So?" Benno said.

"So, nobody can afford to sit across the fence making mad eyes while the wheat rots in the fields," Ward said. "Something has to give. A war would cut too deeply into profits." He took a deep breath. "I think we'll be back on passive alarms and single patrols within a week."

"Opinions?" Benno asked the room.

Stallart was the first to leap into the breach. "I think the boy's partially right."

Hardy looked disgusted.

"I agree this won't go on long," Stallart continued, ignoring Hardy, "but I think Wing's gonna jump. They lost millions on that ship. They have to recoup it somehow. They won't get that kind of money from an indemnity, even if we took the ship. Which we didn't."

He turned away from the advisors and squarely faced Benno. "They also invoked the Code when they blamed us. That is serious shit. They now have no choice but to seek satisfaction, otherwise they'll be laughingstocks. They've trapped themselves. A clan war may be their only way out."

Hardy made a rude noise from the corner.

"Hell, we made it easy for them," Stallart said. "We've isolated ourselves from our friends and allies, at least until the Davies issue is resolved. Everybody, including the Council, is pissed at us. We're way up on the skyline."

Ward watched the advisors round on Stallart like sharks after blood. Even Alma, Stal's most likely ally, didn't buy it.

"We're too evenly matched," she snapped. "They'd need to have us three-to-one on open ground to have any assurance of victory. They just don't have the numbers."

"Lighten up, Alma," Stallart replied, "and forget the textbook for a moment. Look at it from their side. Tactically, it's an open question of who would win, I'll admit that." He raised his finger, gesturing to reinforce his point. "But strategically, they may never have a better opportunity."

Ward fled for an open seat while the other advisors pecked at Stallart. He watched his father from his new vantage, gaining some insight into his style. "He *likes* setting them on each other," he mused to himself, "that way he can sit, observe, and form his own opinions." The hated study suddenly didn't seem as intimidating.

Stallart fought long and hard, grudgingly giving ground under the combined assault of Hardy, Alma, and the others. Ward could tell Benno wasn't buying into the idea of an attack.

Stallart seemed to sense that, too. "Okay," he said, defeated, "but that still brings us back to the issue of precautions."

Benno was ready for him. "No guards," he said firmly.

"Okay," Stallart said, "but what about Ward? He's the Clan Chief's son. He's important. Somebody snatches him and you lose face."

Benno looked at Ward. His eyes narrowed while he considered the situation.

"Shit," said Ward through tightly pressed lips. He kept his face carefully composed while he watched his father chewing on the idea. He knew a tag-along would put a great big hole in his plans to see Seladra.

"Do it," Benno said.

"Shit, shit, shit," Ward whispered. He wanted to protest, to say something. He looked at his father, trying to frame an argument. Benno's jaw was set. The discussion was closed. Ward felt his spirits plunge.

"I'll have Hariman do it," Stallart said, still looking at Ward. "He's good, and they're friends. He'll keep up with the boy."

"Boy," grumbled Ward. "Charming."

Ward contributed little to the debate that followed. He answered when directly addressed, but otherwise kept quiet. Noon crept closer. He began to worry about missing his time with Seladra. He glanced at his watch every few minutes, hoping the aimless discussion would end. His surreptitious glances at his timepiece did not go unnoticed.

"Someplace else you'd rather be?" asked his father in a carefully neutral voice.

Ward realized that Benno must have been watching. His face grew hot. He wanted to shout "Yes!" but that required too many truths to be told. He mumbled something unintelligible and shook his head.

"Well," Benno said sarcastically, "it seems we're boring my son. We probably ought to start the show." He looked at Ward. "Would you kindly tell us the time?" he asked.

Ward was grateful for the dark room. No one could see him blush. "Umm, it's ten past eleven," he answered without looking at his wrist.

Benno put on his headset while a wall section slid back to reveal a view screen. Ward knew the viewer was one of the newest flat-holographic projectors. It had been an import from Earth and hideously expensive. Benno, with his love of gadgetry, had installed it himself. He'd often bragged it was better than anything else on the planet.

He slid a chip into his desk slot and waited for the communications satellite to make connection. Snow blotted out the view at first, then cleared as the signal grew stronger to reveal a woman sitting a desk.

There was a Council flag in a stand behind her desk. Ward saw stars winking in the dark window that formed a backdrop.

She looked well past middle-age to Ward, perhaps in her sixties. Her face seemed firm in spite of the crow's feet around her eyes and the short iron-gray hair that framed a stern expression. The only word he could think of to describe her was "formidable."

Ward looked at his father as Benno adjusted his headset.

"Councilor Thorn? Benno Tuchman here," he said with false joviality. "How is Clan Thorn these days?"

"Well enough, Benno," she answered shortly. "You didn't call me to make clan small talk. What's on your mind?"

Benno sighed. "I'm trying to work something out so that West Hills doesn't fall apart. Wing and I have been dancing around each other for years. I don't understand why this has to be different—why we can't work something out?"

"What do you mean?" Thorn asked carefully.

It seemed to Ward that Thorn was playing with Benno, trying to draw him out. The telltale set of his father's jaw suggested that his thoughts matched Ward's.

"Look," he said tightly, as if to a child, "we've had scraps with Wing since forever, ever since Grandpa shot LeVan Wing." He made a sweeping pass with his hands as he talked. "We brush them back, they brush us back. Status quo restored. We keep things down, fight some duels, everything goes back to normal. Smooth. What's changed?"

"The world, Benno, the world's changed," she answered tiredly. "This thing with the *Stellar Conveyor*, for one. This isn't a few egglayers or a riding ox this time." Her brow furrowed in concentration. "It's a whole starship. Wing's convinced you took it. Not withstanding their pride, they have millions invested."

She paused and looked directly into the viewer. Ward blinked in surprise. Benno simply listened quietly. Ward expected *some* fireworks from him.

"They think you brazened it out from under them," Thorn continued. "They've lost a lot of prestige. They didn't help the situation by howling blue murder, but they *are* the aggrieved party. Someone has to pay, Benno, to restore Wing pride."

Benno growled, "Why does Clan Tuchman have to be the whipping boy?" His voice grew gruff as his temper slipped a notch. "We didn't take the damn ship and I'll kill anyone who says different. Hear me? Anyone!"

"That's your other problem, Benno," she said wearily. "We've known each other a long time." She held up one hand to forestall his protest. "I know we haven't been friends, but listen to what *I* have to say, for a change." She took a deep breath.

Benno stared hard at her, his arms crossed over his chest.

"That stunt you pulled at Assembly pissed a lot of people off," she said in a cold, quiet tone.

"What stunt was that?" Ward heard the heat in Benno's voice.

"Come on, Dad, don't blow it," he whispered.

Thorn fixed Benno with a glare. "You blew Hardesty away in front of God an' everyone."

"So what? I was within my rights under the code," Benno said tightly.

She shook her head in exasperated negation. "Yeah, Benno, you were. And any Law-Speaker you ask will sigh and agree. Stewart made for you, so technically you're okay." She rapped her hand on the desk. "Damn it, Tuchman, the Hardestys don't have a pot to piss in. What do you think the small clans are thinking now?"

Benno lifted his chin stubbornly. "That's not my problem," he snapped.

"Yes," she retorted, "it is. And you made it worse. When Hardesty got up on his hind legs, you checked with Wing before killing him. I've heard that from a dozen witnesses. The message was loud and clear." She turned away from the pickups for a moment, revealing her stern profile. "Tuchman only seems to care about the big clans' rights. Half the small clans think you took the Wing ship. The rest just think you're a menace. They want to see you slapped down before they become the next Hardesty."

Benno looked sharply at Alma. This rehashed their earlier argument almost word for word. The guard chief shrugged.

"I'm going to lay it out for you," Thorn continued, "clear and simple." She faced back to the viewer and stared directly at Benno, her face set. "Everybody, and

I mean everybody, is talking unification." She stood and walked around to sit on the edge of the desk. The pickup followed her and kept her centered in the view screen as she spoke.

"The Council is intended to be more than a referee. Our job *is* to unify this colony. The small fry're talking about banding together. They're afraid of you and the other big clans. Even Wing is talking about lashing up. And Tuchman . . . ?" She frowned. "Tuchman is giving everyone that tired old 'Cross the line of death and I kill you' speech. You're an obstacle, Benno. No wonder everyone thinks you're trouble."

Tuchman's face turned to stone as Thorn lectured. "Are you finished, Councilor?" he asked when she finally ground to a halt.

His voice dripped contempt. "Now that you've given me Wing's line, let me give you mine. I don't want a war. I want this resolved the way things used to be; a couple of duels and we all go home."

"Damn it, that's not enough," she snapped back, "not for Wing, not this time. They want something real." She ran her hand across her forehead, seeming fatigued. "I might be able to work something out, but you have to give me something I can use." She paused and took a deep breath. "Wing is going to want proof you didn't take their ship."

"Go ahead," Benno said, slowly and carefully, "I'm listening."

Thorn plunged ahead. "Wing will want to search Tuchman property for items that were on its manifest. Your gas separation plant, for instance." She paused, waiting for a response.

Benno let her stew a bit. "And?"

She brushed a speck of lint from her sleeve. "They'll want proof you didn't sell the ship. They'll probably want you to turn your books and accounts over to the Council for monitoring."

"I see," said Benno. "Is there anything else?"

Stallart sat down next to Ward and leaned over to him. "She's awfully well informed about what Wing *might* want, isn't she?"

Ward nodded back. "I noticed that."

"Pacify your neighbors," Thorn said. "Make them happy." She held her hand out, imploring him. "Give the Hardestys an indemnity for Stewart large enough for them to get back on their feet. Reduce your patrols to their former level. Make a public affirmation for the Council and the need to unify, and you should be fine."

"Thanks," said Benno in a surprisingly light voice, "next time, kiss me first. We'll be in touch." He closed the circuit. The afterimage of a gape-mouthed Councilor Thorn lingered on the screen a moment.

"The bitch knows I've got a temper," he said as he turned to face the room. "Was she trying to set me off?"

"It doesn't really matter," Hardy said evenly. "If we bend to the search, the audit, or even the indemnity, we show the rest of the planet that Tuchman autonomy is meaningless." He buffed his fingertips on his protective vest and checked the results in the gloom. "Next thing we know we'll have Greenes, McKenzies, and the Sandiford crowd coming from the other side of the planet to piss with us. You give in to this, Benno, and you kiss the clan goodbye." He ran his thumb along his holstered laser. "Besides the Code carries weight only so long as we can stand up for our rights. What happens if we give that up?"

He looked grim. "We'll handle this clan to clan, the way we always have." No one else spoke. Hardy seemed to sum up their feelings.

Ward's father rubbed his finger along his jaw a moment, then reopened the contact to Thorn's office. She looked startled at his sudden return. "I've thought it over," he said.

"No small talk or greeting," Ward mumbled in Stallart's ear, "go Dad!"

"And?" Thorn replied. Ward heard the hope in her voice.

"Go to hell," snapped Benno. "We'll do it ourselves."

He moved to close the contact. She raised her arm to stop him. "Wait. Please, Benno. Just a moment." He hovered one finger over the disconnect.

"Give me three days to work something out," she implored. "Okay? Maybe we can fix this. Just don't do anything for three days."

Benno thought a moment. "Okay, Thorn, I'll give you three days. Then I do it myself."

He closed the contact and turned to Alma. "You'd better leave the guards in place for now." He turned away, then paused. "Not me, though."

Alma bowed her head in acknowledgement.

Ward watched the minutes scroll by as Hardy then led them into a rambling discussion about moving stored crops and grazers in case of war with Wing. They argued about what level of defense they could sustain through the harvest. The only piece of business that interested him was the decision not to issue a general call-up of Tuchman retainers.

He knew mobilization would escalate the already steep costs of the crisis. More importantly, it would immerse him in work and kill any chance whatsoever to see Seladra.

He tried not to fidget as the clock's hands swept towards noon. Just as Ward gave up hope, Benno yawned and stretched. "This chair settin's hurtin' my behind. I'm for lunch. Anybody else?"

Ward bounded to his feet with alacrity and fled the room. He knew he was late, but it was barely possible he could make up the time before she left. Behind him, Stallart and Benno traded a glance.

He'd taken the precaution of staging his supplies:

lunch, a liter of wine, several music crystals, all wrapped in a thermal blanket and stuffed into a hay pile by the side of the ox barn. He tossed the basket into a ground-effect car's cargo box. He slammed the lid down, still irritated at his father's decision to saddle him with a guard while refusing one himself. "Hypocrite," he seethed.

He jumped into the driver's seat and quickly wound the inertial gyroscopes, waiting for them to match before he activated the compressor. He set the altimeter for ground skim and maximum acceleration. The machine wasn't really built for ground-hugging speed, but it did shower gravel nicely as it took off. He took his usual precaution of remaining at ground level to stay below the house's navigation control radar. He dispensed with the added measure of security given by driving off in an odd direction to hide his true destination, then looping around to the fort.

He looked at his watch: twelve twenty-three. "Damn, damn damn!" he cursed, punching the steering yoke in time with his profanity. He knew Seladra had a short fuse and that his being late would set her off. He had no time today for subtlety. He blazed like an arrow for the fort.

Hariman stepped from behind the barn door and watched Ward's dust settle as gravel pattered around him. Stallart joined him a moment later. "Have you got the tracker?" Stallart asked.

Hariman dipped his head once. "Yup."

Stallart shaded his eyes as he peered at the thinning dust that marked Ward's passage. "Well, it's official now. Benno wants him guarded."

"Guarded or watched?" Hariman asked.

"Guarded," Stallart replied.

"Poor kid," Hariman said with a grin. "Its gonna be the last time he gets laid for a while."

"Yeah, well," Stallart warned, "if anyone finds out I've

had you tailing him since he started taking his lunches on the road, it's both our asses."

"I've been thinking about that," Hariman said. "I think it's going to leak, sooner or later. We ought to tell him ourselves."

Stallart pursed his lips, thinking. "You're his friend," he said. "I'll defer to your judgment."

Hariman looked at the small triangle-shaped blip that represented Ward. "He must really have the hots for her today," he said.

"How's that?" Stallart replied.

Hariman glanced at the tracker again. "He isn't doing any of that goofy circling around he's so fond of. Just jetting straight out to her."

"Is he going back to the old bunker?" Stallart pressed.

"Yup," answered Hariman.

Stallart sat on the hay bale and scratched an itch just above his sock. The scent of hay teased his sinuses and made him want to sneeze. "Think it's a snatch job?"

Hariman did a double-take and appeared to be having some trouble keeping a straight face.

"Is there something funny?" Stallart asked.

Hariman tried not to laugh. "No, sir."

Stallart looked at him long and hard. "Well, go after him and make sure he doesn't get into trouble."

Hariman turned away, then looked back. "Do you want me to find out who the girl is? She comes across from Wing to meet him."

Stallart scratched his leg again, considering. "If you can see her without getting caught, but as long as he stays on the reservation, and she comes by herself, I don't really care."

"Okay," Hariman replied.

He sketched a salute and climbed on his ground-effect sled. Stallart watched him blaze out of the compound, his tracker hanging from one handlebar.

Stallart knew that Ward and Hariman had been friends

since before Hariman took up Stallart's weapons trade. He thought he knew why the friendship worked between them, even though their social backgrounds couldn't be more different. Ward appeared to enjoy having a friend who wasn't intimidated by his money or who didn't seem to be looking for a handout.

Hariman had made it quite plain that he had no objection to following Ward and keeping a discreet eye on him to make sure the Clan's heir didn't get caught in a trap right on the edge of Wing turf. Stallart simply assumed Hariman would refuse if asked to observe Ward's activities inside the fort.

Ward arrived at the bunker just as Seladra raised her powerbike's kickstand. She looked at the approaching ground-effect car with momentary apprehension until she identified Ward.

He slewed the vehicle around to bleed off momentum. The vehicle's landing feet gouged the hard earth as the vehicle slid to a stop. Ward popped the driver's bubble canopy and jumped out. She made no move to get off the bike, though she hadn't fired it up yet, either.

"Hi!" he said breathlessly.

"Ward, you're late," she chided. "You said twelve twenty. Its twelve forty-two now."

Ward noticed that she wore the same type of bodysuit she'd worn to the Assembly. It left little to the imagination. Ward's heart beat faster at the reminder of past glories.

"Look, I'm sorry," he half pleaded. "I got held up in one of Dad's forever meetings and couldn't get away."

She looked down at the bike's control console. "I'm taking big chances coming here." She sounded both hurt and angry. "The least you could do is show up on time."

He looked contrite. "I said I was sorry. Let's let it go, all right?" He gestured back to the car, trying to change the subject. "I brought lunch."

She shook her head in negation. "I can't stay."

He looked puzzled. "Why not?"

"My father's getting worried about security," she answered. "All of your troop movements are making Wing nervous."

"Those aren't troop movements, they're patrols," he corrected carefully.

"Not to my dad and the rest of Wing." She looked sad. "I want to see you, Ward, but I'm not going to be able to get away after this."

Ward stepped away from the bike, angry and hurt. "Damn it, Seladra." He kicked the dirt in frustration.

"Ward, please, I have to go." She looked up at him, the curtain of her brown hair partially masking her eyes. "I want you to come to me tonight," she said. "I can't get away from the house. I—I can't bear not to see you."

He thought he saw tears start in her eyes. He looked at her, torn between suspicion and compassion. "Go to you? Where?"

"Please, Ward, come to Wing." Her voice softened. "I'll—I'll find us a place and make it safe, I promise." She seemed on the verge of pleading with him, her eyes shining with tears. His heart melted. "I can make it safe for you," she repeated, then whispered, "please." She paused, and gave him the ghost of a saucy wink. "I'll make it worth your while."

Neither laughed at the weak joke.

"All right," Ward gave in. "Tell me what to do."

She smiled happily and leaned across the bike to give him a damp kiss on the mouth. "Thank you, baby. Thank you."

She settled herself on the bike. "Wait until after moonfall, then come up the old ravine to the path your grandfather used to raid us." Her tone grew more businesslike. She used the toe of her boot to draw a map in the dirt as she described the route. He leaned towards her, trying to steal a kiss. She tossed her hair in exasperation.

"Please, Ward, this is important." She pointed at the map with her toe. "Take the old path and come up to the south barn. The door will be open a crack." Her voice dropped an octave and grew softer again. "I'll be waiting for you."

"Okay," he said, already doubting the wisdom of what he'd agreed to. "I'll be there."

She smiled again and kissed him, this time on the cheek. "I've been away too long already. I have to go." She looked suddenly very shy and young. "See you tonight."

She keyed the powerbike's energy stud and waited for the batteries to stabilize their power flow. Once the bike idled smoothly, she turned and brushed her hand across his lips.

"Wait!" he called. "I have something for you."

She looked vexed a moment and glanced impatiently at her bike's chronometer. He dug the comm-link out of his pocket and gave it to her.

"What's this?" she asked.

"It's a short-range transmitter," he said hurriedly. "I bought a code chip for it. It'll let us communicate privately."

Seladra said nothing as she put the communicator into her pocket. She revved the bike. "*Tonight*," she mouthed, a silent promise.

"*Tonight*," he mouthed back, feeling slightly inane. She fed power to the drivers. The bike accelerated away as Ward stepped back.

He watched until she crossed from the Tuchman estates onto Wing turf. Only then did he turn for home. He didn't like the idea of visiting her at Wing. He tried to see it from her perspective. She'd been taking the risks, coming to see him. Maybe it was fair to expect him to go to her.

He decided it didn't wash. It was one thing to meet Seladra on the sly out in the boonies and quite another to sneak into the heart of Wing. He laughed aloud as he contemplated running the Wing gauntlet. He ran his fingers through his hair and made a wry face.

"Ho, boy," he said to himself. He looked down at the erection tenting his trousers. "Now look what you've gotten us into," he chided.

Half an hour later he pulled unsteadily back into the compound. He'd been at the wine he'd packed for lunch and had tucked a fair bit away. He wasn't paying as much attention as he should have been and almost drove over Hariman before he saw him. The retainer, with his dancer's moves, dodged nimbly out of the way.

"Have a good trip?" Hariman asked.

Ward wasn't fully himself at the moment. "Huh?"

Hariman pressed on. "You blazed out of here after the morning briefing like your tail was on fire. I assume you had someplace to be?"

Ward shrugged. Hariman chose to take that for acquiescence. "I hope you had a good time."

Hariman stepped closer as if to open the cargo box. Ward took two quick steps and placed his hand over Hariman's. Hariman sniffed the air and caught a whiff of wine fumes. "I see," he said, sounding disappointed.

That was too much for Ward. "It's not what you think, damn it! I didn't go off just to drink!"

"Then why did you?" Hariman pressed.

"None of your business!" snapped Ward.

Hariman slipped his hand into his pocket and pulled out the tracker. "Your father ordered transponders put on all the vehicles," he explained. "If anyone steals 'em, we can follow them. You didn't know that, did you?"

"No," Ward said, staring at the small box as though it might bite him.

"Then you should go to more meetings," Hariman chided. He abruptly changed the subject, throwing Ward off guard. "Who's the girl?"

Ward tried to track on the sudden shift in topic, his

head still a little fuzzy. "Girl?" He tried to sound calm, but his voice came out as a squeak.

Hariman looked smug. "Stallart and I fixed some of the sensors in the outlying blockhouses."

Ward's face paled. Hariman held up one hand, laughing at his friend's discomfiture. "Oh, not the visuals, buddy-boy, but we got thermals and motion devices working."

The way Hariman said "motion" made Ward blush again.

"We've known for about six months that you were using them to go spelunking."

Ward stood very still. He was cold sober now, his stomach knotted. "Who's *we*?" he asked carefully.

"Just me, so far." Hariman grinned, a fellow conspirator. "Maybe Stallart."

Ward looked bitter. "Which means my father, of course."

Hariman placed his hand on Ward's shoulder. "Don't take on like that. Your old man was pissed you weren't at the Assembly, but was pleased you were living up to the 'family tradition,' you know." He winked.

Ward wasn't amused. Hariman tried another tack. "Nobody said anything," he asserted. "Really." He tossed Ward the tracker. "Here, keep it."

"You'd just get another," Ward said bitterly.

Hariman frowned. "This isn't going well," he said. "Stallart asked me to keep an eye on you. So I did. I'm doing him a favor." He winked at Ward. "Come to think of it, I'm doing you one, too." He became serious again. "But not your father. I'm supposed to keep you alive, not to spy on you. I tell Stallart what I think he needs to know. That's it."

"Sure," Ward said. "I'm about to test you on that."

Hariman's brow furrowed.

Ward looked at him, half accusing, half pleading. "I need your help. She's Wing. I love her."

"I know," Hariman shot back.

Ward just blinked. He did a good job otherwise of covering his surprise. "You know what? Which?"

"I've followed you to your little love nest," Hariman answered. "She comes across from Wing turf, so she must be a Wing girl. Right?"

Ward's voice mixed anger and disgust. "How long did you say you'd been following me?"

Hariman became defensive. "If you mean peering in the windows while you were screwing, buddy-boy, not at all. I kept an eye out for you and occasionally ran diagnostic tapes in the sensor outlets so the techs wouldn't get *too* much data."

Hariman tried to duck the subject by changing it. "I do have one question. When you say she's Wing, do you mean Wing retainer or Wing kin?"

"I mean Seladra Wing," Ward said, "Gustav's daughter. Big Daddy Wing's own granddaughter." Ward took malicious enjoyment from watching his friend's startled face.

"Wow," said Hariman, after a time. "I'm impressed. You don't do things by halves, do you. Gustav is *not* a nice man. Does he know?"

Ward shrugged.

Hariman exhaled heavily, then brushed his hand through his hair. "What am I saying? If he knew, you'd be dead. The man's a psych case. So's her brother, ol' what-his-name."

"Delius," Ward supplied.

Hariman gave Ward a long look. "She's a beauty, but I'd rather bed a bear trap."

Ward rolled his eyes. "It's given me some idea of how porcupines copulate."

Hariman raised an eyebrow. "How's that?"

"Carefully," Ward said. He rubbed his forehead, uncertain as to how to proceed. "Look, there's a problem . . ." he began tentatively.

Hariman came alert. "Oh, yeah, just one?"

Ward ignored the gibe. "I told her I'd go see her. Tonight. I'm afraid it might be a trap, but I promised."

Hariman looked nonplussed. "Where are you supposed to meet her? At the fort?"

"No," Ward said, "inside Wing turf. Just outside the Wing mansion."

Hariman whistled, long and low.

"Look, I love her." Ward seemed to Hariman to be thinking aloud. "She loves me. It's just . . ."

"Yeah, I know," Hariman answered. He leaned across the cargo box, resting his elbows on the lid. "Going to Wing-land to see her is a lot to take on faith, though." He rubbed the tip of his nose. "Stallart. . . ." He broke off, seeing Ward shake his head in sharp negation. "Hear me out, okay?" He waited for Ward's suspicious nod before continuing. "Stallart's almost alone in thinking there's going to be war."

"No kidding?" Ward interjected sarcastically. "I was at the meeting, pinhead."

Hariman ignored him. "Stal told me while you were gone that he's itching to do a recon job on Wing. He wants to find evidence that Wing is getting frisky. Your dad's forbidden it. He's afraid that'll stir up more trouble if Stal gets caught." He paused, trying to gauge Ward's reaction.

Ward nodded again. "Go ahead."

"I assume you have a map or way to get into Wing?" Hariman ventured.

"Yeah . . ." Ward answered carefully.

"Let's go see Stallart," Hariman pressed. "You take him with you and he'll watch your back. He gets a secure route and a good long look at Wing. You get some security while you're romancing your lady-love. And if we get caught, Stallart'll get us out."

"Who's we?" Ward asked.

"You need someone to drive, don't you?" Hariman grinned and thumped his chest.

Ward thought it over. "What about my Dad? What if we get caught?"

Hariman grinned conspiratorially. "Benno has enough to worry about. And as for getting caught . . . none of us can afford it, so let's not. Okay?"

"I thought you were supposed to keep me out of trouble?" Ward grinned, suddenly feeling easier.

Hariman grinned back. "You'd only sneak off if I try to stop you. This way, you'll at least have some cover."

Ward laughed. "Bastard. Let's go find Stallart."

The three conspirators spent the afternoon feverishly planning. Ward transferred Seladra's described route onto a computer pad, then overlaid Grandfather Abel's attack routes. Hariman arranged the vehicle and laid in the supplies. Stallart had Ward dump his battle armor into the car's cargo box. Stal's position as Ward's trainer made the excuse of taking him out for night exercises seem natural.

They edged out of LaPort just as night fell. Ward sat silently and watched Stallart order Hariman to cruise high enough to get a good registry on the navigation radars before descending to the night-training range. Stallart then had Hariman skim the car back along its course, hugging the trees until they crossed over into Wing territory. It was a simple matter to quickly cruise to the ravine and drop the vehicle in.

Their timing was a bit closer than Ward would have preferred. They had only just gotten the car into the cut when Centauri B made its usual quick passage, dropping below the horizon like a stunned sheep, leaving almost total darkness behind. They covered the vehicle with a thermal blanket and crept slowly up the steep channel, using infrared goggles and fingertips to feel their way along.

Ward quickly gained an appreciation for his PBA's sophisticated imaging capabilities. The IR goggles lacked the armor's lidar rangefinder, causing him to bang his head several times on overhangs and outcroppings that were closer than they appeared. He swore quietly and rubbed his forehead after his second impact. Hariman leered at him in false-color, his bug-eyed goggles and teeth glowing red-black against his face. Ward adjusted his own eyepieces and grinned back.

Hariman led him to the apex of the ravine, then quickly across to the trail. Ward followed, starting nervously as he heard Stallart emerge from behind a bush. Ward hadn't seen him until he moved.

Stallart's ghilli suit damped almost all of his infrared signature, but Ward knew the temperature inside the suit would soon become hellish. Ward had been the recipient of Stallart's woodcraft before and had long since become aware that Stallart was almost unmatched in the boonies.

Stal tapped Ward on the shoulder and gave him a thumbs up. He held up a handful of power cables and ground sensor heads. Ward nodded back. He led Ward and Hariman towards lights winking in the distance between the trees.

Hariman, trailing Ward, wore an ablative poncho over his clothing, intended more to distort his heat signature than to hide it. He walked backwards most of the time, monitoring their trail and sticking flashtabs to trees so they could find their way back to the ravine. The flashtabs would light when activated by a specific radio frequency, then would burn out. They had been ordered from Earth by Benno at Stallart's recommendation.

Only Ward had no infrared shielding. He skulked between the other two, trying to keep Stallart between him and the manor house up ahead. Stallart suddenly froze, then gestured for them to stay. He vanished into the brush.

Ward sat on his haunches and peered into the gloom. The infrared false-colored everything surrounding him, but the ground heat and water vapor released from the trees and brush hung in the air. They distorted the local heat signatures from the cooling trees, hazing the air and reducing visibility. Ward listened intently, straining to hear any unnatural noise. The local leafsawers and thrummers kept up their incessant nocturnal buzz. The harder he listened, the louder and louder they sounded, until the noise seemed overwhelming.

He almost jumped out of his skin when he felt Hariman's hand on his shoulder. Hariman pointed his index finger in the direction Stallart disappeared, then mimed walking with his fingers. Ward raised his thumb, indicating assent, and brushed through the undergrowth.

They crept up on the Wing compound. Ward's nerves felt as if they were afire, and he had to concentrate to steady his breathing. Stallart waited, crouched behind a low hedge of Terran blackberry bushes. He made a pushing gesture with his palm towards the ground. They crouched down and worked their way to his side.

"The barn is a little ways from the main house," Stallart whispered, "and is partially shielded from view by those trees." He tipped his head in the direction of the barn. "The doors face away from the main compound, so you shouldn't have any trouble getting in. There's a lot of light wash around the entrance. The outside light is either broken, disabled, or off, so you shouldn't have to worry about being illuminated until you're in the doorway. Any questions so far?"

Ward shook his head.

"Good." Stallart continued his report. "You can get to the barn doors easy enough. One is open and the interior is already lit. Your optics will fuzz as you enter the light haze and your eyes won't have time to adjust. *Don't linger in the light.*"

Stallart didn't raise his voice, but his low tones grew more forceful. "If you are seen or something goes wrong, haul ass for the car or hit your transponder. Hariman and I'll cover you. Okay?"

Ward dipped his head in a vigorous "yes."

Stallart pointed around the blackberry bushes. "Go get 'em, tiger."

Ward grinned, his teeth red-black in the infrared imaging. He quickly slipped around the bushes and angled for the barn. Stallart slid on his haunches a few paces over, the better to watch the barn and the south side of the compound. He noted that Ward stood up and openly walked towards the barn rather than skulking up to it. "Good job, kid. Make 'em think you belong there," he whispered to Ward's distant back.

He watched Ward approach the door and take off his infrared goggles before slipping inside.

"Hark," Hariman whispered from his vantage point, "what light through yonder barn door breaks?"

Stallart smiled. "There is a certain irony to that, given who he's screwing," he whispered back. "All in all, you were right to keep that little item from me until we were on the property. I'd have pulled the plug, otherwise."

Hariman didn't answer. Stallart scanned the area for guards and saw none. He'd been expecting to see more than he had, but so far there'd been little except the usual roof and grounds walkers. He hoped his luck held.

Something didn't feel right to him, though he couldn't quite determine what it was. He wished he hadn't shackled himself to Ward. He needed to get out and explore to satisfy his nagging worry. "What in the hell am I doing here?" Stallart murmured to himself. "This is a serious mistake."

"What?" Hariman whispered.

"I screwed up," Stallart replied. "This seemed like such a sweet deal. Now I'm seriously regretting it."

"He'd have just snuck off," Hariman reminded him pragmatically. "This way he's got some cover."

Stallart nodded ruefully.

"Here I am, ass deep in enemy territory, while the boss's kid is getting his ashes hauled," he said disgustedly. "I just wish he wouldn't do his thinking with his gonads."

He looked at his watch. Ten minutes, so far.

"I should've given him a time limit, fifteen minutes at the most."

"Don't you think that's a little crass?" Hariman answered, still speaking softly.

"And us squatting in the weeds isn't?" Stallart replied. "He's going to get us all killed if he doesn't hurry."

Stallart checked the body core temperature gauge on his suit's wrist. The diode indicated a hundred and one degrees. He bent to unzip the vanes in the suit's legs. They were made of the same fiber as the rest of the undersuit and would wick collected body heat away and out. The vanes would glow like furnaces in an infrared scope, but that wasn't a problem here with so few guards.

He froze, his hand halfway to his leg. "Shit, that's it!"

His harsh whisper carried to Hariman, who turned on his heels. Stallart twitched a finger at the younger man, calling him closer. "Count the guards, how many do you see?"

Hariman looked back towards the house, his lips moving as he inventoried the sentries. He held up three fingers. Stallart affirmed Hariman's count with a nod of his head. "How many away from the house?"

Hariman sat up a little higher, rising on his thighs to look carefully around him. He turned a complete circle, then held out a closed fist to Stallart: zero.

Stallart leaned in closer to Hariman. "Wing and Tuch are at loggerheads. How many guards should there be?"

Hariman thought a moment, then waggled his fingers. Many.

"So where are they?" Stallart asked.

Hariman shrugged his shoulders.

"Something's going on," Stallart stated. He peered at

each guard in turn. None wore PBA, but that wasn't unusual for beat-walkers. The smear of body heat blurred details beyond a few feet, but there was something odd about the way the guard on the roof moved. Stallart tried to boost the gain on the goggles to improve detail. No luck.

"Did you bring your light-scope?" he whispered to Hariman. The retainer reached into his belt-sack and passed Stallart a short, blunt tube. Stallart checked the power levels, removed the goggles, and held the light-gathering device to his eye. The guard jumped into sharp relief. Stallart used the zoom to bore in for more detail.

The female sentry walked with stiff, heavy movements. She turned and Stallart saw a thick shock of white hair. He frantically turned the tube on the house, scanning windows, doors, and outside areas for people. A few moved in his augmented field of vision, children mostly, but no parents, none of the able-bodied.

This was Wing's manor, the heart of the clan. Where the hell was Wing? Stallart felt his heart thump in his chest. Something was desperately, desperately wrong.

Chapter 3

Stallart broke from cover and sprinted across the open area towards the barn. He kept low and skirted the trees in a ground-eating lope. Hariman remained undercover, wrapped in his thermal blanket while he guarded Stallart's approach.

Stallart hit the wall beside the door and raised his goggles. The exertion had spiked his body temperature and sweat ran freely under the suit. He ripped the chest closure open with an impatient hand and felt the cool air wash over his heated skin.

He turned towards the door, listening carefully. He heard the soft tones of a music player mingling with low murmurs. He drew his Execuline hand-laser and slipped through the door.

He spotted the lovers by the clothing strewn across the hay bales. They were tucked into a pile of soft, fragrant first cut, with a music crystal player and a wine bottle nearby. The girl reclined, naked to the waist, while Ward, still almost fully dressed, nuzzled her small breasts.

"Boyo, you'd have kept us here all night at this rate," Stallart grumbled to himself.

The girl shifted under Ward's weight, her hands cradling his head to her breast. She opened her eyes, saw Stallart, and squeaked.

Ward, to his credit, rolled away and went for his laser.

"Cool your rockets, boy. It's Stallart." He moved to keep

the barn door in view. Seladra covered herself with one hand while groping for the blanket she lay on.

Ward sprang up, angry and embarrassed, fists balled at his sides. His voice sounded harsh, just on the edge of being too loud. "What the hell?"

"Something's going on," Stallart hissed. "Let's get out of here!" He held the Execuline in a careful two-handed grip, ready to fire at anything coming through the door.

"Wha-whad'ya mean?" Ward stammered.

"Get your clothes. We have to get out of here." Stallart had already decided that if Ward gave him any lip, he was going to rag the boy out.

But Ward scrambled to obey. "What's going on?"

Stallart looked coldly at Seladra, who had finished wrapping the blanket around her. She looked to him as though she'd already recovered her poise, even with her disheveled hair and flushed face. "Why don't you ask her?" he suggested icily.

Ward looked a question at Seladra. She shrugged.

"Where is everyone, Wing?" Stallart demanded.

She flipped her hair away from her face and met his eye. "What do you mean?"

"There are three guards, one old enough to be my mother, and no able-bodied people at all in the courtyard." He bent close to her, holding the laser between them like a talisman. "*Where is everyone?*" he hissed.

Seladra looked at Ward, her eyes pleading. "I don't know."

Stallart raised the laser as if to hit her. That proved too much for Ward.

"That's enough, Stal." Ward's voice cut across him like a shot. He looked up, surprised at the unaccustomed authority in the boy's voice.

Ward finished tucking in his shirt and buckling on his gun belt. He squatted on his haunches next to Seladra as she sat huddled in the hay. To Ward, she looked vulnerable and unhappy. Ward wanted to cradle her in his arms and smooth away her hurt.

"Sel, I have to ask. Is there something happening?" he asked gently.

Her eyes met Ward's. She shook her head slowly, but said nothing.

Stallart grunted in disgust. "Damn it, let's get out of here before we get killed, huh?"

Ward stood and gathered the last of his things. Stallart kept an eye on Seladra until Ward was ready, then steered the younger man towards the door. Ward glanced back at Seladra.

Stallart bent his head. "You really should tie her up, you know, to keep her from giving an alarm."

Ward shook his head. "No."

Stallart sighed. "You're definitely your father's son."

At the door, Stallart stepped into the light a moment to signal Hariman. He glanced at Ward. "Are you ready?"

Ward looked at Seladra. She held her head in her hands and appeared to be crying. "Yeah, I guess."

"When you duck out," ordered Stallart, "run for Hariman. Skirt the trees to the west but don't go in. I didn't sweep 'em." He paused. "I'll cover you. Any questions?"

"No." He braced himself to run.

"Go!"

Ward sprinted for the far side of the small clearing, staying well to the covered side. Hariman, alerted by the sudden flurry of movement, jumped to his feet and waved. Ward crossed to him in a flash and crashed into the brush. Hariman, rather than barraging Ward with questions, only drew his laser and sighted back across the clearing towards the barn where Stallart remained.

Stallart kept one eye on Seladra while Ward crossed. He didn't want to get backshot as a result of Ward's soft heart. Stallart contemplated tying her up but knew there were too many things that could go wrong. He almost missed Hariman's signal as he shifted his attention from Seladra. He looked back to her one time.

She raised her head as she fixed the blanket around herself more firmly. Their gaze met momentarily. He saw her eyes were dry. He spat on the ground.

He sprinted across the open ground at a dead run, arriving at the observation point without difficulty. He clapped Hariman approvingly on the shoulder as the younger man finished tucking his poncho into its carrying pouch and readied himself to pull back. He slipped on his IR goggles, and the world suddenly sprang into ghostly, false-colored life once again.

He signaled the others to retreat, pointing to each in turn to indicate the order of march. They returned in the same order they came, Stallart leading and scouting, followed by Ward, in turn trailed by Hariman. Stallart glanced back and saw that Hariman had lagged a moment to ensure they weren't being followed. He knew Hariman well enough to hope Seladra didn't put in an untimely appearance. She'd be laser bait if she stuck her head out while he remained behind.

Stallart thought an ambush unlikely, but had to factor for the possibility. He slipped quickly into the undergrowth, trying to balance speed and stealth. He paused every few random steps to listen. The usual animal sounds and nocturnal noises continued unabated, a clue that nothing lurked in their area.

They moved along their backtrail, moving quickly into the thicker underbrush to smear their infrared outlines. He knew to within a few meters where the ravine ended and he'd maintained his orientation with the aid of the stars and small night clues. He decided they could afford the luxury of burning the flashtabs to make absolutely certain of their path.

He took the transponder from its belt pouch and keyed it to "constant signal." It would ignite each tab as they came within range. The IR firefly glow ignited almost at once. He blessed the Hegemony as he walked quickly towards the flare.

"They may be assholes," he murmured softly, "but they make good hardware." A second tab popped in the distance, then another as each reacted to the transponder's limited range.

Ward heard the first tab ignite and stopped to fumble with his goggles. He smeared the lenses with his sweaty palms as he tried to position them over his eyes. His hands shook from the stress and adrenaline, making what should have an easy task difficult. He got them on after his second try. They misted almost instantly as perspiration trapped underneath the eyepieces condensed.

He ran on, half blind, following Stallart's distant figure and the flashtabs glowing like runway lights. He barely missed careening into a tree head on and did step into a hole while fumbling to follow Stallart. Stallart caught him as he almost blundered into the ravine. He slip-slid down its steep grade as Stallart, abandoning stealth, pushed on ahead for the hidden ground-effect car.

It seemed an eternity before he panted up to the vehicle. His hands stung and his knees were scraped from falls and blunders. The goggles fogged over completely as soon as he stopped, blinding him. He impatiently stripped them off. Darkness closed in. He tried to wipe the moisture away with his sweat-soaked shirttail before he gave up on the whole idea.

He crashed around the car, tripping loudly over a stone as Stallart tried to warn him of obstacles in an irate, hushed voice. Ward, panting and desperate, heard Stallart moving in the moonless night but couldn't see him until he flipped on the red map-light. The weak glow seemed like a beacon in the darkness.

Stallart's goggles glowed an eerie red as the weapons master gave him a long look, shook his head, and returned his attention to prepping the vehicle for flight. "Get your armor on while I do the checklist," he ordered.

Ward obeyed without question. He quickly stripped to his shorts and began to tug and pull his heavy battle armor out of the car's cargo box and onto the dirt. Ward grunted under its weight as it slid out.

Stallart jumped out of the vehicle and began the preflight inspection. Ward knew Hariman had synchronized the gyros before shutting down, saving Stallart the trouble. He watched Stallart check them anyway.

Ward opened the front carapace of the armor, setting the main battery units to preheat the system. Stallart looked over at him, saw him initiating warmup, and swore. "Damn it, Ward, you should have started preheat *before* we left! Now we're stuck for another five minutes!"

Ward looked at him, irritated and stung. "I didn't want to waste battery power."

"Don't give me that," Stallart snapped. "You were in a rush to get to Miss Hot Pants back there. You'd have lost maybe one or two percent of power if you'd have kept the system warmed up."

Stallart grumbled angrily as he reached into the vehicle and pulled out a worn cloth bag. He drew the components of a HEAP pistol from the bag and began assembling it while the engine compressors loaded.

"Shit, Ward, you keep thinkin' with your gonads, some day a little filly is gonna grab them and lead you into a world of hurt."

Ward had no desire to pursue that topic. He pointed to the HEAP gun. "What are you doing with that?" He shuddered. "Cripes, I hate those things."

Stallart held the oversized pistol up as he checked the action and loaded a clip. "This lil' thing?" he replied. "I expected *you* to be our anti-armor. Now I'll have to do it until you get suited."

Ward shuddered again. He'd seen imprint images of the horrible burns inflicted on suits and flesh by HEAP pistols. They were notoriously inaccurate, but when they hit they gave hellish results and first-shot kills. He shivered as Stallart locked a warhead into the barrel.

The weapons master laid the weapon and a bandoleer of reloads on the passenger seat and went to help Ward just as Hariman slipped out of the brush. The retainer gave them a puzzled look and raised his laser to his shoulder. "What the hell is taking so long?" he hissed. "We should be gone by now!"

Stallart used his whole hand to point to Ward. "Lover boy didn't preheat his battle armor. We need more time."

Hariman looked dumbfounded at Ward. Stallart took the coil rifle from the car, checked the ammunition tube and the powercell, and handed it to him. "Why don't you go back upslope a bit and pull security. See if anyone is pursuing us." Hariman looked grim as he took the weapon and disappeared into the gloom.

Ward fidgeted while the suit finished its preheat cycle. It seemed an eternity to him before the ready light glowed green. He quickly locked out the sensor system, preventing the suit from jerking or flexing while he climbed in. He scraped his back as he began to twist and slip against the tight fit, grunting as he tried to work his chest around the encapsulated gyro and balance monitoring mechanism. Stallart whipped his head around at the sound.

"Do you think you could make just a little more noise?" he said in a soft, irritated voice. "They aren't awake in Foundation yet."

"Why does this trash have to be made as a single piece?" Ward complained in a whisper as he worked himself around. "Why can't they be modules, put on a piece at a time?"

"Don't whisper," Stallart said, "the sibilants carry farther. Talk in a lowered voice." Then he shrugged. "You wouldn't have so much trouble getting inside if you'd kept your weight down. The suit is sized for you at seventy-nine kilos, not eighty-three." Ward swore as he sucked in his gut and tried to slide his hips past the narrow waist joint.

Stallart turned his attention back to his portable scanner. "This box should be alive with chatter. Wing usually has lousy communications security. There's nothing here, nothing at all."

Ward activated his servo-systems with his tongue switch and closed the chest connections. Diodes on the wrist diagnostic panels began to wink and glow as the suit's internal software ran through its test sequences. Ward skipped most of the usual checklist, testing only that the boost-packs were on-line and that weapons were operational. He peered intently at his wrist and nodded to Stallart that he was ready.

Stallart whistled softly once to Hariman, calling him in. The retainer trotted in and at Stallart's signal leaned his coil rifle muzzle-up between the two front seats. He popped the bubble canopy and tossed it into the ravine while Ward used his augmented strength to hop into the cargo box.

Hariman slipped behind the wheel, brought the compressors to full, and lifted the car out of the cut on a column of compressed air. The intake fans howled as they sucked air to maintain compressor pressure. Hariman flat-spun the car, orienting it towards where the Tuchman travel beacon should have been. The scanner diodes flickered back and forth, looking for the signal. Nothing. The beacon was off the air. Ward felt his guts wrench in fear. He knelt in the cargobox and peered intently towards LaPort.

Stallart frowned and turned to Hariman. "Take us home, boy. Fast."

The retainer locked the dead-reckoner to the overlay map and engaged the autopilot. The car accelerated towards distant Clan Tuchman, the compressor intake whine rising an octave as the demands on it increased.

"You'd better take us up out of ground-effect," Stallart ordered. "Direct flight'll be faster right now."

Hariman checked his gauges. Ward thought he looked distinctly unhappy. "Stal," he protested, "this car's built to clear rough ground. It's not designed for open flight. I don't think the compressors'll take the abuse if we take the direct route."

Stallart kept one eye locked on the Wing compound. He could just barely see the top of the building over the trees. "We need to be somewhere else right now," he declared. "This car only has to get us back. Fly direct."

Hariman complied and pushed the compressors' angle of attack to the stops. The car bucked forward, jerking and swaying on its own turbulence as it lifted above the ground effect boundary.

The compressor whine shattered the night's quiet. Stallart wasn't surprised to see the glow of an infrared searchlight through his goggles as the Wing responded to the noise. The IR light began to play back and forth from the corner of the main house closest to the escaping car. It scanned futilely back and forth as Hariman pointed the nose down and accelerated away.

"Shit," Stallart swore, "the light's new."

Hariman mumbled something obscene from the driver's socket, then said: "Do you want evasive?"

"No," Stallart replied, "they aren't even close. "Just get us home." Hariman answered by steepening his angle.

Ward fretted through the short flight back to LaPort. The compressors' gimbals and bearings began to heat under the strain of open flight. Ward felt the change in vibration as they warped and reamed out the channels as the demands on them mounted. The vibration built to a clatter that sounded as though someone had thrown a handful of iron pellets in the engine. The car's alarm chimed as they crossed the border of the Tuchman lands.

"We're home!" Ward sighed.

"Not hardly," Stallart grumbled in return.

Hariman aimed for Benno's manor house. Soon they could see ground fires: parts of LaPort and the Tuchman compound burning. As they pulled closer in, a distant explosion bloomed from the side of the manor house, lighting the building with a red-yellow ball of fire. A soft *thud* washed over the car several seconds later. Light from the fires and explosions lit the underbelly of an appalling smoke cloud, giving the hilltop manor a hellish appearance.

Stallart closed his eyes a moment, then signaled Hariman to land away from the house. Hariman looked rebellious.

"You land there, we die," Stallart said to the retainer as he pointed to the manor house. "Whatever happened is over. If the defenders don't shoot us down Wing will if we come screaming in. Angle for my place. It'll be safer there until we figure out what to do."

He looked at the burning building up ahead. "More or less safer, anyway."

Hariman turned the car towards LaPort. The town and house were both dark, the likely victims of a sabotaged power plant. The only ambient light came from the glow of secondary fires. Some of the burning came from shops and stores.

"Looting," Stallart said, gesturing to one burning establishment, "as well as killing and burning. That's Wing, all right."

Ward was silent, hot rage boiling up in his chest.

Stallart looked sadly down at the burning town. They passed over a small park. He pointed out to Ward four corpses lying under a shattered streetlamp and nearby the body of a naked woman. A burning storefront illuminated the grisly scene.

"Look at that," Stallart commanded softly, "and remember."

He glanced back and saw the heat in Ward's face.

"Oh, no, boy, don't get hot. That's the way to an early grave. Get cold and stay cold. Get pissed and get dead."

Ward stared at the woman, limbs akimbo, her torn garments nearby. He could see the blood pool from her cut throat even at their height. He felt his gorge rise. He frantically fumbled with his helmet catches, desperate to get it off before he spewed. He pulled the helmet free just in time to vomit over the side. He heaved and retched miserably. He felt unable to forget the woman, even when the sad scene passed away behind.

Stallart turned in his seat. "Are you all right?"

Ward nodded silently. Stallart reached down and handed him a shop cloth. "Here, wipe your face." Ward cleaned himself as best he could.

The car pitched and yawed as Hariman struggled to hold it on course. "The control gimbals're getting sluggish," Hariman said in response to Stallart's sharp glance. He adjusted the pitch several times before it wallowed back on course.

Ward peered forward as Hariman skimmed the edges of LaPort and angled for Stallart's hut. He tried to focus, make sense of all the carnage, but he couldn't. He'd seen death before, but the naked woman's outraged form represented a casual brutality that shook him to the core. Stallart glanced back and saw Ward's pale face and shaking hands. "Clear the car as soon as we get close enough for the servos. Don't wait for us to land. Use your boostpacks to break your landing if you need to, but don't waste fuel. We don't know when reload might be. And Ward . . . ?"

"Yes," the younger man responded.

"If it ain't Tuch', kill it," Stallart ordered.

"No problem," Ward answered.

"Once we get on the ground, we'll check on my wife and I'll armor up. Then you and I will go through the woods and the trail up to the main house and see what we can do. Hariman, you'll stay with Mona and do as she tells you." He smiled proudly.

"She's young, but she's good. Any questions?" He barely paused. "None? Good."

"Now Hariman, listen up. Mona's got a seventy-millimeter Piat stashed away, loaded with squash-head rounds. We don't want to surprise her." He pointed to a clearing several hundred meters downhill from the hut. "We'll land over there and walk up, so she can get a nice long look at us."

Hariman nodded gravely and aimed for the site, an opening in the trees barely large enough for the vehicle. Ward noticed that they were landing in the same woods where he'd played "Cowboys and Commies" with his friends as a child. It had never occurred to him that he might actually fight in the woods where he'd had so many boisterous arguments about who shot who. "This time," he said to himself sourly, "there won't be any doubt."

Stallart slung the bandoleer over his shoulder and drew the HEAP pistol, careful not to disturb Hariman's coil rifle. He looked back at Ward. "Are you still here?"

"Sorry," Ward answered as the car settled over the trees. He slapped his helmet on and hurriedly closed the catches. He then levered himself over the edge of the car and plunged through the leafy branches as Hariman made his final approach. Right after he left the car, all hell broke loose.

Stallart saw streams of coil gunfire lance up from the middle-left and heard the ring penetrators slicing through the car like a punch awl through leather. He heard Hariman grunt softly and cant the vehicle sharply to the right. The coil gun followed them, stitching the side of the vehicle and reaming out the compressor. Stallart felt the car shudder under the hammer blows as more airfoils shredded the underbody. A few stray rounds whipped through the passenger compartment, one coming through the console between the two men and smashing their coil rifle's ammunition feed coupling. Stallart tried to block the flying spall from the damaged weapon with his arm.

He felt the compressor's fan blades begin to break up as the compression chamber lost integrity. The car lost power and plummeted the last ten feet to the ground. Stallart covered his face and head with his hands, leaned forward in his seat, and waited for the impact. The car hit hard, jolting him and snapping him deep into his seat. He felt a sharp pain as something gave in his back.

The fan began to unspool, hurling pieces of blade through the compression chamber's walls and into the car. Stallart was never more thankful for the thin piece of armor that separated the passenger compartment from the compressor. He felt thumps and bumps and heard the blade shrapnel sing as it daisy-cut the clearing. He realized he'd have lost his legs if he'd tried to bail from the vehicle as soon as it crashed.

Stallart reached out to restrain Hariman, to keep him from getting out while the blades flew. The retainer's head lolled back, eyes open and staring. Stallart saw the nasty exit wound from the tumbling ring penetrator that had passed between Hariman's collarbone and his shoulder blade. He brushed his fingers across the dead man's eyes, closing the lids.

He hit the quick release harness just as a coil gun chattered in the right-hand woods. As he tried to twist in his seat to see the source, a jet of agony lanced through his chest. He cried out and slumped back in his seat, blacking out.

Ward had only just fallen through the trees when he heard the first burst of coil gun fire and the unmistakable *ping-patter* as airfoils cut into unarmored metal. He restrained himself from firing his boost-packs to slow his descent. "No sense in giving them a nice IR target," he said to himself. His training was taking him through the nightmare on autopilot.

His AI flashed a warning as the ground rushed up. He squeezed his eyes closed. "Oh, this is gonna hurt," he whispered. The leg servos whined as they tried to distribute the impact load.

His helmet catches popped loose on impact, the helmet slewing around as he landed. He cursed himself for not having taken the two seconds necessary to ensure they'd been properly closed. He tried to monitor the incoming streams of fire while he fixed them.

The last one closed correctly after what seemed like an eternity, pressing the helmet into the rubber collar and sealing the suit.

Power flooded into the helmet as the interlocks closed and the suit began its diagnostic routines. Ward aborted those with an impatient gesture and reset the AI for enhanced vision. The artificial intelligence selected IR/ambient overlay for optimal imaging and seamlessly merged the two into a clear composite image. His augmented vision approached daylight clarity.

Ward swore at the lost time as he whipped his head around to check his area. He saw that the car had crashed about fifty meters from his landing point. It looked badly chewed. He wanted to radio the car to see if someone might have survived the crash, then remembered Stallart's warnings about communications security and the punishments the gods of war meted out to the feckless.

A physical inspection of the vehicle was out of the question, at least while it was still taking fire from the coil gun and spitting out engine pieces. His enhanced hearing brought him the thumps and bumps of the 7500 RPM compressor going through its death throes. "Damn, nobody could live through that," he whispered.

Another stream of fire lanced out of the trees a little ahead and to the left of his current position. Ward hop-jumped, skirting the clearing and using his boost-packs to leap first into an oak tree's thick, low branches and then to jump from tree to tree, scanning left and right. He could almost hear Stallart's soft voice in his ear saying "If you have three dimensions, boy, *use them*!"

He was able to trace the projectile stream to a single PBA-clad figure. The Wing's unshielded electromagnetic repulsion coil glowed cherry-red in Ward's thermal vision as it heated under the current needed to hurl hypervelocity airfoils. A *hiss-crack* was the only sound the weapon made.

Ward crept up and away along the branch. He prayed the Wing's AI would suppress his augmented hearing as long as the coil gun fired. Otherwise, Ward wouldn't remain undetected for long.

He closed to within seventy meters. His direct line of sight was blocked by the tree the Wing was leaning against. Ward fired anyway, cracking off a dozen rounds.

The recoil rocked Ward's supporting branch, but penetrators ripped through the Wing's tree and kicked up dirt all around. The Wing jumped clear of the kill point even as airfoils still tore great splinters from the tree and gouged the earth by his feet. His helmet scanned frantically at ground level, looking for the source of the shots.

The branch beneath Ward's feet betrayed him, breaking under his weight with a sharp crack just as the Wing looked in his direction. He tumbled out of the tree and was almost cut in half by ring penetrators as the Wing's AI tracked the movement and reacted by firing. Ward rolled to the right, keeping the tree he had already shot between them. He looked accusingly up at the branch and smiled in inspiration as it swayed back and forth, broken but not severed.

The Wing had taken cover behind the shot tree and stepped out only long enough to crank off a few random rounds in Ward's direction. Ward waited for his opponent to fire and step back before he answered, aiming his weapon at the damaged bole.

The water at the point of impact inside the tree exploded under the laser's touch, weakening its already damaged structure. The trunk snapped a meter above the ground, the point of cleavage a broken, steaming mess of splinters. The Wing's AI tried to dodge the falling mass one way, while the fighter tried to move another.

"Dipshit," Ward said. He recalled Stallart's lectures on suit AIs. Ward knew that the AI's programmed reactions were often faster than human hand-eye, but they were limited and could clash with the wearer's desires at odd moments. He was glad that his own suit's AI performed only support and diagnostic functions. He saw the Wing throw up a futile arm as the tree smashed him to the ground.

Ward walked to the pinned fighter. The Wing had drawn his powerknife. He hacked at the treebole, though it would take the better part of a day to free himself that way.

Ward shot him through the faceplate. He tripped the Wing's emergency transponder and ghosted back from the body.

He set himself about a hundred meters from the fallen tree and positioned himself at an angle from the most likely approach route. He now understood Stallart's admonishment to "stay cold." He felt frightened and very alone, but stored his emotions in a corner of his mind that remained disconnected from his actions. Most of his body moved automatically, executing remembered instruction as his mind feverishly planned ahead. The world seemed to move in slow motion as he shifted slightly.

He didn't have long to wait for the Wing troops. A squad of armored figures bounded into the edge of his augmented sight. The first four positioned themselves in a lazy W formation, moving closer as they flickered from cover to cover at the top of the hill. A fifth trailed the others, armed with a multiport HE rocket launcher.

Ward whistled. The weapon fired high-explosive rockets in groups of two and had a forty-round drum magazine. It was bulky as hell, and the rockets could easily gang-fire if the drum's thin walls were pierced. It was a fearsome weapon and rare on New Hope.

Ward felt his spirits plunge. He hadn't expected a whole squad to react and knew he didn't really have the ordnance for a protracted fight. He thought Stallart could pull off a running battle against odds like these, but Stallart was probably dead. Even if he wasn't, Stallart would need armor to fight the Wing PBA and the weapons master's armor was on the far side of Wing. Ward realized at that moment he was truly on his own.

He looked hurriedly back and cursed. He realized that in his zeal for ambush, he'd forgotten to plan a line of retreat. He didn't see so much as a blade of grass behind him for a full ten meters. A large oak beckoned temptingly to him from that distance, but it seemed to be a football field away.

Ward looked back at the Wing troops. The squad had crossed the fallen tree where their comrade lay pinned. The closest was about sixty meters away. The fourth, possibly the squad's leader, bent over the dead man.

The point troop pulled an emissions scanner from an equipment belt and began playing it back and forth over the twelve-o'clock sector.

"Shit," Ward whispered, "no way to wait this out."

He was pretty certain their suit units weren't sensitive enough to detect either his low-level IR emissions or the servos' electromagnetic signatures. A belt unit was another story, however. Ward knew that eventually the point guard would aim the box in his direction and he would be well and truly screwed.

"Back to Plan A, I suppose," he said to himself.

He shifted his coil gun and laser to fire through the

deadfall, looking for all the world like a hunchback in a set of stocks. He peered over the top of the piled trees, touching his chin plate to actuate the feedback crosshairs.

The enemy had the dead man's helmet off and was probing the mess beneath for something. Ward fired the laser and coil gun together, twin streams of death converging.

Ring penetrators scored and pierced the leader's carapace as the laser energy licked out and etched into his leg armor. "Targeting must be off," Ward mumbled to himself as he saw the laser fall below the crosshairs.

He watched, detached, as the impact blew the armored figure back over the trunk, textured foot soles briefly visible as legs flopped upwards. Ward's audio pickups, damped automatically by the AI each time the coil gun fired, came back on in a rush. Ward heard the burning hiss of the leader's boost-pack firing behind the tree. Wood smoke began to drift from the tumbled branches.

The three troops to Ward's left front reacted instantly. He barely had time to duck before ring penetrators zinged through the deadfall to either side. Three smashed into him, slowed by passage through the wood. A spray of splinters rattled against his helmet and carapace.

Two penetrators hit the left elbow joint. The third struck at midarm and glanced away. The triple impact pushed the armor's contact against his arm with some force. The AI interpreted the sensor pressure as a desire by Ward to raise his arm. The servo reacted, jerking it up by the shoulder. The sudden strain on the elbow, coupled with battle damage, blew the joint. Ward felt the wrench as the elbow's servo locked.

He quickly rolled to his right across the open ground, and prepared to sell himself as dearly as he could. Laser fire licked the ground behind him as he frantically sought cover. A beam played across his side a moment, damaging cooling vanes and sending a drip of molten metal and polymer down the outside of the suit. The leg armor conducted the heat inside, overwhelming the insulation and burning his thigh. He stifled a cry as he rolled behind cover.

Laser beams followed him, flicking and flashing as they sought him amongst the boles of several close-growing trees. His breath sounded loud in his ears, amplified by the closed helmet, as he sucked air. The suit responded to his increased demand by pumping higher concentrations of oxygen into his breath-mask.

He popped his head up a moment to locate the enemy. Three were still in their mutually supporting base wedge, two interlocking their fires while the third moved. He ducked as the laser fire picked holes in the trees to either side of his head. He didn't think their fire was terribly accurate, certainly not AI assisted, but it kept him moving and ducking. He rolled again, trying to keep the trees between him and the three. He glanced hurriedly about, looking for the rocket launcher.

Chuff! Chuff! Ward went flat to earth, covering his helmet with his arms as two rockets detonated almost overhead. He knew the high-explosive heads would do serious damage all by themselves, but the three ring penetrators imbedded in the HE matrix would finish him if a rocket got a solid hit. He rolled to his left, then shifted onto his belly as he tried to identify his target. He got a glimpse of the bulky rocket pack as the launcher ducked behind another tree. *Chuff! Chuff!* Two more rockets detonated, the second close enough to rain stones and dirt on his head and shoulders.

"Shit! The bastards flanked me." He bobbed his head up and saw the three working closer to him, apparently using their radios to coordinate their fire. The rocket launcher continued to work around towards Ward's four-o'clock position. He realized they would have him in a crossfire once they were in position. Ward cursed again as he realized he'd have to expose a flank to one element in order to shoot at the other.

Ward set his coil gun to single fire and snapped off a shot at the rocket launcher. He sighted at the trees sheltering the Wings, using the residual heat smear left on the bark by the rocket's plume as a reference point.

He waited for the rocket launcher to emerge from cover. The Wing loyalist moved, almost as if on command. Ward aimed his coil gun, still on single shot, when he heard the popping noise of a twig breaking from his right. He whipped his head around long enough to see Stallart, sealed in his IR ghilli suit, leaning up against a tree on the rocket launcher's far flank.

The older man had a reload for his HEAP pistol clenched in his teeth. He braced his left hand against the tree and laid his firing hand across it. Ward watched the projectile lance off the end of the pistol with a soft *whuff*. Stallart waved pleasantly to Ward as he faded back into the brush and disappeared.

Ward turned his attention back to the rocket launcher. He saw Stallart's projectile through his augmented vision, wobbling in its lazy flight towards the rocket launcher's flank. The Wing's AI must have been loaded with a preset evasion command, one that didn't factor for the additional bulk of the rockets. The armored figure tried to jump away from the tree as the projectile wandered into detection range.

The rocket launcher's heavy pack caught on the rough bark. The delay held long enough to convert Stallart's near-miss into a glancing blow.

Ward saw the shaped charge detonate millimeters from the victim's side in a sun-white burst. In an instant, the Wing was engulfed in a burning ball as his own rocket propellant charges burst and exploded in sympathetic detonation.

Ward saw the body tumble forward, blown towards him by the secondary blast. He could see flames licking out of the joint seals as burning fuel and plastic fed into a channel cut by the HEAP projectile.

Ward turned his attention back to the other three, who had gone to ground when their comrade died.

"Boy, are you still there?" Ward heard in his earpiece.

"Shit, Stallart, am I glad to see you! I thought you were dead." Ward almost wept with relief.

"Not till you see the body, boy, not till you see the body." Stallart's voice turned serious. "Listen up, 'cause we don't have much time. Did you see what they did to you?"

"Yeah," replied Ward. "The flank job?"

"That's it." Stallart's voice crackled in his ear. He sounded a bit winded to Ward. "Now we're going to do it back. I have to get around out of their line of sight." There was a long pause. Ward heard a grunt and splash through the open mike as Stallart crossed a small stream. "The HEAP'll get 'em," he continued, "but it moves too slow. They'll just dodge if they see it coming. I don't have any PBA so *get* jumpy. If you see armor, it ain't friendly."

"Okay," Ward responded. "What do I do?"

"Just keep their heads down, and yours in one piece. Your father is going to be pissed at me as it is without getting you killed."

Ward heard the panting a little louder now.

Ward fired one shot, then another. He was rewarded by a crisscrossing stream of lasers and coil guns that almost took his hand off at the wrist, furrowing the armor before glancing off his shoulder.

"Shit," Ward said to himself. The mike picked it up and relayed it.

"What was that?" Stallart panted between words. His concerned voice was rough with fatigue.

"Nothing," Ward answered. He levered himself around for several blind laser shots. "What's wrong?"

"I don't know," Stallart answered. "I think I did

something to my back when we crashed. Give me a few more minutes."

Ward nodded, then realized Stallart couldn't see him. He ducked back, using his frozen left elbow as a fulcrum to lever himself behind another tree. The small copse looked ragged as the fire stream blew bark and cambium out of the oak to his left. Incoming rounds seemed to slacken a bit to the direct front, then appeared to arrive from his one o'clock position.

"They're moving again," he warned Stallart. "Your way."

The first warhead on the rocket launcher's body cooked off in the intense heat of the fuel fire. It arched skyward, bursting like a Roman candle as it detonated. Others began to go off as well, popping like champagne bottles as explosive compounds overheated.

"Got him," Stallart announced. A moment later Ward saw a bright flash behind a low rise. The *whuff* of the blast carried clearly through the woods.

"How many?" asked Stallart.

"Four down of six known," Ward answered, then added, "there may be more."

"Gotcha," Stallart panted. Ward heard a rattle of coil gun fire further back and pointed away from him. He popped up and bounded forward, rolling. Laser fire spattered to his right, and he cranked off another shot with his coil gun, having forgotten he'd set it to single fire.

"Listen up, boy," Stallart's voice crackled in his ears. "I'm pinned. Bastard's got me wedged in, but can't get at me without exposing himself. There should be two left. You're gonna have to take that one all by your lonesome." Ward heard another rattle, loud through the earpiece and quieter from over the hill.

This time Ward didn't nod but remembered to hit the chin-switch, clicking the circuit twice, acknowledging Stallart's transmission in radio shorthand. He reset the coil gun to burst fire, then moved again, feinting left before rolling right. The Wing's suit either had a better than average predicter built into its AI, or the wearer wasn't fooled by the move. Ward caught a laser blast full in the chest the moment he moved.

He knew suit lasers depended on contact time for their damage. They lacked the coil gun's true penetrating power and so worked by burning through the thermal resistant armor.

Ward jumped and rolled frantically, trying hard to evade the beam's questing destruction. A moment's hesitation let the beam linger and cost him a power conduit along his left side. Another moment took out his main heatsink while the servos slowed from the power loss. He scrambled behind a small hummock and tried to get a burst off at his assailant.

A high deflection shot almost cooked him through the faceplate. It came in from his upper right, above him.

"Shit," Ward cried as he ducked. "Three dimensions. *Three.*" Stallart didn't answer, apparently still bound to his own troubles. Ward used thermal imaging to track the other suit's jump thruster exhaust ports and heat sinks. He finally saw the thermal resonance flicker between the leaves, giving him a general idea of where the other hid.

A laser blast hit between his shoulder and the dirt. Ward felt his skin burn as trapped energy translated to heat and wormed through armor and insulation. Heat sinks were supposed to channel and disperse such incidentals, as well as the suit's own thermal waste. Ward's were slag.

But the last shot gave him a clear idea of the Wing's hiding place. He fired his coil gun, raking the target tree with a sustained burst.

He knew the fusillade was sloppy as hell, but didn't care. Branches fell and leaves flew as he hosed down the area. Entire sections of canopy vanished under the invisible scourge of the ring penetrators. Ward watched his ammo supply dwindle from sixty percent to the low thirties as he cut the tree into ribbons. A figure in Wing PBA tumbled from the tree and landed heavily. It didn't move.

Ward stood up to confirm the kill. He knew standard operating procedure called for a crisscross of rounds, but the Wing looked dead and he didn't want to waste what little ammo he had left on a fallen enemy.

Ward's legs and right arm moved sluggishly. His left elbow remained frozen, laser effectively out of action. There was unrelieved heat buildup, but he knew that wouldn't become a problem for some time. His left side main power conduit was also out, marked by flashing red in his wrist display, while the crossover backups were carrying their full load. His right conduit was green, but had already been working at capacity when the left had blown. He was down to effectively forty-percent power in his limbs. He looked at the narrow band that separated his current effective power level and the thirty percent minimum the servos needed to actuate. He swore.

"No wonder I feel like I'm in molasses," he said to himself.

"Ward," said Stallart, his exasperation clear even over the radio static, "will you quit chattering and come here and help me?" Ward, abashed, moved to comply.

The suit was heavy, requiring exaggerated movements to actuate the systems. He walked by shifting his weight from one foot to the other and moving his leg as a single unit. The system damage worsened as the overstressed crossover circuits began to fail. He looked down at his wrist display again: thirty-eight percent power in his legs. He had plenty of juice, just no way to get it where it was needed.

He thumped to the top of the low rise and took clumsy shelter behind a thick tree. It had been hit several times in the firefight. Deep gouges of white cambium glowed against the dark bark in Ward's enhanced sight.

He clearly saw how the Wing trooper had pinned Stallart in a narrow defile. Stallart couldn't get a clear shot at his opponent as long as he remained wedged in the rocks. The Wing partisan couldn't get to him without exposing himself to the HEAP gun. Neither could attempt escape or try to flank the other without moving up out of the depression and risking a killing shot.

Ward aimed at the Wing as best he could. He had no fine motor control. He compensated first too much one way and then the other as he tried to draw a bead. He attempted to bring up his crosshairs to help him aim. They fuzzed and faded as the AI overrode the request to keep power flowing to the joints and servos. He tried several more times to obtain an accurate shot before he called Stallart.

"Unnh, I got him in sight," Ward reported, "but I can't get a bead on him."

"How's that?" Static still laced Stallart's transmission.

"Suit's bad off. Taken some serious hits." Ward tried again to close his aim. "Nothing doing," he reported.

"What's your status?" Stallart asked.

"Thirty . . . six percent power to the legs, forty-two to arms," Ward answered.

"Shit," swore Stallart, "that's a Mark Four, right?"

"Yeah," said Ward, "the servos'll freeze at thirty."

"Shit." Stallart thought for a moment. "I'll tell you what—can you hit close to him?"

Ward thought about it. "Yeah . . . and?"

"Get as close as you can, then crank off a burst," Stallart said conspiratorially. "We'll see if that will flush him. Understand?"

"Yeah," Ward answered. "I understand that if this goes down twisted, I'll be a sitting duck."

"You and me both, kid," murmured Stallart.

Ward shifted his body left and right, trying to line up

something resembling a decent shot. He frowned as he listened to the joints whine as they struggled to operate under reduced power. He got as close as he thought he was likely to, then fired off a short burst.

The Wing loyalist jumped like a scalded cat. He frantically turned towards Ward and began to pick gouges out of the tree with his laser. Ward saw Stallart emerge from his rock, steady his aim, and let fly with the HEAP projectile. The Wing trooper whirled again and tried to stitch Stallart scrambling back under cover. Ring penetrators and laser beams skipped and glanced near the weapons master as he hurled himself behind a rock. The Wing stepped a little further back and left, exposing himself to Ward. Ward hit the firing key for his coil gun and held it down while jerking his torso back and forth.

Servos whined in protest. The blast of the coil gun overwhelmed their squeals entirely as Ward sprayed the area. Penetrators went high and low, skipping off rocks, plowing into trees, and generally tearing the hell out of the ravine. A few stray shots dinged the other's armor. They did little visible damage but for knocking the Wing trooper over.

Stallart stepped from behind another rock, his face bloody, and fired his HEAP pistol again. The Wing partisan was just trying to get back on his feet when the HEAP round wobbled into contact.

The flash lit up the ravine and Ward saw the shaped-charge core through the Wing's midriff. The Wing, blazing like a bonfire, collapsed in a heap.

Ward looked down at the tableau below. He felt utterly drained.

"Well, that's that," said Stallart with a grin as he came from behind his rocks and headed for Ward. "Let's get you out of that before you freeze up."

An explosion rumbled from the direction of Stallart's hut, a bass *thraruum* that lasted several seconds. Stallart's grin turned to horror as he jerked around towards the cabin. "Oh, God, no! *Mona!*"

He took off at a sprint, dropping his HEAP pistol onto its lanyard as he used both arms to climb the rocks. Ward turned heavily and squeaked after him as the older man shot past him. He quickly fell behind.

Stallart passed the Wing that Ward had shot out of the tree. Stallart's vision was so tightly focused on the house that he didn't see the Wing raise its head and aim its laser. Ward did. He tried to scream out to Stallart to duck, to do something, as the Wing fired.

Stallart's thermal suit gave him some protection from the Wing's suit laser, but not nearly enough. He died instantly as his lungs vaporized under the lazing stream. Ward screamed as he shifted his weight and ponderously brought his coil gun around. He fired even before his aim was true, saturating the Wing with penetrators. He fired, jerking the body and rolling it over as he streamed rounds into it. Pieces began to disintegrate as the suit's structural integrity failed under the hammering. Ward still held the firing key down when the coil gun clicked and whirred, its ammo exhausted.

He tried to move to Stallart, to help him, but his servos began to betray him. His left leg froze as the crossover circuits failed in sequence. He continued a few more feet—step-drag, step-drag—trying to get to Stallart. The right leg servo failed completely. He overbalanced and fell, damaging his communications and boost-pack. He was as helpless as a turtle on its back.

He turned his head to look at Stallart. The infrared residue of the laser shot hovered over his body like an aura. Ward could see the massive trauma even in the infrared.

A distant light drew his attention. He turned his gaze towards the house. His augmented vision began to flicker and fail.

A hand-spot worked its way down the hill towards the

battle site, the first artificial light he'd seen not caused by weapons since the action began. Then his augmented vision failed completely, leaving him blinded to everything except the bobbing light.

The yellow patch quickly resolved itself into a plain looking young woman carrying a Piat, a larger version of Stallart's HEAP pistol. Ward saw that the launching spring had been armed and a finned one-kilo warhead was nesting in the launch cradle. He prayed she didn't assume he was a Wing and liquify him with a single lobbed bomb.

Ward cringed inside his frozen armor as she approached. She prodded his chest with the Piat.

"You alive?" she asked.

"Yeah," replied Ward.

"Too bad. You Wing?"

"No," he answered with alacrity, "I'm Tuchman, Ward Tuchman. Benno's son." He paused. "Can you help me out of this thing?"

She thought for a moment. Then, "Hold still." She pulled a powerknife out of her belt-sack and used it to saw through the chest catches. Air whistled out of the suit as the first gave. Ward shivered at the knife's hum and the memory of the Wing he'd killed using much the same technique. He was almost in tears by the time she cut through and opened the carapace.

She helped him wriggle free and climb to his feet. He felt absurdly embarrassed as he stood in front of her in his skivvies. She looked hard at him. "My husband was with you. Where is he?"

Ward began to cry, great sobs racking his chest. He pointed into the darkness. She turned the light and saw Stallart's ruined form. The hand-spot showed the cruel wound in his back where the laser had penetrated between his shoulder blades. The gas expansion had been minimal, largely due to the fact that most of the exploding steam had carried lung tissue out of Stallart's mouth.

She stepped forward, dropping the light and collapsing across his body. He heard her sobs through his own. They remained frozen, each pouring tears into the raw wounds of their grief. Ward shook and shivered as his adrenaline faded until he looked afflicted with ague.

Eventually, Mona struggled to her feet, attempting to carry Stallart's body in her arms. Tears tracked down her blood-smeared face as she turned heavily and began to stagger up the hill with her burden. Ward tried to help her. She savagely jerked away and struggled on. He gathered up the light and the Piat she had left behind and moved to light her way.

She fell twice while climbing the trail to the cabin. She refused each time to let Ward assist her and insisted on bringing her husband home herself. Once there, she kicked in the half-opened door and went inside.

Ward, aware of his seminakedness, went into the barn to find something to wear. He jumped and almost fired the Piat when an armored figure loomed in the spotlight. In a moment, he recognized Stallart's PBA, still hanging on its maintenance rack. Ward was apparently not the first to mistake the empty suit for a real man: the PBA was riddled with ring penetrator holes and laser scalds.

He found some clean work coveralls and a pair of boots by a workbench. He put them on. The coveralls were much too big and he had to roll up the sleeves several times. The boots were too small and pinched his feet.

He finished dressing and walked out of the barn. He played the light from left to right across the front of the cottage. The cistern in front of the house had blown upwards. Curious, Ward crossed to the edge and peered inside. A dead Wing, the seventh in the squad, lay inside. Ward could tell this one had been female. Her helmet was off, her hair askew. She looked very pretty and very dead to him in the light.

"Blew her up," came Mona's voice from Ward's back

right. Ward turned to her. Her face was streaked with Stallart's blood. She carried a sponge and a bucket half-filled with water. "The rest of them took off down the hill and left her behind." Mona spoke in a monotone, her voice clear and distant. "She ordered me to get her a drink of water. I put a mining charge under my shirt and went to lower the bucket into the cistern. She came closer and took her helmet off. I set the charge and dropped the bucket in the water through the hole. I jumped away as it blew. She was standing on top and fell in."

Mona's voice became even more emotionless as she spoke. Ward watched her with silent, pain-filled eyes.

"I cut the bindings on the hay bale we used as a bench and pushed it in on her. She shot it up, scattering it over herself. She got tangled in the wet straw and baling wire." Mona looked down at the dead girl. "I got Stal's coiler off his armor. I used that on her until she was dead." Mona looked into the cistern and spat.

She looked up at Ward, almost as if seeing him for the first time. "They killed my husband," she said simply, and walked back to the house. Ward followed her inside.

She'd lain Stallart on the wooden table and lit candles around his head. Ward sat vigil for her while she laved her husband's face with the sponge and crooned to him.

Chapter 4

Samuel Denison glanced around the devastated Tuchman compound. An acrid tendril of smoke drifted across the hood of his ground-effect car. He sneezed violently, squeezing his eyes shut against the burning fumes. He looked up at his chauffeur, his normally unlined features deeply creased by a frown.

"I've never seen it this bad, Carol," he confessed, "not in twenty years. They even killed the peacocks."

He pointed towards the smoking carcasses that were all that remained of the lawn's tropical birds. Several laser pits marked near misses around the helpless creatures.

"Mr. D," Carol said, her voiced laced with concern, "won'tcha reconsider the body armor and the laser? I got 'em in the back."

Denison shook his head. "I'm here on behalf of the Planetary Council and I represent one of most powerful clans on this planet. If that and the code won't protect me from the locals, then body armor sure as hell won't."

"Yeah, well, accidents happen," she said.

"Thanks anyway," Samuel said. He reached up and patted her on the shoulder.

"Shit," she whispered, "they trashed the place."

He frowned again, evaluating the damage. "They hit the main house hard," he said. "It looks like they used short-range artillery, maybe mortars, to rip holes in the outer walls. You can see where the short falls tore hell out of the grass."

He pointed to the various damage sites as he continued his assessment. "You can also see the speckling around the upper windows where they used suppressive fire to keep the defenders' heads down before using rockets on them. Anything caught unarmored on the second floor probably died at that point. The backblast marks from the rocket launchers are over there by the rose bushes."

Carol tensed. Denison turned, dancer light and dancer quick, to face the main door. A pair of Wing retainers in combat fatigues and light body armor rolled a wheelbarrow loaded with Tuchman dead out of the house and casually dumped them in a shallow pit.

Carol's voice mirrored his own angry horror. "None of them are armored," she whispered. "They're just babies."

He glanced at three Tuchman women piled together, their flesh torn both by ring penetrators and by the distinctive keyhole-shaped ovals of ferrous sabots. He recognized one of the Tuchman cousins, Vreena, sixteen and studious, only by her distinctive hip-computer. He recalled donating the machine to an intercontinental chemistry competition.

Carol saw the keyholes in the girls' bodies. "Coilers need to be fired within a meter for the iron slugs to hit like that. This wasn't a fight, it was a massacre."

Denison nodded sadly as he watched a pair of body collection teams scour the area. They used cutting torches to slice through the rods that held closed the warped metal doors of the badly burned stock barn. He felt his stomach lurch as they began to haul scorched corpses into the light. Men, women, and children were piled in an untidy heap as the Wing loyalists continued their grisly task. He turned away, sickened both by the dead and by the retainers who laughed and joked as they worked.

Wing personnel in another part of the yard poured petroleum lubricants onto another pile of dead. One bent over. Sam saw a gold necklace glitter in his hand before he fired his hand-laser into the oil-soaked stack. Thick, greasy smoke gathered in a pall and drifted upward towards the overcast sky.

The second Denison car hissed in for a landing, the driver balancing the vehicle tail-down on the compressor streams while Denison's escort detail in full battle array clattered off the ramp. He saw Carol relax fractionally as they flanked Samuel.

"Tawn, what took you so long?" Denison asked the leader.

"We got caught in the Wing holding pattern and had to circle," she answered. Her voice, muffled by the heavy powered suit, conveyed her displeasure. "They were screwin' with us," she griped. "There was nothing else in the sky to wait on."

"That's all right," he said, "you and Carl are here now. No blood, no foul."

"Boss, they raped the place," Carl cut in, his voice flat and angry.

Denison understood the statement as a professional assessment of excess.

Carl pointed over his shoulder. "They've got trucks out back, cleaning it out."

Denison set his jaw. "We'll see about that." He saw a figure in powered battle armor step from the open doorway and walk towards the little group. The guards stepped closer, using their bodies to shield him.

The armored figure stopped well outside their comfort zone. "You're tresspassin'," he growled.

Denison pushed between the two guards. "I'm here at the behest of the Council," he announced. "Take me to your commander."

The Wing trooper thought a moment. "Okay," he said. "Follow me." Denison and his escort followed closely.

The guards knew Sam well enough to detect the emotions he held tightly in check. He walked, head erect, with his hands clasped tightly behind his back. Tawn fancied that she could feel the heat of his anger and outrage through her suit's laminate. "What a waste," she heard him whisper as they crossed the lawn.

She saw the house's front doors, blown inward. Scorched fragments still hung from the warped and twisted hinges. She looked around for evidence of the charge and saw several short extension tubes lying beside the porch.

"Bangalore torpedoes," she pointed out to Denison. "Boss, those are a stone bitch to use."

"Yeah?" he replied. "You mean like sappers?"

"They came ready," she replied.

Denison followed the escort through the blown entrance, noting the armored security doors were retracted.

"Shaped charges against wood doors're as much overkill as flechette rounds on mice," Tawn mumbled.

"I doubt the blast doors barrier would have fared any better," Denison replied. "What do you think, Carl?"

The guard behind his left shoulder, murmured, "Wing must've really caught them with their pants down."

Denison frowned again. "It's not like Benno to get caught short. He's too cagey. Wing had *something*—a spy, a good surveillance team, something that got them on the property unnoticed."

He turned to Tawn. "Have our people quietly nose around and find out how Wing got so close. I don't want a repeat of this on our turf."

They crossed the foyer into the main hall and saw a Wing guard, wearing light body armor and carrying a Tuchman flechette auto-gun, push three Tuchman retainers through the entrance hall and towards the back of the house. Sam saw all were lightly injured and had the dazed, shocked look of those who had experienced extreme violence for the first time.

"Go to the study," the Wing trooper ordered, pointing over his shoulder. He took up station in the entrance hall.

Denison nodded and stepped over a pile of rubble, crossing to the room the guard indicated. He noted that Wing troops had lazed the statues lining the room in wall niches, cutting curlicues in the composite drywall and vandalizing the valuable pieces. The carpets were missing, as were the furnishings. Thick, clotted blood pools dotted the room.

"Sir, over there."

Denison looked where Carl pointed. A tiny slipper lay beneath a corner table beside a burned doll. Droplets of dried blood from an arterial spray spattered the wall above the table.

"Bastards," growled Carl, his voice tight with anger.

"Somebody's got juice." Tawn pointed towards the study. Denison saw a wash of yellow light play across the shattered doorway. He looked up at the skylights that lit the foyer. "Is the rest of the town's power still down?" he asked.

"Yeah," she answered.

They heard a crash and clatter from the study. Carl and Tawn exchanged a glance as Sam stepped forward. He crossed gingerly over a pool of congealed blood and walked through the puddles of sunlight that splashed through the unbroken skylights. A thin trail of dust from the damaged overhead trickled onto the shoulder of his expensive wool suit. He brushed it away with an impatient gesture as he entered the doorway.

He saw that the Wings had blown this door as well. Fragments had traveled across the room and damaged most of the furniture. Shell casings gleamed in the reflected light and scattered iron coil gun slugs lay on the floor alongside blood spatters.

Samuel's eyes locked on Hardy Tuchman, who was tied to a chair in the middle of the room and stripped to the waist. His nose had been broken and a mass of cuts and bruises covered the rest of his face. His chest and shoulders were speckled with small, deep burns. His head hung low, his breathing deep and labored as he tried to draw air. One hand had been tied to the chair arm. The fingers were twisted and wrenched.

Denison looked up from Hardy to see a young man sitting on the edge of Benno's chipped desk. Denison thought he looked typically Wing, with dark, almost black, hair, a thin frame, and a chin so sharp it might cut wood. He wore a touch of rouge to highlight his pale cheekbones and was dressed entirely in black silk. His eyes were bright as he grinned at Samuel.

"I take it you're responsible for this," Denison said grimly. "Which Wing are you?"

"I'm Delius," the boy answered in an affected cultured voice. "But no, I'm not in charge. That would be my father. I just get to talk to the prisoners." He grinned again, showing small, sharp teeth.

"Bastard looks like a vulture," Carl mumbled.

Delius' piercing eyes flicked to Sam, only to be drawn hungrily back to Hardy's tormented body. His nostrils flared. "I take it you are Sam Denison," Delius said. "I was told to expect you." He lit a hand-rolled cigarette and gestured with one lazy hand to the Tuchman family tree set in the back wall. "What do you think of my little changes?" he asked.

Denison saw a black pen hung from a spike rammed into the wall. Most of the names clustered around Benno's were inked through. The Clan Chief's had been almost obliterated by laser bolts. It appeared to Denison that only Ward and Hardy's names were as yet legible.

Delius smiled thinly, then puffed on his cigarette. "I was just about to ask Mr. Tuchman here, again, about the whereabouts of Master Ward," he said pleasantly. "I'm afraid I owe him some money." He giggled.

Denison tried to keep his voice calm and steady. "Don't you think he's had enough?" he asked.

Delius made a show of considering it. "Yeah, I think you may be right," he said at last. He stood up and drew his hand-laser. Tawn stepped quickly in front of Denison while Carl moved to the side.

Delius ignored the guards. "Asshole here may just be stupid, not stubborn." He stepped beside Hardy, grabbed his hair, and wrenched his neck back. Hardy's mouth opened and his pupils rolled back up into his head. He seemed dazed to Denison. A trail of blood and mucus ran from one nostril and into the corner of his gaping mouth. Sam spotted several broken teeth.

Delius peered critically at Hardy, looking like a sculptor deciding where next to place his chisel. "Yeah," he mused, "stupid."

He placed the laser behind Hardy's ear and touched the firing stud. The advisor's head jerked violently and his cheeks puffed out under the discharge. Blood and scalded brains blew out the far side in a cloud of steam, splattering the far wall and floor. Hardy's body jumped and twitched in the chair. Delius giggled again and mimed blowing smoke from the tip of the barrel before twirling it in his hand and reholstering it.

Denison felt rather than heard Tawn raise her coil gun. He placed his hand over the weapon, pushing it down even as he heard the rustle and angry tension in the guards' servos. Carl moved a bit to the left to open his fire lane and position himself to block any shot aimed at Denison.

Sam stared at the body, stunned by Delius' casual brutality and the fact that he so clearly felt he was above the law and the code duello. He made no effort to hide his revulsion.

"Don't like blood much, do you?" Delius remarked

conversationally. He used the tip of his finger to turn Hardy's head and clinically peered into the steaming hole. He trailed his finger in the bloody trickle that ran from the base of the entrance wound and giggled again. "Bastard had it coming."

Denison tore his eyes away from Hardy. "How's that?" he asked, his voice betraying his tension.

Delius shrugged. "They stole a Wing ship. They paid the price." He stared at Denison, his eyes narrowing as though seeing Sam for the first time. "I assume you have some business to conduct."

Denison reached into his coat pocket and pulled out the memory chip. He held it up, reflected light glittering from its crystal matrix. "I've been appointed by the Council to assume receivership of the Tuchman estate until the Planetary Assembly considers the situation."

Delius sneered. "The hell you say. Tuchman forfeited when they pirated us."

Denison flipped the chip onto the burned floor between them. "The Council is even now communicating its wishes to your father and the other Wing leaders," he said formally, as though speaking for a recorder. "It will be best for all parties concerned if I can report that you handed over the keys to the keep willingly."

Delius turned his back. "Go to hell, Denison. This ain't your turf."

Denison let ice and iron creep into his voice. "It is now, Wing. Your claim that your raid was justified under the code died the moment you slaughtered everything that moved." He let his gaze linger a moment on Hardy's body. A tendril of steam drifted from the laser hole. "I saw the barn. The doors were barred from the *outside*. Did you seal them in before or after it caught fire?"

Delius turned back and grinned, unrepentant. "What's the diff? We're reclaiming what's ours."

Denison glanced at two techs who entered through a side door and began removing lightstrips. "The lights?"

he asked, incredulity coloring his voice. "You can't be serious."

Delius' grin grew wider. "It seems the original manifest was incomplete. The *Stellar Conveyor* had a lot of stuff we've only *just* now realized was missing." He winked at Denison. "Like lightstrips."

Samuel ground his teeth. "And *just* when did you discover this?"

Delius waved an airy hand. "Oh, we're getting the new manifest in dribs and drabs. Usually, we find something we think's ours, query the computer, and lo—there it is." He smiled again at Denison. "Strange coincidence, huh?"

Sam tried hard to master his temper. He gestured at the chip. "I assume my duties as receiver as of now. Get out."

Delius lazed back on the desk, stretching like a cat. "I wasn't informed of any Council arrangement. I'll have ta check before I give it over to you." He grinned at Denison, a feral rictus. "You wouldn't want Wing to accuse *you* of stealing, now would'ya?" He mimed aiming a pistol at Denison.

Denison's control slipped a notch. "Threaten me," he growled, "and what Clan Denison'll do to you will make this look like a panty raid."

"*Oooh*, I'm *sooo* scared," Delius snorted.

"Wing's had a good night, boy," Denison said. "Don't wreck it now."

Delius laughed.

Sam mastered his temper, some color returning to his face. "You'd better call your grandfather, boy. The Council's informed him of the receivership."

Delius lazily reached for his comm-link, then thought better of it. "Oh, my goodness," he said with patent dishonesty, "my communication grid seems to have gone down. Doubtless some vile Tuchman treachery." He grinned, showing his teeth. "You'll have to wait, I'm afraid. So sorry."

Denison unclipped his comm-link. "I'll use mine." He spoke a few soft words into the grille and waited. He heard a *hiss-pop* as Carol routed the short-range unit through the ground car's more powerful set.

"Hello, Efram? This is Sam Denison." The guards and Delius listened to the one-sided conversation. "I need to speak with Wing himself." There was a slight pause, then Denison continued, a slight frown on his face. "Well, too bad he isn't feeling well. I assume you got the Council's pronouncement? . . . Yes . . . ? Then be advised I've assumed my duties. Tell your brat to pull out."

Delius tapped a switch on his belt. Efram's voice boomed loud in the room, startling the guards.

"Well, Sam, my friend," said Efram in a hearty voice, "it isn't that simple. Wing is claiming indemnities against Tuchman."

Denison laughed in surprise. "Indemnities. Whatever for?"

"Why, for wrongful death, of course," Efram answered smoothly. "Nineteen brave Wing men and women lost their lives recovering Wing property. We want danegeld for it."

Denison felt like he had been hit with a brick. "You can't be serious. You attacked Tuchman. You've killed hundreds, you've looted the property, *and now YOU WANT TO GET PAID FOR IT*?"

"Basically, yes," Efram purred. "We can make a compelling case for it, too." He smoothly shifted gears. "We'll accede to the Council's edict without complaint *if* you agree to discuss reparations, as 'caretaker' of Tuchman, at the next continental assembly."

"Fine," Denison said. "Whatever. Now clear out."

A Wing retainer slipped through the side door. "We think we found Ward Tuchman," he announced.

Delius leapt to his feet, his feigned indifference gone. "How?"

"The Tuchman cars had transponders," the tech

replied. "We found a signal coming from a clearing a couple of kilometers away. It matches one associated with Ward." He held a piece of paper. "I've got the coordinates."

Delius jumped off the table, his face split in a predatory grin. "Got him!"

"Wrong." Denison's voice cracked like a whip. "Give that to me."

The retainer backed away, clutching the paper to his chest.

"Carl, get the paper," Denison ordered. The guard stepped towards the shaking tech, his hand held out. Denison saw Delius reach for his belt.

"Touch that control box and you die," Denison snapped. Tawn stepped forward, her cell gun pointed at Delius. "I don't know what brand of hubris made you let us in here unescorted," Denison said dryly, "but I think I like it that way."

Carl snatched the paper out of the tech's hands and carried it to Denison. Sam glanced at it before he put it into his pocket. "Sorry, this location is part of the Tuchman holding," he said smoothly, "which is under my protection."

Delius looked like a cat denied a mouse. "Bull!" he snorted.

"Efram," Denison called, "explain it to him."

"Come home, Delius," Efram's voice ordered. "We'll take this up at the Assembly. Tuchman isn't going anywhere."

"You must be joking!" Delius demanded to them both.

Denison set his teeth. "After what you did here, be assured, I'm deadly serious."

Efram broke in. "We got part of what's ours, son. Don't screw it up."

"Yessir," Delius replied in a surly tone. He signaled the techs to precede him out the side door. They gathered up a satchel of lightstrips and something that looked suspiciously like a computer core. Delius stopped at the dead lamp by the door and peered at it intently. "Why yes," he smirked, "I think that's Wing's, too." He unscrewed the strip and dropped it into the basket. "Tsk, tsk," he said as he exited, "Tuchman'll steal anything not nailed down."

Denison heard Efram's voice chuckling through the speakers. "He's a precocious lad, isn't he?" Sam closed the contact before Efram could irritate him further. He raised his right hand and rubbed his temples to clear his thoughts. "At least they didn't take the porta-lamp," he said, sighing. "Tawn, get Vito and some of the boys up here. We need perimeter security. Carl, go out back and make sure these rat-bastards don't take everything. I have to go see Ward Tuchman and see if I can't head this off before it gets worse."

"You're not going by yourself," Tawn retorted.

"If he sees armor," Denison answered tiredly, "he's going to run or shoot. I don't need either right now. Besides, Carol'll be with me."

"That cupcake'll do you a *lot* of good," Tawn scoffed.

"No arguments," he said, "please?" She nodded stiffly.

He turned away from Hardy's body. "See he gets buried and get some windows open. It smells like an abattoir in here."

They heard the patter of feet and crashing noises above them as Wing troops ran from room to room smashing whatever they could lay their hands on.

"Boss," asked Tawn, "are we gonna take this shit?"

Denison turned towards her. "Yes, my friend, we are." He looked at Hardy. "Word of this is going to get out, and a lot of people are going to be angry. Our job is to keep the lid on." He turned away towards the door leading into the main hall. The bright sunlight beckoned to him. "For our own sakes."

Carl and Tawn paced him through the house and back

across the lawn as he reeled off instructions. "Check the larder, see what Wing left. There are going to be some hungry people here soon. Use whatever you need from our stores to get people fed and sheltered."

He popped open the passenger bubble before Carol could scramble out and around to his side. "Also, try to roust a doctor. There are a lot of injured." He gave the lawn a final look. "You'd better ask Jedda if she and her engineers will drive up and have a look at the sanitation and power situations."

"Boss, do we bill it back to Tuchman?" she asked when he finished. "It's gonna cost a lot to feed and doctor somebody else's retainers."

Denison looked around at the battered estate, the piled bodies, and the burned buildings. "We'll try, eventually. I'm not sure the locusts left us a whole lot. For now, we just have to stabilize the situation. We'll worry about the bills later."

"Okay," Tawn replied, "we'll keep the lid on."

Denison slid into the passenger seat. Tawn lowered the bubble and secured the closure. Carol lifted the ground car up and settled on a circular course while Denison handed her the slip of paper. She smiled, locked the course into the navigation computer, and cued the auto-drive.

He fretted the few minutes until the car settled in on a course towards the clearing. He worried that Wing's orgy of killing would create more animus than he could control. He hated having to bury the bodies and clean up someone else's mess. He was well aware that if Wing had done to Clan Denison what they had done to Tuchman, he wouldn't rest until *all* the perpetrators were dead. He frowned distastefully as he mulled over the implications of talking young Ward out of doing exactly what *he* would do under similar circumstances.

The car landed. Carol looked up at him, concern in

her eyes, as he got out. "Mr. D, you want I should come up there with you?"

"No, thank you, Carol," he refused gently. "I'll be fine. Just keep the compressors warm."

She didn't look happy but offered no further protest.

Denison turned and walked towards the only sign of life, a small cottage on a hill with a thin plume of smoke rising from the chimney. He saw the crashed car and angled towards it. He saw the corpse lodged inside and wondered briefly if it was Ward. The age seemed about right. "Naw, it can't be that easy," he said as he turned away.

He saw the first fallen body and noted the haze gray Wing used to camouflage its powered battle armor. He scanned around and saw several more crumpled forms. He hoped against hope to find a corpse clad in Tuchman livery. His estimate of Ward rose as he tallied the body count. "Not bad, kid," he said. "A whole squad by your lonesome."

He climbed to the top of the hill and immediately saw Ward sitting by a fresh grave. The boy looked exhausted as he cradled a shovel in his hands. A woman sat beside him, her face puffy and swollen from crying. She was a little heavy and very plain, and with her mousy hair askew and her swollen eyes she looked to Sam like fifty kilometers of bad road.

"Ward?" Denison asked.

The young man raised his head. "Who's asking?"

"I'm Sam Denison of Clan Denison. I'm here for the Council."

"So?" Ward said heavily. The woman didn't stir.

"Come, Ward, walk with me. We have to talk." Ward allowed Denison to help him to his feet and guide him along a broad path. Denison watched the butterflies flitting about, feeding from local flowers. Denison knew most of the insects would die, drawn to the pretty blooms to consume the toxic pollen. The realization did nothing for his mood. "Let me begin by expressing my regrets for the attack. I find Wing's actions repugnant," he said sincerely.

"I should have been there," Ward replied, his voice ragged with agony.

Sam frowned and shook his head. "Then you'd be dead." He paused, realizing he was dodging the real subject. "Listen, Ward, the Tuchman estates have been placed under my care."

Ward stood stock-still, startled. "For who, for Wing?"

Denison sighed to himself. "I've assumed receivership of the Tuchman estates on behalf of the Council . . . at least until the continental Assembly decides what to do. It took a lot of fast talk and Council threats to brush Wing back."

He paused, waiting for a response from Ward. Nothing. The boy sat, listening, his face guarded. Time to try another approach. "Councilor Thorn told me what happened." He inhaled once, heavily, before continuing. "She apparently made a deal with your father to try and calm this down."

"Yes," Ward said shortly. "I was there."

"Good," Denison said, rubbing his chin with his hand, "then you know more about that than I do." He steepled his fingers. "Thorn called Wing and tried to make the same deal. Wing asserted that Tuchman fighters were massing near the border." He took a deep breath. "Thorn called me to come down and check out Wing's allegations. I was on my way when they hit."

He brushed his hair back with his hand. The fine blond-white hairs settled perfectly into place. "A lot of people are angry. Nobody wanted an all-out clan war."

Ward looked stricken. "How—how bad is it?"

"It's bad, son," Denison said slowly, "real bad. Wing did a lot of damage, killed a lot of people."

"My family?"

Denison saw no reason to sugarcoat it. "Dead, so far

as I know." He saw Ward's jaw muscles clench as the boy fought for control. Denison wanted to take advantage of the moment before grief overwhelmed his shock. "Your father and I were never friends, but I respected his talents. We lost a good man there."

"They're dead? They're all dead?" asked Ward in a whisper. "How?"

Denison shook his head, then told a lie as he recalled Hardy's battered face. "I don't know exactly." He moved quickly to safer ground. "I know Wing claims they are, and I can't think of any reason for them to lie." He gave Ward a moment to let the implications sink in.

"The magnates," Denison continued, trying to ease Ward away from the subject of his family, "the councilors, everybody—wants this to quiet down, has wanted this to quiet down since the beginning. I . . . we want it to end here. It's in your best interest, too, Ward, to let it end."

Ward, his voice bone-dry with grief, answered, "How could it possibly be in my best interest?"

Denison examined his manicured nails. "The most likely scenario is that Wing'll be heavily sanctioned for this, charged a lot of fines as punishment. They'll say the raid was done without sanction by subordinates who got out of control. They'll save face under the code if they punish the miscreants themselves. They'll give up all further claims on Tuchman assets."

"That's supposed to make up for what they've done?" Ward's voice was dark with bitterness.

"No, not really," Denison responded honestly, "but it's the best you're going to get. Nobody senior in Wing will be punished, and LaPort will be held in sanction for a while." His voice flattened as he tried to hide his own distaste. "Push Wing into a corner, and they'll have no reason to deal."

Ward looked at him, long and cold. "Thanks for the party line."

"The Council wants this *done*," Denison retorted. "No more killing, no more fighting. Wing went too far. We all agree on that. But we see no purpose to continuing the cycle."

He looked sidelong at Ward, trying to gauge his reactions. He let his voice harden. "That includes backing Wing into a corner. Subordinates will take the fall for the clan leaders. Nobody big will get hurt."

"I see," Ward said, his voice as hard and cold as ice.

"Ward, what Wing did was unconscionable, but it has to *stop*." Denison tried to put a comforting hand on Ward's shoulder. The younger man pulled away. "Nobody wins, not even you, if you continue this."

"How's that?" Ward asked, his voice like ashes. "What've I got to lose?"

Denison chose to answer indirectly. "Look, Ward, if you behave yourself, it's possible that in four or five years the Council will restore LaPort to you, once they think you'll abide by the code duello. Then you can restore Clan Tuchman to its rightful place. You can rebuild what you had." He ventured a smile, let his voice soften and become cajoling. "I'll help you. Denison is powerful; we have a lot of money. We'll do what we can to get you back on your feet, *if* you wait it out. Don't make it worse now."

Ward snorted cynically. "How much worse can it be?"

"A lot worse. You could be dead. And if you get frisky, Wing'll arrange it for you." He looked at Ward's face. "You are the last of your line. You have a certain responsibility to stay alive and lead your people. You *are* the Clan Tuch Chief, *de facto* if not *de jure*."

Sam rubbed his brow. "If the Council thinks you're hell-bent on revenge, they'll never let you have LaPort back. They'll find a tame sixth cousin and elevate him or her in your place. Cousin X will be so grateful, they'll do whatever they're told, even if it's peace with Wing."

Ward spat on the ground. "Never!"

Denison expected that response. He'd have felt the same way in Ward's shoes. His respect for the younger man rose a notch. He knew his interests at the moment, however, lay in keeping the peace and keeping Ward down.

"This is the deal," he said, sympathy fading from his voice. "You go to LaPort and behave yourself. I'll set up an account for you with Denison funds. You can live comfortably until the Council decides you can handle Tuchman without precipitating a war."

"Why your money?" Ward asked. "Why not Tuchman?"

"If I give you cash money, Tuchman money," Sam sighed, "you'll just use it to go and get yourself killed. I can keep you on a short leash with a Denison chip." He took a credit plate out of his pocket and set it on the bench between them. "This will work for services, but not cash." He slid the plate across the bench with his fingertip.

"What about my armor?" Ward asked defiantly. "I can't defend myself without it."

"Or attack with it," Denison countered. "I'll extend the protection of the Council and my clan to you. Wing won't cross that. They think they've won; they don't want to mess it up now."

"Didn't they win?" Ward asked bitterly.

"Yes, they did," Denison answered as he stood and brushed the dust from his trousers, "for now. They won't get off scot-free."

Ward looked up at him, then down at the chip. "What would you do in my shoes?"

Denison dreaded the question. "I'd take it easy," he lied. "I'd go to LaPort, get a room and a girl, and be a good little church-going boy. I'd take a great big bite of this shit-sandwich, pretend I liked it, and pressure the Council like hell to get my own back."

"What about my family and the rest they killed?" Ward

tipped his head towards the distant grave. Mona still sat hunched over, her head in her hands.

"The dead are dead, Ward," Denison answered sadly, "you need to look after the living. I'll be in touch." He walked away, angling across the woods and down the hill to the distant car.

Ward looked down at the plastic plate, then at Denison's retreating back. He picked up the lightweight polymer and weighed it in his hand. He flipped the card into the bushes with a curse and a savage gesture.

Mona looked up at him as he returned. "So?"

Ward looked down towards the clearing. He heard the distant whine of a car lifting. "Denison assumed control of the Tuchman estates. He offered me forty pieces of silver to behave myself."

"What are you going to do?" she pressed, her voice as flat as his.

Ward kicked at the dirt at his feet. "I can't go to LaPort. Denison'll have that sewn up tight by now. And I sure as hell can't go home." He winced. "Complein looks like my best bet."

"Why?" she asked.

"It's on the Tuchman estates. Denison promised me protection as long as I stayed on the reservation." He sighed bitterly. "What his protection is worth, I don't know." He looked at the distant horizon and saw smudges of smoke still rising from the town and Benno's house. "Also, Complein's essentially autonomous. It's got its own government and laws. They used to piss the hell out of my dad every tax time. He saw the Compleiners as a necessary evil, but I know he'd have liked to send in the troops on more than one occasion. I think he would've if he thought he'd get away with it." Ward's smile faded. That hit a little too close to home. "Denison won't be able to keep me under his thumb there, and that group of hardheads'll defy him if he tries to get them to do it."

He pressed on, trying to stem the sudden tide of grief. "It's also one of the biggest towns in West Hills. It'll be easy to get lost among ten thousand people until I can get organized."

Mona shifted in her seat and looked up at him. "What will you do then?"

His voice turned bitter. "Payback."

"Then I'm going with you."

Ward stared at her. Her placid face belied the intensity behind her words.

"Why?" he asked sharply.

"You're going to kill Wings. I'm going to help you," she answered. She brushed her fingers along the dirt mounding her husband's grave. It was an oddly sensual gesture, like a woman combing her fingers through her lover's hair.

"Why do you think I intend to kill Wings?" he asked, bemused. He bent down and laid his hand over hers to stop her. She used her free hand to lift his away and resumed her combing gesture.

"Why do I think the sun will rise in the morning?" she retorted. She contemplated the neat furrows in the grave's soft loam. "I want every Wing on the planet dead," she said in a voice so devoid of emotion that Ward wondered if she was serious. "It's for my husband, you see."

She smoothed the furrows flat, an abruptly practical gesture. "What do you plan to do for money?"

He tipped his head towards the valley. "I'll strip the suits off the dead down there. A couple are in pretty good shape. They'll be worth a lot to someone in Complein. Enough to get my armor fixed, at least."

She smiled grimly. "Then we kill?"

"Yes." He paused. "Do you have a car or something we can use to haul the armor?"

"Yea," she replied, "we've—I mean, I've got an old wheeled crop hauler we can use."

He looked at the smudge of smoke still rising from LaPort. "Then soonest begun, soonest done."

They collected the balky vehicle and powered slowly down the hill to the first of the dead Wing troops. The wheeled truck was obsolete, its solar cells pitted and corroded as it labored to pull in enough sunlight to power the electric engine. Ward thought he heard at least one bad bushing as the truck jerked and tugged under the load.

Ward watched with fascinated horror as Mona jointed the stiffened bodies with her powerknife, spattering herself with gore. The dismembered corpses slid easily out of the suits. Their bodies went in one pile while the armor was stacked in the truck's bed.

Ward crossed the clearing to the crashed car once they'd finished stripping the dead. He looked at Hariman's body a long while. "I'm sorry, my friend, that I can't give you a decent burial. I'll do the best I can for you." He used a piece of wreckage to lever open the small front access hatch. Inside were two cans of emergency fuel and a survival kit. Ward took everything.

He poured one can of fuel onto Hariman, soaking the car and the body. He then lit a flare from the survival kit and stood a moment, contemplating the bright flame.

"Good-bye," he said as he tossed the brand onto the vehicle. He stepped back as the flare hit the cargo box and rolled down into the crushed driver's compartment. The flame lit the fuel with a loud *whoosh* and fire engulfed the front half of the vehicle. Ward turned his back on the pyre and walked away.

He saw as he returned to the truck that Mona had already settled into the driver's seat. She watched impassively as he poured the second can onto the pile of dismembered Wing dead, then fired it with his handlaser.

"Isn't that better than they deserve?" she asked. "I'd rather leave them for the crows." Ward laughed without humor and climbed into the passenger seat, pausing only to fling the empty fuel can away. "I'd hate to poison innocent crows," he said as she turned the truck back upslope.

They stopped at the stone cottage just long enough for Mona to collect her weapons and a small bag Ward was certain contained mementos of Stallart. He wondered how best to broach the subject of Stallart's armor. Mona saved him the trouble.

"I need you to help me get Stal's suit out of the barn," she said.

"What do you want to do with it?"

"Sell it," she replied. "I won't fit in it. Stal would want us to use every asset we can muster. He'd never forgive me if I just walked away and left it."

Ward took a deep breath and went to help her. They gently lifted the battered suit into the truck bed. Mona carefully wrapped it in cargo blankets while Ward familiarized himself with the control yoke. She never looked back as he eased them out onto the dirt track that led to the LaPort-Complein road.

Ward fretted for the three days it took to reach the trade town, but he suspected that their slow passage was the reason they evaded any nets placed for them. Most everyone with a choice on New Hope flew or skimmed. Denison and company likely assumed that the fugitive Ward would try a fast getaway. They couldn't know that Mona's truck was old, barely functional, and conked out as soon as the sun showed the first inclination to setting. Ward and Mona therefore merged easily into the rest of the second-rate traffic and so avoided the multiple patrols that flew overhead. Ward concerned himself more about being jumped for the valuable power suits they sat on than he did with being picked up by Denison's grunts.

And late each night he brooded, staring at the stars

and plotting his revenge. Still, the lengthy trip *was* useful in that it allowed him to rough out a plan before they reached town.

They arrived at Complein midway through the fourth day. The outer wall was a single thickness of plastic brick, painted to look like stone. Ward recalled that the Compleiners had built it in Abel's day as a symbolic divider between the Tuchman estates and the free city. The relationship between burg and bailey had been turbulent over the years.

The trade town needed access through Tuch lands to move its goods and maintain its economy, as well as for the protection a powerful clan offered. Ward had seen first-hand the advantages Tuchman gained from Complein through proximity and local jobs. Ward considered the situation to be win-win, even though he understood his father's irritation every time he saw the forbidding wall.

Ward hoped that enough time had elapsed since Benno's last spat with the town. He knew the issue had been especially thorny: proportional shares of the cost of local patrols. Ward remembered seeing Benno white with rage when the Compleiners asserted that their fair share was zero since Benno had to patrol the region anyway. Relations had deteriorated when Benno threatened to blockade the place until they paid up. He fretted as Mona pulled the truck into the short line of traffic waiting to be granted entry to the town.

The PBA-equipped guard standing by the sheet metal gate looked Ward and Mona over carefully as they rolled up to the gate. "All right, hold it right there!" the guard demanded. "Are you Tuchman?" he said as he looked at Mona's faded clan colors.

Ward leaned out of the cab and mopped his sweaty brow. "Yup."

"You best keep rollin', then," the guard ordered, "unless you got goods. We don't take no charity cases."

He jerked his thumb, vaguely indicating an area on the far side of the town. "There's a camp over yonder for you lot."

"I got goods," Ward snapped.

He jerked his thumb towards the truck's tarp-covered cargo box. The guard flipped the tarp back to reveal the power suits piled within. Flies and sawlegs still swarmed over the crusted blood.

"You do this?" asked the guard, indicating the load.

"Pretty much," Ward responded laconically.

The guard stared at the suits a moment longer. "Damn, boy, least you could've done was wash the blood off."

Ward shrugged, uncaring. "Didn't figure it would affect the price none."

The townsman looked ill. He jerked his thumb over his shoulder. "Move along."

"Thanks," replied Ward dryly. "By the way, who'll give me the best price in town for this stuff?"

"Well," the guard replied slowly, considering. "Wing's spending money like its goin' out of style. Don't reckon you'd want to try selling them these, though? Prob'ly need to scrub the paint off first before tryin' 'em, though."

"I don't *think* so," Ward said tightly. "Anybody else?"

"I'd try some of the independents down on Tinker's Row—they'll give you the best price on a hot suit."

"The suits aren't hot," Ward argued, "all taken in fair combat."

The guard glanced at the blood-encrusted armor and saw the HEAP burns. "Yeah, right," he said skeptically. He waved them through.

The sights, sounds, and smells of Complein immediately assailed Ward as the guard opened the gates. People crowded the gate's courtyard, a small fragment of the multitude that called Complein home. Children from five clans played stickball together alongside two youths in city colors who sold lemon punch from a stand. Ward saw clan colors he'd only heard about—MacAvoy and MacKensie from Idleford, dark-eyed Ulundu, Singh Clansmen with their turbans and ritual knives—and tradespeople from across the planet. It made the Hills Assembly seem to him like a yokels' gathering or a county fair.

They rolled through the square and saw a man in Complein greens performing three-card monte for a couple in Tuchman red, gold, and blue. They watched the rubes plying the Complein man with plastic credit chips while trying to guess the hiding place of the red queen. Ward noticed two of Complein's toughs lurking nearby, looking deceptively bored. Ward guessed the two Tuchman retainers would soon find themselves playing until they were broke, whether they wanted to or not, with no recourse to the police. The Complein constabulary believed in *caveat emptor*.

Mona poked him in the ribs. He followed her glance and saw two Tuchman women exchanging pleasantries with a pair of Wing youths. The Wing men were being free with their hands, patting and touching the woman. The Tuchman girls appeared to be encouraging them.

Ward went hot and cold all at once. He wanted to leap from the cab and flog all four—the Wing men for touching his kin, and the Tuchman women for permitting it. Mona muttered something obscene and started to slide a HEAP projectile from her bandoleer. Ward placed his hand over hers. "Not yet," he said, his own voice tight with anger, "not until we're ready."

She tried to jerk away. He held his hand over hers until she stilled. The vehicle ground slowly past, the solid tires hissing against the extruded silicate paving. The girls' playful protests and giggles burned in Ward's ears like a brand. Mona quietly seethed, her broad face tense and closed. He glanced back in time to see a Wing retainer place a credit chip in the Tuchman woman's hand. She led him away with a smile. He forced down a hot jet of rage.

He turned his attention back to the street in front of them while his anger cooled. He peered into the thick crowd, looking for danger or enemies in the eddies of people that made the trading lifeblood of Complein flow. Men and women, children and adults, clan and city, scurried about, buying and selling with feverish abandon. Two women had a fiery debate on the merits of genetics and sweetness as they haggled over the price of a head of lettuce. A Vargas woman argued with intensity with a boy over a bushel of bakeroots. They were surrounded by fifty other loud hagglers and gesticulated wildly as they shouted over the din. The cacophony of the street threatened to overwhelm him.

They passed close by a man sweeping the concrete sidewalk in front of a watering hole called the Pigswiller. The place looked clean and well lit, in spite of its tawdry name. Ward leaned down from the wagon to address him.

"Excuse me. Can you tell me how to get to Tinker's Row?" Ward asked the sweeper.

"Yes," the sweeper replied.

Ward waited a moment for the man to say something else. The elderly gent ignored them and concentrated on his broom strokes.

"Will you tell us?" demanded Ward, his voice short and impatient.

The old man made a rubbing motion with his thumb and index finger. "Depends on what it's worth to ya."

Ward dipped into his belt-sack and pulled out two small denomination tokens. The old man grinned and whipped out a scrap of paper and stub of pencil. He drew a quick map and handed it to Ward. "Thankee for the business," he chortled. Ward laughed ruefully as he examined the map. Tinker's Row proved to be a cross street two blocks ahead.

The street was crowded with independent dealers content to haggle the week away, or so it seemed to Ward.

He fought long and hard for the full value of the Wing armor and still found himself worn down and settling for half its worth. He gritted his teeth at the end. The tinker barely restrained a smile as he wrote out a map and a draft for Ward to take to his credit bank.

They found the bank in short order, underneath a signboard reading FIRST NAT'L BANK OF SATTERJEE. A smaller, hand-lettered card on the door read OPEN DAILY, MOSTLY. Ward might have laughed under other circumstances. He climbed down from the truck's cab. He stepped up to the door.

"Do you want me to stay here and guard the truck?" Mona asked.

Ward looked at the junker. "You must be kidding." He turned and pushed through the batwing doors.

Satterjee's place looked like a dump to Ward. The only illumination came from the sunlight angling in through the slatted windows. The air was stuffy and dusty, with no appreciable effort being made at climate control. Dust also lay thick on the rolltop desks. A single hinged gate separated the small patron's area from the working areas. The noise of a fly buzzing in the room and the *Clop, Clop* of an archaic grandfather clock in the corner were the only noises.

Mona, following close behind Ward, dipped her head fractionally after her eyes had become accustomed to the light. Ward followed her gaze and saw a camera positioned in the far corner where it could sweep the room. Beneath it winked a ready diode for a mounted laser. Ward looked again at the dusty room, this time noting the cracks in the façade.

The rolltop desks had power cables snaking from their corners and were linked by thick fiberoptic conduit.

"He's gone to a lot of time and trouble to appear low rent, hasn't he?" he said quietly.

"Indeed I have, young man."

Ward looked up in surprise while Mona cleared to the

side, her hand on the HEAP pistol. Neither had seen how Satterjee entered the room. The banker looked bald as an egg to Ward, except for a thin fringe around his ears. He wore an old-fashioned string tie, a loose white shirt, and a long, hammerclaw coat. Pince-nez glasses perched on his stubby nose, threatening to fall off at any moment. He looked as though he'd just stepped out of a nineteenth-century tintype, a portrait of a frontier bank master.

His eyes, full of bright humor and intelligence, locked on Ward. Mona might not have existed as far as he was concerned. He wiped his mouth fastidiously with a checkered napkin. "Can I be of assistance to you, Mr. . . . ?" Satterjee asked politely.

"Tuchman," Ward supplied. "Ward Tuchman."

Satterjee dropped his napkin on the desk as he came forward. Mona relaxed fractionally, but kept her hand on her pistol. Ward looked around once again. He pulled out the draft. "I need this cashed."

Satterjee used his hip to push through the swing-gate and came forward to examine the check. He frowned when he saw the signature and the sum. He read the draft carefully. "You're Benno's son? That Ward Tuchman?" Satterjee looked at Ward again, very closely, as if memorizing every detail. Ward nodded once. "Yes."

"Um, pardon me for being indelicate, Mr. Tuchman," Satterjee asked carefully, "but may I ask where you came by this?"

"What business is it of yours?" Ward replied sharply.

Satterjee seemed embarrassed. "Well, I'd heard that the Tuchmans were, um . . . a bit down on their luck right now, a bit vulnerable. Rumor has it your clan got cleaned out by Wing."

"I don't follow," Ward said. He was puzzled, but had a sinking feeling he knew what was coming.

Satterjee steepled his hands in front of his face. "The

Wings have been using Tuchman bank codes for the last forty-eight hours." He shifted his feet uncomfortably and gestured towards the roll-top desk. "Sam Denison's been tryin' to stop it. I've seen Council injunctions all over the bank-net, blocking the codes' use. If this check serves one of those coded accounts, I can't touch it."

He held his hands away from his sides and shrugged, an admission of helplessness. "So far, Wing's been able to stay ahead of the Council. If I cash this, it could also post to one of your clan's corrupted accounts and disappear into Wing coffers."

Ward's shoulders slumped. "What do we do?" he asked in a defeated voice.

Satterjee smiled. "I'll cash it here and log it onto a new account that I'll set up for you in this bank. You'll be able to keep the money as long as you don't post it to the network. My name's good for credit in this town, so you can have one of my credit chips for local shopping. I'll deduct charges from the outstanding balance, plus a fee, of course."

"Of course," Ward repeated. "How much is the fee?"

Satterjee jerked his head, a birdlike gesture odd for a pudgy man. "Two percent."

Ward snorted in disbelief. "I figured five. Why the charity?"

Satterjee looked pained. "Look, you Tuchmans don't know what it's like. You don't push to run this town like others do. These other trade towns are just cash cows for the local clans." He sighed. "Complein isn't like that, at least it didn't used to be. Denison seems willing to let the status quo be. I'm not sure Wing will. It doesn't cost me anything to help you, and maybe help myself. You'll owe me and someday I can collect."

Ward thought it prudent not to mention his father's machinations or his attempts to control Complein. If Satterjee saw him as a white knight, that was the banker's business and Ward's windfall. "All right, you wanna help me," Ward said after a moment, his voice skeptical. "Then tell me where I can get my armor fixed."

"Carlo Theisiger," Satterjee answered without hesitation. "He's got a repair shop in town. He's a private duelist who made good." Admiration colored the banker's voice. "He's the best."

"Never heard of him," Ward replied.

The banker took the check and sat down at the rolltop desk. The simulated wood grain top rolled back on silent hinges to reveal a modern computer terminal. Satterjee logged on and began running numbers. Dozens of characters flickered across the screen as the terminal ran batches of satchel codes.

Satterjee gestured to the numbers on the screen. Every ten seconds another number flicked onto the top, displacing the one below.

"What is that?" Ward stared in fascination.

"That's Wing," Satterjee answered, "trying to run the numbers out on Tuchman accounts. Benno was good, but he never counted on Wing getting into his mainframe." He rubbed his fingertip across the top of the desk and frowned at the thin gray smudge of dust he collected. "They'll be able to crack all his codes eventually. My guess is they've gotten about forty percent of Tuch's assets so far." He turned back to Ward. "Benno squirreled away a lot of stuff in bizarre places. It's going to take Wing quite a while to get it all."

"How do you know all this?" Ward demanded. "You weren't Dad's banker."

Satterjee tapped the computer console. "That's true, I wasn't. But I watch the nets. Your dad liked to play here, too."

"Can you monitor Wing?" Ward looked grim.

Satterjee dipped his head like a bird going for a worm. "Sure. Why?"

Ward looked intensely at the screen. "Someday I'm

going to reclaim every credit." He looked at Satterjee. "I'll need to know exactly what was taken."

Satterjee licked his lips, waiting for Ward to pay off.

"I'll pay you a three-percent commission on everything we recover from them," Ward said.

Greed lit Satterjee's eyes. "Done," he said at once. They shook hands. He smiled warmly at Ward. "Three percent is a lot more than the job is worth, you know. Why so generous?"

"Right now I need friends," Ward answered. "I have to be willing to pay for them."

Satterjee bobbed his head again.

"Now," said Ward pleasantly, "will you tell me how to find this Theisiger?"

Chapter 5

Ward sat in Carlo Theisiger's plush visitor's chair and stared at the 2-D portraits of his wife and children. Window sills and elegant lamp tables proudly displayed childish artistic efforts in crayon, fingerpaint, and daubed modeling clay. He looked around the lushly appointed office. The happy images around him brought the loss of his father into sharp focus. He fought back tears.

Theisiger puttered behind him as he worked a hissing, steaming piece of machinery mounted on the wet bar. "How do you like your espresso, Ward?" he asked in a low, cultured voice. "My wife gave me this gizmo last Founder's Day, and I'm still learning how to use it." He brought two cups over to the desk and handed one to Ward, who peered at the thick, heavy liquid filling the bottom.

Theisiger smiled easily. "Try it." He tipped his own mug back and tapped the bottom to coax out some of the thick sludge. Ward heard a distinct *glop*. Theisiger made a face and wiped the corner of his mouth with one thumb. "Then again, maybe you shouldn't. It's pretty horrid."

He grinned again. Ward had only heard about Theisiger from Satterjee, whose description had been flattering, to say the least. Ward had expected to meet a physical giant with massive pectorals and a towering ego who enjoyed killing for a living. Instead, Theisiger was slim, of average height and weight, and appeared to Ward to be a quite unassuming man in his forties.

He had an engaging lop-sided grin, blue eyes, and a thick shock of unruly brown hair. Ward had a hard time reconciling the family images with the occupation.

Of course, Ward was one of Terra Nova's aristocrats, so he didn't know much about the lives of *any* Terran on the planet. He was aware that recent immigrants from Earth usually staffed the automated factories and did the simple repetitive tasks that clanfolk wouldn't. Some clan chiefs employed Terrans as liveried menials, simply as an item of conspicuous consumption. But Benno Tuchman had never been like that.

Theisiger appeared to have done extremely well, for someone from Earth, someone who was clanless and with no prospects of ever joining one. For a native Terra Novan, the fastest way to rise was through attachment to a clan leader. Practical training in negotiation skills, and the patronage of a powerful clan, could make a local lad a very big man when he returned to his home district. Ward knew his friendship with Lupe Vargas wasn't without political benefits for Lupe. Of course, associating with someone like Ward could be extremely dangerous, too. . . .

But always at the bottom of the social structure were the newest immigrants. It didn't help their status that everybody knew that the Hegemony had been infiltrating spies and potential saboteurs among the more recent ships. But Theisiger was clearly no menial, no factory worker. So far as Ward could see, Theisiger had forged his own bloody path to success without the help of any clan, and now he was enjoying the easy life.

Theisiger graciously took Ward's untouched mug and set it on the edge of the desk. He sat in his own chair, touched a button on his desk, and the window behind him polarized and the room darkened. Ward heard the high-pitched whine of sonics vibrating the window to prevent their conversation from being monitored by sensing lasers or shotgun microphones.

Theisiger looked at Ward curiously. "I have to be honest, my shop is very expensive. How do you plan to pay?"

"I've got money," Ward replied shortly.

Theisiger raised his eyebrows. "Rumor has it that Wing cleaned you out."

Ward dipped his hand into his shirt pocket and pulled out Satterjee's credit chip. He tossed it on the desk for Theisiger's inspection. The duelist picked it up and turned it over in his hands.

"I guess the word is wrong, huh?" Ward said acidly.

"Guess so," Theisiger answered. He dropped the chip into the reader and bobbed his head as he read the balance. "If Satterjee says you got money, then money you got."

"When can you fix my suit?" Ward asked.

Theisiger rubbed the edge of the chip reader with his fingertip. "I'm not sure I can."

"Why not?" Ward demanded.

Theisiger gave him a neutral look. "Well, for starters, I'm collecting a handsome retainer from the city."

Ward's expression grew dark. "So?"

Theisiger held up one hand. "I have an ethical obligation to represent their interests. I wouldn't be doing that if you used a suit I fixed to go tear-assing around the city hunting Wings. The city is off limits for clan fights. It's a city ordinance."

Ward looked angry. "I see. You belong to them."

"No," Theisiger smiled, "I belong to me. I just rent myself out." He became more serious. "I've worked hard to establish myself here and I won't risk that."

"What would it take for you to do the repairs?" Ward asked.

Theisiger thought a moment. "Give me your word that you'll respect Complein's law and take your spat outside the city."

Ward raised his eyebrows. "Or?"

Theisiger looked sober. Ward saw a hint of the steel that lay beneath his genial surface. "I'd have to call you out to restore my good name."

"Maybe I don't want to kill Wings," Ward ventured, "maybe I'd rather give you some competition."

Theisiger laughed and shook his head. He raised his hands in mock surrender. "Okay, okay," he said, laughing, "you got balls, kid. I like that." He gave Ward a long, appraising look. "I'll tell you what. You agree to keep it out of my backyard and I'll fix your suit for you. How's that?"

"How much?" Ward pressed.

Theisiger glanced at the screen again. "Eggbert just finished the diagnostics. You've got a blown main line, a bad heat sink, a locked elbow, and various chips and dings." He tipped his head from side to side as he tallied the damage. "I'll tell you what, I'll do the whole nine yards—fixin', bench testin', and AI upgrade—for thirty-one hundred, plus parts." He grinned. "Hell, I'll even paint it a spiffy color."

Ward's looked skeptical. "That's a little light, isn't it? I figured you'd hit me for five thousand credits up front."

"The final bill might be more than that by the time we finish," Theisiger warned. His expression grew troubled. "Some of what Wing did at your place is leaking out. It was pretty heinous. I figure you need a break. This is the least I can do."

"I don't want charity," Ward replied stubbornly. "I'd rather pay the full load, if it comes to that."

"You couldn't afford the whole boat, not even with this." He tapped the chip in the reader. "Just consider it my contribution to clan justice. Okay?"

Ward sat tugging at his lip as he thought it over. "Okay."

Theisiger stood up. They shook hands, a polite, businesslike squeeze without any of the macho posturing Ward expected. Theisiger took a fresh chip from his desk and plugged it into the reader next to Ward's. "I'll take nine hundred now to order parts and start work, with the balance due on completion. How's that?"

Ward nodded. "More than fair. When'll it be done?"

"I'd give it three or four days," Theisiger replied. "We've got our own fabrication shop so we don't have to order out much. Egg's inspection didn't show any structural problems." He gestured to Ward with his fingertip. "I want you to meet Egg. You'll see your armor'll be in good hands."

He stepped across the office to a russet-colored curtain that covered one wall and touched a button. The curtain slid silently back, followed a moment later by the soundproof glass door. Ward followed him onto a balcony that overlooked the shop floor.

Techs in bright clothes moved between the shimmery white cubicles. The only splashes of color that relieved the otherwise sterile working areas were calendars and pinups on the walls. Music pumped out of hidden speakers. Ward saw a dozen or so power suits in various states of disarray littering tables in the work spaces while specialists clustered around. Ward's impression was of a happily buzzing hive. He looked around approvingly until he noticed several of the suits on the tables were Wing gray.

"I didn't know you fixed Wing suits," he said, his voice cold and angry.

"I fix anybody's who pays me," Theisiger replied coolly. "I just charge different amounts." He looked at Ward's expressionless face. "*Very* different amounts."

He led Ward down the stairs and between the cubicles to one occupied by a massive man with a *cafe au lait* complexion and a chest-length beard encased in a plastic sheath. The man turned as they entered. Ward craned his neck upwards. He saw the tech's cool, intelligent eyes taking his measure.

"Egg," Theisiger said, "meet Ward."

They shook hands, Ward's almost disappearing inside Egg's huge paw.

"I have to ask," Ward said, "what's the plastic thing?"

Egg laughed. "It keeps hairs and skin flakes out of the circuits. We all wear hair caps. I'm the only one with a beard, though."

He gestured Ward and Theisiger over to his work area. The table, made of steel and plastic, looked to Ward like an operating theater. Racks of instruments stood by, ready to be used. Ward's suit had been cleaned and placed on the table, arm and leg restraints holding it firmly in place. Ward saw that Egg had already opened a number of the access panels and had the guts of the suit strewn across the table.

Theisiger listened to the music wafting from the worktable's speakers. "Mozart?" he asked.

Egg grinned. "Dvorak, actually." He turned towards Ward. "I want ta thank you for giving me the chance to work on a *real* suit." He drummed his fingers on the side of Ward's gutted suit. "All I've been servicing is junk—retread partials and early model Phisters. These Mark Four's are pieces of sweet engineering."

Theisiger laughed and clapped Egg on the arm. "I wanted Ward to meet the man who's gonna make his suit right. I worry when my armor's been played with by someone I don't know." He looked at Ward. "You have no idea how many people I've fought whose maintenance techs got them killed."

Ward nodded soberly. He watched Egg turn back to the suit and open a hydraulic shunt in the locked elbow. His fingers moved delicately, giving Ward the impression of Egg as more surgeon than mechanic. Hydraulic fluid dripped like blue blood into a small plastic catch basin.

"I'll start by checking this for metal filings or bits of actuator sleeve. That'll help narrow whether this failed from battle damage or was something else."

"Seems fairly straightforward to me," Ward retorted. "I got hit there by airfoils. I'd say that counts as a likely culprit."

Egg looked patiently back at him. "Maybe, maybe not. I get paid to eliminate 'maybe' from the equation. He's been shot up, all right, but you never know what kinds of problems are lurking under the battle damage, just waiting for a chance to bite you in the ass."

"He?" Ward asked in an amused voice.

"Sure, Mr. Torchman," Egg answered, "all these suits, they got their own personality. Some are he's an' some are she's. They all hurt when they come in here."

"I see," replied Ward in a tone of voice that suggested exactly the opposite, "and by the way, that's Tuchman, not Torchman."

Egg was engrossed in dripping the hydraulic fluid into a portable centrifuge. "Sure thing, Mr. Torchman."

Ward looked at Egg again before he nodded to Carlo. "Yeah, he'll do."

Theisiger touched his elbow, steering him out of the work area. "Let's go back to my office and finalize a few things." He turned to Egg. "Make Ward here happy, okay?"

"Will do, Mr. T," Egg replied.

Ward followed Theisiger back to his office. Theisiger saw that he seemed troubled. "Is there a problem, Ward?"

Ward tugged at his lip. "I was surprised at how fast Egg got to business. We'd only just met. That's downright rude back at LaPort. I thought we'd talk about the weather or something."

Theisiger sat in his chair. "This is town, Ward, not clan. You clan folk can afford to be lazy; you've got a safety net that'll make sure you eat. Town folk don't have that. For us, time is money. Small talk here is rude; it means you don't value other people's time."

"Then why are you 'wasting' time with me?" Ward asked, irked by the duelist's view of clan life.

Theisiger grinned. "I'm the boss. I bring in the clients. If gab is what it takes to get the deal, then I gab." He looked at his watch. "I do have to go, however. If you'll tell me where you're staying, I'll keep you posted on how things're going."

Ward looked embarrassed. "Well, I only just got into town. I haven't had time to find a room."

"Hmm," said Theisiger, stroking his chin, "I'll tell you what. There's a boarder hotel near here. The Lager House. It's clean, cheap, and just across the square." He pointed towards the front of the building. "Go out the door you came in, look south, and you'll see it. The three story white building with the big windows, porch, and pillars. If you don't like it, leave a message where you will be stayin'. I'll be in touch."

Ward realized the interview was over and made his farewells. He left Theisiger's office and returned to the truck. Mona sat slumped in the passenger seat, staring at a 2-D of Stallart. She wept silently, fat tears rolling down her cheeks.

He took his place behind the control yoke and steered for the whitewashed Lager House. He parked in the side lot and stepped up onto the broad veranda. The porch opened onto a brightly lit, whitewashed registration area. The lobby was cluttered with glass tables, wicker and wrought-iron chairs, and fake Persian rugs. The inn seemed far more folksy and pleasant than the flophouse image Ward had gotten from Theisiger.

A heavyset woman with a large wooden cross dangling between her ample breasts waited behind the desk. Ward didn't think she looked very impressed with him. "I need two rooms with a connecting door," he said without preamble, "and a private bath, if you have one." Theisiger's warning on local mores seemed to hold true. She made no comment at what seemed to Ward to be rude behavior.

The woman looked over his shoulder at Mona, who

still sat hunched miserably in the wagon. "Married?" she asked.

"No," Ward replied.

"We don't put up with unmarried sex here," she admonished, "so if you wanna shack up, go do it somewhere else." She started to turn away.

"We're kin," Ward lied. "Cousins."

She looked him over carefully. "All right," she said grudgingly, "that's different. I can give you two together on the third floor. No private baths, though. There's a fresher at the end of each hall, by the stairs. How long do you plan to stay?"

"I don't know," Ward answered, "perhaps two weeks. Perhaps longer, depending on how much it costs."

"The damage is one-fifty a room. Three hundred a week for the both of you. Pay me for three weeks now," she demanded. "I'll expect payment in advance if you want to go week to week. I'll keep one week out for damage and theft."

Ward handed her his credit chip. She ran the numbers and gave him a receipt. "I'll expect another three hundred two weeks from today if you plan to stay longer." She saw Mona coming up the stairs, her small bag cradled in her arms. "No cussing, no spitting, no loud music, no pets, *and no sex*," she said loudly.

"Umm, what're the taproom's hours?" Ward asked timidly.

"Five until ten-thirty," she answered. "We don't tolerate drunkenness here." Ward blew out his cheeks as she turned away, her cross clattering on the faux-teak registration desk. Ward grabbed the plastic room cards and fled, trailed by a slightly baffled Mona.

A half-hour later he stood naked in the middle of his room, trying to wipe away thin soggy scum of sonic-loosened skin and dirt from his body. "That harpy!" he swore. Mona came though the door, saw him standing naked, and turned away.

"What happened?" she asked.

"She cut the flush cycle to about thirty seconds," Ward complained. "It's not nearly enough to rinse off the dead skin."

"I've never needed more than a half minute," Mona replied.

Ward ignored her. He made a face as he looked at the dirty residue in the towel. "I've got a headache, too. I'll bet the bitch detuned the sonics to save power." He swore again.

They both jumped as Ward heard an authoritative knock on the door. "Now what?" Ward growled as Mona fled through the connecting door. She pulled it closed behind her, leaving it ajar the slightest bit.

He dropped the dirty towel over his holstered laser, hiding it on the single bed. He wrapped a clean towel around his middle and walked to the door. He jerked it open, expecting to be face-to-face with the proprietress. He saw instead an official-looking woman in Complein green backed by an average-looking Asian man wearing a constable's uniform.

"Umm, give me a moment to get dressed?" he said as he opened the door.

She looked him over, her expression frankly assessing. "Don't worry about it, Mr. Tuchman."

Ward watched the constable's gaze flick to the corners and across all the likely ambushing spots. His features were grim and unsmiling as he rubbed one scarred hand over his shock baton's grip. A Mark III laser adorned his right hip. He took up station outside the door as she stepped past Ward and into the room. He tried to close the door. The guard placed his hand firmly on the wood and shook his head.

He left it and followed her, his hand clutching the towel around his middle. "How did you know who I was?"

She looked smug. "Complein has relatively few clan

leaders on the lam at the moment. The gate guard reported a Tuch rolling in with a wagonload of Wing suits. Samuel Denison's been burning up the airwaves looking for you. It wasn't hard to figure out."

She extended her hand to him. "I'm Sandia, by the way, city Council representative for the seventh ward."

Ward almost lost his towel as he moved reflexively to shake her hand. Her grip was firm and dry, a business-like clasp. Her eyes, full of mirth, danced over his scantily clad form. She made no comment about his dress. He felt his face begin to heat as he blushed.

"To what do I owe this visit?" he asked.

She turned away to the bed, lifted the dirty towel, and looked at the laser hidden beneath. "My, my," she said as she dropped the towel back over the weapon. "Well, Mr. Tuchman, that depends on why you're here." She flipped her brown hair out her eyes with a casual gesture.

He looked sharply at her. "Just to get my suit fixed, maybe a little longer. Then I'm on my way."

She smiled. "Maybe. Maybe not."

Ward didn't care for her tone. "What the hell does that mean?" he snapped.

"What happens next is really up to you," she replied. "Denison wants you back or safely out of play. How we answer his polite request depends on you."

"I don't follow," Ward said grimly. "I've already promised not to fight in the city, unless I'm attacked, of course. What else do you want?"

She smiled at him. "Your father had some rather possessive attitudes about our city while he was Clan Chief. We want those clarified."

"What do you mean by 'clarified'?" Ward asked.

"Well, for starters," she answered, "we want a guarantee that Tuch won't dun us for crossing clan lands, claim taxation rights, or assert we have to contribute to local patrols. In short, we want our independence, once and for all."

"Let me get this straight," Ward answered grimly. "You want to live amongst us, do as you please, and not be expected to share any of our burdens, even as you draw the benefits."

"Yes," she said simply, "we want to have our cake and eat it, too."

"I'm not really in a very good position to keep my end of any bargain I strike, you know," Ward replied.

"You're the last surviving Tuch," she said with a shrug, "at least according to Denison. If you get your clan back, we'll hold you to our little agreement."

"Why aren't you talking to Denison, then?" Ward pressed. "His receivership gives him effective clan leadership right now."

"We are," she answered simply. "He's not biting. We figured we could wring a permanent concession from you once you realized we had you over a barrel."

"I appreciate the honesty," Ward answered dryly. "What if I don't agree?"

She cocked her thumb at the door. "Then Hsing outside will detain the two of you in these rooms until Denison's people arrive and take you into custody. Your little adventure will be over."

Ward sighed. "We call that blackmail back home."

She smiled. "Call it whatever you like. Give us what we want and you will be entitled to asylum in Complein, as long as you obey our laws. Hsing will slip into civilian clothes and become your bodyguard. He will follow you everywhere, report on your movements, and make sure you don't stray from the path of the righteous."

"I see," Ward said, "I don't have much choice, do I?"

"Not really," Sandia replied. "What will it be?"

"All right," Ward said, "I agree to your terms. How do we make this official?"

"You just did," Sandia answered cheerfully. She held up a palm-sized imprint recorder. "I taped our little talk.

I'll record it as legal as soon as I leave. In the meantime, Mr. Tuchman, allow me to offer you refuge in Complein."

"Thanks," he said dryly. "Are you happy?"

Sandia never stopped smiling. "Just doing my job, Mr. Tuchman. I'm sure you understand."

She walked back to the door and called the guard in. "Hsing, meet Mr. Tuchman. He's accepted our generous offer. You'll be his guard while he's here." Ward warily shook his hand. She smiled at Ward again. "Just consider him your first friend in town." She walked towards the door. "Just the city's elders looking after a guest."

Ward waited for her to leave, then looked at the constable. "Well, guy, you want a chair or somethin'? You're going to be out there a while."

Hsing sighed and looked at where Sandia had gone. "Sure," he replied.

Ward got the chair from the desk and carried it out into the hall. "Here you go."

Hsing looked at him intently. "Thanks."

Ward went back into the room and closed the door. He laid down on the bed, still wrapped only in a towel, while his mind whirled through the day's events. The seductive comfort of the bed captured him almost at once. A giant yawn slipped free.

"Damn," he said, "I've been pushin' too hard. Got to conserve my strength." He felt his energy bleed away as the soft bed, the warm shower, and his long-suppressed fatigue took their toll. Hsing's presence outside the door even contributed its small part. He relaxed for the first time since the attack on LaPort and was almost instantly asleep.

He awoke briefly as Mona curled up beside him, fully dressed. He listened to her crying softly until the tide of fatigue washed over him, dragging him down.

* * *

Ward stayed in close contact with Theisiger, monitoring the pace of the repairs while he prowled the city. Hsing remained with him, pacing him step for step and following him everywhere except into lavatory stalls. Ward resented him until the first time he saw Wing toughs gather. They stalked the pair on several occasions, trying to catch Ward alone. Hsing's credentials and extendable stun baton ran them off each time they got too close. Ward quickly realized he'd likely have been knifed without the guard's stolid presence.

Hsing's low-key contacts allowed Ward to fish for information in places he wouldn't have dared go otherwise. He spent his evenings trolling various taphouses near the hotel, buying drinks and listening for pieces of news he could use to begin his revenge. He knew he'd have to start small and reasoned to himself that it would provide him with his first opportunities.

He'd chosen to lurk in the Speakeasy for his third night of trolling. The bar was a dive of the lowest sort, smelling of urine and vomit and inhabited by the absolute dregs of humanity. Only Hsing's air of authority protected them.

"This is stupid, Ward," the guard hissed as Ward rolled a filthy beer glass between his hands. "I can't guarantee your safety here. Let's go somewhere else."

"No, it's perfect," Ward retorted. "Listen!" He gestured towards two men who stood talking a few steps away. Hsing turned his head and saw a grog-soaked retainer in soiled Tuchman colors.

"So anyway," the drunk chattered, "I was workin' the plot down by the old border, what was Tuch' 'afore Wing hit us, when I seen smoke comin' up."

He leaned in closer to the bar and took a long pull of licorice-colored beer.

"Then I went down by the stream, and that's where I saw it."

His friend, less far gone, queried, "Saw what?"

The drunk's face clouded, and he made a rude noise at his friend's obtuseness. "The Hardestys. Down fish farmin'. In the old gap between Wing and Tuch' lands. Wing blew it up." He made a billowing gesture with his hands. "Ka-bloom! Fish and shit everywhere, fallin' out of the sky. I thought I was gonna split ma' gut right there." He laughed gassily. "Ol' damn Hardesty looked like a kid who lost his lolly-pop. Little Delius pervert Wing was up there giggling like a fool. He called Hardesty out, right then and there. Gave him a week to move off the plot or get buried on it."

He broke off, seeing Ward staring at them, obviously listening. "Hey, mister, got a problem?" he said with angry aggressiveness.

Ward smiled. "Naw, 'course not. Tell you what, let me get you two another round."

The drunk looked as though he wanted to make an issue of it. Hsing loomed up over Ward's shoulder. "Is there a problem?"

The drunk dropped his gaze. "Thanks for the tip," Ward said to them. "This'll cover your drinks." He put a small stack of low denomination coins on the table.

He took a deep breath as soon as they were outside. "Damn, that feels good. I got my hook!"

Hsing looked troubled. "Mister Tuchman?"

"Yes," Ward answered. "What is it?"

"You're gonna get in bad trouble if'n you keep this up," the guard said. "You know that?"

"I won't be the only one," Ward answered grimly. He gestured for the guard to precede him back to the hotel. "Home, Jeeves."

Hsing sighed and went on ahead. "Mr. T, what exactly are you tryin' to accomplish?"

Ward, still savoring the clean air after the bar's dank miasma, shadow punched the wall as they walked. "I'm like a dagger," he said, "pointed at Wing. Most daggers break when they hit armor. I can't afford to break. So

I have to wait until Wing gives me a chink, a gap I can exploit to hit them. This thing with Hardesty is the first clear target I've seen."

"What are you going to do?" Hsing asked.

"I'm not sure yet. The Hardesties are scum, but they might be useful to me. I may just go up and stand in for them." Ward's grin got broader. "Hell, yes! That'll do just fine. I'll cut Hardesty a deal. I just hope Egg gets the suit finished soon. I don't know how long ago Delius made his challenge."

"You realize I'm passing everything I see and you tell me on to Sandia, don't you?" Hsing asked.

"Yeah," Ward answered, "the easier I make your job, I figure the more leeway you might give me, if I were to need it."

Hsing blew his breath out slowly. "Fair enough, I suppose."

Ward entered the workshop the morning Egg had promised the suit. Egg met him at the door. "Is it done?" Ward said without preamble.

"Yeah," Egg said tiredly, "I was up most of last night putting the finishing touches on him. We'd better go down to the test facility and try him out."

"Is that necessary?" Ward replied. "I've got things to do."

Egg bobbed his head, his plastic beard holder cracking against his chest. "Sometimes little bugs show up during testing that were missed during the bench repairs. The only way to find them is to put the suit through its paces. If you want to skip that phase, then it's your problem, not mine." Ward thought it over a moment, then agreed with poor grace.

Egg led him to the cubicle where his suit had been stored.

The technician smiled at Ward's sharp intake of breath as he opened the curtain.

"It's beautiful!" Ward cried. "What kind of paint job is it?"

"Theisiger calls it 'tiger stripes,'" Egg answered. "We had to sandblast away the old paint to inspect for hidden damage, so we repainted. Carlo wanted you to have something special. We used olive drab, gray, and matte black. The black is infrared dampening, so you'll get some benefit in IR."

"Damn," Ward whistled, "it sure as hell *looks* lethal."

"It is," Egg said. "Why don't you put him through his paces? I'll be in the testing room."

Ward clumped in a few minutes later, his shoulder dusted with plaster. Egg watched him lurch around the obstacle course several times, stumbling into walls and barriers. Theisiger came in and stood next to Egg just as Ward staggered into a heavy plastic barrel.

"How's he doing?" Theisiger asked.

"He keeps overcontrolling the servos," Egg said. "Maybe I should have told him I boosted the system sensitivity."

Theisiger demurred. "No, he should figure that out for himself. Oops, here he comes. Put on your happy face."

Ward stumped over to them. He swore in frustration as he fumbled with the helmet catches.

"The damn thing doesn't work!" he swore as he removed the helmet. "I can't control it for shit."

Egg laughed. "I played with the AI and boosted the servo sensors. They're more delicate, respond more easily. You've got ten percent faster reflexes. You just ain't used to them, yet. You've got better IR vision and augmented powercells, too."

"Try it again, Ward," Theisiger suggested, "this time with a lighter touch."

They put Ward through his paces until they were satisfied he could control the new suit at least moderately well. Ward's glower faded as he learned the more subtle movements that the modified suit required. He grinned broadly as he skipped and dodged between the barrels and obstacles. His final test was a precisely controlled boost that landed him within a half-meter target circle.

He whipped his helmet off. "All right!" He turned and saw Theisiger and Egg walking towards him. Theisiger wore a heavy equipment satchel that rattled as he moved.

"What all did you guys do to it?" Ward asked. "I can barely tell where you put the patches."

"Your new power conduits are forty percent more efficient," Egg supplied. "They've been cross-wired. Either path will handle the suit's full load. You won't have any more power-down failures."

"Thanks. You guys did a great job." He grinned at Theisiger. "Look, I'm ripping you off. Thirty-one won't near cover it."

Theisiger held up his hands. "Naw, it's okay." He smiled. "You're a walkin', jumpin', Wing huntin' package of certified death and destruction, kid. Go drum me up some business, okay? Just not in the city."

"There's got to be somethin' I can do for you," Ward said.

"All right," Theisiger said, "give me first dibs on any future suit contracts."

"Done!" Ward declared.

"It'll be expensive," Theisiger warned.

"Less expensive than people dying in bad suits," Ward responded.

Theisiger slipped the satchel over his shoulder and held it out to Ward.

"What's this?" Ward asked, looking bemused.

"Tools," Theisiger replied, "and a maintenance manual. This way you can pull your own first echelon repairs in the field. There's a checklist taped inside. Follow that like a religion and you'll be at peak performance every fight."

"Thanks," Ward said sincerely, "I really appreciate this."

"Not a problem," Theisiger said. "Stop by the armory on the way out and get yourself a couple of coil gun cassettes. Main power is full up and Egg added an auxiliary jack that will let you recharge from house current."

Ward shook their hands and walked away to the changing area.

Egg sighed. "He's just like his daddy."

"Well, I hope his temper is better," Theisiger replied, "or he'll be dead, too."

"Did you get the payment from Wing for those suits we patched together?" Egg asked.

"Naw," Theisiger answered, "and doesn't look like we're going to, either. They say the repairs were substandard."

Egg swore. "That's why you gave Ward the suit for a song!"

"Yeah," Theisiger replied, "let's just call it 'Carlo's Revenge.'"

Ward and Mona were well clear of Complein by nightfall and camping under the stars when Mona came and sat next to him. "Which Hardesty are we going to help?" she asked.

"It's kind of hard to tell," Ward answered dryly. "They're cousins, but they've all got the same parents. I think this one's Steven."

"Steven?" she repeated, "Wasn't he Stewart's brother, the man your father killed at Assembly? What makes you think he'll accept your help?"

"Wing's breathing down his neck," Ward explained. "He's too broke and too screwed to turn us down."

"I don't follow," Mona replied.

Ward tossed a pine cone into the fire and watched it snap and pop as the seed pods within burst open. "Wing apparently feels free to police their borders with us. They're running squatters off what used to be no-man's land. My dad used to rant about Hardesty all the time."

"Why did he put up with them?" she asked.

"He didn't have a choice," Ward answered. "If we'd sent forces down to clean them out, Wing would have reacted with their own troops to keep an eye on us. Any stray fire from our side would have landed in Wing and possibly started a fight. Dad hated Stewart, but not enough to go to war over him."

He poked the fire with a stick. "Most clans would have cut a deal and run them off together, but that wasn't possible with Wing. So Hardesty lived safely in the crease, at least until last week."

"What are we going to do?" she asked.

"We'll go and talk Steven into letting us stand in for him when Wing comes back. He's not in a position to refuse. That'll keep us within the code duello."

Mona seemed satisfied. She began fieldstripping and cleaning her Piat by the firelight. Ward saw she'd collected a small supply of duplex antitank rounds. He whistled silently. The duplex rounds were designed for armored vehicles rather than people. They wouldn't even leave a grease spot behind if they hit PBA. He watched her attaching a small, bulky-looking object to the bottom of the Piat with gray duct tape.

"What's that?" he asked.

"Imprint camera," she replied. "It's got an integrated uplink, built to interface directly with satellites."

Ward looked puzzled. "Why?"

"You're gonna kill Wings," she asserted. "After the first couple or three innings, they're gonna say you're cheatin'." She checked the camera mount. "This'll record the duels and transmit the data to the Council. It's got a wide-view visual pickup, and audio. It'll record everything." She set the weapon down carefully beside her. "I got us four more with tree staples."

Ward smiled at her ingenuity. "It never occurred to me to record the duels."

"This'll keep 'em from declaring open season on us," she said deliberately, "and it'll show any cheating they do to us."

"We have to travel hard tomorrow," Ward said. "We're running out of time."

They awoke before dawn, ate a cold breakfast, and then had to wait for the sun to rise enough to power the truck's pathetic photocells. Mona patiently listened while Ward ranted about forgetting to buy a new vehicle. The swearing proved unnecessary. Even at the truck's sluggish pace, they arrived at the Hardesty plot well before noon.

Mona looked at the gray surroundings and the thin trail that branched away from the silicate road. "What a shit-hole!" she declared, looking at the scraggly trees that grew alongside the roadstead.

"This was one of the first places we exploited," Ward said. "Dad brought me down here when I was boy and things were better with Wing. He called it a legacy from Grandpa Abel's time. We exhausted the soil and cut all the trees." He shook his head. "We learned resource management from disasters like this. Dickerson hasn't. They've run their land down so far, it probably won't come back." He swept his hand across the bleak landscape. "This area will probably recover, but it'll need to be left alone a generation or two."

Mona stepped down from the wagon. Her lip curled as she sniffed. "I'd be careful if I were you. Some of those piles alongside the trail are excrement, I think."

Ward suppressed a shiver as she tucked the loaded HEAP pistol into her waistband at the small of her back.

She looked at him as he climbed down. "Aren't you taking a gun?" she asked.

He held up his shirttail and showed her the Execuline

he'd nested there. "I don't want to display it. This is going to be hard enough without toting in the open."

She acceded with a nod of her head and extended her hand, indicating he should precede her. He started up the thin trail and across the low rise. The fecal odor grew stronger as they crested the rise. Clusters of sawlegs hummed angrily as they passed.

He paused a moment at the top of the hill to survey the camp. The heart of the place looked to be a hardscrabble shelter made of smooth river stones cemented with mud. The shelter had been built with a single door against a rough tumbledown of stones. A ragged piece of cloth flapped in the doorway. It seemed a pathetic defense against the weather. The whole area looked gray and unpleasant.

Mounds of stones piled almost five meters high lined the ragged watercourse, telling Ward that the creek had been dredged at least once. A thin brook gurgled between two placer mounds and meandered through the campsite to join the main stream.

Ward could see the remains of a dam that had been built between two tailings piles. The ruins of a small paddle-wheeled generator lay beneath the remains of a small spillway. The machinery was chaff, apparently obliterated by the same charge that had scattered the weir's stones across the dismal hillside. Ward saw a mudline that indicated the downstream area had been hit by a moderately sized flood.

Several people emerged from the hovel as he and Mona started down the hill. A man led the sad procession, armed with a piece of bent pipe. Two women walked behind him, one heavily pregnant. She carried an infant and leaned on her companion, a thin, sallow-faced woman. An array of children puttered along behind, bickering and squabbling as they poured out to see the newcomers.

Ward frowned at their poverty. His own travel-stained

and dirty clothing was still two steps better than the ragged coverall the man wore. The two women looked cleaner, if no better dressed. They wore faded flower-pattern sack dresses that looked as if they had begun life as curtains. The eight or nine children were barefoot and wore various castoffs and pieced together rejects.

"This is disgusting," Mona whispered. "Why do they choose to live this way?"

"I'm not sure they chose to," Ward answered out of the corner of his mouth.

The man stopped about twenty meters from Ward, on the far side of the thin creek. "This 'ere's our land!" he shouted, brandishing his pipe.

"What a hick," Ward said softly. Then louder, he answered, "No, this is Tuchman land."

"Ah'l we want is to be left ah'lone," the man shouted as Ward picked his way along the creek bottom, looking for a place to cross. As he stepped into the water, Ward mimed putting his hand to his ear. The Hardesty man yelled again and smashed the pipe down on a rock. Ward heard Mona move behind him. He looked back and saw she had drawn the HEAP pistol and held it in front of her in plain sight. Hardesty backed away from the weapon, looking more sullen than threatening.

"What do y'all want?" he demanded as Ward gained the far bank. His manner struck Ward as simultaneously defiant and skittish, much like a kicked dog.

"My name's Tuchman, Ward Tuchman," Ward said.

"So?" the squatter asked suspiciously, "you Tuchmans ain't nuthin, not since Wing put you down!"

Ward suppressed a surge of anger. He heard Mona scrambling over the rocks, possibly to keep her line of fire clear. Ward bit back a hot retort and instead tried to speak calmly. "That's part of your problem, isn't it?"

Hardesty's rheumy eyes narrowed. Ward caught a whiff of sour beer and stale sweat. "Wha' do ya mean?" the squatter asked.

"Without Tuchman to hold Wing off, you got no protection here whatsoever." Ward pointed to the broken fish weir. "Too bad." His voice dripped insincerity.

The thin woman stepped from behind the man. Ward thought she had the hard face of someone who'd seen a lot of bad times. "You bastard!" she hissed at Ward. "Your ol' man killed Stewart, left mah sister knocked up without a husband. Left three children, too. Who's gonna feed 'em and take up for 'em?"

Ward shrugged and met her eye. "Not my problem." His voice held no compassion. She rocked back, surprised by his blunt statement.

The man glared at the woman and tried to seize the initiative from her. "What're y'all doin' here?" he demanded again.

"Business," Ward answered. "Can we talk?"

Hardesty looked hard at Ward, then nodded his head once. He seemed to deflate as his angry front crumbled.

Ward and Mona followed the family back into the camp. Ward watched as Hardesty pulled a brown bottle from his pocket. He glanced quickly to see if either woman was watching and took a long swig. The level inside looked severely diminished when he lowered the bottle from his mouth.

Ward waited until they were in the camp and the children had been rousted before he got down to business.

"I hear Wing's threatening to push you out of here," Ward stated.

"Yup," the man replied, "and we ain't got much choice." He sighed heavily, an expression of self-pity. "Don't got no armor. Don't got no desire t' die." He sighed again. "Guess we'll just move along."

Ward exhaled. Hardesty's beaten dog routine would get old fast. "Look, asshole," he said unsympathetically, "you always got choices."

"Yeah, that's what Stew thought, too," Steven answered.

"How's that?" Ward asked.

Hardesty patted his pocket to make sure his bottle was where he had left it. "My asshole brother thought he'd just ally with either ya'll or Wing. He figured that if one of you'd support him, we'd all be safe." Bitterness and anger chased across his worn features. He picked at a scab on the back of his dirt-streaked hand. "He chose Wing, those bastards. He thought they'd gotten the upper hand and would win th' drag-out between ya'll. Guess he was right, for all the good it did him." He looked bitterly at Ward. "So my asshole brother goes to kiss Wings' ass by settin' up Benno in front of the whole district." He spat. "Bastards left him to twist in the wind."

Steven Hardesty's anger ran out of him like water from a spilled glass. He stared apathetically at the toes of his rotten shoes. "Ain't nuthin' to do," he said sullenly.

"I see," said Ward. "You just fold up and die, then." He looked contemptuously at Hardesty. "Coward."

Steven looked at his feet. Ward caught a whiff of him as a slight breeze stirred the camp dust. The man reeked of sweaty fear, anger, and alcohol.

Ward tried again. "Wing gave you a week to clear out, right?"

Hardesty nodded. "Delius and his boys'll be back the day after tomorrow. We either git, or I accept his challenge and git kilt."

"Go ahead and accept," Ward said. "I'll stand in for you."

Hardesty's voice had grown muzzy from the liquor he'd consumed. "Why zat?" he slurred. "You'll jes' get kilt, too."

"I'll represent you," Ward said, trying to bring Hardesty around. "I'll be your ringer. You won't have to die."

He knew Steven had to verbally agree to Ward's proposal for him to be legal under the code as Steven's champion. It had never occurred to Ward that a simple "yes" would prove so elusive.

Hardesty shrugged, uncaring. "Why bother? We'd just get kilt." Ward sighed. He turned to Mona, his hands raised in defeat.

The sallow-faced woman stormed out of the shelter and walked up to Hardesty. "If'n you don't do this, I'll stick you mahself," she shrieked. Ward and Mona both stared at her, startled by her vehemence. She vibrated with anger. "We're as good as dead as it is. You pass this up and ah swear 'ahl cut your goddamn throat mahself."

The old man just let her temper wash over him. "Ah've followed you goin' on five years now," she blazed. "An' every time someone raises a hand, you fold up an' quit." Steven's eyes were unfocused. "Then you come back an' beat the shit outa' me. Ah'm tired of it." He looked away.

She slapped him once across the face, hard. "You look at me, you bastard!" He brought his hand to his red cheek, apparently surprised that she would actually hit him.

Ward saw the anger build in his face like a summer storm. The woman stared at him defiantly. He raised his hand and punched her hard, swinging his fist in a wild roundhouse that connected with her temple. She fell to the sand, holding her head.

Ward saw a trace of blood on her face and heard Mona snarl. He held his hand up to stop her.

Hardesty stared down at her, nostrils flaring as he panted. "Bitch," he said tiredly.

The woman glared back defiantly. "Ah swear ah'll kill you," she said. "Ah'll cut your damn throat and take over the family mahself. Ah'm tired a' runnin, and if you don't take this deal ah'l cut you, no matter how long it takes."

Hardesty raised his hand as if to hit her again. She

didn't flinch. Her eyes bored into his face. His anger drained away and his hand fell to his side. "Suit yourself," he said apathetically. The woman grinned in triumph. Ward smiled and looked at Mona.

"Got it," Mona announced. "It's imprinted."

"Great," Ward said. "We're on our way."

Chapter 6

Mona stood in the middle of the dueling field, her 70mm Piat clasped tightly in her hands. "Can you see them?" she asked as she peered back to where he hid, shading her eyes from the dawning sun.

"No," Ward replied testily, "I put the damn blind down too low. I can't see where they landed. I spent too damn much time walking the field and not enough trying to figure out how I was gonna get on it." He shifted around, trying to see over the low rise that blocked his view of Delius' ground car. "What are they doing?"

She touched one hand to her headset. "Nothin' yet. They're still passing the bottle around. Delius is trading nips with his cronies." He heard the laughter from the Wing contingent across the field. "I think they're waiting for something," Mona continued. "One of them keeps looking at her watch."

"Damn, I wish I could see them," Ward griped. "How many are in battle armor?"

"Two," she replied. "One has his helmet off. He looks like a hawk."

"That would be Delius," Ward answered, remembering the few times he'd seen Seladra's brother. He glanced up quickly as a second ground car flashed in low and settled next to the first, out of Ward's sight. "What's going on now?"

Mona waited a moment. "I've got two more in sight. One looks like a driver, the other one is bald. They're walking towards me. Delius is following." She waited a moment. "I'd start the cameras now if I were you. I think the show is about to start."

Ward stepped over to the rack of plastic-covered transmission equipment that remained hidden behind the blind. He ignited the chemical generator and brought the four hidden cameras on-line. He checked the signal from the orbiting communications satellite. "I've got a clear image. Can you point the wide angle at them so I can see what's going on?"

The image in the monitor bobbed and weaved as Mona lifted the Piat. Ward felt his stomach lurch as the camera settled on the small group walking towards her. He saw they had just crossed the stream that bisected the forest, rough, and open ground that made up the dueling field. He could just make out the red and white boundary markers in the far distance behind them.

Delius shifted the helmet he carried under one arm. Ward saw a suspicious-looking bulge on the right side.

"What's he got on his helmet?" Ward asked.

"I'm not sure," Mona answered, "I think it's a camera. It's too short to be a laser."

"Sounds good," he answered. "Have they figured out you're not Hardesty?"

"No," she answered, "I've got the sun directly behind me. They can't see shit."

Ward, still looking through the monitor, saw them squinting and shading their eyes as they tried to take the measure of the figure standing in the middle ground. All except Delius, who walked towards her, seemingly unconcerned.

"He's wearing a sun-filter," he warned. "He must have it squidged all the way down to look directly at the sun. He'll figure you out in a moment." Ward grinned. "That filter's a two-edged sword. He'll be blinded as soon as he looks away."

Ward watched Delius stop and point to Mona. Ward

couldn't hear what he said, but the other two turned towards him.

"Who's the bald guy?" she asked.

Ward looked at the monitor. "That would be Efram Wing. He's Wing's pet Law-Speaker. Dad thought he was a pissant."

"What's he doing here?" Mona asked, perplexed. "Hardesty isn't worth that kind of attention, is he?"

"No," Ward answered, "the spear carriers at the car are enough to run the squatters off. I'd guess Efram's here to make sure Wing stays legal and doesn't piss off Denison."

Mona seemed puzzled. "Denison? Why would they worry about him?"

"He's the receiver for Tuchman," Ward answered, "so technically he's an aggrieved party, too. Half of Hardesty's camp is on Tuch lands. I think Efram's here to make sure that Wing's activities don't bleed over onto Tuchman turf and abrade Denison's sensibilities."

"I don't follow," Mona answered. "Wing already invaded once. Why should they care about the border?"

"Clan Denison is a big player," Ward said, "bigger than Wing. Wing knows that pissing with them is bad juju. And Denison's got the backing of the planetary Assembly. Much as Dad didn't like to admit it, the Assembly acting together can make it rougher on any one clan. Efram won't want to make Denison lose face, not over a pissant like Hardesty. He knows Denison would have no choice but to respond to a border encroachment, and that's the kind of trouble Efram can do without."

"I wished I'd kept up on politics," Mona replied. "Stal didn't like to talk shop at home. Can't we set Denison against Wing and watch them fight it out?"

"I'd like to know how," Ward answered. "It'd make my life easier. But Denison's too smart for that, damn him."

"Who the hell are you?" Ward heard through the

camera's audio pickup. The view in the imprint camera bobbed low and swung high as she shifted the Piat.

"I'm the second," she said to the man. The gun camera settled down. Ward saw the armored figure at an angle and off center, hands on his hips.

"Where the hell is Hardesty?" the man snapped.

"He couldn't make it," Mona replied coolly, "so he arranged a stand-in."

Delius snorted. "Damn coward doesn't have the brains to pour piss from a boot." He looked at Mona. "Well, bring on your ringer. Let's get this started."

"Not so fast!" snapped Efram to Delius. He turned smoothly to face Mona. "We've got a legal affair to settle with Hardesty. Are you empowered to talk for him?"

"Yes," she snapped. "He says he's legal, that the border area is fallow and unclaimed. Your claim has lapsed."

"That proscription is obsolete," Efram said with a yawn. "They voted that clause out eons ago. Is there anything else?"

"Yeah," Mona answered. "Go to hell."

Efram pursed his lips. "Well, we will consider that insult as proximate cause for a duel. Do you retract your words?" he said formally.

"No," Mona replied.

Efram gestured to Delius. "My kinsman desires to seek redress for the injury done to me. Does that satisfy convention?"

Mona nodded once. "Yes."

Efram gave her a long, assessing look. "Where is your principal?"

Mona's voice seemed tense to Ward. He hoped she would hold together long enough to finish the encounter. "He'll be along in a minute," she said tightly. "Just as soon as we nail down terms."

"Bullshit!" injected Delius. "The fight's 'come as you are' and s'posed to go at dawn. It's past that now."

Efram half-turned towards Delius, an exasperated

expression on his face. Delius made a rude gesture with his hand. "No," Efram said, his voice wary, "I think a discussion of terms is a very good idea right about now. What did you have in mind?"

Mona ticked off the points on her fingers. "Just the standard stipulations. No reinforcements, resupply, or outside aid. Suit systems only. They fight till one yields or dies."

"Fine," Efram answered.

"Can we get this over with?" Delius snapped. "We're burning daylight."

Efram looked at him, clearly vexed. "We agree to your terms. Bring out your principal."

Ward was already up and walking towards the small group before Mona turned and waved.

Delius, with his sun filter, was the first to see Ward's lethal-looking suit. "What the hell is this?" He turned to Efram. "He's got a custom suit. The bastard's loaded for bear." It seemed to Mona that Delius looked like a deer caught in a spotlight. His bravado melted away as Ward walked leisurely towards the middle ground.

Efram looked worried as he squinted into the morning light. "Who's that?"

"Hardesty's champion," she replied slowly, some of her equanimity returning. The way she drawled out "champion" made it sound like "champ-een."

Efram fought hard to maintain his poise. "I wasn't aware Hardesty knew anyone who could spell 'armor' much less owned any." Ward suspected Efram was playing for time, trying to give Delius a few moments to get organized. "I don't recognize the paint. Who are you?" Efram asked Ward, pitching his voice to carry across the rocky field.

"No one of importance," Ward replied.

"Why are you here?" Efram pressed.

"You blew up Hardesty's fish weir," Ward replied. "I happen to like fish."

"W-wait," Delius mumbled. "I-I'm n-not ready to fight a suit. M'battery's only got sixty percent power, an' I've only got half ammo." Efram rolled his eyes and flashed Delius a look of contempt.

Ward relaxed a trifle when he saw that the bulge on the side of Delius' head was indeed a camera and not something more lethal. "Too bad," Ward said with patent insincerity. "I think you said this fight is 'come as you are.'" He grinned inside his own helmet as he gave Delius' own words back to him.

Delius pouted. "This isn't a fair fight. I think you should at least give me a chance."

"Just like the one you were going to give Hardesty?" Ward answered.

Delius made no answer.

Ward held up his arms to display his shoulder-mounted coil gun magazine and unshielded laser. "Time to bring out your shit, boy," he said quietly.

Delius shook his head, clearly unhappy. He turned to Efram. "Can't you do something?"

The Law-Speaker looked unhappy. "No. You put your foot in it. It's all legal."

Delius removed his sun-filter and fumbled with his helmet, taking several tries to get it secured. Mona and Efram walked around their principals, checking equipment.

Delius held up his arms, displaying his own cassette. Ward saw that Delius' configuration matched his own: a Mark III laser, coil gun, and jump pack. The seconds stepped back.

Mona broke open her Piat, cocking the launching spring as she bent it in an "L." Ward watched as she loaded the launcher with a heavy-duty duplex grenade. Efram stared at her while she loaded the weapon. He removed an Execuline from his coat and inspected it.

"Don't you think that's a little heavy to back your man with?" he asked.

"Naw," she replied laconically, "I rarely need a second shot."

Efram shook his head and indicated the sidelines.

Ward turned and walked back to his own starting line, his helmet polarizing almost instantly as he faced directly towards the rising sun, blanking almost all of the ambient light. He couldn't see his feet and stumbled once or twice as he walked. He grinned. His ordeal would end as soon as he got to his starting position. He knew Delius' was just beginning. He heard the warning whistle just as he hit his own mark, two hundred meters away from Delius and on a direct line. He whirled and crouched.

Delius pivoted to his right, using his AI to track Ward and lay down a slashing burst with his coil gun. Ward jumped up and back, triggering his thrust pack to lift him back and over Delius' stream of ring penetrators. He looked like a high jumper stretching for the bar. Ward fired his booster again, using its power to flatten and lengthen the curve of his jump.

Delius continued to hose the area around Ward with the coil gun, spraying penetrators into the trees and hillsides as he fought to bring his weapon on target. Ward knew optimal use of the coil gun called for short, controlled bursts while the AI or operator assessed accuracy and made changes. Delius kept his feet firmly planted while he attempted to pivot and hose Ward. This suggested to Ward that Delius depended almost completely on his AI for tracking information. Like Ward, Delius couldn't face the sun and see the field at the same time.

Ward lengthened his leap as he stretched back and looked for the ground. He saw it rushing up. He cued the AI to "target" by clicking the suit's tongue switch. The crosshairs came up and settled on Delius. Ward back-flipped, using the heightened reflexes in the suit. As he landed, he fired his laser, licking the ground around Delius. It was enough, but just barely. Ward staggered to a landing, some twelve meters from his starting point.

Delius tried to turn to face the incoming fire, but his polarizer was still set too high. The faceplate damped the painting laser, making the killing beam invisible to him. Ward saw him fumbling with the control knob on the side of his head to open up the visor while trying to evade the lasers he couldn't see. He stepped once, twice, then stumbled on a rock and fell. Ward played the beam over Delius' exposed knee and thigh for several seconds before Wing could scramble down a bit of scree and roll out of sight.

Ward didn't even bother to seek cover. It was painfully obvious to him, as well as to any bystanders, that Delius was hopelessly outclassed. Egg's modifications only made the disparity worse.

Ward heard Delius crank off another long burst. None were even vaguely pointed in Ward's direction. He smiled to himself. At the rate Delius was wasting rounds, he'd overheat his coil gun's electromagnet.

Delius scrambled out from cover, pumping out a long stream of airfoils as he tried again to overwhelm Ward with a sheer volume of firepower. Ward dove gracefully for cover, then bounded back to his feet. Lasers and ring penetrators skipped and skittered along the ground as Ward struck Delius with an offhand laser shot. The bolt vaporized the surface of Delius' laminate PBA, knocking him over backwards and behind the scree. Ward realized he had inadvertantly pushed Delius into a perfectly good defensible position.

Delius disappeared from sight behind the mound, then briefly appeared on the far side. He probed twice, seeking to pinion Ward with his coiler. Both times Ward beat him to the punch, scattering dirt and stones around his head, spoiling his aim and making him duck. Ward stood poised, waiting. He saw a puff of dust and heard a slight shuffle, but Delius refused to emerge again to risk Ward's superior fire.

Ward leapt forward and up, using the boost-pack to skim the terrain as he sought a spot from which to flank Delius. He sprinted for a promising hummock and was surprised that Delius didn't at least try to bring him under fire while he crossed open ground. He rolled behind the hummock and pointed his coiler at the scree. Delius fired twice, quickly, then scrambled behind the loose stones and shingle to keep the mound again firmly between them.

"Damn," Ward swore. Delius could keep the rock pile between them and drag the fight out indefinitely. Ward scanned his map and saw that he had to circle wide around to flank the Wing champion, while Delius only had to scramble a few meters to restore the status quo.

He looked around and saw a smaller, knee-high outcropping a quarter-circle from the hummock. His eyes narrowed as he glanced from the scree to the outcropping and mentally judged the angles. He quickly switched from targeting crosshairs to his terrain map and set his AI to plot the deflection angle necessary to bounce rings off the outcropping and into Delius' lap. The AI's solution churned out a few seconds later, marking the correct deflection as a red line on Ward's computer map.

He popped his head over the side of the hummock and fired a few desultory laser beams to keep his opponent's head down. Delius showed no inclination to respond in kind. Ward braced himself on one knee and sprinted for the red line marked on the map.

Delius fired, his own coiler appearing briefly over the top of the scree as he tried to shoot without exposing himself. Ward recalled Stallart's terse lecture on the practice of weapons fire without direct AI inputs. "Long on security, short on accomplishing anything worthwhile."

Delius' airfoils whined and hummed as they passed, none close enough to seriously worry about.

The red line flashed amber as Ward crossed it and the crosshairs settled on the computer's firing solution pipper. Ward keyed his coil gun, slamming a stream of airfoils into the outcropping. The heavy stone shattered under the hypervelocity tungsten projectiles, scattering shrapnel behind the scree pile. More importantly, ring penetrators ricocheted off the churned stone and began peppering the area where Delius hid.

He grinned at the glint of armor that shone around the edge of the scree. Delius had shifted around the mound to try to shelter from both the glancing rings and Ward's direct fire. Ward fired a quick burst, snapping the air over Delius' exposed shoulder. The armor slid out of sight and Delius' coil gun probed around the edge of the scree. Ward concentrated his fire on the menacing weapon, but Delius was a hair faster. Ward had to scramble to one side and dive sideways as Delius' wild shots pelted the area.

Ward's motion sensor blipped, placing a target in range. He raised his head and saw Delius fleeing for the tree line, using his boost-pack to augment his running speed. Puffs of blue flame seared the grass as Delius loped in great strides, chewing up ground as he sought cover. A small fire started in his wake.

Ward sighted carefully, using his AI to lead his opponent. The crosshairs settled on the middle of Delius' retreating back. Ward fired the laser again, conserving his precious coil gun loads. He played the beam across Delius' pack, landing two sustained shots on one fuel tank. He saw a plume of something, either compressed air or boost-pack fuel, vent from the back of the suit. Delius tumbled as the plume knocked him off balance. Delius tried to get a shot off at Ward, aiming his own laser low and sweeping it back and forth along the low rise. Most of the beams plowed into the dirt, scalding vegetation and causing micro-explosions as water trapped in roots and soil flashed into steam.

He moved in slowly, weapons ready, and looked to his left where Delius had crashed into the woods. Ward could see the point of entry by the smoldering saplings and small trees. Delius had moved farther than Ward figured he'd be able to go, but Ward could hear him crashing about in the undergrowth. Ward activated his coil gun sight and placed the feedback tracker on the underbrush, locating a source in a cluster of clinger bushes.

Ward bet that Delius would emerge from the bushes at any moment: Ward knew that clingers tended to grab onto anything that moved near them. They would grasp whatever passed until they dried out or lost traction, an admirable survival strategy, in Ward's view.

Ward saw the forest side of the cluster shiver and shake just before a vegetation-covered head emerged and a hand reached out to claw the clinging, crawling creepers away. Delius tore his way out, covered from head to toe with short tendrils of writhing vine. "I can't decide whether he's lucky or smart," Ward whispered to himself, "the creepers're better camouflage than the haze gray and the plants'll soak up some laser fire." He shook his head. "Even assholes get lucky once in a while."

He kept his head down as he tracked Delius' slow progress upslope. The Wing had gotten clear of the creeper and was working his way from one tree to the next. He'd pop his head up, take a quick look, then bound up from the same spot he'd peered over. Ward knew that a quick peek was a fine thing to do, provided Delius had done it from some place other than his starting point for his next advance. It served Ward well as a semaphore.

Delius hopped up again and sprinted forward. Ward enhanced his magnification, centered his crosshairs, and poured gouts of laser fire into Delius. The Wing champion staggered and stumbled as the laser bolts picked at his armor. He fell again. Ward poured on the coal, firing twin streams of rings and lasers into Delius' exposed armor. He heard a bubbling shriek and saw Delius fall onto his side and roll onto his back.

Ward sighted on Delius' head, adjusting his magnification to place the crosshairs on the smoking hole in Delius' faceplate. Time seemed to slow as he exhaled slowly and touched the firing stud.

BA-whoom! Ward ducked involuntarily as the close blast shook the trees. He looked frantically back at the pillar of smoke and fire that rose from the lower ground. He zoomed in on Mona as she painfully brought the Piat down from her shoulder and slowly reloaded. He panned back and scanned in on the blast site. A single armored arm landed just outside the point of impact.

"Nobody goes in!" Mona screamed at the Wings, her voice exploding in Ward's ears until the AI dampened down the speaker grill. "Nobody goes in, or I'll blow you to smithereens, too!"

One of the Wing gunmen jumped for her, screaming "You *bitch*!" Efram jumped in front of her, forcing her laser rifle down, and shouting "*No!*"

Mona brought her own weapon up. "I'll vaporize the lot of you here and now!" she snarled.

Ward turned back to Delius and swore again. The Wing had gotten his shit together and had crossed his index fingers over his head, the universal sign of surrender. Ward considered ignoring it and killing the bastard until he remembered the camera alongside Delius' suit. God only knew what that was linked into. It would be just his luck to tie into a public circuit.

"Hellfire!" he swore as he turned bitterly away from the writhing Delius. "It's done," he said as he turned towards the clearing. "Mona, tell 'em to come get their boy."

He walked slowly down the slope and crossed the

dueling field towards the Wing contingent. Efram gestured to the two gunmen to tend to their fallen leader as Ward approached him. Mona fell in at Ward's flank, favoring her sore shoulder as she covered him. Efram stood, pale and shaking as Ward stalked closer.

"That bastard wouldn't have died," Mona said, "if he'd have stayed out of it."

Efram looked down at the smoking hole that was all that remained of the gunman. "Who the hell are you?" he demanded of Ward in a voice hoarse with shock.

"I'm Benno's son," Ward answered without inflection. He gestured around the field. "We've imprinted and transmitted this little fracas to the planetary Assembly staff and the Council. Just to show we respected the proprieties. As have you, I'm sure."

Efram's voice shook. "Listen, you little shit. You'd best be just glad you didn't kill Delius. You'll pay for what you've done here, though, you be sure of that."

The two retainers had inflated a stretcher and were carrying Delius back slowly. He lay still, apparently unconscious.

Ward ignored him. "I claim victor's spoil."

"Oh, yeah?" commented Efram slowly.

"It's my right," Ward asserted, pointing at Delius and the former Tuchman ground car. "Put his armor into my car."

Efram frowned sourly. When the two gunmen had brought Delius back to the vehicles, Efram ordered them to set the stretcher down, then assisted the toughs in removing the PBA from Delius' recumbent form. The twisting and pulling ruptured delicate vessels and Delius began to bleed. The bloody stump of his left leg rasped across the inside of the armor as the toughs slid him out of the custom PBA, wrenching scream after bubbling scream from Delius' tormented body. One of the men carrying the stretcher turned away and puked.

Ward looked on impassively as Efram, his natty suit

marked with gore, manhandled Delius onto the stretcher. Ward leaned down carefully and trained his laser at the PBA, severing the shot-up left leg from the suit. He flipped it into the surprised hands of a gunman.

"Here," Ward said, "you forgot this." The man looked into the armor piece and blanched. He could see the top of the severed femur and the ripped meat around it. He handed it silently to Efram and turned away. Efram, much tougher than he appeared, wriggled the leg free of the laminate. He cradled the limb in his arm like a baby.

"You haven't heard the last of this," he said to Ward softly, barely above a whisper.

"I hope not," replied Ward.

The Wing people began to back away, unwilling to turn from the scene.

"You didn't kill him," Mona announced flatly, disapproval heavy in her voice.

"Wasn't expedient," he replied. He picked up the suit's knee joint and tried to flex it. "I hope I didn't damage the joint," he commented, "that'll considerably raise the cost of repairing it. No profit in busted armor." The Wing retainers trying to stop Delius' bleeding paled. One looked as though he might be sick again.

They stood together and watched while the larger Wing vehicle lifted off. "Well, we have a replacement for the truck now."

"Yeah." She almost smiled. "What'll we tell Hardesty?"

Ward looked around the bloody, torn field and grinned at her. "He'll figure it out."

They collected the cameras, transmission equipment, and Delius' bloody armor, loading it all in the ground-effect car's cargo box. They lifted off and left the dilapidated truck sitting alongside the border road.

Ward was surprised to see a small crowd waiting for their return as they powered in towards a landing outside Complein. Most of the assembled two-score people wore tattered Tuchman colors and appeared to be from the refugee camp outside of town. They surged towards him as he brought the vehicle into a landing a short distance from the south gate and slowly powered towards the customs queue outside the gate.

Ward blinked in surprise as the people, mostly men and children, rushed up to the car in a laughing, joyous throng. The men slapped his back and shook his hands, while the children ran grubby fingers over the side of the vehicle and the windscreen. Several of the adults held their brats up so they could see him. Ward was utterly taken aback by the babbling congratulations.

"Well done, boy!" said a grizzled farmer as he pounded Ward's back. "Kicked some Wing ass!"

"Ya gonna do it s'more?" another demanded, then shadowboxed the air when Ward nodded his assent. The crowd made him uncomfortable. He felt closed in and oppressed by their unwashed weight. The gate guards forced their way through the cluster of Tuchman supporters.

"Anything to declare?" demanded the first guard, trying to stick to his script.

"Yeah," Ward replied. "Striped suit's mine. Other one's a spoil."

The guard flipped the blood-soaked tarp away from the cargo box and exposed Delius' mauled battle armor. The sight triggered another round of cheers from the crowd. Adults and children pushed and shoved to touch the Wing PBA.

"Can we get this over with?" he plaintively asked the guard.

The gate guard seemed sympathetic. Ward couldn't tell if that was really the case or the man simply wanted the refugees away from his post. "Yeah," the guard replied, "where're you stayin'?"

"Lager House," Ward answered.

"Go ahead, then," said the guard. "We'll send the custom statement there. Just fill it out."

Ward's eyes narrowed. "I didn't have to do paperwork with the last suits I brought in. What's changed?"

The guard shrugged. "Sam Denison's insisted we track customs revenue. So now we fill out the forms."

Ward frowned. "I don't follow."

The gate officer shrugged again, his voice muffled by his battle suit. "Part of the city's free-holding status came from the agreement to share customs data with the Tuchman liege. The city Council felt that infringed on its sovereignty and ignored it. Your family was never in a position to enforce it."

Ward frowned. "I didn't know there was a free-holding agreement." He looked sharply at the guard. "Why the sudden urge to abide by the agreement now?"

The guard shrugged again. "That's no secret. Wing's agitating to 'adjust' the border to include us. We're faced with a choice of Wing or Denison. Denison looks like a better deal." He paused. "You Tuchs were pains in the asses, but you pretty much left us alone. Wing'll offer us no such luxury if they take over, so we suck up to Denison, give him what he wants."

"I see," Ward said grimly. "Can you get these people away so I can leave without frying anyone?" The guard nodded again and began to shoo the onlookers back to give Ward adequate clearance to lift off. Ward breathed a sigh of relief as he brought the vehicle up. The crowd below cheered thinly. Ward ignored them and entered the city, skimming low over the wall as he entered the local traffic patterns.

He dropped the suit at Theisiger's along with instructions for its repair, then proceeded to the hotel. Mona had arrived a few minutes before and sat on the steps outside. He envied her. She had sailed through the crowd and entered the city unmolested. Hsing stood next to her, talking pleasantly. Ward wasn't the least bit surprised to see the constable. He landed in the small lot off to the side of the inn and walked around to the front.

"Hello, Hsing," he called as he walked up to the veranda. "How's life treatin' ya?" The big guard grinned.

Mona looked up. "What happened at the gate?"

"I don't know," Ward said. "It was weird. All those people pulling and tugging at me."

"You'd best get used to it," came a voice from over his shoulder.

Ward turned and saw Theisiger approaching, carrying a small cooler. The duelist opened the rotating top and began removing several bottles of frosty ale. He passed them around, with only Hsing demurring.

"How's that?" Ward asked once he'd tipped his bottle. The beer was ice cold, with a pleasant bite against the back of his throat.

"You were on the Tri-dee, all morning," Theisiger informed them. "Local press feed tapped in on the signal you beamed the Council. Everybody in West Hills with an antenna and a receiver saw it." He made a mocking half-bow. "You're a celebrity now. Clan Tuchman hasn't had a whole lot to cheer about." He sipped his beer. "You gave 'em something, a hit back. It makes 'em feel less like victims now that they know someone on their side is still swingin'."

Ward frowned. "I'm not doing this for them."

Theisiger frowned. "So? They benefit too. What's wrong with that?"

Ward shrugged, unhappy. "That fight was *mine*. I don't especially feel like sharing it with the whole damn district."

Theisiger's eyebrows shot up. "Actually, a lot of people contributed to your little win." He pointed at Mona. "She covered your flank and blew away the asshole who might otherwise have back-shot you while you were engaged with Delius." He cocked his thumb over his shoulder. "Egg did the maintenance on your suit that got it ready."

He frowned. "Hell, even Hardesty helped. He agreed to let you stand in for him." Theisiger drained the last of the bottle. "Nobody works in a vacuum, Ward. Everybody owes someone, somewhere."

Ward looked abashed. "I'm sorry. I didn't mean it that way. It's just . . ."

Theisiger relented. "Yeah, I understand. . . . Look, why don't you get out tonight, blow off some steam? I hear the Pigswiller's a nice place. Clean and cheap. I'll stop by for you about six."

Ward finished his own beer and handed the bottle back to Theisiger. "I'll think about it." He went inside.

He used the 'fresher, ignoring the grating vibrations as the poorly tuned sonics loosened the dirt, oil, and sweat that had collected on his skin. He turned quickly in the brief rinsing cycle, trying to wash away the loosened dirt before the water stopped. He managed it, but just barely. The stream ended just as he sluiced the last of the whitish brown scum from his legs. "Gotcha!" He laughed, feeling better than he had since the attack.

He swaggered back to his room, riding the adrenaline rush of victory. He knew he was in a fey mood and wanted to take chances. Hsing waited for him patiently in his chair outside the door, a newsfax folded up on his lap. "Let's go out!" Ward announced.

Hsing looked up at him, his expression one of distressed surprise. "You can't be serious. Not again."

Ward skipped around him, doing a boxer's shuffle in his towel as he opened the door. "I'm in a mood to have fun, my friend," he said. "Anyway, I need food. What do you know about the Pigswiller?"

Hsing shrugged, noncommittal. "The ale's okay, and it's ten steps above those other places we went." He shook his head. "I don't think this is a good idea. Wing'll be pissed off about what you did. They may come after you here."

Ward went through the door, then turned back to face

Hsing. "That's what I have you for, isn't it?" He closed the door.

Hsing snapped his newspaper. "Stuck up little shit," he muttered, then went back to pretending to read his 'fax.

Theisiger collected them around six while the westering sun still hung low in the sky. He introduced them to his wife, a tiny auburn-haired woman with a smile on her face and the Devil in her eye.

Hsing relaxed when he saw the woman. Ward suspected Carlo wouldn't have brought her if he thought there was danger. He looked from the bodyguard to her and met her eyes. She stared back at him boldly.

"So this is Ward Tuchman," she said to her husband. "I saw your duel this morning. It made the news."

"Yeah, I took care of him pretty quickly!" Ward replied, always ready to impress a beautiful woman.

"You're going to have to do better than that if you expect to win many fights," she declared.

"What would you know?" Ward snapped. "I thought I did all right!" So much for scoring with Carlo's wife.

"You got lucky," she replied coolly. "He was second rate. He should have been a pushover."

Theisiger stepped in before the situation degenerated. "Julia here is the only duelist who ever beat me three times running in the Continental Eliminations." He smiled down at her, his eyes so full of love Ward thought he was going to be sick. "She let me yield."

"Let's get going," he grumbled. "This is getting out of hand."

They walked the few blocks to the Pigswiller, arriving just as the streetlamps came on. A small sign taped to the bat wing doors said PRIVATE PARTY. Ward looked a question at Theisiger, who answered by shooing him inside.

Ward was first struck by the noise and crowd as he entered. The place was packed shoulder to shoulder with people in Tuchman colors. Red, gold, and blue bunting hung from the lights and vibrated to the thumping of the music coming from hidden speakers.

A cheer rose up from the happy throng as those nearest the door saw him and passed the word deeper into the bar. Friendly hands grabbed him and pulled him into the depths before Hsing could interpose himself. Ward permitted himself to be led, bemused at being manhandled so gently.

A barmaid slapped a glass into his hand and sloshed it full of nut-brown ale from a pitcher. Ward barely had time to thank her before she swept away. One of the revelers grinned at him. Ward hefted the glass.

"Who do I pay?" he asked the man, yelling to be heard above the din.

"It's on us, Master Ward," the man yelled back, showing a gap-toothed smile. He pointed to his mouth. "I lost half m'teeth to a Wing in LaPort, 'twas good to get some back." Ward paused, torn between irritation and amusement. "It's good to see you standing up for us little guys, you know?"

Another hand slapped his back. A man, quite drunk, stared at Ward with owlish intensity. "That was great, what you did to that bastard," he said. "I used to think you was all high an' mighty, livin' up there in the big house, and lordin' it over us." He weaved a bit. Ward grabbed his lapel to keep him from toppling over. "I was kinda' glad when you got yours, it kinda' brung you down. You know?" He scowled, losing his train of thought. "Then Wing sacked us, an' I saw what havin' no liege was like." He stopped again. "I'm all for ya, boy. Kick some names and take some ass," he concluded, and staggered away. The cheering, chanting crowd swallowed him up.

Ward turned back to the gap-toothed man, his confusion evident. "I think he meant 'kick some ass and take some names,'" the man said dryly.

"Thanks," Ward said, extending his hand. "What's your name?"

"Bender," the man yelled, almost leaning into Ward's ear, "Nate Bender. Used to be a teamster till Wing hooked m' truck." Ward shook his head and looked around the room. The people he'd seen before as refugees and runaways, barely more acceptable than Earthers or clanless Freemen, he saw now as people.

Theisiger appeared behind, clapping him on the shoulder while he leaned down to talk into Ward's ear. "They're just folks, Ward, uprooted and displaced, same as you. They need something to cheer about. Don't be an asshole about it."

Ward looked at him.

Hsing reappeared, worming his way between a loud group at a nearby table and one of the barmaids. The drunks were replaying portions of his fight on a holo-projector and were cheering as Ward shot down the fleeing Delius. They ran it back and forth, hooting and yelling each time the laser licked Delius and blew the coupling in his back. Ward made a grim face and tried to slip away from Nate and Theisiger.

"Hey, Master Ward," Nate said, trying not to let desperation leak into his voice, "you need a trucker, you let me know, huh?" He tried to press a card into Ward's hand. Ward reluctantly accepted it. "I'm working as a day laborer over in the mill, but I drive real good. I got kids." Ward tried a half smile. It failed miserably.

That proved the pattern for the evening. Each time he slipped away from one group, edging towards the door, he was accosted by another retainer or associate. He heard fifty versions of the same story, with each drink pressed into his hand. He eventually gave up and settled in a dark table to drink his fill. Hsing kept close by and doubtless damped down the press of people, but the chairs at the table never had time to cool between supplicants. It seemed as though everyone wanted something from him, something more than he was willing to give. Each time he wanted to yell out "Go away," he saw Theisiger's cool, measuring eyes.

Ward's patience was just about exhausted when a tall, thin man in his early forties slid into the chair. Ward looked up resignedly at him. The balding fellow sipped neatly from a glass. He looked to be completely sober, a state that only Hsing shared. Ward saw that his coverall was clean and pressed. Ward, sick to death of hard luck stories, growled in the man's face, "What'cha want me to do for you?"

The farmer looked back at him, unfazed. "It's what I can do for you that's important," he replied coolly.

His blunt answer piqued Ward's curiosity. "How'z that?" The beer slurred his words a little.

"This is how I see it," the man said. "You had no cause to help the Hardestys, other than the fact they were up against Wing." He peered at Ward, trying to gauge his reactions. "The fact they were hopelessly outgunned didn't mean shit. You stood in for them because they were convenient. Right?"

Ward slouched in his chair and shrugged, noncommittal. "Could be," he replied. "So what?"

"So I got a hook for ya," the man continued, more earnest as he made his pitch. "I've got a neighbor named Conners. He's a Wing ally. Not big, but not small either." He held his breath a moment while he gathered his thoughts. "My father's estate got quartered when he died. My three sisters and I each got a share. Conners bought them all out through a third party, cut them and their husbands a deal. Now Conners has me surrounded."

Ward tipped his head a little, interested in spite of himself. "And?"

The man looked bitter. "I'm supposed to have a right of way across the land that was my pap's, but Conners and his Wing friends blew up the connecting road. I have to fly in and out. They shoot at anything cruising over. I can't get my stock to market."

Ward rubbed his chin. "How many head do you have?"

"I got a hundred beeves, and about the same of pork," the man replied.

"Why should I get involved?" Ward asked.

The rancher smiled at him, ready for this question. "I'm Tuchman. The link's distant, but solid. You're just looking out for your retainers, just like you were looking out for your land with Hardesty. It's all perfectly legal."

"What do I get out of this?" Ward asked, grinning now.

The rancher smiled broadly. "You get to kick Wing's ass twice running. I'm legal, I got my right of way in my daddy's will. They hit me, then they're pirates. You can do anything you want to as my protector. All according to the code."

Ward smiled back. "I like it," he said. "If you're playin' me, I'll kill you."

The rancher grinned and stuck out his hand. Ward shook it gravely. "What's your name, anyway?" Ward asked.

"Basileikos," the man replied. "They call me Basil for short."

"That's odd," Ward said, "My mother's mother was a Basileikos."

"So's mine," the rancher replied dryly. "We're distant kin."

"Why didn't you lead off with that?" Ward asked.

"No point," the man responded, rubbing his bald head. "I had to show how this venture would benefit you. You don't seem the type to do favors."

Ward smiled. "Let's talk," he said, rising from his seat, "where there are fewer ears to hear."

Hsing followed them out into the night, projecting an air of disapproval at the two scheming men.

* * *

The next morning, Ward watched from a distance as Basileikos stormed into the cattle market. He wore the partial armor that was the best he could afford. Ward had been quietly horrified at the condition of his suit. It looked to have been assembled from at least two other junked partial sets. The bastard engineering that Basileikos used to keep it marginally functional impressed Ward. In spite of its shabby condition, the servos were clean and oiled, for all that they were worn—the mark of a precise, careful man.

Ward, observing from his vantage point, couldn't smell the alcohol on Basileikos, but knew it was there. Ward had carefully poured a generous libation into a gauze pad sewn into the man's cloth headpiece before they slid him into his suit. Basileikos' voice boomed out of his scratchy speaker as he put on his drunk act.

"Conners! Where are you?" he shouted. "Come out here!" Ward smiled. Basileikos had informed him that the Conners family rarely came into Complein. Ward knew that calling Conners out publicly would ensure that the message would quickly worm its way through the grapevine to the intended targets. Complein's tradespeople were some of the best rumormongers on the planet. "Conners!" Basileikos shouted again. "I'm bringin' my stock out in two days." He seemed to weave, apparently far the worse for drink. "I'm usin' a damned transport 'cause you blew up my road. Don't even think about violatin' my right of way! I'm armed an' you betta not violate m' rights."

Two guardsmen appeared on cue to escort Basileikos away, frog-marching him out of the square to the paddy wagon. They helped him inside and then drove four blocks to where Ward and Hsing waited. The guard looked grim as he opened the door to let Basileikos free.

"How was I?" Basileikos asked as he stepped down.

"Lousy," Ward answered with a laugh. He gestured down the street to where the Tuchman ground car idled.

Mona sat in the pilot's seat. "Your chariot awaits, sir. Let's get you some decent armor." He turned to Hsing. "Thanks. I really appreciate this."

The guard looked away. "Just don't let it get out that you talked me into this."

"Fine," Ward answered with a laugh. "In the words of the poet, 'Let's go kick some names'!"

Chapter 7

Ward stood by the upper end of the transport's cargo ramp. A runnel of itchy sweat rolled down his back. He cursed, then grabbed the support post as the floor tilted.

"We're on our way," Mona announced over the public address system. "I'm going to swing us around so Basileikos' main house is on our right when we cross Conners' turf."

Ward looked at his time display. "How long until you think they'll hit us?"

Basileikos shrugged inside Delius' armor. "I figure they'll do it while we're still inside Conners' territory." His voice turned bitter. "It'd really screw things up if we crashed outside the area they'll claim we trespassed."

Ward ran his hand over the new camera array mounted on the side of his helmet.

"What's that contraption?" Basileikos asked, pointing at the rig.

"Theisiger's tech put it on for me. It's an idea I copied from Delius Wing that'll let me keep a first-person record for the Council's consumption. God only knows what he was doing with it." He twisted his neck from side to side, testing the feel of the camera outfit. "Egg did a great job of balancing the servo outputs. I can't even tell it's there."

"How well will it work at night?" Basileikos asked.

Ward drew up short. "Well, it has an ambient light collector and a modest infrared capability."

"Good luck," Basileikos replied. "It's going to be darker than a moneylender's heart under those trees, especially with moonfall as early as it will be."

"Damn," Ward grumbled, "I didn't think of that."

Basileikos, his faceplate raised, leaned around his stanchion and grimaced. He gripped the post firmly and licked his lips. Ward watched him flinch as Mona jigged the ground-effect transport over small terrain irregularities, jostling the cattle and human occupants. The tranquilized animals lowed uncertainly, but otherwise remained placid.

"What is it?" Ward snapped as Basileikos fidgeted again. The rancher raised his eyebrows.

"Sorry," Ward mumbled, "nerves."

Basileikos smiled, the corners of his mouth twitching. "Damn suits have no amenities," he answered, "especially these new ones." He looked down at his arm. "I want to thank you for lettin' me use it. I guess I'm lucky that me an' Delius are almost a match, huh?"

"Yeah," Ward answered distantly, "well, the paint job's new, so take care of it." He looked at Basileikos. "What exactly do you mean by 'amenities'?"

"I have to *go*," Basileikos answered. "Now!"

"It's got a relief tube," Ward answered.

"Those fail all the time," Basileikos replied. "I've no desire to get m'self electrocuted."

"Yeah," Ward agreed, "mixing free liquid with electricals ain't a real bright idea. It's worse for the women, though."

Basileikos shifted his weight. "Yeah, how's that?"

"Think about it," Ward answered.

"Oh, my," Basileikos said after a moment. "What do they use, a catheter?"

"Or worse," answered Ward. "You don't really want to know." He looked at his time display again. "It shouldn't be long now." He grinned at Basileikos. "Then you can go."

They crossed another series of low rises. Basileikos' face grew progressively whiter. "Mona, do you have to fly over *every* hill?" he asked plaintively.

Mona's voice, carried electronically from the bridge socket two levels up, sounded testy to Ward. "No, I'm trying to hold to that squiggly line you called a course. It ain't easy in this pig-boat rental. And yes, until you give me a better line to navigate, I'm going to have to take every hill. Just be glad we don't have to do this from the ground."

Basileikos looked plaintively at Ward. "I gave her the best I had. The path marks my right of way."

Ward shrugged his shoulders. "Don't worry about it. She's wrapped a little tight 'cause she's trying to fly nap-of-the-earth in a converted ore carrier. It'll pass once she gets out of this ripple-back country." He thumbed the PA call box by his shoulder. "Any contacts, Mona?"

"Naw, nothing yet on the displays." She paused. "Still another forty-seven hundred meters to go—" A crackle of static cut her off. "Tally-ho, boys, I've got three . . . five . . . heat spots."

"Where'd they come from?" Ward demanded, trying without success to keep the strain out of his voice. Basileikos looked pale as he snapped his faceplate down.

"I don't know," Mona answered. "Maybe thermal blankets or something. Infrared count is up to about a dozen so far."

Ward frowned. "Can you pipe it down to me?" He reached over for a fiberoptic interface cable and plugged it into the universal jack on his chestplate. Data flooded into his suit's heads-up display. "I got 'em," he announced to Mona. "Can you get me an energy scan?"

"In this tub?" she answered. "No can do."

Ward glanced at the formation. Fifteen heat spots, all displaying the telltale thermal patterns of powered battle armor. "I think they plan to ring us," Ward advised her. "Most're still out of position. They'll wait until all are ready before they hit us."

He felt the transport's left side slump and shudder. Ward didn't need the suit's augmented hearing to pick up the ripsaw noise of ring penetrators fired from the starboard side of the transport.

"Got any more bright guesses?" Mona said sarcastically from the bridge. "They just shredded the number three compressor and the left wing. I can't maintain lift with just three pods until I retrim."

"Okay," Ward said grimly, "set it down before they do more damage." He looked at Basileikos. "The thing we have to do is sort out the leaders. Once we take them out, the rest'll be easy meat."

Basileikos nodded once.

Ward mimed with his hands as he spoke. "Remember, when we hit, you break left. They're in a rough circle. We'll cut through on one side and see if we can draw them after us. They'll hopefully get strung out enough that we can take them piecemeal. Egg installed improved IFF transponders, so your suit will lock out if you target me. Don't worry about friendly fire."

They hit hard a moment later, the left side dipping as it struck. The carrier rocked as the leveling jacks balanced the load.

"What's the count?" he yelled up to Mona.

"Total still looks like fifteen heat blips," she answered, preferring to yell rather than to key the PA. "I used the radiation detectors to approximate an energy scan. Most're leaking power like sieves. Four are scattered ahead, four in the port quadrant, and seven to the rear and starboard. Be careful—two look like they might be worth a shit."

Ward grinned at Basileikos. "Ready?" he asked.

Basileikos looked pale. "Fifteen to two ain't good odds."

Ward grinned. "Better than fifteen to one, anyway.

Just remember to keep moving. You slow down, an' they'll be on you like a pack of wolves."

Basileikos nodded again and swallowed nervously.

"Basileikos!" boomed a voice from outside. "Surrender your vessel! You're trespassing!"

"Mona," Basileikos called, "plug me into the external speaker. And kill the bay lights." The cargo hold plunged into darkness.

"We're callin' you out!" the voice boomed again.

"Go to hell, Conners!" Basileikos said tightly, boosting his voice through the ship's PA. "I got rights!"

"You got nothin'!" Conners' replied. "Either you come out or we come in! Which'll it be?"

Basileikos voice rattled with nervousness. "I'm comin' out. Don't hurt me."

"'Course not," Conners' voice dripped honey, "we're just gonna have a little talk."

Mona tripped the cargo ramp. The long hatch unsealed, then lowered one end to the ground. Stray bits of straw blew away in the engine wash of the three functioning pods. Ward looked at Basileikos and placed his hand on his shoulder in a gesture of comradeship. He pointed to the door.

Basileikos jumped out into the night. Ward moved to follow, trying to clear the ramp and break right. He took two running steps before he was wrenched off his feet. He fell heavily against the side of the ramp and spun around, hanging by his chest. He groped frantically a moment before he grasped the fiberoptic cable still hooked to his auxiliary jack. He pulled sharply on it, trying to rip free. He swung a moment before the connection parted with a snap, dumping him onto the roadway's asphalt surface.

"That was stupid," he said to himself as he shuttled his vision into the infrared spectrum and glanced around. Basileikos had jumped to his left as instructed and crouched in the shelter of the ramp. Ward watched as he cranked off a long laser burst against the nearest Conners suit. It flared brightly as the laser penetrated the flexible metal laminate, then ballooned outward.

"Hey, that was a goddamned Phister!" Ward said, startled by the ease of the kill. "Pieces of shit."

Ward scrambled under the ramp's lee. Incoming fire licked its top, answering Basileikos' opening burst. Ring penetrators glanced off the ramp's upper slope and caromed inside the ship. A cow bellowed.

"Dammit Ward," Basileikos swore between bursts, "those are my damn beeves!"

"Okay, let's go!" Ward shouted as he ducked a tight stream of airfoils and lasers. One ring penetrated the hydraulic strut next to the rancher, spraying him with fluid. Another foil glanced off his armor, the ramp, and into the cows above, stirring them to the edge of panic.

"Mona!" Ward shouted. "Now's the time!"

"Hold on to your hats!" Mona called. Ward heard the transport's three remaining compressors begin to cycle, blowing air underneath the stubby wings to create lift. Flickering fire shifted upwards and at the craft as Conners troops tried to prevent the vehicle's apparent attempt to escape.

Mona ran the lift fans up and angled them as far under the craft as the pods would allow. Dust, pebbles, and debris began to whirl around; Ward swore as a piece of asphalt banged off his helmet.

"Basil! Are you still gettin' her telemetry?" Ward called as he scanned to his right. Fire hadn't slackened much, but the lasers were attenuating in the dust and the aerodynamic ring penetrators were having some trouble in the strong winds.

"Yeah," the retainer shouted back, "where do we go?"

"There," Ward said as he pointed his laser and fired, "that's your landmark! I'll cover you!"

Basileikos jumped to his feet and sprinted for the thicker trees alongside a burning bush. A single Conners figure rose from cover to challenge him. Basileikos burned him with a concentrated stream of laser fire. The metal mesh Phister swelled like a sausage in a microwave as the water flashed to steam.

Ward poured stream after stream of rings and lasers into the hidden Conners people on the ramp side of the craft. He ignored those behind him, hoping Mona's engine storm would provide adequate cover. A quick glance at his HUD confirmed that the Conners troops appeared generally content to remain undercover.

Basileikos hit cover a hundred meters from his starting point, well away from his precious cattle. He crashed to earth and began pouring his own fire into the troops pressing in on Ward's right.

"All right!" Basileikos panted in Ward's earpiece. "It's your turn!"

Ward saw that the returning fire was beginning to thicken as more Conners troops worked their way around from the far side of the transport. A chattering cartridge rifle joined the ripsaw coil guns and *hiss-crack* of the lasers burning through the air.

Ward rose to one knee and paused to set his AI. The tracer stream appeared again. The AI tracked the tracers to their source and plotted crosshairs on Ward's faceplate. He overlaid his coil gun's sight pip and keyed off a quick burst. His augmented hearing picked up the sound of a crashing body from the cacophony around him.

"All right, Basil, I'm going. Cover me!" He jumped up, the storm of fire intensifing as he stepped out into the open, but most of it seemed hopelessly inaccurate, random firing for the sake of expending ammo. Ward trotted to cover about halfway to where Basileikos sheltered, his airfoil stocks seriously depleted, but his suit essentially undamaged by his passage.

The distance to the next scrap of cover seemed impossibly long. Ward took a deep breath.

"Come *on*!" Basileikos cried. Ward heard the transport's engine pods behind him begin to redline. One abruptly shut down, its banshee wail quieting to a hum. A second followed, then the third as Mona gingerly reduced power in the drive systems. The duststorm cleared, freeing the few remaining Conners troops on the carrier's far side to reengage.

Ward jumped forward as a rocket lanced in from his right. His AI proximity warning chimed. He did the first thing he thought of and fired his boost-pack.

Ward shot to the left of the smoldering bush, aiming for a piece of ground that had seemed promising when viewed from beneath the transport's landing strut. He was almost on top of it before he realized that the expected hole was little more than a shallow depression. He cut his pack and moved on toward Basileikos, his proximity alarm chiming again as ring penetrators cut into the trees on either side. A laser struck him as he ran, but the contact time wasn't sufficient for anything more than superficial damage. A distant scream told him that one Conners round, at least, had pierced another's armor.

"Get down!" Ward yelled to Basil, who was up and shooting. "Three seconds. Three!"

Basileikos plunged to earth as another rocket blazed overhead and exploded against a tree. Ward's AI damped down the glare of a third explosion.

"Move to your front right!" Ward panted. "And stay down. That damned rocket is gonna chew you up."

"Where the hell is it?" Basileikos cried. "I can't even see it."

"Damned if I know," Ward answered, "somewhere behind *that* group over there." He punctuated his statement by blazing off burst towards the right hand group.

Basileikos gathered himself and kneeled. "I'm going!" he yelled. Ward rose and poured fire into a small copse. There was a bloom of fire and a sharp rapping explosion. Basil bounded up and forward, landing behind a tree thick enough for some shelter. "You haven't done this much, have you?" Ward remarked dryly.

"Does it show?" Basileikos asked, spacing his words between snap shots. "So what do we do now?"

"We keep moving," Ward said, "until we can take the leaders."

"Give me some covering fire, then belly crawl after me," Basileikos suggested. "There's a ravine behind me. It isn't much, but it'll angle us back to their right. We can maybe bushwhack 'em from there."

"How do you know that?" Ward asked.

"This land was all my pap's, before Conners got his lunch-hooks on it. I grew up here. Cover me." He slithered out of sight, between two trees, the trail of bruised leaves and disturbed earth clear even to unaugmented sight. Ward waited a few moments, then scrambled. Laser fire picked holes in the air above his head. He settled in behind some cover and angled back to face the Conners forces finally advancing to meet the unexpected threat. This was supposed to have been an easy ambush for them. Ward smiled to himself.

He fired a short burst, then two longer ones, switching weapons to simulate the fire of two men. Spatters of laser fire lanced in from his right, striking splinters and puffs of steam from nearby trees. First one, then another, crashed to the earth as the lasers and airfoils chewed through their trunks. His proximity alarm chimed as his suit's AI registered the trees' falling. Pine needles showered down. Another stream of ring penetrators struck sparks on his near side as the point element of the left-hand Conners force crept close enough to engage his position. He ducked as a barrage of laser bolts from two directions passed overhead.

"Okay, we've managed to get them to move. But I'm in a crossfire here," Ward called out.

Basileikos' voice panted in his ears. "All right. I'm in position. That gully isn't as deep as I thought it was. You'll have to stay down. It won't take even those cowardly bastards long to figure out what happened."

Ward fired two short laser bursts, then scrambled back, sliding along the ground until he tipped forward into a shallow runoff track. He pulled himself along it, scrambling on elbows and belly and hearing a continuing hail of fire into the position he'd abandoned.

He saw the bottom of the ravine flattening out into a small floodplain, the darker hillside erosion material glowing redly against the background as it gave off more residual heat than the lighter alluvial material.

"Okay, I'm at the bottom," Ward said. "Where are you?"

"I'm a hundred-ten meters off your left side as you leave the gully, beneath the pine with the split trunk. I've got two almost directly between us, trying to work their way upslope. You'll be in their line of sight if you pop up now."

Ward exhaled heavily, then looked back up the hill. The fire above him seemed to have slackened a bit. "I think something's happening back there." The slackening fire doubled and redoubled again, rising to a crescendo as rocket after rocket burst into the abandoned position. The copse glowed merrily as secondary fires blazed.

"If they didn't know we'd vacated before, they will in a few moments," Ward said. "Okay, we've got to get rid of these two so I can get out of there. You fire on them first, I'll get the other one. As soon as both go down, run like hell. Okay?"

"Got it, boss."

"All right," Ward answered. Ward carefully glanced around the lip of the ravine. He saw nothing until the rancher opened up with his coiler and airfoils left heat traces in the air as they connected Basileikos to his victim. Ward heard a flurry of crashing and the rancher's shout, dampened by the suit's AI to a dull roar, in his ears. "He's coming towards you!"

Ward saw a single figure fleeing. The Conners retainer fled along the edge of the floodplain, emerging from cover to sprint more quickly along the edge of the cleared ground. Ward took him with a short burst and watched with horrified fascination as the man tumbled and rolled in the sand. Ward quickly skirted the base of the hill, pushing hard to make Basileikos' position before a Conners man arrived to return the favor.

Ward dived down near where the rancher lay, panting as he tried to draw air into oxygen-starved tissues. "How many is that?" Basil asked.

"I'd mark it at something between five and seven, not counting the ones we'll pick up who try following us down the gully."

"Damn, this is hard work," Basil said. "Wish I could just rest a few minutes!"

"Not till we're clear," Ward replied, "otherwise we'll rest forever. Get up and follow me. They'll be hot after us, especially after they realize we capped two more."

"You're right. They'll be starting down the gully soon," the rancher commented, "if they haven't already. We'll have a chance to catch one or two more right at the mouth if we hurry."

They got up and began to move along the edge of the treeline at a dog trot.

Basileikos led for about a hundred meters, then pointed out a spot along a shallow ditch. Ward moved under cover. Basileikos paged him moments later.

"Here they come!" Ward raised his head to see a pair of heat spots working their way down the ravine. Basileikos had led Ward to the vantage that allowed him to see the lower half of the runoff track and track the infrared signatures of the Conners retainers probing their backtrail.

Basiliekos waited until the first had almost reached

the bottom of the ravine before he raised himself up and sighted in. Ward roused himself to one knee, but his first burst cut high, the second low, before the suit gave him a solid target lock. The second Conners retainer, backshot as she tried to scramble back up the hill, tumbled into the floodplain and lay writhing and screaming. Ward pumped a short burst into her, putting her out of her misery.

He moved away without comment, leaving Basileikos to follow him. The cattle farmer kept up as best he could, but still fell behind twice. The second time Ward waited until he'd caught up. "We got at least seven, maybe nine," Ward informed him.

"What do you suppose they're going to do next?" asked Basil.

Ward thought a moment. "Half missing, wounded, or dead, and with nothing to show for it." He pursed his lips. "If I were a chicken-shit Wing lackey, expecting easy pickings and instead getting us, I'd give serious thought to running away just now. Is that what you think's going to happen?"

Basileikos bobbed his head. "That makes good sense."

Ward looked back towards the grounded transport. "Mona?"

"Don't bother me right now," she hissed, "I've got at least one, maybe two inside the ship. I'll call you when I can." Basileikos turned towards Ward, then straightened abruptly. Before Ward knew what was happening, the rancher had slammed into him. Ward, caught completely off guard, was bowled over backwards. He hit hard, his temple striking the padding that Egg had thinned to accommodate the camera. Lights and stars exploded behind his eyes, and he heard a vast roaring noise.

Control returned in a rush as he felt himself starting to retch. He fumbled for his helmet and managed to get it off just before he vomited into the grass. Acrid smoke mixed with the smell of bile. He looked dazedly around and saw that the small clearing he lay in was blackened, lit only by a line of burning leaves that crept outwards from where Ward lay. Basileikos loomed in the darkness.

"Are you all right?" he asked, squatting down. Ward, still dazed, looked up at him.

"What the hell happened?"

Basileikos voice sounded strained as he knelt beside Ward. "Sorry I hit you so hard. Rocket Boy got the drop on you. I saw the flare just as he fired. I tackled you. You were out cold almost five minutes. How do you feel?"

"Sick," Ward answered. "Did you get him?"

"Yeah," Basileikos replied. "I took one close hit, but the secondary explosion when his rockets gang-fired turned him into a grease spot and took out the two with him. The sidekicks had chump suits."

Ward put a hand to his throbbing head and tried to sit up. Basileikos helped him recline against a tree trunk. Ward focused blearily. "Are you okay?"

The rancher shrugged wearily. "I'm leaking fluid from my right knee and shoulder, but other than that, I'm in pretty good shape."

Ward dipped his head, trying to slow his accelerated breathing. "And Mona?"

Basileikos tipped his chin towards the distant transport. "She lured them into an access corridor, then dropped a wrench between them. One killed the other, then Mona hit her with that damned HEAP gun."

"Her?" Ward repeated dumbly.

"Yeah," Basileikos said, "I think it was Conners' daughter. Blond bimbo. Mona thinks she might fit the armor. She's running a systems check right now to see if the transporter's going to go anywhere."

Ward leaned over to retch again. "Look, Basil, I'm

sorry I blacked out. I wasn't much good to you back there."

The rancher forestalled him. He opened his helmet so he and Ward could talk face-to-face. "Don't worry about it. It was mostly my fight, anyway. You gave me the tools to do the job and got more than half of them! Besides," he said, grinning, "it ain't over yet."

Ward looked puzzled.

"By my count," Basileikos continued, "there are still a couple out there for you. I'm going to lose system integrity in about twenty minutes. I figure that'll be enough time for you get your shit together and start hunting again." He grinned again. "I'm guessing all they have are cheap metal mesh Phisters. Your laser can cut through those. It should be duck soup."

Ward tried to laugh but the act only made him ill. "Do you still have to go to the bathroom?" he asked.

"Naw," Basileikos answered ruefully, "I pissed myself a long time back."

Basileikos glanced up and closed his faceplate. Ward saw a figure moving into the firelight. Mona knelt just outside the circle of light. "Is there any special reason you guys are jaw-jacking while two more are still out there?" Ward saw the barrel of a burp gun projecting from her improvised cloak.

"Where'd you get that?" Ward asked.

She pointed with her shoulder towards the carrier. "About half of them carried these instead of suit weapons." She smiled. "I 'liberated' it." She held the machine pistol up for Ward's inspection.

"That's an Uzi, isn't it?" Basil asked.

"No," Ward replied, "it just looks like one. It's really a coil gun. The electromagnet is hidden inside this square housing." He pointed. "The magazine is the usual ring tube." Mona obligingly pulled it out and showed it to him. Ward continued, "You'll get a nice seven-millimeter ring job with this."

Mona slammed the clip back in its well and pulled the bolt back.

"By the way," she said, "I found these for you." She tossed a pair of coil gun cassettes on the ground between Ward and Basileikos. "I thought you could use some reloads."

Ward bent to pick one up, then almost overbalanced as a wave of dizziness set in. Basileikos gripped his shoulder as he weaved. Ward shrugged him off as he went to one knee. He covered his continuing disorientation by carefully picking up one magazine and handing it to Basileikos.

The rancher rotated his coil gun's safety bar ninety degrees away from his body, disarming the weapon. He popped the cassette release, freeing the partially used magazine. He inserted the fresh case, checked the diagnostics diode, and rearmed the weapon.

Ward held his hand to his helmeted temple.

"Are you okay?" Mona asked.

"Yeah," Ward asked, "I just hit my head." Mona looked worried. He quickly changed the subject. "How many were there?" "Fifteen," she replied. "You know that. You really *did* slam your head! I've confirmed thirteen dead. Two are still out there somewhere." She pointed with her chin in the general direction of the transport. "I found what I think are heat traces from some vehicles. They're parked hull down about a half-klick due north. They must have covered them with thermal blankets or something. I've got nothing on infrared."

"What about . . . ?" Ward used his chin to point back to the transport. Mona grinned and gave him a thumbs-up. "We'll never see our security deposit again, but it'll take us to Complein."

Ward heard Basileikos swear. He turned, almost overbalancing again as a ground car did a quick liftoff. Mona brought her weapon up before she realized that it remained hopelessly out of range. They watched it stagger across the sky, dipping and swaying.

"Gyro's aren't synchronized," Mona commented clinically as the car weaved and dipped. "The engines are reacting to bad data. They might not make it home." Basileikos' blue-green laser licked the bottom of the car, spalling the paint and burning a landing foot.

"Hold it, Basil!" Ward said, placing his hand on the rancher's arm.

Basileikos sounded puzzled. "What the hell?"

Ward pointed to the car as it lurched across the sky. "That'll lead us back to their camp, *if* we give it a chance," Ward explained. "We can go clean out the pirates' base."

"All right. Let's do it!" Basileikos enthusiastically pumped his arm, then cursed as it stiffened into place. "Damn seals are blown. I'm not going anywhere."

Ward tried to rub away the pain in his head. "Fade back to the transport and cover it. I'm going after that other car."

Basileikos nodded once, silently, then turned back towards the carrier.

Ward followed Mona towards the hidden Conners vehicles, stumbling a bit as dizziness overtook him. Mona, her face set, matched him stride for stride.

"Where are you going?" he asked her.

"With you," she replied. "You can barely stand up." She looked him in the eye. "You're gonna kill Wings. I ain't gonna try an' stop you from doin' that, but I don't want you gettin' killed 'cause you crashed."

"I can handle it," he said stubbornly.

Mona stood her ground. "I fly you, or I'll take the transport and follow. Either way, I'm going."

Ward stared at her a long moment before he relented. She quickly led him to the vehicle and brought the engines on line. "This is going to move like a pig compared to what you're used to," she announced, "so don't ask for any fancy tricks."

He strapped himself in while she took off, pivoting the car as it turned to follow the Conners vehicle.

"Damn," she swore, "can you track them? The lidar in this thing is out and I've got no ranging capability."

"Yeah," he answered, "steer right a bit. You're almost on line with them." Waves of disorientation washed over him. He held his helmeted head in his hands a moment until the dizziness passed. He squeezed his eyes shut, trying to clear his head. "Do you have a baseline figured?"

"Yeah," she answered, "they're all over the sky, but I think I know where they're going."

Ward blinked his eyes rapidly to clear his vision. "Okay, nothing fancy. We'll do a fast landing—get in and get out. I'll call you for pickup."

Mona smiled to herself and boosted the engines to overdrive. A bad bearing inside the right compressor set up a noise that cut through Ward's helmet and into his brain. Mona started to whistle a tune.

"What the hell's that?" he asked tightly.

She grinned. "'The Working Man's Blues.'" She looked over at her gauges. "Two minutes to ground zero. Here we go!"

Ward saw the lights of the Conners steading through the trees a few moments later. He saw a shower of sparks from the refugee vehicle's rear as the damaged landing foot collapsed. One Conners retainer jumped out of the car and ran for the whitewashed main house. Other members of the extended family, drawn by the noise and spectacle, wandered out of the clustered outbuildings and towards the damaged car.

Mona lifted the car's nose to bleed off airspeed before she put it into a steep bank. Ward had only a few moments to size up the layout of the dozen-odd outbuildings before she flared into a combat landing.

He unsnapped the safety harness and sprang out of the craft. She waited only until he had both feet on the ground before she pulled the controls into the pit of her stomach and lifted the car vertically.

Ward knelt while she blazed away, waiting for the debris raised by her engine wash to clear. He quickly spun towards the Conners car. The second Conners retainer scrambled out of the vehicle and into his line of sight. He shot the man through the faceplate with his laser.

A part of Ward's mind cried out in horror as he glanced left and right in search of the last retainer. His vision swam as dizziness threatened to overcome him again.

The first of the crowd poured around the other car, stopping in shocked disbelief as they saw the twitching retainer on the ground. Ward waved the laser at them. They melted back. Ward took two deliberate steps towards them and watched with cynical amusement as they scattered before him like chaff on the wind.

Ward moved purposefully through the thin crowd, searching for the last retainer. He entered the first barn, using his servo-boosted strength to kick the door in. The door, made of flimsy wood laminate, blew completely off the hinges and tumbled back into the room. Ward ducked back, afraid of an ambush, and counted to three while he listened with ringing ears for movement inside.

He glanced quickly in. Bales of piled hay blocked his view and provided ample places to hide. He stepped into the doorway and fired his laser into the first bale. It burst into flames. He shot each in turn, eliminating their use as ambush points as he searched for the last Conners fighters. He figured he would have flushed out any additional people with PBA by now. The conflagration he caused was what Stallart would have called "useful collateral damage." The barn quickly caught fire, the bales exploding like bombs.

He torched each barn and outbuilding in turn. One barn held a young couple locked in the throes of passion. He frowned, recalling his own dalliance with

Seladra. He rousted them, calling "fire in the hole!" just before he shot. He laughed to himself as their naked buttocks disappeared into the night.

The entire compound had burned within a few minutes, with the sole exception of the main house. He crossed from the last building, a print shop, to the now scorched lawn that led to the mansion. Overhead lamps, strung like beads on a string, bobbed and danced in the heat. One distant strand went dark in a shower of sparks and fell as a support post burned through.

His headache returned in full force, piling dizziness and disorientation onto his throbbing temples. His vision fuzzed. Portions of his field of vision remained clear while others blurred and fogged. He hunched over, his hands on his knees, as he squinted up at the two-story building.

Made of whitewashed concrete, the main house looked to him to be a cheap imitation of a plantation house. A peaked roof angled down onto a shallow overhang supported by plastic colonnades that ran the length of the house.

Ward stopped a moment as he surveyed the best way to penetrate the house. He didn't see any perimeter or interior defenses, but that didn't mean there weren't any. The numerous first floor doors and windows were a little too obvious and would doubtless be guarded. He paused, at a loss. Stallart's words rang clear in his head, "Use your resources, boy. Up and down are as valid as left and right."

He inspected the second-story windows. They were wide, didn't seem to be screened, and were within high-jumping range. Most were lamplit. "Upper floors are usually broken up into smaller rooms that'll be easier to clear," he whispered to himself. "Corners are best."

He checked his boost-pack fuel. It registered better than three-quarters full, plenty for this run and several more. He backed away from the outer wall, the better to begin a good takeoff run.

He tried to shake off his momentary confusion as he positioned himself and began his sprint. His brain seemed to be immersed in cottage cheese. He sprinted towards the second-story corner window, aware he drifted a bit to the right as he ran. Once at speed, he leapt for the window, using his boost-packs to correct his angle and power him through the plastic-laminated glass. A single laser licked out, missing by a wide margin.

He hit the lower left corner of the windowsill with his shoulder, turning his headfirst launch into a sloppy tumble. A laser cracked above his head as he rolled. He slipped on a pile of clothing and fell in a heap. He whipped his laser up while he flailed free.

The crosshairs centered on a young boy, perhaps ten years old, holding a laser in his shaking hands. A stain spread down the inside of his pajama leg as he looked with terrified eyes at Ward. Ward shifted the laser upward and fired a blast into the drywall above the boy's head. Debris rained down, galvanizing the child into motion. He dropped the weapon and fled.

Ward untangled himself from the clothing and got to his feet. He leaned heavily against the bedpost, feeling it flex under his weight. He tried to wipe away the cobwebs that settled in front of his eyes. He smashed the solitary glowing lightstrip, plunging the room into darkness. His AI shuttled back to infrared detection. A small secondary fire smoldered in the wall, marking the laser's impact. It began to spread slowly. He heard shouts and cries from below as the household's residents reacted to his entry. He sprang for the door, dishing in the drywall with his weight as he peered into the hall. The midpoint of the hall opened into a broad stair leading down. Doors and painted portraits alternated along the corridor. Deep green carpet covered the floor and offset the imitation walnut used liberally as trim.

It didn't take him long to clear the floor, smashing into

each room in his zeal to find the hidden Conners fighter. Numerous smoke and heat alarms twittered in the aftermath of Ward's assault as laser shot after laser shot started small fires. He grinned as he surveyed the damage. "All clear upstairs. Back Wing and get bit."

He went over to the stairs and knelt to peer into the open area below. "Ain't no way I'm goin' down those stairs," he said to himself.

He found a section of hall floor about five meters from the stair. He fired his laser into the carpet, setting it on fire. He played the beam back and forth, burning swatches in the polymer and scarring the plastic floor beneath. Smoke and heat alarms began to scream in earnest as the thick black clouds rose from the scorched fibers.

He aimed his coil gun in a tight circle and made short passes across the exposed floor. The ring penetrators chewed into the plastic flooring, weakening it as they ripped into the level below. He lazed the ragged edges of the hole he made, melting polymer and widening it a fraction more. Portions of the beam seared the area beneath the hole, incidentally clearing his landing spot of any toe-poppers, small mines, or proximity charges. The smoke from the burning carpets interfered with the beam, attenuating its power and diffusing it. A blue-white haze glowed around Ward.

He dropped to the floor below. He whirled on landing, establishing that no ambushers lurked nearby. He quickly scanned the main room as a whole. It seemed to be empty, except for weapons dropped on the floor. Ward scanned the floor for micro-thermals. Most of the foot tracks pointed towards the front door, suggesting the defenders had broken and run.

He assaulted the first floor the same way he had the second, firing to clear each room. A dozen men and women shouldered past him as he kicked in the door to a meeting room, all screaming and shrieking as they fought to escape. Ward grabbed one of the men as he tried to push past.

"Where is he?" Ward bellowed, his suit augmenting his speech.

"Wh-hoo?" the man stammered as Ward held him suspended a foot off the ground. The rest of the shrieking crowd disappeared around the corner.

"The armored man, the fighter!" Ward bellowed again.

"I d-d-dunno," the man begged. "Puh-puh-please let me go." Ward shook him like a rag doll, jerking him so hard the man bit through his tongue. Blood spattered his shirt and Ward's front.

"Lie to me again," Ward snarled, "and I'll bust your head. *Where is he?*"

The man, numb with fear, pointed towards the basement. Ward tossed him aside. The man cried out and stumbled away, his right shoulder slumped forward and down.

Ward passed through the large dining room, trying to recall if he'd seen a basement access. He reasoned the most likely spot for one would be in the cooking area, where they would need ready access to stores.

He kicked in the kitchen door, frightening a woman who brandished a butcher knife. "Where's the basement?" he demanded. She pointed silently to an open rectangle. The door stood ajar, its back lined with plastic cans. Ward crossed to it and scanned the risers for microthermals.

A single laser arched up, burning into the painted ceiling. Ward glanced up and saw a red-rimmed scorch mark as the paint curled back in the heat. He pulled his head back a moment to consider. He discarded simply jumping into the basement and trusting to luck. The confines were too narrow for a scream-and-leap style assault, and in his present state another blow to the head would likely render him brainless. He took another look down and almost lost his head. The second shot gave him enough data to calculate the fugitive's position. Ward looked across the kitchen to above where he thought the Conners probably lurked, braced himself, and fired both laser and coil gun through the floor between his feet. He sustained his fire, criss-crossing the floor laminate with tight X patterns until he was convinced he'd covered the whole area. He dumped the rest of the coil magazine, stopping only when the ripsaw of the massed hypervelocity rings fell silent.

Ward waited a moment, listening for some sound from the basement. He crept over and peered down. The Conners lay pulped, his metal mesh laminate pierced in half a hundred places. He stared at the corpse, unable to tear his eyes away until he heard Mona's insistent, almost frantic voice. "Boss! Boss! For God's sake, can you hear me?"

"Yeah," Ward replied. "What's up?"

"The whole place is going up. You'd better clear out!"

He crossed the kitchen in two bounds, using his servos to bound around obstacles. The AI fired the boost-pack in quick spurts to offset his tendency to overbalance. He saw the back door standing open and rushed through it.

He looked back at the house as he fled across the grass towards cover. The entire second story blazed brightly, throwing showers of sparks into the night sky. Conners people still ran about, some trying to organize firefighting details, others simply trying to escape. The first barn Ward had burned collapsed in a crashing roar as the inferno engulfed it. A few people stared at Ward, numbed shock warring with fear.

"Dustoff, Mona," he ordered as he sprinted for the landing pad. The car came screaming in just as he arrived. He jumped in.

"Glorious," she whispered, "absolutely glorious."

Ward saw her flashing eyes in the firelight. His

attention faded as soon as he settled in his seat. He fumbled unsuccessfully with the straps.

"Are you all right?" she asked, seeing him slouch.

"I dunno," he said, "I'm havin' a hard time thinkin'."

She lifted off and quickly set the auto-nav for the cattle carrier. "Come here," she ordered. He obeyed, twisting himself in the seat. She unsnapped his helmet and removed it. He tried to help, but his hands felt as if they were encased in gauze. She impatiently pushed them away. Ward felt ridiculous.

She snapped on the car's interior light. "I don't see any blood. Did you get hit?"

Ward shook his head, trying to clear it, then winced as another lance of pain sliced through. "Just m' head." She frowned, then turned his face with her hand and peered at him.

"Hold still," she said as she reached across him to secure the safety restraints, "I don't want you fallin' out." She used the opportunity to peer at his pupils. "Shitfire," she swore.

"What?" Ward asked, still muzzy.

"Your pupils are different sizes. I bet you got a damned concussion." She swore again and pounded the steering yoke with her hands. "You need a doctor," she declared. "Now. Shit!"

"Call Theisiger," Ward suggested. "He'll know somebody."

"*No!*" Mona snapped. "He's got his own agenda. We need somebody *we* can trust." She gripped the yoke and stared straight ahead, talking more to herself than to Ward. "We'll go to LaPort. There'll be doctors there we can see, clan doctors. They'll look after us."

She boosted the ground car's speed to maximum, the bearing reminding them of its irritating presence. Ward tried to escape the grinding squeal that cut through his head like a knife. It seemed to him like an eternity before Mona brought the car into a fast landing cycle near

Basileikos, who sat on the ramp of the carrier next to his frozen armor, looking forlorn.

He looked up, startled by the fast approach. A burp gun he'd appropriated appeared as the Conners vehicle slid to a halt. His features relaxed when he identified Mona. "What's up?" he asked, concern coloring his voice.

"Ward's hurt," she snapped. "I've got to get him to a doctor."

"Okay," Basileikos responded. "What do I do?"

Mona looked at Ward, who struggled to maintain his focus. "Umm," Ward said, "take the suits to Theisiger. Tell him to salvage what he can and sell the rest. Keep one of the partials for yourself once it's fixed." He frowned, trying to order his thoughts. "Make sure Theisiger knows about all the incidental damage to that suit." He slumped back into his seat and closed his eyes.

Mona turned back to Basileikos. "We'll be in LaPort. We'll contact you through Theisiger if we need to get a hold of you."

"Okay." Basileikos grinned. "It's been a pleasure. Call me sometime, we'll do it again." He offered his hand. She shook it firmly, her grip seeming to him to be neither masculine nor feminine. The first ghost of a real smile played about the corners of her lips.

"We'll do that."

Basileikos stepped back, shading his eyes from the bright strobes as she turned the running lights on and boosted out of the clearing. She opened the throttle up all the way.

Ward began to drift in the lulling rock of the craft as small nocturnal temperature changes created minor turbulence. His eyes began to close of their own accord. He felt exhausted. His head drooped.

"Ward!" Mona called sharply. "Don't. You got a concussion. You can't go to sleep."

"I know," Ward replied distantly. "Talk to me or something, wouldn't you? Give me something to do."

Mona looked perplexed. "What should I talk about?"

"Tell me about yourself," Ward replied.

Mona looked embarrassed at first, but then began to speak as Ward's attention drifted and his eyelids began to droop. Ward fought hard to focus on each word she said as she spoke, haltingly at first, of her life.

Ward didn't know much about her, only that she was Stallart's wife. He'd come to rely on her stolid dependability, but often she just seemed to fade into the background. Ward didn't think she was very bright, that only her intense hatred of all things Wing disrupted her bovine nature.

She described her life, her feelings of being one of life's "also-rans." She talked of how Stallart had changed that. The great Tuchman weapons master had been noted for his wit and humor, and he picked her when he could have had any girl on the estate. She was perfectly happy to follow his lead and live away from the manor house. She'd been happy, perhaps for the first time in her life, during the time they'd been together. Ward realized that Wing had changed her the instant they'd shot Stallart down. They'd destroyed her life. He understood then the essential difference between them. He had something to go back to. She did not.

Ward hadn't realized the depth of her anger, the extent of her hatred, until that moment. She would say anything, do anything, kill anyone without remorse, if it brought suffering to the Wings. Ward's feelings ran pretty much along the same lines, but seeing it in someone else made it seem ugly.

They crossed most of the distance to LaPort. He could see the street lamps up ahead and recalled his last flight into the town. He listened as Mona came into LaPort's traffic control and asked for landing instructions. She cleared the name of the family's physician from landing control and guided the Conners car towards his home.

Doctor Silman waited for them near his private landing pad. He was dressed and carried a green canvas bag in both hands. His home and dispensary were ablaze with lights. Four guards in olive drab and gray Tuchman fatigues stood by, their shotguns at the ready. Each had a Tuchman patch sewn on the right shoulder and had the hard face and calm eyes of the trained professional.

Silman rushed up to the vehicle the moment it touched down. He drew a penlight from his pocket and began to examine Ward. One guard hurried over with him. The rest kept a wary eye on Mona.

"What's goin' on?" she asked, indicating the guards with her chin.

The chief guard looked at her, frowning at the burp gun. "We're here to keep an eye on the doc. We didn't know if it was a trap or legit." She nodded, understanding their caution, but still looking uncomfortable.

Silman broke into her ruminations. "He's concussed, all right. Possibility of a skull fracture." Mona looked worried. Silman rushed to reassure her. "He should be okay. His head is as hard as his daddy's. We can treat him here." He turned to the lead guard. "Dave, will you get him out of his armor and inside, please?" He gestured back to the ground car. "And get this thing out of sight, will you?"

The guard grinned and waved to his companions. He was short, no taller than Mona, and had a freckled, boyish attitude that seemed at odds with his receding hairline. Two other guards came forward, a statuesque redhead, the other a tiny brunette with a splint covering her nose. They helped Ward get out of the vehicle. They didn't have the strength to force his servos to move, but they could guide his weak steps. He tottered towards the dispensary. Mona followed, head turned to watch the third guard slip into the car's control seat. The guard appeared thin, almost skeletal, to her. He'd cropped his hair so close to his skull that Mona had a hard time telling what color it was supposed to be.

He brought the vehicle into a low hover and skimmed it away towards a copse of trees. He barely brushed the top of the close-cut lawn, keeping the landing feet scant millimeters above the ground. Dave noted her watching the driver.

"He's a show-off," the guard chief told her. "One of these days, he's going to bend somebody's car but good."

"What's he do?" Mona asked.

"He used to be a sniper. Moonlights now as Doc's chauffeur. Worked for Benno hunting poachers and rustlers. Lost everything when Wing hit." He shook his head mournfully. "Just like the rest of us. Doc took us in."

He started towards the main house. Mona walked with him. The guard seemed a bit uncomfortable to her.

"Look," he blurted after a few seconds, "we owe Doc big, you know. But we're Tuchman first. We heard about what you're doin'. You need us, you call us." He paused. "There's a few more of us, too, who'd like another crack at those bastards."

Mona looked at him carefully. "Got any suit time?" she asked.

"About three hundred hours," Dave replied. "Mostly partials. Served on a reaction team for a year, before I came up as a gamekeeper."

"And the rest?" Mona asked.

"The driver, Garibaldi, has an eye for deflection like nobody's business." Dave grinned. "He prefers a 12.7mm solid-slug rifle. I've seen him hit poachers at ranges better than three kilometers." He pointed towards the house. "Clarissa, the redhead, is a demolitions expert. She's set charges for most of the mining consortia on New Hope, before she joined us. Ludmilla is a take-down artist. Hand-to-hand. She's had the most suit time of all of us—almost a thousand hours, I think."

"That's good to know." Mona grinned at him. "I'll talk

to the boss. I think we can use you." The guard smiled back. "You may have to wait a bit. We're real short on cash right now."

The guard continued smiling. "Not a problem. This is a good gig here. Let us know when you want us."

She let it go. Making promises wasn't her department. "Got any coffee?" she asked.

"Yeah," he answered, "it's in the guardhouse. I'll show you." They crossed the yard in silence and entered the dispensary.

They saw Ward's bloody armor lying on the floor. The two guards were nowhere in sight, apparently having returned to their regular posts. Ward sat on an examination table, wearing only his underwear. Blood from his nose had leaked down along his throat and neck, matting in his chest and tracing a dried rivulet that ran to his waist and stained his underwear.

She watched the doctor position a scanner over his head, using the self-stabilizing derrick assembly to hold the device still. Dave paused and turned towards her as Silman touched keys on his control pad. The scanner began to hum as it ran images of the inside of Ward's head through a sophisticated computer setup. After a moment, an image began to compile on the screen. Even to Mona's untrained eye the small mass on the back of Ward's head looked abnormal. It glowed redly. A color bar along the right side of the screen showed the elevated temperature of the area.

He saw her staring through the open doorway and crooked a finger to call her in. She obeyed sheepishly. The doctor shifted the console around so both she and Ward could see it. "There it is." He pointed to the red mass with a finger. "One middlin' serious brain cramp."

The guard chuckled. Ward didn't seem particularly amused.

"Can you fix it?" Mona asked. The doctor and Ward both looked at her.

"Sure," the doctor said with a shrug, "program the machine here, and it'll use microprobes to reduce the swelling, relieve the vascular distress, and generally make everything all better."

"Do it," Mona demanded. Ward frowned.

"Look," she said, turning towards Ward, "you can't afford to be out of action. You decide you want to convalesce and Wing'll blow you away." Ward looked as though he wanted to assay an opinion. She prevented him from speaking. "We don't have time for this. How long do you think it will take before someone figures out we're here?"

"About ten seconds," came a voice from the hallway. They turned as a group and saw Samuel Denison standing in the doorway, covered by one of the Tuchman guards.

"Mr. Denison," asked Dr. Silman carefully, "what brings you here this time of night?"

"My people track the local landing control," Denison replied casually. "I like to know who's in town." He pointed at Ward. "Ghengis Khan here scotched Conners, wiped them off the map. Thirty minutes later an unidentified Conners vehicle asks for landing instructions in LaPort. It wasn't hard to figure out."

Silman looked worried. "Don't worry, you're all safe," Denison reassured them. "I'm your insurance policy. Wing's been kissing my ass over the issue of indemnities so much that I'll need surgery if I stop too fast. They won't touch me, regardless of the provocation." He looked long and hard at Ward.

"Get your head fixed. I'll be in the other room. We have to talk." Ward nodded. The doctor draped him with a blue surgical cloth while the rest retired.

"This won't hurt a bit." The doctor grinned at Ward.

"That's what you told me when you set my leg when I was six. 'It won't hurt a bit,' you said," Ward replied sarcastically.

"And did I lie?" the doctor asked.

"Hell, yes!" responded Ward.

"Well," said Silman, "this won't hurt a bit."

Two hours later Ward scratched the medicinal patch on his upper arm as he looked about Silman's office. He still had a slight headache, or would when the analgesics wore off, but the concussion had been reduced to insignificance.

Denison hefted the pouch of imprint chips in his hand. Most were still warm from their time in the reader. The crystal marked Ward Helmet Cam sat in Silman's viewer, unspooling its record. Ward watched as Denison silently reviewed the crystal. Samuel's face grew increasingly grim as watched the replay of the evening's events. He looked up when the screen went blank. His frown covered nearly the lower half of his face.

"What do you have to say for yourself?" he asked as he took the last crystal out of the reader and dropped it into the pouch.

"I stayed completely inside the law. Basileikos had a legal right to be there. We were set on by bandits." Ward crossed his arms in front of his chest, defiant in the face of Denison's disapproval. "I only responded as any right-thinking clansman would."

"How's that?" Denison scoffed.

"My kinsman was in trouble. Bandits violated his rights and were threatening his life," Ward shot back. "I did what I had to in order to help him."

Denison wasn't convinced. "In a situation you contrived?"

Ward shrugged. "Basileikos had to move his cattle. The bastards had him ringed. They'd have gotten him sooner or later. We just picked the time of the confrontation. We did nothing to coax them beyond what they'd have done anyway."

"I suppose that justifies burning Conners out?" Denison challenged.

"Yes," he replied angrily, "some of the bandits flew to what was presumably their hideout. I pursued and finished takin' 'em down." Ward paused, silent a moment. "The fire was collateral damage." The last had seemed too strident, even to his ears. "Look," he tried again, "I was by myself. The whole place could have been an ambush. I had to make sure I was covered. That meant shooting up anything that looked like it might be dangerous. The only people who got hurt at the compound wore suits. Nobody else got hurt."

"Don't you consider getting burned out to be 'getting hurt'?" Denison snapped.

"Win some, lose some, I suppose," Ward answered. "They're alive, aren't they?"

Denison seemed not to hear. "You realize that Wing is going to claim the carrier was trespassing. They are also bound to assert that the destruction of the Conners homestead was itself an act of banditry."

Ward shrugged, unfazed."I've got the camera records." He lifted his hand, miming holding a bag. "If the Wings want to support bandits, that's their business. I've got the record on my side. You saw the ship's recorder, heard when they called Basileikos out. He's got his father's will deeding him that right of way. We're covered." He tipped his head up and grinned. "If Wing wants to pursue the matter, then you, Mr. Samuel Denison, as the legal head of Clan Tuchman by the decision of the august and wise planetary Council, will be responsible for my defense." Ward delivered the last with an ironic wave of his hand and a half-bow to the seated Denison.

Denison seemed torn between fury and amusement. He rocked back in his chair, his face a study as he considered the implications of Ward's statement.

"I was brought here," he began tightly, "to assume the receivership in order to restore calm to the West Hills District. My specific intention was to stop a war, not get drawn into one! With the situation so delicate with the

Hegemony, we can't *afford* any major dissention on this planet." Sam felt his control slip. "You've managed to box everybody in, haven't you?"

Ward shrugged.

Denison held up his index finger. "One. The planetary Assembly will have to take your side if the Wings go to the law over the Conners' deaths. You'll show them what you've shown me and they'll have to back you. They'll grit their teeth, but they'll take your side. They'll sanction Wing for not policing Conners themselves."

He extended his middle finger. "Two. If they don't go to the Council, then they'll admit their guilt by not seeking legal redress. Their other retainers will wonder if Wing'll leave them hanging like Conners if it drops in the pot sometime."

His ring finger joined the other two. "And three. If Wing comes after you privately, then you're entitled to the protection of the Council. The Council will back you out of concern for its own prestige." He closed his fist. "No matter what Wing does, they're screwed."

Ward brought his hand to his cheek and faked a shocked look. "Really? Goodness, that hadn't occurred to me." He smiled broadly.

Denison leaned back in Silman's chair. "Ward, I can't figure out if you were smart or lucky in pulling this off." He smiled ironically. "As your designated protector, I'm advising you to stay on the estate."

"Advising?" Ward asked dryly. "You're not ordering me?"

"I'd like to," Denison answered honestly, "*if* I thought you'd listen. Frankly you're too much a loose cannon to try and keep against your will." His smile faded. "If you go back to Complein, Wing'll surely kill you." He shook his head. "That'll just bitch things up worse for me. I'm having a hard enough time getting this mess sorted out as it is."

"Your concern for my health is touching," Ward said

sarcastically. "Okay, I'll stay on the reservation, probably in one of the outlying buildings, at least for the time being." He gingerly felt the tender spot on the back of his head. "Frankly, I can use the down time." He paused a moment, drumming his fingers on the chair arm. "I'll send Mona back to Complein for supplies. I don't want to use anything from the house."

"I think it would be better for all parties concerned if you stayed up at the main house," Denison urged. "It'll be safe for you there."

Ward laughed without humor. "It wasn't safe for my kinfolk, was it?"

Denison growled and got to his feet.

Ward rubbed his fingertips across his temples. "I haven't been back since before the attack. I don't think I could bear to see it right now."

Denison paced to a window. "That raises a delicate point, though." He held up the chip from Ward's helmet camera. "What would you say to someone who saw both that tape and the aftermath of what Wing did at your place?" He tossed the chip on the table. "They look a lot alike, you know. Wing might have contrived a situation to justify certain excesses against Tuchman. So you, in retaliation, contrive a situation to justify certain excesses against Conners." He pretended to balance two objects in his hands. "It's kind of hard to sort out the good guys from the bad, isn't it?"

Ward crossed his arms over his chest. "There's a difference," he replied tightly. "They started it. I'm just playing by their rules."

"Ah, I see," said Denison, "and that justifies everything?" He opened the door. "I'll be in touch. Stay out of trouble."

Ward looked at his retreating back, his mouth half open. "Yeah," Ward said softly, "it does."

Chapter 8

Gustav Wing rolled his eyes as his comm-link buzzed. He looked at his armor's time display, then hit the tongue switch that completed the circuit.

"Yes, Efram," he asked tiredly, "what is it now?"

Efram's voice sounded nervous and irritable. "Is it done yet?"

"No, it's not," Gustav replied, "we're still sneaking up on the little bastard. It's going to take a while."

"It's past midnight already," Efram replied petulantly. "What's taking so long?"

Gustav tried to sound patient. "If we go charging in, we'll blow it."

"Damn," Efram fretted, "how did I let you talk me into this?"

"Simple," Gustav replied, "we may never get another shot this good. He's holed up in an outbuilding. No guards, no alarms, and no witnesses."

"This has gotten out of hand," Efram whined. "Do you have any idea how much heat I'm getting?" His voice became accusing. "You didn't tell me you were taking thirty people."

"Relax, the hard part's over. Everybody got across the border and into position without being detected. All we have to do now is stamp out the vermin and come home."

"What about Denison?" Efram said. "We aren't up to the kind of party he can throw. He'll know it was us."

Gustav laughed. "Knowin' and provin' is two different things. We brought enough liquid explosive to make sure that when we're finished there won't be so much as a molecule left of Mr. Ward Tuchman!"

"Gustav," Efram pleaded, "be careful. We can't afford any more screw-ups."

Gustav grinned wryly. "I do have some practice at this, you know. *I* did the plans for the Benno raid, and *I* hired the scouts who made it possible. So, please don't lecture me."

"What the hell are you in such a good mood about?" Efram snapped.

Gustav laughed into the microphone. "The thought of the last Tuchman leader vanishing in a giant red mist makes me positively giddy. Who would have thought that Benno's wild son would turn out to be so damn organized? I'd prefer the little bastard to die slowly and painfully, but I'll take what I can get."

"Damn it, don't get sidetracked," Efram replied. "Our asses are on the line here." Gustav rolled his eyes as Efram continued. "You guaranteed Skywing that a decapitation strike would eliminate Tuchman and recover the *Conveyor*. You were wrong on both counts. Now you've promised him that this hit'll do it. If we screw this up, Wing's gonna put us at the head of his shit-list."

"Don't worry about it," Gustav said reassuringly.

"You can afford to be complacent," Efram snapped. "You're the boss's kid. There's no chance of you getting exiled. The rest of us can't afford to take that for granted."

"Look," Gustav replied, "even if there is an exiles' list being drawn up, it'll be small fry. Nobody close to power. You'll be covered."

Efram exhaled loudly. "Can you do that?"

"I covered my daughter, didn't I?" Gustav answered tartly. "Sel missed her raid assignment and her squad got wiped out. She's still around, isn't she?" He waited a second for Efram's answer. "I'll cover you, too. Don't worry."

He watched the last of his assault elements move into starting position. "Look, I have to go. The troops are almost ready." He snapped the comm-link off. "You, my friend," he whispered, "are about to wear out your usefulness."

He switched his radio to the scouts' channel. "We're ready for you. Go ahead."

"We're moving." The mercenary's voice sounded hollow and distorted, a product of their encryption system.

Gustav looked at Kate, his second, and saw disapproval on her face. "I take it you don't approve?" he asked.

"Mercs are trash," she said angrily, "spies with no family histories. We shouldn't have to hire out. It makes us look like we can't handle our own business."

Gustav looked at her. "I am not in the habit of explaining myself," he said testily, "but I will this once to further your education." He took a deep breath. "I see no reason to purchase an expensive capability when I can rent it for a fraction of the price. The scouts did an exemplary job of preparing the briefing packets that we used to take down Benno. My son, for all his bragging, accomplished what he did because those *spies* did their jobs. They did more to cut Wing losses than the rest of you put together."

Gustav turned towards her, eager to show off his superior knowledge. "Their mission is to sneak in, scan the area, and get out. That's all. Their only contribution to the actual fight'll be to leave a low-light camera behind that we'll use to monitor the shack before the attack. We'll do the real work, the fighting."

She bobbed her head, accepting the rebuke. They stood together, waiting for the scouts to report. A quarter-hour passed before the radio broke squelch. "One to Base."

"Umm, talk to me," Gustav replied.

"Roger two bogies," the scout reported. "I confirm two battle suits set on standby mode. Do you copy?"

"I got it," Gustav answered. "Is there anything else?"

"Roger," the voice continued, "the target is a single sod line shack dug out of a hillside. It has one door and one window. Do you copy? Over."

"Gotcha!" Gustav replied. "Anything else?"

"Negative," replied the scout. "We're placing the camera now. Give us fifteen minutes to get back. Don't jump the gun. Out."

"We'll stay put," Gustav affirmed. He switched to the general frequency and waited for a break in the constant chatter.

"Listen up, everybody," he ordered. "Tuchman's in a sod shack at the target center. Everybody goes on my signal. I'll personally lead the assault through the door. Nobody enters before me."

He switched back to his command channel and turned towards Kate. "Got 'em trapped like rats." He punched the air with his fist, unable to restrain his exuberance. "Now do you see what spies can do?"

She shrugged. "Maybe. How exactly did your agent track them?"

"Well," he gloated, "one of our people saw the girl in a shop in Complein. He followed her to Theisiger's, where he found the car they stole from Conners. He attached a transponder and we followed her here. Simple."

The scouts returned at that moment, slipping past the command party and shedding their thermal blankets like snake skins. They glowed cherry-red in the IR spectrum as the suits vented heat. Gustav heard the whir of the intake fans as they drew air into the filters to replenish their depleted oxygen reserves.

He moved to join them. They connected the cable to the monitor and watched as the image of the sod shack settled on the screen. He clearly saw the building in the low-light camera's green and amber tints. It stood against a low hill on one side of a small clearing about fifty meters across. The Conners vehicle stood just inside the tree line.

He opened his faceplate. "Good job," he offered. "I'll see you guys get a bonus."

"We should," one said dryly. "We deserve it."

Gustav grinned. "I like a man who knows his own worth." He paused. "Keep an eye on the screen. Call me if anything changes."

One of the scouts looked up briefly. "Can do."

Kate walked over and peered over his shoulder. "Boss, is it a good idea for you to kick in the door yourself? We've got people trained to do this."

Gustav shook his head. "The little bastard took my son's leg. I'm gonna take his head. Personally." He smiled at her worried expression. "I've got a double layer of appliqué. By the time he cracks through that, he'll be strawberry jam." He checked the monitor one final time, then used his command override to silence the babble on the general circuit.

"Now listen here. Keep your intervals and don't bunch up. Your jobs are to make sure he doesn't escape. Nobody enters the clearing except me and my flank guards. I'll kill anybody else I see in the open." He paused. "And stay off the damned radio unless you've got something important to say."

He stepped out, walking slowly through the woods towards the clearing. He glanced at his HUD and was pleased to see the platoon slowly closing on the line shack. He saw they kept good intervals, minimizing Ward's chances of escape. His mood got even better during the few minutes it took to cross the woods to the tree line.

Gustav called his flank guards to him while the rest of the assault party hunkered down behind trees. He checked his HUD to ensure the entire platoon was in position around the shack. He looked at Kate and the guard. "Remember," he hissed, "I go first." He sprinted across the open area for the right door frame.

He hit, followed by Kate a second later on the left. She braced herself against the left door jamb. The flank guard positioned himself behind Gustav. Gustav nodded to her and shifted directly in front of the portal. He waited a heartbeat, then kicked the door with all his strength. It disintegrated under the impact, flinders scattering into the room beyond. Gustav flashed his suit light into the room and saw bags stacked from floor to ceiling. "Nitrated fertilizer," he read aloud. "What the hell?" He looked at Kate just as he heard a metallic *snick*. He pulled her in front of him with desperate speed as the world went gray.

The scouts saw the flash of the explosion a second before the rumbling *powm* swept over them. One looked at the other. "Shit, man, I told you I thought I detected something else."

The other merc, just as shaken, replied, "I guess I should have passed that along to His Nibs." He looked back at the rising fireball. "We'd better get out of here and call the boss. He wasn't expecting this."

The first scout gathered up his monitor. "What about my camera?" he asked plaintively.

"You and your damn cameras," the other one replied. "Let's go!" They fled for the vehicle park.

Ward Tuchman slid the blanket back over his head as the last of the assault force pushed on up the slope.

"Well, you were right," he said softly, "they didn't find us. We've only got a few minutes to get ready before the sky falls in." He slid along the ditch a few meters until he found his suit. He stripped, opened the carapace, and began to slip inside.

The entire western horizon flashed yellow-white. A

second later a bass rumble washed across them, followed by a thin rain of debris. "Damn," he swore, "that was quick." He saw Mona's naked form slip past as she moved to her own suit, a partial rebuild from pieces salvaged from Conners' daughter. She slipped inside and closed her carapace while Ward was still trying to work his paunch through the tight midsection. He looked at her.

"I wish you'd said something about being able to use a suit," Ward groused. "It'd have made life easier."

"You could have asked," she retorted. "I was Stal's wife. Did you think the role was purely ornamental?"

Ward heard the bitterness in her voice and bit back his snide response. "I'm sorry," he answered lamely, "I didn't think."

He wedged himself into the suit with much straining and grunting. He closed the carapace and looked around at the rosy glow of the secondary fires. "Damn," he said, "I guess Stallart was right. He said that nitrated fertilizer was as good an explosive as HE."

Mona made a face. "Stal didn't much care for informal bombs. He said it made demolitions too easy." She shifted her weight. "I hope the truck is okay."

"I doubt it," Ward replied. "Five barrels of liquid Cepex stacked on top of a ton of fertilizer don't leave much. I figured on a nice blast, but *damn*!" He looked at the glow again, entranced. "Remind me to thank Theisiger for the Cepex." He looked at her. "Going shopping was a nice touch, too. It distracted any watchers while the crew loaded the barrels."

Mona shrugged, seemingly embarrassed by the attention. "We'd better go mop up," she said, trying to change the subject.

Ward looked skeptical, but followed her towards the clearing. "I'm not sure anything could have survived that," he said doubtfully.

They detected a pair of fleeing figures almost

immediately. "Oops," Ward apologized. "Sorry. You were right. Again."

She turned to him. "You don't listen to a word I say, do you?" She raised her mounted coil gun and began tracking the fleeing troops.

"No," Ward ordered, "let them go. They're running away, probably back to where they left their trucks. I think if we give 'em a little time, maybe they'll show us where they left 'em." Mona looked disappointed, but acquiesced. They stood quietly a few minutes before they saw a small craft rise above the trees and skim away.

"Got it!" Ward announced in a triumphant voice. He marked the spot on his HUD's terrain map and turned back to the blast site. They crossed the distance in less than a minute, using their boost-packs to augment their running.

Ward stopped and stared as he took in the entire panorama. The packed explosive had been focused by the contour of the hill into a shaped charge that had scooped a crater a hundred meters wide and ten deep. Whole trees lay scattered like pickup sticks around the perimeter of the blast. Bodies in PBA lay tossed like dolls in a windstorm in all directions.

Mona whistled softly. "I'll bet they heard it in LaPort."

"The hell with LaPort," Ward retorted, "I'm betting on Complein." He heard a faint moan on his aural pickups. "I'll be damned," he said in an amazed voice. "There are people alive here."

"Well, let's clean up," Mona suggested. Ward nodded distractedly, then walked carefully in the direction of the sound.

She pulled out a device that looked like a cross between a hook-knife and crowbar.

"What the hell is that?" Ward asked.

"A little thing Stallart made," she replied grimly. "He called it a 'can opener.'" She mimed levering a helmet catch. "We'll see."

They crossed to the first body; it was missing its right arm.

"I think he's dead," Ward said as he moved to draw a bead on the Wing retainer.

"I want to try this out," Mona insisted. She levered the crowbar between the partial suit's shoulder joint and the underlip of the helmet. Ward heard her servos whine as the system fought the strain; the rivets popped as the helmet latch gave way. Mona continued her levering movements, setting the hook-knife into the soft tissue beneath. The body didn't move.

"I guess it works," she said as she withdrew the dripping weapon from the dead Wing's neck. "Next!"

Ward stared at her. "That's gruesome."

She shrugged. "So?"

"Good point," he said as he gestured for her to precede him to the next candidate.

The woman in the second suit struggled feebly as Ward and Mona came into sight. Her faceplate had been ripped away and she bled from her eyes and ears, but otherwise seemed more stunned than hurt. She tried to bring her laser to bear, but couldn't get control of her arm. Ward covered her while Mona approached the woman. She stepped on the woman's twitching hand before she raised the hook-knife over her head. The woman silently pled. Ward looked away as Mona brought it down hard, using her servos' augmented strength to boost the impact energy. Ward heard her strike two more times before the woman's heels stopped drumming the torn earth. He tried to wish away the sound of her head breaking from his memory. It sounded to him exactly like a flower pot dropped onto a tile floor.

Mona held the hook-knife out to him. "Do you want to try it?"

Ward felt his stomach heave. "No thanks," he replied, "you go ahead." He turned away, trying to control his nausea. He heard another crunch behind him as she "cleaned" another Wing suit. He turned towards her as she began to whistle "The Working Man's Blues."

She stopped by another body. He looked away.

"Hey, Ward, you have to see this!" she called.

"No, thanks," he answered, "I'm fine over here."

"No, really," she pressed. "This one's got a Wing badge."

Ward whirled his head around. "Retainer or family?"

"Family," she answered. "And I think he's alive."

Ward sprinted over to where she stood. The man lay on his back, his right arm missing and his chest plate dished in.

"What's that stuff around the edges of his chest?" he asked. She bent down. "It looks like a layer of appliqué, maybe two or three together."

He took Mona's tool and used it to lever the remains of the faceplate up and away.

"I'll be damned," Ward said. "It's Gustav Wing himself." He took a broken piece of appliqué armor and held it next to Gustav's lips. Breath fogged it at once. "And the son of bitch is alive, too." He looked down at Gustav. "You can stop pretending now. We know you're awake."

Wing's eyes opened and focused slowly on Ward. "Well, boy, we meet at last." Gustav coughed. "The explosion was a nice trick."

"Glad you liked it," Ward replied grimly. He raised the crowbar. "Any last thoughts?"

"Yeah," replied Gustav, "I have to know. Where were you that night?"

"I thought you knew," Ward answered. "I was screwing your daughter. Where were you?"

Wing closed his eyes a moment, pained. Ward's heart leapt in his breast. He'd wanted to believe Seladra hadn't been involved in the attack. Now he knew.

Wing opened his eyes. "Where was I?" he replied, coughing deeply. "I was killing your family." He gasped for breath a moment. "I thought you knew."

Ward felt rage wash over him in a red tide. He dropped the crowbar and leveled the coil gun at Gustav's face. "When you meet Benno Tuchman in Hell," he snarled, "tell him his son hasn't forgotten." He held the firing key down, pouring airfoils into Gustav's head until the helmet disintegrated and only a bloody hole remained.

Mona looked at him as he raised his smoking weapon. "You could have killed him without destroying the most valuable part of the suit, you know."

Ward shrugged. "We can afford it." They walked together to finish off the last of the moving figures in the distance. They showed no mercy.

When they left the blast area several hours later, Ward left a note on one of the three abandoned ground cars.

> Sam,
>
> Thanks for guaranteeing my safety on Tuchman property. I'm sure you know how much your promises mean to me. Gone back to Complein with the salvaged armor. Consider these vehicles as my contribution to the cause.

* * *

Carlo Theisiger walked into his rear courtyard and saw Ward, red-eyed and groggy, examining two headless Wing suits suspended from a wash rack. He noted with approval that their battery packs and computer cores had been removed. He slid two bottles of iced tea out of his hip pockets. "How many this time?"

"Twelve suits, more or less complete," Ward replied, "and pieces of about eight more."

Carlo handed him a bottle. They stood together a moment before Ward scooped up the garden hose and began spraying away the dirt, blood, and leaves that clung to the suits.

Ward gave Carlo a toothy grin. "Thanks for the boom juice, by the way."

Theisiger affected a deep, twangy accent. "Aw shucks, twern't nuthin'. Cepex is as common as water around minin' camps. Jest happy to oblige."

Ward smiled at Theisiger. "We were lucky. Mona remembered the sod shack from an old training exercise her husband ran. Somebody stored fertilizer in it some time back and forgot about it. It was pretty decomposed. We stuck the stuff you gave us on top of the bags, set the detonator, and *ba-whoom*. We really overdid it." They laughed together. "That detonator was a sweet piece of work." Ward asked, "Can I get more?"

Theisiger shrugged. "I got it as a gift from a friend for services rendered. I haven't seen many like it."

"How does it work?" Ward asked.

"Mass and pressure sensitive." Theisiger demonstrated with his hands. "Either come to within a certain distance or break a trip laser and the solenoid closes. Two seconds later you're on a one way express back to old Earth!"

Ward's laugh faded as he saw the unhappy expression on Carlo's face. "What's up?"

The duelist took a deep breath. "I got a call from the Wing of Skywing himself this morning. The old man wants to hire me to rub you out."

Ward whistled softly. "So the Patriarch of Clan Wing is getting personally involved?" Ward tried to keep his voice neutral. "What was the offer? Maybe I can counter it."

"I don't think so," replied Theisiger. "He offered me a figure somewhere north of a hundred thousand."

Ward whistled and continued to play the garden hose over the two suits. He stared at the flowing water for several minutes before he spoke. "That's a lot of beer money. Are you going to take the job?"

"Can you give me a reason why I shouldn't?" Theisiger took a sip of his tea.

Ward looked at him carefully, trying to see beneath the calm exterior. "Hmm, Wing certainly has the money," he answered bitterly, "even if it is covered with Tuchman blood. And they do pay cash." Ward tried to essay a smile. "Maybe you should be worried about how the fight might turn out?"

Theisiger shook his head. Ward laughed thinly, fully aware he didn't stand a chance against Theisiger. He chewed on the implications of Wing's offer. They had offered Carlo a fortune. "I can't really see any reason not to take the contract," he confessed at last.

"I can," Carlo replied.

Ward almost dropped the hose. "How's that?"

"I emigrated from Earth almost two decades ago to get away from that velvet prison they call life there." He gestured around him. "I came here. I married local, my kids are local. I've even served as a member of the city Council. Hell, I've made a fortune here." He sighed bitterly. "Egg tells it best. He usually fakes a heavy slave's accent." He shuffled a bit, mimicking the big tech, "Ah'm still fed in de' kitchen when massah summon me to the big house to fit him fo' de' new suit." He spat on the ground. "I am a talented and rich man, but I've been treated like shit for the past twenty years by the Wings just because I came from Earth. Hell, the bastards still owe me money for a contract job I did last spring!"

Ward turned back to his hosing, angling the water stream up into the crevices while the suits slowly turned. "Us Tuchmans've treated you pretty badly, too."

"And you Tuchmans, if it comes to that," Carlo agreed, "but not by you. I owe you that, boy. I can't kill you." They shared a smile.

"Well, I'll be damned," Ward said under his breath. He left the hose to run down the drain while he grabbed a heavy brush and worked the last of the stains loose.

"I'm glad you're cleaning up the suits before you turn

them over to Egg," Carlo offered. "He can be a handful when he's upset."

"Yeah," Ward said dryly, "I heard. He complained to me that last batch of suits I sent were still dripping blood. He rather sarcastically advised me to make sure I clean the brains out first before turning them over to his delicate care."

Carlo held the suit still while Ward scrubbed. "Look, Ward," Carlo said pensively, "if the Wings want to kill you, they'll get someone else to do it." He paused, his brow furrowed with worry. "A hundred thou will buy a lot of talent."

Ward shrugged and handed Carlo a brush. "There's a tough spot over there." Carlo set to it with a will.

Ward sat at the bar in the Lager House's taproom sipping a lemonade when Theisiger entered. The duelist stepped over to him. "Finish your drink. We're going for a ride."

Ward looked at him in puzzlement. "What's up?"

Carlo looked at his watch. "The ringer Wing hired is coming in this afternoon. I want you to get a look at him."

Ward took a careful sip from his glass. "Who is it?"

"We're short on time," Theisiger said. "Let's talk in the car."

Ward paid the tab and followed him out to the small wheeled vehicle that sat in front of the inn. Ward laughed. "You drive one of these? I thought battery cars were obsolete."

Carlo looked defensive. "It's cheap, easy to operate, and cheap to repair. I don't need anything bigger."

Ward laughed as he squeezed inside. Theisiger started the vehicle and turned south. He gripped the control yoke tightly. "The fellow's name is Marble. He's as good as me, maybe better. He works out of Foundation."

"How'd you find out he was coming?" Ward asked.

Carlo glanced at the rearview mirror. "I do the odd

job for the city Council. Traffic control usually tips me when somebody special is coming in. Marble filed a flight plan. He's supposed to arrive in about an hour."

"Damn," Ward answered, "that was fast. I expected to have two weeks to get ready, not two days." He sucked air through his teeth.

Carlo slipped his hand into his shirt pocket and fished out an imprint chip. He gave it to Ward.

"What's this?" Ward asked, holding up the chip.

Carlo shrugged. "It's everything I could remember about Marble from my days on the circuit. I'm told he hasn't changed much."

Ward let the moment pass, then casually put the chip in his pocket. "Tell me about Marble."

Theisiger ran his fingers through his hair. "He wears a heavy Higgins custom model layered with either double appliqué or ablative lacquer. I'm not sure which." He braked to let an oxcart cross in front of them. "He moves more slowly than he should and his jumps tend to be lame. He usually just sort of stumps after you."

"What makes him so tough?" Ward asked.

"He's got an eye for deflection like nobody's business," Carlo responded grimly. "He's very accurate and doesn't go for general hits. His usual tactic is to move towards the center of the field and plink away at the joints." Theisiger looked in the mirror again. "Stand off and he burns you with his laser. Get in close, and while you're trying to shoot through all that crap he's got glued on, he's turning your knees into fritters. Try to wait him out and he's content to just chip away." He grinned, the smile of one professional acknowledging another. "He's an arrogant bastard. He's also as good as he thinks he is."

"Damn," Ward said, "what do you suggest I do?"

Carlo looked at him, a ghost of a smile playing about his lips. "Run away."

Ward frowned. "I need advice I can use."

Carlo pressed the accelerator button, easing the

vehicle around the cart. "Put double appliqué on your joints. Leave your carapace alone; you'll need to shave weight to stay nimble. Replace your laser. It won't be heavy enough to cut through his armor at short ranges, and you won't be able to match him for ranging shots. Take something else instead."

Ward looked worried. "Like what?"

Theisiger shrugged. "A second coil gun, maybe. Or something more exotic. I don't know." He looked up at Ward. "Get in close, hit him with everything you've got, and pray."

"Do you think that'll work?" Ward asked.

"You're fast, you're younger than he is and you're lucky, but no, I don't really think it will," Carlo replied. "Your best chance is to get it over with quick, before he has a chance to work you over."

Ward looked out his window.

Carlo glanced at Ward and saw the worried frown. "He usually travels in a great big ground-effect truck, all decked out in lights and gingerbread. Looks like a roving whorehouse. You'll see for yourself in a few minutes."

Ward looked at him. "How are we supposed to get in close enough to see him without being seen?"

"Easy." Carlo laughed. "He's the only duelist I know of with a publicist. He asked for landing instructions on a commercial channel. Half the citizens and all the media heard it. There'll be a good-sized crowd by the time we get there."

Ward shook his head.

"Didn't you used to have a guard?" Theisiger asked. "I figured you'd have a shadow."

"They loaned me one of their constables to make sure I honored a deal," Ward answered dryly. "I haven't seen him since I got back from blowing up that platoon."

Theisiger rolled up to the south gate and presented his identification to the guard, who waved them through. Carlo touched a button on a small panel over his head.

The canopy went quickly gray, then twilight dark. He smiled at Ward's questioning look. "Polarization'll make it harder for us to be identified."

"I don't understand," Ward said.

"Look at all the Wings," Carlo said. "Thick as scavenger weed on a trash pile."

"Where?" Ward asked. "I don't see them."

"They're on the far side of that crowd. Look where the barrier tape is strung between the trees along the edge of the clearing."

"Damn," Ward said as he followed Theisiger's gaze. "There must be a couple of hundred people out there. What are they waiting for?"

"They want to see Marble's Traveling Circus and Freak Show," Theisiger said acidly.

"I take it you don't like him," Ward commented.

"The guy is *weird*," Carlo said. "Here he comes now." He pointed up through the bubble canopy.

Ward saw the truck as it first cleared the trees. "That's really ugly."

The large ground-effect transport lumbered in low, the bastard child of a mated circus wagon and limousine. Heavy chrome gingerbread gilding brushed along the sides. Hologram lions and predators leapt and cavorted as flickering lights played along the truck's flanks. The compressor pods rotated as speakers blared martial music. Blue and green smoke poured from small ducts set in the tips of the stubby wings.

Ward cringed. "Talk about tacky."

"Yeah," Carlo answered, "as the poet once said: 'It takes a lot of money to look this cheap.'"

The vehicle made two wallowing passes over the field, trailing smoke, before it settled in for a landing. Wing troops moved quickly towards the access as a gangplank descended with a trumpet fanfare.

"That's Marble," Theisiger said, pointing his finger. "The one in front with the long black hair."

Ward peered at the man and almost laughed. The wiry man who led the entourage down the ramp had long oiled hair that fell to his waist, accentuating slim hips and overly broad shoulders. But he moved with a dancer's grace. Theisiger handed Ward a set of binoculars and lightened the canopy.

Ward watched as a grim-faced Efram led the Wing delegation to the ramp. They spoke together a moment before Efram turned away. "I'd give anything to know what they just said," Ward said wistfully.

Theisiger didn't respond.

Ward watched as Marble stepped away from his entourage to greet people behind the tape. "You'd think he was a celebrity from the way that crowd is behaving."

"In a way, he is," Theisiger replied. "It's still in poor taste to tape duels for public consumption. Some duelists, like Marble, make their own imprint recordings and sell 'em to collectors. It gives him a certain following." He frowned as though tasting something bad. He pointed with his chin. "But the money is an excuse for him."

"He looks more a like a sideshow freak than a big-time duelist," Ward noted.

Carlo smiled. "He *is* a touch flamboyant."

Ward whistled. "Did you see the woman in the back? That dress couldn't be any tighter."

Carlo pulled a small card out of his pocket and consulted it. "She's listed on the manifest as a 'private nurse.'"

"A 'nurse,' huh? She's beautiful, like a queen."

Carlo gave him a sharp look. "You need to stay focused on the small matter of surviving."

Ward nodded. "Ho, my."

Carlo darkened the canopy again. "Seen enough?"

"Yeah," Ward replied, "take me back. I think I may have an idea."

They returned to the Lager House in silence. "How exactly will this happen?" he asked in a subdued voice.

Carlo looked up at him. "He'll contact you and will probably call you out."

"Thanks," Ward replied distantly.

"Study the chip," Carlo called out. "It includes a lot of things that might help."

Ward walked away from the car and entered the building, his head down. Carlo started the vehicle and smoothly pulled away from the inn. "Good luck, Ward," he said. As he rounded the corner he saw four expensive ground cars discreetly parked by the Inn's service door. He stopped the car and crossed to the first vehicle. He swore as he saw the discrete Wing logo on the door. He ran for the service entrance.

Ward crossed the threshold and nearly bumped into a huge chest. "Pardon me," he mumbled as he tried to sidestep. The person stepped with him. Ward, irritated, looked up. His eyes locked on the man's Wing logo. His hand dropped to his laser.

"I wouldn't do that if I were you," a dry voice rasped.

Ward whirled his head and took in the reception area crowded with Wing gunmen. Two moved slightly, revealing an old man between them. He looked to Ward to be in his nineties, frail and supported on either side by the huge gunners. Ward saw his bent, shaking legs and realized he couldn't stand unaided.

The old man's face, the color and consistency of mellowed parchment, cracked into something like a smile. Ward saw his resemblance to Seladra as the old man stared at him. A wisp of sparse white hair fell over his brow. One of the men smoothed it back.

"Are you done starin', boy?" Wing of Skywing whispered. His voice, as dry and thin as a desert breeze, hissed over pale lips.

Ward took a deep breath. "What do you want?"

"I wanted to see the brat who's killed off more of my

family than the plague and Io combined," the old man rasped.

"And?" Ward asked, raising his chin.

Wing looked around at the staring faces in the reception room. "Let's go in there," he said, raising a shaking finger to point into the bar. "More quiet, more privacy."

Ward turned and walked into the taproom. The barkeep fled for the service door as she saw the entourage enter and two bodyguards took up station by the door.

Ward settled in a chair at the bar, trying desperately to maintain his calm front. The two escorts carefully lowered Wing into a chair and took up waiting positions at their elder's elbows, each staring at Ward with bovine concern.

Wing smiled, his face splitting into a horrible riotus. His skeletal hands gripped the chair arms. "I'm here to offer you peace, boy, to give you a chance." His intent look made Ward feel like a rabbit facing a wizened eagle. He shivered involuntarily.

"How's that?" Ward swallowed, trying to wet his parched throat.

"This war must cease," Skywing began, voice growing stronger as he warmed to his topic. "The cost has become too high for both our families." He coughed dryly, making no effort to cover his mouth. "We Wing have buried fifty of our kith and kin because of you."

"You started it!" Ward charged.

"We were provoked!" Skywing snapped, momentarily loosing his composure. Ward started to snarl back a retort. He allowed himself to be cut off by Skywing's upraised hand.

Skywing picked at a scab on the back of his hand. "It does us no good to fight like school children. What is done is done." He met Ward's eye. "However regrettable." He turned his head and whispered something to one attendant. The guard looked around and nodded.

"Here's what I'll give you, boy, as the price I'll pay for peace."

"What's your offer?" Ward said.

Wing smiled, his face splitting again into a rictus. "We drop our demands for indemnities for the nineteen Wings who died at your house. We'll also ignore the damages to Conners' home and blood money for Gustav." He licked his lips, his pale tongue flicking briefly out like a snake sampling the air.

"Not good enough!" Ward snapped. "That's all money you'll never see anyway."

Skywing pursed his lips. "I'll order an immediate exile from the district for all persons directly involved in the attack for a three-year period. Wing will also support your immediate elevation to head your clan." He opened his clenched fists, palms out. "Its a very generous offer, Ward. We'll even throw in some mulct for the LaPort raid. We're also amenable to some kind of bloodgeld." He leaned forward. "In exchange, Wing admits no wrongdoing." He rubbed his palms on the chair's arms. "What do you say?"

"No," Ward replied. "It's not enough. My family is dead, and you offer a three-year exile in exchange. The rest is window dressing. Do you really believe that I'd let *you* back my claim to the clan?"

Wing smiled. "Frankly, Ward, yes I do. Benno would have lived decades if he hadn't provoked us. This way you get to be Chief of Clan Tuchman while you're still in your prime." He laughed dryly. "There are certain advantages to being young, let me assure you."

Ward looked at him, his expression torn between anger and disbelief. "No deal," he said bluntly. "Go to hell!"

"Then die!" Skywing snarled. "Marble will kill you. That's the way it ought to be, anyway." He seemed to transform. Malicious energy poured from him, powering his words. "Marble will finish the job of wiping your rancid name from this planet, of killing the last of your breed!"

"If that's how you feel," Ward replied, his voice icily furious, "then why did you come here?"

"Seladra insisted I give you a chance to save yourself." Wing's voice softened a note. His eyes remained fixed on Ward, hard and cold as twin sapphires. "That, and you spared Delius' life."

"That's a mistake I won't make again," Ward replied.

"I thought I could talk sense into you." Skywing's voice calmed, his mouth softened as he made one final play. "Seladra thinks highly of you. She thought you would see how generous my offer is."

"Not hardly." Ward crossed his arms over his chest.

"Die, then," Skywing said, his voice full of disgust. He looked up at his attendants. "Get me out of here."

Ward waited until Wing and his entourage were gone before he collapsed into a chair. He turned abruptly as the service door opened. Carlo stepped out, an Execuline laser in his hand.

"How'd you know?" Ward asked.

"I didn't," Carlo replied. "I saw the cars parked out back."

"Thanks." Ward slumped in his chair and massaged his neck. "Did you hear the whole thing?"

"No," Carlo replied, "I only came in for the tail end." He took a deep breath. "Shitfire, boy, you don't do things by halves, do you? What'd you do to piss him off?"

"He offered me a deal," Ward answered in a flat voice. "He said he'd see me installed as Chief of Clan Tuchman. I didn't take it."

Theisiger looked baffled. "I thought that was what you wanted—to get your clan back."

Ward propped his hands on his knees and hung his head.

"Yes." He paused, confused. "No." He looked up at Carlo. "Hell, I don't know anymore."

"Well," Carlo replied pragmatically, "you'd better figure it out quick. The train carrying your last way out of fighting Marble just left town." He looked gravely at Ward. "Unless you get lucky, Ward, he's gonna kill you."

Ward looked down at his hands. They had begun to shake and nothing he could do would make them stop. Theisiger saw Ward's trembling. He put his hand on Ward's shoulder. "I'm goin' back to the shop now. I'll make sure Egg has your suit ready."

Ward looked up. "Thanks, Carlo."

Theisiger pursed his lips. "Look, Ward, you'd better stay inside. I think Wing's gonna be after you. It won't be safe on the streets, especially since Complein appears to have pulled your guard."

Ward tried to grin and failed miserably. "Yeah, okay."

He kept to the corner of the bar, sipping a beer that grew steadily warmer as the afternoon wore into evening and the taphouse's clientele filtered in. He attempted to eat a hamburger. His stomach, tied up in knots of worry, refused more than a couple of bites. He set it down in disgust just as a shadow loomed over his table. He looked up expecting to see Theisiger.

"You must be Ward," Marble said pleasantly. He leaned over the tabletop, placing his hands where Ward could see them. "The two-dee imprint they gave me doesn't do you justice." He smiled. "Do I need to upset your food in your lap, or can we dispense with the preliminaries?"

"No, I think we can skip that," replied Ward, licking his lips. "It's pretty obvious you're calling me out."

Marble tipped his head back and laughed. "Did you really say 'calling me out'?" He chortled again. "How . . . quaint." He grinned. "Did you have any specific time in mind?"

Ward wasn't amused. "No, anytime you choose will be fine."

Marble smiled again. "Very gracious of you. Hmm ... in keeping with the 'calling you out' motif, how about if we do it tomorrow at high noon?"

"Fine," Ward replied tightly. He recalled the field where he and Delius had fought. "There's a place near here I'd like to use. It's got open and rough ground, trees and creeks."

Marble raised one eyebrow. "Don't you have a municipal field?" He drummed his fingers on the table. His smile never wavered. "In Foundation, we've got artificial dueling fields with movable terrain features, barriers, and the like. Do you have anything like that here?"

"Yes," Ward answered, "but it's nothing as fancy as what you're used to, I'm sure."

Marble grinned. "That'll do fine." He stretched his long fingers out on the table. "Just so long as we have *some* terrain variety. I'd like to avoid a bare field. There's no science to that kind of slugfest, no *passion*." He yawned. "It's just, ho-hum, pistols across a table." He looked keenly at Ward. "Don't you agree?"

Ward shrugged. "If you say so."

Marble smiled again. "Now that we've gotten that out of the way . . . what say you join me for dinner tonight?"

Ward looked startled. "You can't be serious."

Marble winked at him. "Oh, I'm very serious. I've got a fantastic chef. Why don't you join me?"

The image of the woman on the ramp flashed unbidden into his mind. He laughed humorlessly and rubbed his fingers across his forehead. "What the hell, I've got no place else to be." He stood and got his coat. "At least until tomorrow."

Chapter 9

Marble led Ward between the temporary shelters that served as bedrooms for his entourage. Ward glanced inside one partially open curtain and saw a pile of futons and comforters nested in silken splendor. He inhaled, catching a tantalizing wisp of lavender and rose. Marble grinned as Ward turned away. "Haven't you ever seen a boudoir before?"

"I thought that was a fancy word for bedroom," Ward said self-consciously.

Marble rubbed his ear. "A bedroom is where people sleep. A boudoir is the sanctum sanctorum of the feminine heart."

Ward pretended to listen to Marble's running commentary on eighteenth-century Persian rugs and tapestries. The details quickly faded and he found himself staring at the waterproof fly-sheets that roofed the encampment while Marble lectured on some minute detail of warp and weft. Marble led him towards yet another tapestry. Ward braced himself for another lecture and was pleasantly surprised when Marble abruptly pulled it aside. Ward, startled by the sudden gesture, peered inside and saw a formal dining area open to the night sky.

"I see it's set for three," Ward asked. "Who's the third?"

Marble buffed his fingers against his shirt. "Judith," he replied, "my version of the odalisque."

Ward looked confused. "I don't understand."

Marble gently steered him into the tapestry-lined room. "It isn't important that you understand, only that you enjoy."

Ward studied the dining area as he entered, noticing the insect repulsers attached to the candelabra. He looked closely at the heavy oak table and matching velvet-backed chairs and decided they were real. A heavy silver ice bucket chilled a bottle on the sideboard while salvers steamed delicious odors into the air.

Marble gracefully motioned him to the head of the table. "It's for the guest of honor, you see," he said smoothly. He sat to Ward's right and pressed a small button set into the table. A woman emerged from a small opening Ward hadn't seen before.

He tried not to stare. She wore an elegant burgundy dress that clung tightly to her lush figure. A shawl was pinned to the back of her head by twin diamond hat pins that matched her elegant earrings. The shawl draped across her shoulders, covering most of her bodice in shimmering silk. Her raven-dark hair peeked around the edges of the falling curtain, emphasizing her dark complexion. She wore only a hint of rouge on her high cheekbones, while her eyes had been smudged with kohl. Ward swallowed reflexively.

Marble smiled at his discomfiture. "Judith," he said pleasantly, "this is Ward."

"Hello, Ward," she said softly. Her rich contralto did nothing for Ward's racing heart and fractured equanimity. She moved to her chair. Ward stumbled to his feet to hold it out for her. "Thank you," she said softly as she took her seat. Marble looked bemused.

Servants appeared from behind cunningly concealed doorways to open the wine and set appetizers before the diners. Ward found the food was as strange as it was exquisite. He made the mistake of inquiring about a dish only once. He wasn't sure if Marble was serious when he answered, "Dormice roasted in olive oil with sesame and poppy seeds."

The meal itself seemed to be a mirror of Marble himself. Each dish vied with its predecessors for strangeness and delicious eccentricity. Ward tried to relax and enjoy the food while at the same time attempting to fend off Marble's probing questions. His grunts and monosyllabic answers did little to protect him from Marble's gentle interrogation. Ward felt like a peeled onion before the salad course had finished.

Judith said little. She answered if spoken to directly, but otherwise kept her gaze locked firmly on her plate.

Ward's patience survived the main course, but expired as Marble picked through a plate of cheeses held out to him by a servant. "Why are you giving me the third degree?" he demanded.

Marble smiled, slow and lazy, as he forked a wedge of cheese onto his plate. "The fight is like the dance." He turned his head to Ward, tugging his lower lip with a thumb and forefinger as he spoke. "And the dance is like the sex. The sex is the consummation, you see."

He frowned at Ward's baffled expression. "I get to know each of my partners before we dance, before we fight. I get to know them so that at the moment it ends, at the moment of consummation, I absorb their souls." He dropped his hand to his lap. "Or, if they kill me, they absorb mine." He giggled, high and shrill. "By finding out as much as I can about you now, I'll know where to best fit your soul tomorrow."

Ward stared as Marble continued, "You can't imagine the release at the moment my partner surrenders life to me, the moment when I feel their souls leave their bodies, seeking a willing vessel. It's better than sex." The servant held the tray out for Ward. "Cheese?" Marble asked solicitously.

He giggled again. "Whomever takes my soul is in for a hell of a surprise. I've got forty others in here with me." He tapped his breastbone. "The one who finally beats me will need a big heart to hold all that karma."

Ward stared at Marble as if the man had suddenly grown horns.

"It's okay," Marble said after a moment's thought, "I realize this is all new to you. But you'll soon be in good company." He giggled and tapped his chest again. "It's too bad really. It would have been nice for you to consummate at least once before you joined me." He sighed. "Ah, well. *Asi es la vida.*" He gestured to Ward's glass. "How's the wine?"

Ward, totally flustered, mumbled, "Umm, it's fine, I guess."

Another servant stepped to Ward's side, bearing a silver tray. Ward looked down. His jaw dropped. The tray held several hypodermic needles loaded with colored liquids, as well as a selection of pills and powders.

"Would you like an after-dinner mint?" Marble asked gently.

Ward looked at the needles. "No, thanks."

"Your loss," the duelist said as the servant moved to his side. Marble selected a needle from the tray and rolled back his lace cuff to reveal a plastic shunt set in his lower arm. He jabbed the needle into the plastic, then pressed the button activating the tiny compressed air cylinder. He leaned back into his seat, his head pressed against the chair back.

"Nothing to slow my reactions, of course." Marble giggled softly. The servant moved to stand beside Judith. Marble rolled his head to look at her. She refused to look at the tray.

"Ju-dith," Marble chided. She took a deep breath and selected a pill from the tray. She swallowed it without water and closed her eyes. Ward thought he saw a sparkle of tears caught in her lashes.

Marble smiled beatifically. "That's a good girl. Now dance for us."

Judith did as she was bid, rising gracefully from the table and undoing her hat pins. The shawl fell to the floor. She spread the puddle of silk into a rough square with a single deft motion of her foot.

She slipped tiny bells from a hidden pocket onto her fingertips and began to chime them slowly. She danced in time with herself, swaying to the rhythm of the muted clappers. Ward felt his blood heat as he watched her sensual movements. He tore his eyes from her and looked at Marble. The duelist stared at him. "She dances for you, you know," he said cryptically. "My gift to my karma." He looked at his watch. "I'd best get you back. It's getting late." He turned to the servant who stood by with the tray. "See Mr. Tuchman gets back to his hotel." Marble rose from his seat. "Please, finish your wine, first." Ward stared as Marble took Judith's hand and led her from the room.

Ward was still thinking about her the next day as Egg talked him through the suit's latest modifications. The tech quickly became exasperated with his inattention. "Look Ward, if you don't pay attention here, you ain't gonna' learn this. An' you'll be another notch in pretty boy's belt."

"Yeah, Egg, I heard you. I'm sorry," Ward apologized, "let's go over it again."

Egg rolled his eyes. "I altered the AI to accommodate the changes in mass and weight distribution. The suit shouldn't feel any different to you. I put double appliqué on the knee and elbow joints, and repainted and lacquered the front carapace. The extra paint won't help much, but it can't hurt."

Ward crawled into his armor. He stood and stretched, testing the servo mechanisms. "It feels different somehow," he judged.

Egg shrugged. "Can you live with it? If not, I can fiddle with the software a little."

Ward flexed his arm, swinging it around in an arc over his head. He heard a rasping sound as he brushed the roof of the temporary shelter.

"Damn it," Egg growled, "I told you. That rocket launcher is about ten centimeters longer than your laser. It won't take much abuse. I don't see why you chose that, anyway."

Ward shrugged. "It's an idea I got from the fight at the Conners place. I can't manage a rocket launcher pack, but this three-shot rail might just give me an edge. I don't really expect to hit anything with it. I'm hoping to keep him busy with the rockets long enough to get close and rip him with my coiler. I think I can turn his arrogance against him. And Carlo did suggest I use something more serious than a suit laser." He looked at the device. "It looks different. Did you do something to it?"

"If you'd been listening, you'd have heard," Egg said with some heat. "Auto-loaders are notoriously unreliable. I took it off. What you have there is little more than a launch rail and three sets of spring clips. You already know about the secrets built into the rail."

Carlo, armored in his flat-black suit and carrying a helmet under each arm, slipped through the door. "Are you ready?"

Ward tried to smile but couldn't manage it. "Yeah." He looked at Carlo. "I'm glad you came. I need all the friends I can get today."

Thesiger looked embarrassed. "I talked to Mona. I'm going to second you on this one."

Ward looked relieved. "Thanks."

They shook hands. Ward marveled at Theisiger's precise reflexes and whisper-silent servos. He felt lumpish in comparison. Carlo handed him his helmet and led him out of the shelter and towards the dueling field. They heard the babble of the crowd even before it came into sight.

Theisiger made a rude noise. "Looks like we got

several hundred out there. The idiots don't seem to realize the friggin' rounds don't magically stop at the edge of the fighting ground. I'll bet some ignorant asshole gets himself killed." He looked back at Ward, his face apologetic. "Sorry."

Ward dismissed it with a wave of his hand. "What time is it?"

Theisiger looked at his suit's chronometer. "About ten till." His expression grew somber. "Are you ready?"

Ward shrugged. "Yeah, I guess. I studied that tape you gave me. It helped. I hope it's enough."

Carlo handed him his helmet. They walked around the protective berm and were greeted by a thin cheer. Ward grinned and waved as he saw Tuchman banners surrounded by a thick knot of unarmored retainers.

Denison and two guards waited by the edge of the field. The receiver carried his helmet from a strap hanging from his pectoral plate. "Good morning, Ward," he said pleasantly.

Ward ignored the greeting. "Why doesn't Tuchman have armor?"

Denison met his eye. "Too risky. Tempers are bound to be short, and I don't want another 'event' between Wing and Tuch."

"Dammit," Ward protested, "duels are *dangerous*. What happens if some stray projectiles wander over that way?"

"Then somebody gets killed," Denison replied evenly. "I didn't think that would bother you."

"It bothers me," Ward said. He saw Juana Park standing nearby, the sixty-year-old spinster who'd been Chief Housekeeper at La Port since before Ward was born. "Juana," he called, "go tell all the Tuchman retainers in that crowd to get under cover. Tell them I *order* them as head of the clan to get under cover."

Juana nodded crisply and strode off. Ward felt an unexpected relief. That was one thing he didn't have to worry about. Nobody was going to argue with Miss Juana.

A cheer rose from the Wing end of the field. He turned towards the sound. A silver ground car came in hot and fast, flaring at the last second to a perfect, glass-smooth landing.

"That driver's good," Denison commented.

"She should be," Ward said dryly. "I taught her that landing. That would be Seladra, I think."

Theisiger took a spotting scope from his equipment pouch and handed the device to Ward. He squinted through it. Seladra jumped out of the car.

His heat skipped a beat as he saw her familiar figure. She stepped around to the passenger side carrying a cane. The scope blurred a moment as the auto-focus shifted. Seladra reached inside the ground car to help someone out. He handed the scope back to Carlo with an unhappy grunt.

"Delius is here," Ward said angrily. "Somebody put his leg back on."

Theisiger pointed with his chin. "Old man Wing is here, too. Look for the two morons who look like football goal posts, Wing's right there between them." Ward raised the scope to his eye again and saw Skywing, flanked by his attendants. Some of Marble's staff stood nearby, but not Judith.

Carlo's wrist alarm chimed. "Five minutes to high noon, Ward," he said. "We'd better get out there."

Marble appeared from his temporary shelter just as Ward and Carlo walked out onto the field. The crowd quieted expectantly. Ward studied Marble's armor, noting the puffy appliqué work and the bizarre paint scheme. The duelist used a complex mix of shimmering, shifting hues to blot out most of his armor's surface details.

"What kind of camouflage is that?" Ward asked. "He'd stand out like a whore in church."

"Look again," Theisiger said. Ward watched Marble

walk through the waist-high dry grass that dominated the middle ground. His lower legs seemed to vanish in the standing hay as he passed through.

Ward whistled. "How's he do that?"

Theisiger grinned. "In pure Marble style. The pattern is made up of tiny dots of pure color, with contrasting colors sprinkled in to 'activate' it. It's weird, but it works."

"Ever the pointillist?" Theisiger said dryly as Marble joined the small circle.

"Theisiger? Carlo Theisiger?" Marble smiled. "What are you doing here?"

"I live here," Carlo answered.

Marble scratched his head. Ward saw he'd coiled his long hair at the nape of his neck in a tight chignon.

"Why'd they send for me, then?" he asked.

Theisiger shrugged. "Whim. Mine."

Marble laughed softly. "What's your gig?"

"I'm seconding for the boy," Theisiger looked meaningfully at the Wing contingent, "to ensure fair play."

Marble laughed aloud, tipping his head back as he chuckled. "We all want to see fair play." He looked Ward over carefully, noting the launch rail. "Unorthodox. Might work." He glanced at the appliqué covering Ward's joints and waggled a finger at Carlo. "You've been talking," he accused.

Ward used the opportunity to scan Marble's equipment. He was pleased to see that Marble carried no external stores. He appeared to be armed with his usual coil gun and laser. Ward glanced at his boost-pack. It didn't seem to be augmented in any way, in spite of the substantial weight penalty imposed by the appliqué.

Carlo moved to stand between them. "You both know the rules. Use only what you brought. No reloads. No fresh batteries. The fight continues until one of you is dead or . . ." He trailed off and looked at Marble. "Or yields?"

Marble pursed his lips. "No."

Theisiger sighed. "It's to the death, then. Go to your sides. High noon is in ninety seconds."

Ward ran quickly to the red-taped trees that marked his entry point, scanning the field as he went. The field was a regulation square, four hundred meters on a side, with a spectator area along the southern boundary. Trees and bushes, planted in singles and close stands for variation, covered the northern quarter. The eastern and western ends were also tree shaded and thickly grown with the same native underbrush that lay in clumps throughout the center ground

Mid-field lay open, checkered off by low rises and depressions, to provide both cover and fast action. The grass had been left to grow high in places to complicate the lines of sight. The open ground was flanked on the east and west side by lines of berms that ran the length of the field. The mounds on Ward's side ran north-south in long ribbons, while those on Marble's were divided into hummocks positioned in three staggered rows like spots on a die.

Ward stepped into his ready box and crouched down where the spectators couldn't see him in the grass and underbrush. He quickly stripped off one of the rocket reloads as well as the top four centimeters of the launching rail. The rail split down the middle along a cleverly concealed hinge. Ward angled the makeshift bipod to cover an area of the field unobscured by the low rises. He could see about two hundred meters downrange, roughly half the length of the field. He propped the rocket up and armed it, removing the safety retaining wire and activating the IFF transponder. He heard the hum as the free-floating seeker head uncaged.

He heard a high-pitched sound horn blast from mid-field. "Time to go to work," he said to himself. He patted the rocket. "Don't let me down, baby."

He broke cover and ran northwards along the length

of the last berm, trying to put distance between himself and the rocket. He sprinted along the smooth ground, noticing the faint trail left by fighters before him. He used his artificial intelligence to track Marble on the display, setting the system to alert him when the duelist moved. The alarm chimed almost immediately as Marble sprinted across his section of rough terrain and into the middle ground.

Marble took the first berm on the east side of the field, slowing visibly as he negotiated his way past it. The earthworks provided cover only along the east-west axis. They made excellent north-south fire lanes. Ward glanced quickly behind him as the implications of the terrain became clear. "Damn," he said, "not even a bush to hide behind." Ward looked to his right and saw the red boundary flags looming close by. "I boxed myself in." He closed his eyes a moment. "Idiot."

Marble continued to track him, permitting Ward to remain under cover while limiting his options. Ward had a glimmer of Marble's strategy. He thought the duelist would be content to remain under cover while backing him into a corner. He realized his only escape would be to bolt across Marble's line of fire. His other option would be to suffer Marble's slings and arrows from a distance.

He looked around frantically. "Think, damn it, think!" He tried to control his wild breathing as he watched Marble clear the second berm, still moving perpendicular to Ward. The duelist accelerated down the second slope, across the open ground, and up the third hill. Ward watched his progress slow to a crawl. His boost pack huffed, bleeding air from the fuel-feed lines.

"That's it," Ward cried. He looked up at the soft, bulldozed berms. "The bastard has to climb!" He monitored his display, waiting for Marble to crest the third berm. Ward fired his boost-pack the instant Marble reached the top. He blasted to the top of the first rise, landed, and fired his boost-pack again to carry him towards the duelist. He extended his rocket launcher, praying for the warbling tone that indicated the seeker had found its target.

Marble whirled with a speed that belied his heavy armor and fired before Ward had done more than step over the first rise. The rocket acquired its target. Ward launched it as Marble's fifth shot splattered into his armor, charring the paint. The eighth shot hit the rocket in mid-body. Its fuel packet detonated, slamming Ward's arm hard enough against his side to damage the launch rail. The explosion tossed Ward sideways like a ragdoll. The remainder of Marble's fusillade missed by a handsbreadth as he tumbled to his right.

He rolled heavily, continuing his rightward movement and trying to keep his coil gun out of the dirt. He flailed through several ungainly and desperate revolutions before rising to his feet on the crest of the berm. His left boot crumbled the soft ground. He felt it slip away a half-second before he overbalanced and fell backward. His arms windmilled as he plunged to the ground below. He saw the yellow beams of Marble's painting laser cut the air above him, missing by millimeters as they pursued him. Only the mass of the berm spared him their lethal touch.

He hit the ground heavily, landing about two meters from his starting point. He lay a moment before fear and adrenaline forced him to his feet. He fled along his earlier course, seeking now to put distance between himself and Marble. The duelist dropped back below the crest of the third berm, keeping the mass of two earthworks between them.

Ward paused to inspect the launching rail. The single remaining rocket's fins and attachment point were intact. He whistled silently. Had the laser hit the HE payload rather than the fuel cell, it could have set off the hypervelocity penetrators. They'd have gone in random directions, but an airfoil at that range would have been fatal.

He ran on, using the berm to his left as a shield. He fired his boost-pack to open up some distance between himself and Marble. The duelist appeared content to stump along in his own good time and remain two berms away.

Ward scanned his terrain map, zooming in to examine details of the northeastern corner of the field. He saw that the berms faded out on the north edge of the field. "Maybe I can slip around the ends," he mused, "and stay off the damned crests."

Ward waited until he saw flags ahead as well as to his right before he made his move. He rounded the end of the last berm and sprinted along the narrow strip of flat ground along the northern edge of the field. Marble's dot accelerated.

Ward crossed the edge of the second berm. Marble topped his own rise and moved to a line just below the crest on the far side of the third berm. Ward leapt, firing his boosters to cover the intervening distance. He plowed into the ground behind a scrap of cover as Marble came into sight.

He jerked his coil gun up to fire a stream even as the duelist was already shooting. Ward felt pieces of appliqué being shot off his elbow joint even before his own weapon was on-line. The impacts disturbed his own targeting, preventing a solid lock-on. He fired anyway, trying to disrupt Marble's aim. Ring penetrators sprayed into the dirt, up into the air, everywhere except where Marble happened to be.

Ward saw the duelist duck and roll over the top of the berm he sheltered behind, then felt his left knee heat up as laser shots hit. He jumped up, taking twin bolts in his heat sink before he could scamper to safety behind the next berm. Ward cursed as harassing fire flashed past him from behind. He scampered past the west, running along the narrow channel at the north edge of the field. Marble plinked him from behind, goading him on.

Ward cleared the last of the berm with a diving leap and a generous boost from his pack. He landed on his feet and sprinted for the trees on the far side of the open clearing. He made it to the first small copse without further harassment. He looked at his elapsed-time meter and swore. "Four lousy minutes." He looked at his internal suit graphic. The heat sink symbol flashed amber, showing minor damage.

He tracked Marble's blip on the screen. The duelist had moved to the end of the berms and crept from one to another, rolling over the sloping ends. Ward tried a snap shot as Marble came over the next to last.

The duelist popped up and over, moving so quickly that Ward's first burst wasn't even close. Ward aimed where Marble rolled, expecting him to reappear. Marble reversed his position, peeping up from where his feet had been. He coolly shot into the tree Ward crouched behind, missing Ward's head by a handspan.

The bole split in a flash of steam. Two shots, then two more, ripped into the breach, widening and deepening it. Ward stumbled back as another shot hit higher up, and the tree fell. He scrambled back out of the tree's way, flailing his arms as he tried to maintain his balance on the rough ground. Marble rose from cover and coolly aimed. Ward whipped his arm across his faceplate as Marble fired. The laser bolt smacked into his elbow, piercing the outer appliqué and flinging Ward back.

Ward bought time behind a wild stream of airfoils as he sought cover. He slid into a shallow depression and loaded his remaining rocket, straightening the tip of his bent launch rail. "Okay, time for plan A. I hope this still works," he whispered as he tried to fit the rocket into its grooves.

The AI chimed a warning as Marble's graphic shifted

positions. Ward twisted himself around, looking for a fallback position. He saw a low rock wall and a deadfall he could use for cover long enough to retreat further. He leaned his coil gun arm over the top of the depression, the better to contest Marble's crossing. The duelist burst from cover.

Ward rose up on one knee and aimed, his torso exposed as he tried to track the wildly dodging Marble. The AI beeped as it assembled a firing solution. He fired, hosing the duelist with a long burst. Marble tumbled as hypervelocity penetrators gouged chunks out of his appliqué. He fired on the roll, his bolts striking the imprint camera mounted on the side of Ward's helmet. Ward felt his neck jerk as the impact overcame the servos. A second shot, following hard upon the first, gouged deeply into his shoulder appliqué before it plowed along his collarbone. The bolt stripped away the protective paint and lacquer before it angled up and slapped into the remains of the camera mount.

The right half of the suit's visual field began to spark and shift as power to systems fluxed. Ward rolled backwards and ran for the rock wall, diving over it as more laser bolts slapped into rocks below and behind him.

He quickly checked his suit graphic and swore. The camera's power fittings had been ducted through the couplings that fed his right visual receptors. He cursed helplessly as the right eye fuzzed and scattered before settling down. His AI chimed again, indicating Marble had moved. He looked at the display, swearing again as the duelist moved under the cover of the first trees.

Ward pulled back again, using a culvert to buy time. Marble crept after him, maintaining a rough seventy-meter distance. Ward used the low, rough terrain to stay out of Marble's line of sight. He dodged behind a pair of low hills, then slipped back into the culvert. He slid along its length, using the inch or so of running water at the bottom to help his damaged heat sink flush away waste thermal energy. He heard the sink's vanes scrape on the river stones lining the culvert.

The stones gave him an idea. He climbed back up the concrete, grabbing protruding roots and branches to pull him upwards until he reached his earlier vantage. Marble had paused, going to cover as Ward reversed his direction. Ward realized as he settled into position that he and Marble were less than fifty meters apart, separated only by the two low hills.

Ward scooped up a handful of river rocks from the culvert in his left hand. He kept his coil gun extended as the AI searched for a target. He flung the rocks across the tops of the hills and was rewarded by a crackle of laser fire as they tripped Marble's proximity alarm. Ward grabbed a second handful and sprinted from behind the culvert towards the lee of the low hill to his direct front.

He hit the base of the hill and launched himself into a flat dive that carried him into sight of the location where Marble had engaged the stones. Ward pelted the area with rocks to distract his opponent, then popped into sight. Nothing. Marble had already moved.

He checked Marble's location on the HUD. The duelist's position hadn't changed. He looked desperately around and saw a small box on the ground where he'd hidden. He dove to his right, the first stream of lasers cutting the air where he had been only a moment before. He flipped his feet underneath him and rolled to one knee, where he cranked off a long burst at point-blank range at Marble. The duelist dodged, beating Ward to the snap shot once again. The laser hit his elbow again, burning away the last of the appliqué and knocking his coil gun wide.

Ward pushed off with his planted foot, trying to escape the searing laser fire. Marble used the opportunity to pick through the appliqué on Ward's left leg, stitching him from ankle to hip as he fled. Ward desperately arched backwards into the air, pursued by laser beams that picked at his joints and carapace.

Ward tried to fire at Marble as he crossed over the apex of his lazy back flip. Marble's laser continued to etch him as he tumbled, inflicting hit upon hit as Ward rolled helplessly in the air. The impacts distorted Ward's trajectory enough that he landed on his knees on the far side of the low hill. His strained neck servos whined as his head rapped the ground.

Ward sprang back, ready for Marble to crest the hill. He reacted to a flicker of motion on his right side. "Damn!" he swore as his vision flickered again. A glancing bolt from his front left staggered him.

Ward went to one knee, battered by the impact. The duelist's laser cut his upper arm again, striking almost the same spot as it had before. Ward's return fire missed completely. Another bolt hit his shoulder, straining that servo. Ward broke and ran over the ridge line.

The trees thinned behind its crest, fading from clusters to single boles not quite wide enough to hide behind. Ward skipped behind one, then another, as Marble slogged after him, cranking off shot after precise shot.

Ward cursed in frustration as his knee and elbow graphics flashed amber, indicating minor damage. He knew that while Marble's laser didn't have the power to cut through his armor at range, the aggregate damage would eventually reduce his servos' efficiency and render him helpless. Then Marble would be in a position to "consummate" his victory over Ward. Well, Ward had known that's what he'd be up against the first time he ran through Carlo's tape, and Marble didn't seem to think Ward deserved any change from business as usual.

Ward dodged back behind the last of the trees, aware that Marble had stalked him over three-quarters of the field and had backed him almost into open ground. He glanced hurriedly back at the closest hummock, set some forty meters from the last of the trees.

Ward took a deep breath, then popped his head from behind the tree to check Marble's position visually. The duelist remained still about a hundred and fifty meters out, working his way along the last small cluster of trees as he attempted to enfilade Ward. Ward blasted him with airfoils and watched as the duelist scampered for cover.

Ward turned and ran for the closest circular mound. Marble abandoned his own cover as he paced Ward. Ward turned, attempting to get a firing solution from his AI while Marble was in the open. The duelist leapt to cover and maneuvered between tree trunks, skipping and skirting the edges in such a way that Ward couldn't get a clear shot.

Ward ran to the first circular mound as Marble made it to the tree line. Ward harassed him, firing short, tightly controlled bursts as his ammunition dwindled. The duelist began to plink back, pressuring Ward with near-misses into abandoning his forward position and falling back to the small mound at his rear left.

Marble ducked from behind cover, sprinting for the berm Ward had only just vacated. Ward, surprised, launched himself into the air, using his boost-pack to clear the top of the dirt mound, Marble ran crouched, out of Ward's direct line of sight as he scrambled over the top of the hummock. Marble popped over the top of the hump. Ward extended his missile rail and was immediately rewarded by the warbling tones as the warhead locked onto Marble's electronic signature. He keyed the missile's firing stud. It leapt away, accelerating in the blink of an eye. Marble's AI took over the duelist's suit, executing an automatic defensive subroutine. Fast, too fast for human reflexes, the AI keyed Marble's boost-packs and jerked him out of the way. The warhead curled to the right in a vain attempt to track him. It arched past its target, still angling to the right, then straightened out as it homed in on the spectator stands. Ward dove for cover as he heard a distant boom and faint screams from the bystanders. Three ring penetrators had just done someone no good.

Marble slid around the edge of his sheltering mound, blazing with his laser to prevent Ward from attempting to close the distance. Ward fled, avoiding the battle armor equivalent of machine guns at ten paces. He fired short bursts as he retreated, his airfoils killing grass and scattering dirt, but leaving Marble unscathed. Marble spattered him with laser fire, striking joints and servos, but continuing to avoid general body hits. Ward checked his watch, then broke and ran when Marble planted his feet and raised his own coil gun.

Ward fired his boost-pack as he rolled, trying to get under the impending lance of airfoils. He dove for cover as the first rings flashed past him. One cut along the back of his leg armor, curling away appliqué and suit armor like carrot peelings. The dirt mound gave him a moment's respite. He landed heavily, his right knee servo whining and flexing more deeply than it should have. Ward glanced down at his knee.

The entire joint was wet with fluid. He tried to wipe the encrusting dirt away and succeeded only in smearing it more deeply into the grooves cut by Marble's deadly accurate fire. He checked his diagnostics and saw the joint's efficiency had fallen to eighty-one percent. He fumbled in his pouch for a tube of joint seal and slathered it on, hoping that he'd plugged the leak.

His proximity alarm chimed again, indicating Marble had moved. Ward looked back and saw the long lines of mounds beckoning to him.

Open ground lay to his right, dotted only by high grass and the occasional patch of Terran bramble. The first of the long rows of berms beckoned from the far side of the open two-hundred-meter space.

Ward looked at his HUD. Marble moved to Ward's left, flanking him and trying to force him into the open field. Ward tried to keep the earthwork between him and Marble, but quickly realized this allowed the duelist to position himself to move more easily from hump to hump. Ward felt his position eroding badly. Marble had him boxed in. It was time for plan B.

He looked back across the field, trying to calculate how far he'd have to run before his concealed rocket fired. His proximity chimed again as Marble closed another twenty meters and dodged behind another mound.

Ward abandoned the earthwork, using it to push off as he sprinted across the field. Laser shots cut close to his right, then his left as he dodged wildly. He covered most of the open field in the first five seconds, using his boost-pack in an extended burn to push him forward. A laser bolt passed between his neck and shoulder. He dove to the ground and sheltered in the high grass about fifty meters short of his most optimistic projection of the missile's line of fire.

Coil gun rounds began to search the tall grass. Ward rolled to his right as a burst passed perilously close. He rolled again, hoping to put a little more distance between him and ground zero. The hay fell in swaths around him, reminding him that the grass had a defensive value equal to paper in stopping airfoils.

He sprang up on his left knee, preparatory to another sprint, then pushed off. He felt the joint blow as he overstressed both the original leak and the hastily applied sealant. He heard a loud *pop!* and fell headlong into the hay. He looked around. His lower right leg dripped blue hydraulic fluid. The joint stiffened into rigidity a moment later.

He staggered up, desperate to reach cover. A single ring penetrator glanced off his boost-pack, bursting the pressurized fuel tank and vaporizing much of the remaining liquid. Several more penetrators chewed into his suddenly thinner back armor before he turned around. The vaporized fuel exploded, driving him forward and smashing him to the ground. He lay dazed for a moment then climbed to his hands and working knee. His right leg remained stretched out behind him. The dry grass around him began to burn, marking the explosion's center with a thick pall of smoke.

Ward's right visual display failed completely as an airfoil glanced off the side of his head. Ward staggered to his feet and stumbled forward, dragging his right leg. His eyes remained fixed on the distant line of berms ahead. Marble paced him from a hundred meters out, still firing single shots, herding him toward the spectator stands.

Ward passed the first berm and turned towards it, setting himself. He felt exhausted.

Marble came abreast of the first long berm. Ward saw a white plume out of the corner of his left eye. The hypervelocity rocket arched towards the duelist, angling in to him from a point just outside his visual field. Marble's AI fired his boost-packs, flinging him to the right. The rocket missed cleanly. The duelist staggered as he landed, a momentary lapse that presented Ward with the flank shot he had been waiting for. Ward hit the firing stud as Marble, cat quick, began to whirl.

The airfoils savaged the duelist's boost-pack and thinner flank. The impacts spun Marble around, presenting his rear armor to Ward. The boost tanks failed, dumping fuel and oxidizer that almost instantly exploded as it touched the pack's hot plenum chamber. Marble managed to keep his feet underneath him through the initial barrage, and even attempted to get his own coil gun on line as he braced beneath Ward's fire.

The exploding fuel blew him off his feet. Ward hammered him with more rounds as he fell and landed facedown. Ward continued to pour rounds into his unmoving body until his magazine went dry and the coil gun hummed quietly to itself.

Ward collapsed as he heard a furor from the distant

crowds. The duelist's body lay still and unmoving. Ward felt utterly drained, too exhausted to even roll onto his back. He lay, content to suck oxygen in great shuddering gasps while his heart trembled and his limbs spasmed uncontrollably. He blacked out, only to awaken to a proximity alarm chiming in his ear. He started, frightened that the last few minutes had been a dream and Marble still pursued him. He struggled to rise as somebody loomed over him.

"Ward, stop it! It's me, Mona!" she shouted into his aural pickup. He stopped thrashing and let her roll him over, aided by several others. His vision sparked and failed as he saw a group of several dozen crowding close. She gently removed his helmet, his sweat-soaked head falling back into the dirt. One of the crowd kicked dust in his mouth as the onlookers jostled for position. He choked and spat as the dirt clotted his already dry mouth.

Then Theisiger was there, a squirt bottle in hand. He shouted the well-wishers back and helped Mona raise Ward to a sitting position. His vision grew dim. He heard a distant voice yelling, "He's going out." A burning, pungent odor filled his nostrils, snapping him back to full alertness.

Carlo held a straw to his lips. He bobbed his head gratefully, drawing the warm water in and rinsing out his mouth. He spat, most of the water trailing down his front. Mona unhinged his front carapace. He sighed gratefully as cool air washed over his chest.

Theisiger jubilantly slapped his back, his armored hand strong enough to rock Ward even inside battle armor. "You did it, boy! You did it!" he yelled.

Ward looked wild-eyed as the cheering crowd swarmed across the field. "I didn't do it. The rocket did it." He looked up at Theisiger. "He had me, dead to rights." He watched two small boys kick at Marble's corpse, then run as one arm settled under their abuse. "I got lucky."

The armor's front carapace folded back. Mona wrinkled her nose at the heavy ammonia smell that poured out. Ward had wet himself sometime during the fight. Theisiger looked up at a young girl clasping a blanket to her chest. She stared wide-eyed at Ward.

"Excuse me, miss, may I have that?" Theisiger gestured for the blanket. She dropped it into his open hand and scampered back to hide behind her mother's skirts. Theisiger laughed without humor. The blanket, like everything else mother and daughter wore, was woven in the colors of Clan Tuchman. He wrapped it around Ward, who slithered free of his dead suit.

Theisiger supported Ward with one hand under his elbow while Mona ducked her head under his other arm. They half carried, half dragged him through the jubilant throng to the temporary shelter.

"What'd you think?" Ward croaked to Carlo.

Theisiger shrugged. "Neat strategy. Got him to underestimate you. And that was a good shot, there at the end. When it counted."

The crowd in front of them grew suddenly still. It parted almost as if by command. Ward looked up and saw Wing of Skywing standing before him. They made an odd pair, both too weak to walk, held upright, aided by others. Ward would have laughed at the irony under other circumstances. The corridor of peering faces grew silent as the tension built.

He roused himself, relief and fury vying for dominance. "Who's next?" he shouted at the Wings. He raised his finger and pointed at Skywing.

"Are you next?" he half screamed, half shouted. "Who wants to die next? 'Cause you're all gonna die!" He choked back a sob, still crazy with the residue of battle fury.

Wing looked at him with mixed pity and disgust. "All we want is to live in peace with our neighbors," he said tiredly. His voice, in contrast to Ward's, sounded soft and reasonable. "Too bad you won't let us." He turned away, helped by his assistants.

Theisiger and Mona helped him to the shelter. He saw a pair of Tuchman guards standing outside. He stared at them as Mona passed him and went inside. The taller of the two men balanced his auto-gun on its shoulder sling while he raised his thumb to Ward.

Dr. Silman waited inside, his portable kit laid out and ready. He examined Ward in the confined space while Theisiger shrugged his armor off, not the least bit concerned about being naked in front of Mona or Silman's female guard.

The physician ran his diagnostic equipment over him, seemingly more concerned about his head and chest than the rapidly purpling bruise that covered his entire left knee.

"No continued swelling. Good," Silman murmured as he worked. He ran the scanner over Ward's chest. "Heart's a little fast and thready. Hmm, drink a lot of electrolytes and stay off your feet for a couple of days. You'll be fine." He pulled out his pad and scribbled something on it.

"What's that for?" Ward asked.

"I'm prescribing you two of my guards." The doctor laughed. "Pardon the bad joke, but you are going to need some serious protection after today. Garibaldi's my driver. He's a fair hand with a gun. Dave is a suit man, and more likely to be of use to you than he is to me at the moment."

Ward looked up in confusion. "Don't you need them?"

Silman smiled. "Not to put too fine a point on it, Ward, but you're on the skyline right now. I'm small beer next to you." He turned to Theisiger. "He's in good shape, better than he has any right to be in, actually. The concussion is almost completely reduced." He gathered his equipment and headed for the door. "Where do I send the bill?"

Carlo pointed at Ward. The physician laughed as he went through the door, trailed by the guard.

One of the door guards stuck his head in the door a few moments later. "Hey, Mr. Tuchman. I got about thirty people out here. They say they wanna help. What should I tell 'em?"

Ward looked at Carlo, confused. "I haven't a clue."

Theisiger, a towel wrapped around his waist, stepped into the breach. "Tell 'em Ward thanks 'em for their support. Have them round up a detail and go secure the dead man's armor and possessions. They're clan spoil. Also, get everybody's name who's out there. Ward'll want to know who to reward for their loyalty."

The guard looked at Ward for confirmation. Ward smiled tiredly. "Sounds good to me. Tell 'em Clan Tuch's on its way back." The guard backed out.

Theisiger dropped the towel and struggled into a loose coverall. "It probably wasn't a good idea to make promises you may not be able to keep." He grinned. "But then again, you have been on a roll lately." He looked at the door. "Speaking of loot, Ward, you'd best get back to Marble's camp. The equipage is worth a bundle and it's arguably part of the spoils." He ran the towel over his head, then combed his hair with his fingers. "I'm pretty sure Marble didn't have any kin, so there's no one to contest you for it."

"Okay," Ward replied, "we'd better go." He sat up gingerly. "Damn, I'm stiff."

Mona turned to Theisiger. "I'll go on ahead and check the van Marble brought for traps or bombs." She looked at Ward and grinned. "Don't you think you ought to put some clothes on first?" She wrinkled her nose. "And mebbe a shower?"

Ward looked at Theisiger, who tapped his wrist meaningfully. Ward stepped out of his towel and into another coverall and slip-on shop shoes. "No time for that," he answered.

Ward started towards the van under his own power, but had to accept Mona and Carlo's help when his legs began to cramp. The taller of the two guards approached, his broad face growing concerned when he saw Ward wincing in pain.

"Is there anythin' I can do?" he asked.

Theisiger hooked a thumb at the watching crowd. "Yeah, keep an eye on these people. They got no guns and no armor. Somebody might take it in their heads to jump 'em." The guard smiled and turned away.

"He's a good man," Carlo said as the guard walked toward the crowd. "I like him."

Ward's cramps became worse once they were in the van. Mona and Carlo traded places so that Mona could sit in the back with Ward. He stripped off the upper half of the coverall at her command. She set to work massaging his aching shoulder muscles. Ward tried to protest, but the unexpected note of authority in her voice cowed him. He lay on an impromptu pad of cargo blankets while she worked her hands deep into his back and shoulders. He cried out several times as she abused several especially tight lumps.

"Quit whining," she said after his third protest. "This is supposed to hurt. I'm squeezing the blood out of the muscles. You'll feel better in the mornin'." She went to work on his cramping thighs and calves next, pressing out the tight knots and working the muscles until the rigid tenseness dissipated. Ward held his fist in his mouth and bit down to keep from crying out while she worked.

Carlo called helpful instructions and mimicked Ward's bleats as he flew towards Marble's base. He brought the van in next to the camp just as Mona reached for the shop cloth to towel the sweat from Ward's shoulders.

"Look alive!" Carlo called out as he made one pass over the compound. "It looks like one of Marble's cars beat us back." Carlo looked from his driver's console into the cargo deck. "Anybody bring any guns?"

Mona leaned over and produced her burp gun.

"Figures," Theisiger said dryly. "Ward?"

Ward shook his head. Theisiger tipped his head towards an athletic bag behind the driver's seat. "There's an Execuline in the bag. Gimme it, along with a couple of extra batteries." He looked around for a place to put them. "Just lay 'em on the seat." Ward rooted through the bag for the weapon and power cells and set them in the passenger's chair.

"What about me?" he asked Carlo. Theisiger glanced around the cab, his eyes locking on a folded shovel racked with the rest of the emergency gear.

"Get that entrenching tool. Unfold the handle and the blade." Ward did as he was told, bafflement on his face. "Now, fold the blade partways, so the tool looks like an 'L.' Turn the locking ring until it's secure." Ward held the tool aloft. It was surprisingly heavy. The hard, pointed blade formed a decent chopping edge. Ward whistled.

"Something I learned from my grandfather," Theisiger said evasively.

Ward looked amused. "I'll bet. All I learned from mine was not to play three-card monte."

Carlo brought the van in at a steep angle, flaring out at the last second for a baby-smooth landing just like he'd seen Seladra do. "Not bad," Ward said dryly.

Theisiger looked hurt. "Not bad for a first time, you mean. How'd you do your first time?"

Ward grinned. "I almost put it in a lake."

Mona sprang out the right-hand cargo door the second the landing gear stopped rocking. She cleared the area, checking for threats while keeping the business end of the burp gun pointed at the camp. Carlo came around the far side of the car, his laser held low and his pockets bulging with batteries. They started towards the main camp area. Ward limped after them, his stiff knee twinging against the abuse.

A scream tore the air. Carlo burst into a run. Ward followed as quickly as his knee would permit. Mona trailed a few steps, the better to place Ward between her and Carlo.

"I'm not sure I remember my way around that rat maze!" Ward called.

"Don't worry about it!" Theisiger replied. He ran to the nearest hanging tapestry and pulled it down, revealing the room behind it. Carlo crossed the carpet to the far wall and tore it down as well.

A woman's voice screamed again. Carlo pointed with his laser in the general direction of a temporary shelter standing in the middle of the camp.

Ward called them to the left and led them around between the shelters. He knew his way from there, having absorbed a bit more of Marble's tour than he thought. He heard a heavy blow land on flesh.

"Shut up, bitch," a man's voice growled.

Ward burst into the boudoir and stopped suddenly. Mona and Theisiger crashed in behind him, almost knocking him over.

Three of Marble's servants surrounded a fourth—Judith. Judith had a dark bruise forming on her cheek, a line of blood trailed from her nose. A hard-faced woman held Judith's arms pinioned over her head. Ward's eyes flicked over Judith's exposed breasts, anger building into rage as he saw the bite marks around one bruised nipple. One man had hiked her skirts around her waist while a second fumbled with his fly. Three parallel bloody scratches ran down his cheek.

All three looked up in surprise as Ward, Mona, and Carlo stood clustered together.

"Hail the conquering hero," the woman said sardonically. The first man dropped his head and slapped Judith again. She cried out and kicked at him as she tried to writhe away. The woman held her arms tighter and laughed.

"What the hell are you doing?" Ward asked, death in his voice. The first man sat up.

The second one dabbed at his bloody face. "You gennelmens, and lady," he said as an aside to Mona, "can have firsts if ya wants." He licked his lips and touched the scratches. "Bitch got fire. There's plenty to go around."

He saw Ward's lips thin into a grim line.

"I mean," he blustered, "it's not as though she matters. She's an immigrant from Earth, not even one of us at all."

Carlo moved to Ward's side, his feet slightly apart. Ward never saw his hand move. One second the servant stood there, his hand pressed to his groin, the next he slumped to the ground with a neat hole in his heart. Carlo held the Execuline at shoulder level, a wisp of coolant gas venting from the barrel sleeve. He glared at the two holding the woman on the bed.

"I'm giving you a chance at a fair fight," Carlo told them conversationally. "You want it?" They looked at each other and scrambled for the exit on the far side. Carlo shot them down as they ran. Ward looked at him, surprised.

"They were clanless scuts," he said grimly. "It's not as though they mattered."

"I've got one question for you—" Ward began.

"Shoot," Carlo replied, the corners of his mouth twitching up in a smile.

Ward grimaced at the bad pun but pressed ahead. "How do you do that? Whenever I've seen anyone get shot with a laser, the steam explosion usually blows bits everywhere."

Carlo put the safety on and slipped the battery cover open. He deftly swapped power cells, then stuck the laser in his pocket. The butt protruded far enough for him to be able to draw it at need.

"Trade secret," he replied. "I'll tell you later."

He used the tip of his index finger to point to the girl. Judith had arranged herself while they talked, folding her legs under her and holding her torn bodice closed with her hand. She stared silently at Ward. He thought her eyes looked a little wild, but she seemed well under control considering that her would-be rapists were still cooling on the floor.

Judith stared at him for a long moment. She dabbed her fingertips to her nose and looked at the thin smudge of blood. She slid her legs gracefully to the edge of the futons and rose to her feet. Ward watched her, the entrenching tool hanging by his side.

Judith slid her shawl from where it lay on the corner of the bed and dropped it in front of her. She used her foot to swirl it into a square. She stepped into it and began to dance. Her eyes never left Ward's face. Ward, entranced, heard neither Theisiger's quiet word to Mona nor the grotesque sounds of the dead being moved outside for disposal. All Ward knew was that Judith danced, and danced for him alone.

She allowed the torn bodice to fall, exposing her abused breasts as she swayed and twisted. Ward felt his throat go dry and his heart hammer as he stared at her nipples, now aroused. She shed each layer of clothing, adapting her dance to accommodate each piece as she removed it. He stared at her like a stunned sheep, unable to move and barely able to breathe.

In the end, naked, she beckoned to him.

He rushed into her willing arms and embraced her. She returned his hard kisses, unzipping his coverall and pulling his clothing away from him. He pulled her down onto the shawl.

She cried out as he entered her and held him close as he tried to pull away. "Gently, baby," she whispered to him, "gently."

Chapter 10

Satterjee looked from the printed manifest to the van loaded half full of carpets and tapestries. "I won't have any trouble selling any of this." He looked around approvingly at the camp, now denuded of its hangings. "Most of this stuff'll go fast, in fact."

Ward mopped his sweaty brow. "That's good. I was starting to worry about cash." He turned and showed the banker to a hastily erected awning. "I'm really glad you could come out so early."

Satterjee mopped his brow. "Actually, I'm glad you called me when you did. There's a small money matter I'd like to take up with you."

Ward looked curious. "Oh?" He gestured Satterjee to a chair. The banker collapsed into it gratefully, fanning his face with his hand.

Ward looked contrite. "I'm sorry I didn't tell you we'd be outside. I hope I didn't ruin your suit."

Satterjee flipped his hand. "Not a problem." He opened his briefcase and removed a thin file folder. "I've managed to line up financial support from some people who want Wing hurt."

Ward opened the file. "Whose money?" He whistled as he looked at the single sheet of paper inside. "Is this right?" he asked incredulously. "Half a million credits?"

Satterjee looked smug. "The figure is correct. Five hundred thousand credits to start, and as much more as you need. Let's just say it comes from secret Wing enemies."

Ward looked skeptical.

Satterjee pressed on. "Look, Wing is desperate. You've hit them from every side *and* killed their pet ringer." He loosened his tie. "You've backed them into a corner."

"What are you leading up to?" Ward asked impatiently.

Satterjee leaned forward, placing his elbows on his briefcase. "I think Wing's going to try something wild, maybe even an assault on you here in Complein. And he'll use all his forces."

"That'll finish 'em," Ward argued. "They couldn't take the strain or the animus from the other clans."

"You're finishing 'em too," Satterjee retorted. "They can't take that strain much longer, either." He ran his hand along the edge of the case. "Ward, your dad didn't think they'd risk the consequences and attack *him* either. Look where he is."

Ward bristled.

The banker cut him off. "Am I wrong?"

Ward thought a moment. "No," he said tiredly. "All right. You've made a good point." He rubbed his chin. "What's that got to do with the money?"

"You need your own stead, Ward," Satterjee answered bluntly, "and your own retainers. You've played the part of the guerrilla leader admirably. Now it's time to get some legitimacy."

"I think I've done pretty well!" Ward snapped.

"You have," Satterjee agreed, "but it's time to move up. You've gained a hell of a reputation since LaPort. You can gather fighters to your banner easily, enough to match Wing. *If* you can pay them." He shrugged. "You can't do that with the estate in receivership and Denison sitting on the piggy bank."

"How does this work?" Ward asked, indicating the folder.

"That is just the beginning," replied Satterjee as he

tapped the page. "I can get more, as much as you need to get back on your feet." He smiled. "Once the Wings are crushed and you get your lands back, you can pay back the advance." He spread his arms wide. "Interest free."

He leaned across and flipped the paper over. Ward scanned the document and looked up. "This says only that you're the originator of the funds. Why?"

"The document has to be registered for authenticity," Satterjee responded smoothly. "I'm already a known associate of yours and a banker. "Who better to advance money to you?"

Ward held the paper a few minutes, rubbing it with his fingertips while he thought. "No deal," he declared.

Satterjee looked stunned. "Why not? It's a sweet deal."

Ward looked skeptical. "A little too sweet. I don't understand it."

"What's to understand?" Satterjee cajoled. "I front you some money. You use it and give it back. We're even."

Ward looked uncomfortable. "I might have gone along if you had bled me on the interest, or set up ruinous terms." He frowned at the document. "This is too easy. You're already getting three percent of what's recovered from Wing. Why don't you want a piece of this?"

Satterjee opened his mouth to answer. Ward cut him off. "I don't much care what I have after this is over, so long as I get Wing." He looked at the file again and handed it back to the banker. "I thought I'd have to mortgage the farm, the cows, and my pet turtle for a fraction of this."

"Let me get this straight," Satterjee replied, astounded. "You're walking away from all the money you need to finish this *because it's free*."

"All I know," Ward answered, "is that some secret somebody is making this offer for unknown reasons—maybe reasons I can't accept." He met Satterjee's eye. "I'm not too sure about this 'secret enemies' business, either." He stood up and began to pace. "The Wings made themselves pretty damned disliked after what they did to my dad. Nobody's been at all secret about that. Quite the opposite, in fact."

He smiled bleakly. "But everyone with the most reason to be pissed, like Denison and the Council, have all been trying to get me to back off. They want this to quiet down. They want unity." He pointed at the paper in Satterjee's hands.

"This *contract*," he said, "gives me carte blanche to continue the fight as long as I want. The Council staff would be the last to want more open war—and that's just what this thing does." He hardened his voice. "No deal. Not until I know more."

Satterjee smiled uneasily, acknowledging defeat and dropping the subject. He pulled a second file from his case and handed it to Ward.

"Well, then, here's my report to date on the search I've done for your family's assets. I've managed to trace about a third. Most has been spent, but it'll provide the basis for an indemnity suit against Wing." He allowed a bit of his disappointment to leak through. "*If* you're ever in the position of being able to pursue a case." He grinned, a bit of his earlier ebullience returning. "You'll note I've already billed you my three percent. I've registered it as a debt account. I'll charge you interest on the balance due, if it'll make you feel better."

Ward smiled. "No, that's okay. Three percent is about right, I think."

Satterjee laughed. "Too bad I didn't realize before I could skin you for more off the top."

"Would you like to join us for lunch?" Ward asked. "We're still getting the kitchen figured out. The menu's a bit bizarre, but we're managing."

"You're living here, then?" Satterjee asked, looking around at the small dome complex.

"Yeah," Ward replied, "me, Mona, and the guards. Theisiger comes and goes."

Satterjee looked at his watch. "Speaking of going, I have to be off. Thank you for your time."

"No problem," Ward answered. "Are you sure you can't stay for lunch?"

"What's on the menu?" Satterjee asked

Ward rubbed his stubbled cheek. "Candied squid, braised artichoke hearts, champagne, and something in tins that looks like raspberry jelly on toast."

"I think that would be the caviar," Satterjee offered.

Ward shrugged. "Sure you won't join us?"

"Sorry," the banker replied, "fish eggs make me sick." They stood and shook hands. "If you change your mind about the loan, Ward," the banker said, "give me a call."

"I'll do that," Ward agreed. He turned away towards the kitchen shelter. "Fish eggs. Who'd have thought?"

Ward started awake, his heart pounding. He groped under the pillow and felt the handgrip of the concealed Execuline. Judith shifted a little in her sleep, rolling deeper into his left shoulder and pressing her breasts against his side. Although sated by her earlier in the evening, he felt himself stir.

He made a face as his heart rate slowed to something approaching normal. "You're jumpy as a cat," he whispered to himself. "Relax." He had just started to drift back to sleep when he heard a low buzz from his bag. He slipped his arm carefully from beneath Judith's head. She grumbled softly as she burrowed towards the warmth, but didn't awaken.

He padded over to the small bag that held his personal effects. He opened it and quietly rifled the contents, looking for the source of the noise. He lifted his shaving bag and saw the comm-link, twin to the one he'd given Seladra. It blinked up at him and buzzed softly.

He grabbed it out of the bag and pressed it to his skin to try and muffle the noise before it woke Judith.

"She's got to be close to call me," he whispered. "I'm sorry, Judith, but I have to go." He bent and disentangled his clothing from her skirt and blouse. He dressed quickly, slipping his shoes over sockless feet.

He stepped out of the shelter and into the waning moonlight before he keyed the comm-link. "Seladra?" he whispered.

"Oh, Ward!" she said, her relief evident in spite of the lousy speaker. "I'm so glad you answered. I need to see you."

"Why?" Ward asked cautiously.

She sounded as though she was about to cry. "Please, Ward. I've missed you."

He looked back at the shelter, then out into the night. His heart went out to her. "Okay," he said at last, "where are you?"

"I'm on the west side of the big truck," she replied. He stepped around the shelter and saw her standing just outside the tree line. She wore shimmering white that reflected the moonlight like a beacon.

"Don't come any closer," he warned. "There are sensors planted. You'll set then off."

"Okay," she replied, "I'll wait here."

Ward crept through the camp towards the security hut, glad that he had agreed to remote the alarm system to the guards' quarters. He stepped inside the shelter and used Marble's elaborate equipment to scan the area. Nothing registered in the banks of detectors except Seladra, still at the clearing's edge, and her car's engine cooling a kilometer away. "If she's got backups," Ward mumbled, "they're the stealthiest folks on the planet." He looked at the winking lights and diodes. "Now, how do I get out without waking the camp?"

He looked around the console, seeking inspiration. His eyes alighted on a knife switch labeled MASTER OFF.

He tore away the protective tape and pulled the switch. The room plunged into darkness.

He left the security hut and quickly crossed the open field. He saw her wave as his form emerged from the gloom. "Please, baby," he whispered, "let this not be a trap." He took a deep breath and walked towards her.

She stood still as he approached, her eyes hidden by her bangs. "Seladra?" he said as he neared. "Sel?"

"Oh, Ward," she cried softly as she flung herself into his arms. "I've missed you so much!" He disentangled her arms from around his neck, and holding her by the elbows, pulled her away. She looked hurt and confused.

"W-what's wrong?," she asked.

He brought his finger to his lips, then pointed back at the compound. She nodded and followed him back into the brush, her arms crossed over her chest. He held a whipping branch away from her and gestured for her to precede him. She surprised him by demurely accepting his help. He'd expected her to give him hell for assisting her. He waited until they'd gone far enough into the woods for her luminous form to be concealed from the camp by intervening trees. He could see the open canopy of her two-person vehicle in the distance.

He stopped and turned towards her. She sprang into his arms, gripping his neck tightly. "Oh, I've missed you!" They held each other a long moment. Gradually, Ward relaxed his embrace. Seladra let him go, wiping away something away with the back of her hand that looked to Ward suspiciously like a tear.

Ward sat on a fallen tree and patted the space next to him with his hand. She sat, placing her hands awkwardly in her lap. She noticed Ward watching her and twiddled her fingers clumsily. Ward frowned. Seladra wasn't by nature awkward.

"I just painted my nails," she apologized, "and didn't let them dry long enough."

"That's not like you," challenged Ward. "You don't usually go for all the paint and powder."

She looked at him, meeting his eye fully for the first time. "I'm doing it for you, Ward," she said ominously.

"Is that why you came?" he asked. "For me?"

"Yes," she replied, "and to get you to call off your vendetta. My father thought you took the ship. He was convinced the evidence was in LaPort. He couldn't find it."

"There was nothing to find," Ward answered grimly.

"Now he's dead," Seladra continued. "You killed him." She rocked back and forth, holding her nails carefully away from her skin while she clasped her upper arms. "Brrr, it's cold," she complained. She lifted a corner of her white gown and worked it between her fingers. "This thing isn't built for warmth, you know." She looked at him. "Would you hold me?"

He wrapped his arms around her, feeling her thin body tremble.

"Another ship is missing, Ward," she declared, startling him as she spoke into his ear. "It last signaled as it entered the Centauri system. Then . . . nothing." She huddled deeper in his embrace, her arms wrapping around his. "The ship's funding came from a cartel based on the Sandiford Peninsula, on the other side of the continent. The three clans involved have all been *very* hostile to the Hegemony." She buried her head in his shoulder. "I think they took it."

"Who're 'they'?" Ward replied.

"The Hegemony," she answered. "The damned Earth government. I think they're behind the piracy, trying to stir up trouble." Her voice faded to a whisper. "It worked with us. Your father dead, my father dead, all on account of the Hegemony."

"Wrong," Ward said harshly. "Wing killed my family, not the Hegemony."

Seladra looked miserable. "And now it's happened

again over in Sandiford. I heard that even my grandfather is willing to privately admit that the attack on your family was a mistake."

Ward laughed harshly and pulled back, taking his arms from around her. "Is that why you're here, another ploy by Skywing to buy me off?"

She looked hurt and angry. "No! I came 'cause I wanted to see you, to hold you."

Ward looked wary. "And that's supposed to make it all better?"

"It's a start," she replied quietly, still whispering.

Ward stood up and faced her."No! It's not," he said angrily. He leaned towards her, placing his hands on either side of her seated form, his face millimeters from hers. "Your family did what they did. Nothing will bring back my kin." His warm breath brushed her lips. "You can't just say, 'Ooops, sorry, we made a mistake,' and expect everything to be all better. It doesn't work that way."

"Then how does it work?" she asked sadly.

"Your folk will pay the way mine did," he said from between clenched teeth, "unless you all pack up and leave West Hills."

She looked at her feet. "I saw Delius' pictures from the attack, all the dead. Is that what you mean? Women, men, children, all dead?"

Ward stood silent a moment, caught in a trap of his own making. "Yes," he said in a defeated voice. He straightened and walked away.

She stood up and carefully approached him. She placed her arms around him, embracing his unresponsive body.

"I think I still love you," he told her, his voice sad and rough, "but that won't make me change my course."

She kissed his throat. "I know," she whispered, her lips feeling the pulse of his carotid artery. "I want you so badly." She looked at him, pleading in her eyes. "I've missed you so much. Please, Ward? One last time before I go back to my family?"

He kissed her. She hugged him hard, pressing herself against him with desperate urgency. He felt himself responding to her, felt the heat for her growing inside him. He wasn't sure who made the first move, but they fell together to the ground. She helped him remove his shirt while he opened her dress. Then they were naked and together. In the moment they joined, Şeladra raked her nails down his spine, as she always did.

He felt the sharp pain instantly dull, then lost all sensation in his back. "What the . . ." His eyes rolled up into his head.

She wept as he collapsed in her arms.

Chapter 11

The bright sun lanced into his head, rousing him from his stupor. "Please let this be a dream," he said. He ran his tongue across his gummy teeth. His back hurt and his joints were stiff, all evidence of a long night on an unforgiving surface. He looked down at himself. His clothing was gone. He was dressed only in a ragged, filthy pair of shorts.

He looked around, squinting against the bright sun. He lay in what appeared to be an oxcart's cargo box. He caught a whiff of animal and heard a cow lowing in the distance.

He tried to roll to his left and sit up, but was brought up short. He gagged against the sudden pressure against his throat. He brought his hand to his neck and swore as he felt a heavy metal collar. He couldn't see it, but it seemed to be an iron affair secured by a rivet. It was attached to a rusty length of chain that ended at a short wooden post nailed to a base welded to the floor of the wagon.

He shifted his body enough to sit up. "Well," he said dryly, "that explains the sore back." He looked around. "I'll be damned," he said as he took in his surroundings, "I'm in a damned camp of Freemen." Several of the nomadic herdsmen stared at him. A breeze gusted through the camp. Ward gagged as the stench of unwashed bodies and uncured hides washed across him.

The Freemen laughed. "He don't gonna smell to good

hisself after a few weeks in that there box," one said. The other nodded sagely. "Hey, civilized! You gonna find out how real men live. Maybe you trade with us now?" They laughed again.

"Damned scavengers," Ward growled.

The first Freeman laughed again. "Don' you get high an' mighty with me. I don' got no chain aroun' my neck!" They walked away, still chortling.

Ward glanced around the camp. He saw his wagon was one of another thirty or so, parked a few meters from a small watering hole. People and animals competed for the brackish water. He guessed there were about fifty adults in this group, but it was hard to be sure. He saw a tiny girl, no more than thirteen or fourteen, hugely pregnant. He had some trouble deciding whether to count her as an adult.

His bemused detachment faded as he saw Seladra. She wore a white blouse, cream-colored jodhpurs, and riding boots. She stood face to face with a dark, swarthy Freeman, an old-fashioned cartridge assault rifle slung over her shoulder. She displayed several clips while the Freeman gesticulated wildly.

They argued briefly before she gave him the rifle and the ammunition. They walked towards the wagon while the man loaded his rifle. The Freeman didn't look particularly happy to Ward. "Now, listen here, Khan," Seladra said to the man, "I want you to keep him here *alive*. Until further notice."

The man grumbled something Ward couldn't understand.

"I've already paid you," Seladra snapped, "that fine rifle and a stock of ammunition. I'll give you more shells to keep him here."

"The gun's obsolete junk," the man retorted, "not enough t' cover our expense."

"What expense?" Seladra retorted with a harsh laugh. "All this rolling flea farm has to do is feed him and keep him from escaping." She let a hint of anger color her voice. "The rifle *is* old, but it's in good shape. Better than any of the junk you have here."

Khan looked slyly at her. "What's to keep me from mebbe takin' this rifle and killin' you?"

They were close enough for Ward to see that what he'd mistaken for a dark complexion was in fact caked dirt.

"The same thing that's going to keep him alive," she replied grimly. She pulled a portable transponder from her pocket. "Don't think I didn't come here covered." She approached the wagon and fixed the transponder to the side. "Not that I need it, but that device is my insurance policy." The man scoffed and shifted the weapon a bit on his shoulder. Other nomads began to cluster around Khan. One of them licked his split and broken lips. He smiled, revealing a mouthful of rotted teeth. Seladra didn't seem fazed.

"My family can track you wherever you go. You assholes can be plotted the same way we plot ocean currents." A bit of her humor returned. "Although the currents move faster." She crossed her arms. "You won't touch me. If you do, my family will track you down. Every last one of you."

"I know," Khan interjected, "an' kill us." He sounded tired, as though he'd heard that threat before.

"Not quickly," she replied, "but sure as hell painfully."

Kahn thought a moment, then acquiesced. He hissed at his supporters. The group began to break up, although the split-lipped man still stared at her hungrily.

Seladra turned to the wagon. Her eyes met Ward's fierce gaze. She looked away. "I'm sorry it's come to this," she said sadly. "I can't just let you kill my family. No matter what they've done, they don't deserve that." Her voice faded. "I didn't want it this way." She looked up at him, her expression as soft as her high Wing cheekbones and proud nose would allow. "Please believe me."

"Not hardly," Ward rasped, and turned his head away.

He heard her sigh. "Keep him alive, Khan. Or else."

Khan laughed without mirth. "That's what you're payin' me for, ain't it?"

"Don't you forget it!" She walked away. Ward watched her go. He curled his arms around his bent legs and rested his forehead on his kneecaps.

His chain rattled. "Hey, boy! Hey!"

He looked up and saw the split-lipped man holding a loop of chain in his hand. "She's got a nice ass," he said. "I wouldn't mind some of that action." He licked his lips obscenely. Ward dropped his head to his knees again, trying to shut the man out. The man jerked the chain hard enough to pull Ward over on his side. Ward gagged and grabbed for the chain, trying to ease the pressure.

The man pulled the chain harder. "Don't you try ignorin' me, boy," he raged. "I'll bust your head!"

Hiss-crack! The chain went slack as the man hopped back, howling. Khan stepped into Ward's line of sight carrying a bullwhip and his shiny new toy. "Damn it, Nuys, leave 'im alone or I'll whip you agin'."

Nuys lifted his head from his crouched position and snarled, "You watch your back, Khan man, or your little bird might get hurt." Khan raised the whip again. Nuys scuttled back and fled.

Khan turned to Ward. "You okay?"

"Yeah," Ward replied, massaging his throat.

"Stay that way," the head man said, and walked away.

The negotiation with Seladra proved to be the only stop of the day. The band traipsed onward, the pace set by the thin oxen. Everybody walked except Ward, even the smallest children, surrounding Khan's two wagons and his herd of a dozen or so pathetic cattle. The family kept their eyes cast downward as they walked. Ward watched, puzzled, until he saw a boy dart down and pick up something squirming in his fingers. Ward looked away as he bit its neck and dropped it in a satchel.

Ward spent considerable time attempting to sort out the family's organization. Khan's family appeared to consist of an older woman, two younger women, two younger men, and at least a half-dozen children. The relative ages were hard to decipher, the product of a harsh, dirty, and malnourished life.

Khan could be either the children's father, grandfather, or both at once. Ward suspected their sexual relationships to be quite messy by his standards. He tried to picture a family tree in his head, but ended up with something that looked like a bramble.

Khan's family moved in the center of a cluster of similar groupings. Men and women wandered away to hunt or gather and rejoined the band at what seemed to be random intervals. The other family groups seemed to follow if they liked, or to depart and join as they wished.

Kahn approached him late in the afternoon, carrying a piece of cargo blanket. "Git yerself under cover. You look like a boiled crawdad."

Ward, his nose and shoulders already blistering, accepted the blanket gratefully. He unfolded it and recoiled in horror as lice and fleas crawled freely over it. He hurled it away with a sound of disgust.

Khan laughed when he saw the discarded blanket. "You'll learn. Bugs is jest a little pain compared to the sun."

Ward looked at Khan. "My bladder's full to bursting."

Khan shrugged. "So? Piss off the back. That's what we do."

The day's travels seemed to end when Khan dropped his bag and sat. The family immediately stopped where they were. Some made rude shelters while others started fires from coals. They barely waited for the flames to settle into coals before spitting and roasting lizards and small animals caught during the day. Other families pressed on, making a little more distance or simply searching for a slightly better place to camp. The herds wandered within the rough pattern of campfires, eating the native plants and the sparse Terran grass. They quickly grazed out the area.

Ward watched Khan's two young men set up a small ammunition factory. One turned a brass casing on a crude, hand-powered lathe, shortening it to fit a smaller rifle. He then took the cut down casing and slid it into the chamber of his bolt action rifle as far as it would go. He rammed the bolt home again and again, forcing it into the chamber until the casing's neck fit tightly enough for the bolt to lock. He then extracted the round with a small chisel and peered at the brass. He used a crude file to swage away the excess metal.

The second man took the bits of brass shavings scavenged from his partner's work and sprinkled them into a tiny bubbling pot of lead. He quickly poured the lead into a mold and pressed it firmly closed. He took the cartridge case, tapped out the expended primer, and fitted another from a carefully hoarded tin with a homemade priming tool. He filled the casing with a lumpy yellowish powder, then tapped the mold against a rock. A single rough bullet tumbled out. He quickly filed the spall away, catching the excess grains on his work cloth. Ward watched, fascinated, as the two men completed four cartridges in an hour's work, before they ran out of lead.

One of Khan's women brought Ward his first food of the day. His growling stomach grew silent as he saw his dinner. The lizard had been cooked on a spit until its skin split.

"No, thanks," Ward said as she offered it to him.

"It's good eatin'," she said, rubbing her belly.

He refused it again. She shrugged and bit into the lizard. Ward winced and looked away as he heard her crunching through its tough outer skin. She walked away and sat with the other woman a short distance from the wagon. Ward soon became painfully aware they were watching him like an animal in a zoo.

Ward had just begun to doze, still sitting up, when a hand grabbed his hair. It wrenched his neck and smacked the back of his head against the wagon. Ward scrabbled his hands against a hairy arm, trying to free his aching skull from the other man's grip. His head smashed repeatedly into the cargo box's rim until his eyes filled with stars and he dropped his hands.

"That's better, boy," Nuys' harsh voice whispered in his ear. "Your pap done me wrong. Ah'm gonna do you like he done me." He slammed Ward's head against the rim again.

"Look, Mama," Ward heard in the distance, "Nuys is at the wagon!" Ward heard the faint flurry of motion, then the sound of slaps and blows. Nuys released him. Ward slumped into the box. He raised his aching head over the rim and saw Nuys kicking the woman. She lay still, making no effort to either escape or defend herself. Ward cleared his throat to call out when he heard the click of racking back the bolt of an automatic rifle. He whipped his head around and saw Khan aiming at Nuys.

"Git away from her!" Khan demanded.

"He done me wrong!" Nuys protested, pointing at Ward. "I'm here 'cause his pap hated me!"

"You're here 'cause you raped a Tuch' girl an' broke her jaw so she couldn't talk," Khan answered. "You threw her down a well and left her for dead. You'd have been shot if you hadn't escaped."

"You bastard!" Ward hissed, drawing Nuys' gaze.

Nuys looked at him with loathing and raised his fist. Ward heard the *snick* as Khan took the safety off his weapon.

"You get away from here," Khan threatened, "'afor I shoot you." Nuys looked at the rifle and backed away.

"You think you're so tough?" Nuys snarled. "Let's just see how good your pissant rifle is against m'suit." He turned and stalked away.

Ward looked at Khan. "He's a rapist and you let him stay here?"

Khan looked unconcerned. "He's a Freeman now. He ain't done my family no harm. What he done elsewhere ain't my problem."

"Does he really have battle armor?" Ward asked.

"Yeah," Khan replied. "He likes to show it off every now and again. I ain't real sure it works, though, so don't get no ideas."

"What if it does work?" Ward challenged. "You're going to let him stay?"

Khan shrugged. "Ain't my place to tell him to stay or go." He snorted and spat in the dirt. "B'sides, ain't a whole lot around here lower than him." He glanced at Ward. "'Ceptin' you." Khan seemed to think this was funny. He strolled away, the rifle cradled in his arms, chortling at his joke.

It soon became obvious to Ward that while Nuys was a Freeman and entitled to go where he chose, he wasn't particularly well liked. The other family groups avoided him in camp and kept away from his meager wagon and mangy herd while they traveled. They quickly gathered their children whenever he stalked through camp.

Khan's family soon settled into a routine concerning Ward. Khan looked after Ward the same way he did his cattle, without affection, but as an asset to be protected from unnecessary danger. The women of the family cared for and fed him, especially a younger girl named Kit. She stayed with him as often as she could, bringing him food and taking away his waste pail. She seemed to be about twelve and very thin, but had taken a lively interest in him.

Ward wasn't entirely certain about Freeman customs, but her signals were damn near universal. If she meant what he thought she meant, then she'd run the risk of looking like the pregnant fourteen-year-old. The very idea made Ward blanch. The thought of bedding any child that young repelled him. The fact that she was filthy and had lice didn't help.

Nuys badgered him only once in the week that followed. Khan had taken a paint pot and gone out to tar the sores that appeared on several of his cows. Most of the family drifted after him, holding the animals in place while he smeared the rough salve on their bloody flanks. Nuys leapt to take advantage of the family's momentary inattention.

Ward sat up as he saw Nuys approach. "I thought you'd be around," he said conversationally. "Screwed any little girls recently?"

Nuys' split lips skinned back to reveal his rotting teeth. "Naw," he replied, "looks like the only one screwed around here is you." He laughed at his own joke. "B'sides, none o' them bastids'll touch me while I got m'suit."

"I wouldn't proud that around too much if I were you," Ward warned. "Even if it works, you'd only be able to lord it over them until you go to sleep." He drew his finger across his throat.

A rock zinged past Nuys' head. They both turned. Kit, about twenty meters away, stooped for another stone. "Now you git away from him!" she cried as she threw. It went wide, almost hitting Ward. Nuys stared at her, licking his lips. "Someday," he said, and backed away.

Ward lost track of time. He lost weight. Sores broke out on his legs and buttocks from the constant pressure of sitting. Biting flies attacked the pustules while he slept, spreading the infections. He ate whatever they placed in front of him, wolfing down the half-cooked portions. His skin crawled with filth and lice. He wrapped himself in the blanket at night, unconcerned with the bugs and germs it carried.

The wagons clattered on in their interminable way and Ward lost track of the days. One particularly hot and dusty afternoon, Ward was trying to doze in his rusty, smelly bed. He eventually surrendered and sat up, wincing at the pain from the sores. He watched Khan and his men preparing for a hunting trip as they loaded their rifles and saddled three of the sturdiest-looking oxen. They angled away from the main body around noon. Ward watched them slowly shrink in the distance until the heat haze obscured them entirely.

He realized he wasn't the only one watching their departure. He turned and saw Nuys cross between Khan's two wagons. His heart beat faster as he saw Nuys carried a large-bore hunting rifle. The Freeman had attached a sleeve bayonet hammered from a piece of pipe. This was what Ward had been waiting for.

Nuys snarled as he came around behind the slow, ox-drawn cart. Ward pulled back as far as he could, trying to keep the post and its meager cover between him and the Freeman. Nuys, pointing the rifle with one hand at Ward's middle, tried to climb on the back of the moving wagon. Ward looked around at the other Freemen wagons. Most of the other families simply gawked, while a few looked away. No one moved to help.

Nuys levered himself up into the wagon's bed. He continued aiming the rifle at Ward's midsection. Ward moved back as far as he could, putting the pole between him and Nuys. It wasn't much, but if the turncoat stepped within eight feet of Ward now, Ward could at least try to reach him with a lunge towards the rifle's muzzle. Nuys grinned, his rotted teeth visible, then screamed.

He tumbled backward off the wagon, dropping his rifle as he fell. Ward jumped forward, almost hanging himself as he groped for the weapon. He grabbed it by the bayonet, cutting his hand. He recovered it, cradling its comforting weight in his arms. He glanced over the back of the wagon and saw Kit standing over Nuys' flailing body. She raised a crude axe and struck him. Nuys screamed once, high and shrill, then lay still.

Ward stood up, swaying as the oxen plodded along the hardpan. He raised the rifle and opened the breech enough to see the shell within. He closed the action, snapped the safety off, and aimed at the middle of the post.

Snap! The hammer fell on a dud shell. He quickly worked the stiff lever, ejecting the dead round and racking another into the chamber. He brought the weapon to his shoulder just as one of Khan's women reached the back of the wagon. Kit trailed her, still carrying the ax.

Ward pulled the trigger. *Ka-whoom!* The rifle jerked and slammed into his shoulder. He stumbled back, deafened and stunned by the rifle's concussion. Oxen and cattle bolted on either side and wagons scattered as surprised drivers tried to get control over their frightened beasts. The oxen pulling Ward's wagon bellowed and lurched forward, throwing him off balance.

He stumbled backwards, taking two stutter steps before he jerked the chain rigid against the weakened post. He windmilled his arms desperately a moment before the post snapped cleanly in two, tumbling him off the end of the wagon and into the arms of Khan's startled woman.

He fell heavily on top of her. She didn't move as he got to his feet and reeled. Kit, still holding the ax, stumbled towards him. She stopped in confusion as he hefted the post with his left hand and brandished the rifle in his right. He awkwardly bent and worked the lever action again, holding the barrel between his knees. He had no way of knowing if another round chambered. He hefted the rifle and waved it at the two remaining women. They fell back in confusion. The older woman screamed at the men in the other families to help.

"Ain't our problem!" They laughed.

Ward stumbled through the moving wagons towards Nuys' cart. He leapt into the cargo box and whipped away the tarp. He saw an abused set of obsolete battle armor lying nested among Nuys' personal effects.

He looked up to see consternation amongst the Freemen as they realized his intent. He saw wagons stopping and men with firearms dismounting.

He quickly opened the front carapace and flipped the main power coupling from STAND-BY to ON. He fidgeted as he waited for the diodes to wink, indicating the system had power. Nothing. He checked the energy cells and saw they held a fifty-six percent charge. He almost cried in frustration. "Why the hell isn't there any juice in the system?"

He looked up and saw the Freemen closing in. "Think, damn it, think!" He opened the power cells' housing and saw the corrosion buildup on the inside of the attachment sleeves. He quickly unplugged the battery contacts and worked them free of their connection points. He rubbed them shiny with a piece of cloth and reattached them. He heard the actuators hum as they began to draw power. He shed tears of joy as he closed the battery cover. The diagnostic diode winked as the system performed its internal checks.

He looked up. Two Freemen, braver or more stupid than the rest, skulked towards him. One emerged from cover, then ducked back as Ward raised the rifle to his shoulder.

The suit began to beep softly, indicating that the system had completed the diagnostic run. He checked the results, looking down at the suit while pointing the rifle at the two Freemen. System efficiency read eighty percent, the coil gun was dead, the boost-pack's fuel tanks were empty, and the laser indicated marginal use. He smiled happily. "I guess I should be glad anything works at all."

He slipped his legs inside the suit, then swore venomously as the chain around his neck rattled. "How the hell am I going to get rid of this?" he asked himself. H eyes locked on the suit's laser. He closed his eyes wearily. "Oh, this is going to hurt," he murmured as he crawled back out of the armor.

He reached inside the suit, bending the arm in a forty-five degree angle. He twisted his neck shackle around so the rivet and chain lay just in front of his left ear. He placed the shackle over the end of the laser and reached into the suit as far as he could. He could just tickle the laser's firing key. He closed his eyes, took a deep breath, and toggled the laser.

He thought at first he'd shot himself. Blinding pain arched through his neck and shoulder as bits of molten metal spattered him. He fell back, bringing his hand up to cover the worst of the wounds. He screamed as he seared his palm on the red-hot neck shackle and then again as he pulled the ends of the collar away from his neck.

The laser bolt galvanized the Freemen into action. Several clots of men began to drift towards him, as unenthusiastic as they were uncoordinated. Each Freeman seemed eager to hang back and wait for his fellows to take the lead. The two in front, made of sterner stuff, charged forward. Ward brandished the rifle at them. They both chose to sprint at once, rather than one supporting the other. Ward aimed at the Freeman on the left and pulled the trigger. He heard a *pfaff*, rather than the rifle's full-throated roar, as the round misfired. He was reasonably certain the bullet lodged in the barrel rather than dribbling out the end.

Ward ducked as the right-hand man worked himself far enough around to blast away with an archaic shotgun. The pellets left jagged, irregular holes in the thin metal of the cargo box before they ricocheted off the battle armor and into the sky. He heard the man cursing as he tried to reload his weapon.

Ward slithered over to the armor and opened the front carapace enough to slip his legs inside. He wriggled around until he found the hip sockets, then wormed his feet into them. He placed his hands along the sides of the chest opening and hauled himself in while trying to stay below the level of the cargo box. He quickly reached for the helmet.

A second shotgun blast ripped through the cargo box just as he sealed the suit. The man with the shotgun popped his head over the rim of the box. Ward kicked at him and missed, his joints moving too sluggishly to make contact. The man tumbled back with a cry as Ward sat up in the back of the cargo box.

He looked through the streaked faceplate and saw the Freemen warily circling him, holding their weapons in front of them like talismans. One raised his rifle and fired. The rest followed suit, showering Ward with a ragged fusillade of bullets, bits of iron, and shotgun pellets. Several Freemen screamed and fell, the victims of their companions' bad aim or ricochets. Ward covered his faceplate with his arms and waited for the barrage to stop.

The wagon began to look like a leaky bucket. Ward heard the ox tethered to it bellow and collapse, victim of a wild shot.

He triggered his laser in the general direction of one cluster of Freemen and was rewarded by screams as the badly tuned weapon found its mark. The painting laser didn't seem to function at all, providing Ward with little feedback as to where his shots hit.

The Freemen broke and ran as he levered himself over the top of the cargo box. He awkwardly clumped to the edge of the cluster of wagons, then out into the wastelands. A few shots followed him before the bulk of the Freemen went back to their wagons. Ward looked back only once to see a tiny figure clutching an ax and standing on the edge of the plain.

He checked the suit's navigation equipment. The battle armor's AI had been obsolete at the time Nuys had taken it. The navigation consisted only of a positioning display and an inertial compass. The display was both out of date and lacking a zoom function. It placed him about three hundred kilometers from the nearest civilized habitation and almost a thousand from Complein.

He cycled through the suit's communications systems. He wasn't terribly surprised to find them all dead, the victims of neglect. His only working system was an obsolete line-of-sight communications turret mounted over his eyes. He laughed grimly.

He stumped off towards Complein, all too aware of the trail he left. "A blind man with a congested bloodhound'll see that," he said to himself. He pressed on into evening, growing increasingly weary as his pain multiplied. The day's travel would have been punishing, even without his various wounds and sores. The suit's reduced efficiency hurt him as well, battering him bloody as it moved around him.

Ward recalled Stallart telling him that "powered armor must either lead or follow." Ward knew that the suit's AI attempted to reduce pressure on all the contact sensors to zero, moving the suit around the body as it reacted to pressures placed against the sensors by the wearer. He had never realized just how much the system depended on abrasion and trading pressures. The hours of repetitious movement first irritated Ward's dry, filthy skin, then raised welts and blisters that broke, and finally abraded the flesh beneath. Every step became more agonizing than the last. The pain from his worn flesh joined the throbbing hurts of his burns, scrapes, and infected sores.

His right knee joint failed without warning, a mirror of his combat loss during the fight with Marble. The joint bent, straightened, then refused to move again. Ward found himself shifting his weight from side to side as he dragged the useless leg. That caused additional abrading against his genitals that triggered its own agony.

The sky darkened. Ward used his laser to zap dinner, a long-tailed lizard. A second shot opened it along its length, exploding its internal organs. A third shot cooked it as well as a Freeman campfire. He held his gorge as he ripped pieces of half-cooked flesh from its backbone and stuffed them into his mouth. The salty meat compounded his intense thirst.

He switched to the suit's sensors after dark, then almost fell down a steep ravine. The light intensifier goggles and infrared suit systems lacked depth imaging. He checked for a lidar or millimeter wave system that would provide a three-dimensional display. He wasn't surprised to find the suit had neither.

He quickly realized that stumbling around in a two-dimensional world full of things one could fall into would be pointless, if not fatal. He worked his way down into the narrow defile he'd almost explored headfirst. He discovered a narrow north-south gully at its base. The steep walls sloped vertically the last several meters, except where landslides of talus piles had slid into it, making natural ramps that permitted egress. The north end of the gully grew thick with branches and fronds that overhung the sandy stretch. A smaller rivulet fed the southern end.

He slaked his thirst by licking the trickling water from the rocks. He made a fire from several pieces of dry wood collected from the stand at the north end. Wriggling out of his armor, he used the firelight to inspect the rivulet more closely. Barely enough water leaked from between the rocks to wet the sand below, much less to form a pool.

Using dampened handfuls of sand to scrub his tattered body, he washed himself in spite of the lack of water. His burned hands stung and swelled from the abuse.

He removed his shorts, flinching as the material pulled away from his infected flesh. He soaked the soiled clothing, pressing the cloth to the rock to wet it, then wringing it out. He wrinkled his nose at the stench. He wanted to throw it away, but it was the only protection he had from the battering of the frozen joint.

The only part of his body he dared not touch was the deep burn on his neck. It leaked and throbbed with every heartbeat. He screamed the one time he probed it with sand. Its fire stayed with him constantly, burning strong and fierce, and spiking whenever a drop of perspiration rolled into the wound.

He finished his ablutions, waiting until his skin dried before he brushed the last of the sand away. He felt better for having cleaned himself, even though he hadn't done as much as he would have liked. He ran his hands over the sodden cloth of his shorts, feeling the scabs trapped in the material. His flesh crawled at the thought of putting them back on.

He carried the garment back to where his suit lay, a tumbled mass in the dark. He picked a number of fronds by touch from the copse at the far end of the gully, hissing as his burned fingers touched the leaves. He jammed the fronds into the soft earth above his suit, soon making a crude shelter for the night. He hung the shorts on a frond and slithered back into the suit.

He settled inside, only then noticing the feel of the sand against his back. "Great," he said to himself, "one more thing to piss me off." He closed the clamshell and put his helmet on but didn't seal either. He keyed his tongue switch from ON to STAND-BY, the better to conserve energy. In spite of his pain and his fear, he fell asleep at once, comforted by the warm crackle of the fire. His last thought was of breathing free air, even if it smelled.

The bright sun streaming through the fronds awakened him. He tried to sit up. The suit wouldn't move.

He almost panicked at first, thinking himself trapped in immobile battle armor. Reason returned and he remembered the tongue switch. The armor came alive under his touch. He sat up, the front carapace swinging open. He closed it and looked around.

The fire had gone out. Ward glanced across at the eastern face of the gully and saw something shimmering on a ledge several meters above the gully floor. He slipped out of his armor and walked over to his dried shorts. He held them up, still stiff and crackly with ingrained dirt. He cringed at the thought of wearing them.

"Better to go naked," he told himself.

The shimmer came from behind a jumble of rocks along the gully's overhung east side. A small talus pile led up the left side to the overhang; the ledge in front of it was a sheer drop of several meters to the sand below. Ward very carefully climbed up the pile, rising on one knee to look inside. His heart hammered and he almost fell when he recognized what lurked within.

He knew that New Hope's giant amoebas were very rare and very dangerous. He recalled from his biology classes that they weren't really amoebas, but they looked and acted like their microscopic namesakes, even to the point of asexual reproduction. Ward knew that they tended to be drawn to thermal registrations or sonic vibrations.

This one looked to him to be a respectable member of its kind. It was several meters long, with a tough, transparent outer layer that revealed the actions of its internal organs. It appeared to be torpid. Ward breathed a sigh of relief. It would likely remain still until warmed by the heat of the sun.

He scrambled back to the battle armor and climbed in. He brought the power levels up and stood, wincing as the thigh joint again rammed into his testicles. His calves still felt on fire from the previous day's exertions. He stepped, feeling his hurts multiply as the suit reawakened the aches and pains. He sighed as he looked up the slope he'd descended the night before.

"There has to be a better way," he grumbled. He followed the dry watercourse down the gully, working himself between the two narrow flanges of rock that had tumbled across the gully's mouth, almost hiding it. He saw his tracks from the previous day cross almost directly in front of his concealed spot. He squeezed between the fallen rocks and moved to recapture his trail to the top of the ridge line.

A glint of sunlight on metal drew his eye down to the lower terrain he'd crossed the day before. He shaded his face and used the suit's limited zoom to focus on the reflection. He locked in on three Freemen. They appeared to be tracking him, moving along his trail with dogged persistence.

Ward leaned against the rock, shaking his head at the odds. He knew his suit desperately needed a rebuild. He was too worn down by the previous day's exertions to sustain a chase. His bird-footed hobble wouldn't get him far against three men who knew the wastelands far better than he.

"I can hold 'em off forever, or at least until I have to eat or sleep." He held the laser up. "And you, my friend, aren't accurate enough to hit a barn at ten paces."

He looked back at the inviting shade of the gully. "When in doubt, hide," he told himself, "and step very carefully around the amoebas." He scrambled back up the ravine as quickly as his tired body would allow. He laid down beneath the impromptu shelter and climbed out of the suit. He gathered a pile of leaves and put that beside the armor, then lay down in it to imprint the leaves with his body. He struggled to his feet and ran to the copse.

There, he snapped another frond, wet it, and dragged it across the fire pit and the bed of leaves. He then swished the frond in front of him as he slipped back behind the small cluster of greenery. He found what he sought: another trickle that fed the local growth. He hid behind a moss-covered overhang and waited through the balance of the morning and on into the afternoon.

The Freemen wandered down the steep side of the ravine, following Ward's trail late in the day. Ward had fallen asleep several times while he lay in the fronds, grateful for the rest, but afraid they would take him by surprise. He needn't have worried. Khan announced his arrival by raising his assault rifle and firing several rounds at the suit. The first several shots were wide of the mark before he put a round into the open carapace.

They warily entered the campsite, pointing at Ward's tracks and the heavy drag marks of the wet frond. Ward saw them talking and gesturing amongst themselves, but he was too far away to understand their words. They seemed to be arguing. One of the younger men pointed at the places where Ward had dragged the frond. The other man ignored him and started towards the copse where Ward hid. Khan called him back.

The younger man half turned, stopping alongside the talus pile. He turned to argue, shouting back at the others: "That birdshit's trickin' us. He din't get et by no 'meba." Ward had to fight hard to suppress a groan. Then sudden movement above the Freeman caught his eye.

The Freeman looked up just as the glistening giant amoeba fell on him, knocking him to the ground and engulfing him before he had a chance to cry out. The westering sunlight had apparently fallen on it long enough to rouse it, and the Freeman's shouts had marked him as a target.

Ward crammed his fist in his mouth to keep from making a noise. The transparent outer flesh provided no concealment from the actions of its internal organs. The Freeman trapped within screamed silently and kicked as organelles spewed the digestive juices that would jelly him for easier consumption.

The other two Freemen ran up. Khan fired a dozen rounds into the thing, mercy-killing his fellow but accomplishing little else. The effect on the amoeba was no greater than an equivalent number of rounds fired into a bowl full of gelatin.

Khan gave up in disgust as the amoeba, with the man's face pressed against its side in a death rictus, slowly crawled towards its lair.

"There's a whole herd about!" the older man cried, on the edge of panic. Khan looked at him, his face full of disgust.

"All right, I believe you. The critter ate him." He looked at the suit again, then swore. "Ah should've killed that bastid Nuys when ah had the chance." He looked at the slowly moving amoeba. "That bitch is gonna kill me!"

Khan looked morose a moment, then trudged back to Ward's trail. He started to grunt and struggle up the steep ravine, backtracking his earlier course. He'd resorted to using the rifle butt as a walking stick to help him get a purchase on the steep earth. The other man bent to recover the fired shells. He tried to angle in towards the dead man's rifle, but thought better of it when he saw how close to the rock ledge it had fallen.

"Come on, damn it!" He looked even more unhappy than Khan, and glanced back several times at the lost rifle, but he stumbled after the head man. Ward waited for them to pass over the top of the ravine and move far out of sight before he allowed himself to relax even a little.

He crossed back to his armor and looked inside. The rifle bullet had entered at a steep angle and ricocheted around the inside of the suit, destroying sensors, systems, and even the thin padding that protected the contact points. He hoped the suit would hold together for one final task.

The amoeba had survived Khan's rifle without apparent discomfort. "I wonder how it'll like laser fire," he said with a feral grin. He climbed slowly to his feet after getting back in the suit. The internal gyroscope had been shot away. He stumbled and fell several times as the system's primitive AI, unable to compare feedback and sensor input, sent random compensations to the servos. It seemed to Ward as if he were walking on marbles. He bashed and bruised himself several times before he gave up and simply crawled on hands and knee. His right leg still remained rigid behind him.

He eventually pulled himself high enough up on the talus pile to see the thing, lying recumbent in its lair. Ward saw the internal workings through the evening gloom. Ripples surged along its sides as it swilled its prey in a soup of digestive enzymes. Ward brought his laser up and pointed it at the amoeba. It didn't move, not even when he shot it.

The beam hit its middle, losing coherence in its fluids as the laser's energy expended itself into the amoeba's body. Water flashed into steam, exploding the middle third of the creature. Matter drenched the front of his armor, mixed with pieces that were identifiably human. He closed his eyes and screamed, firing until the laser's safety interlocks closed to prevent the weapon from overheating.

He opened his eyes. The thing was dead, burned and lazed into a puddle. He shined his map light into the ledge's dark recesses. He almost crowed with glee as he saw the Freeman's inorganic equipment, apparently expelled by the creature. He recovered the man's ratty, open-toed boots, equipment pouch, water bottle, and found the rifle. He worked the bolt until he was certain he'd cleared the magazine. He was pleased to see four shells, two homemade, littering the sand. He collected his filthy shorts, piling the shells inside the cloth for safekeeping until he dressed in his rags.

Abandoning the PBA, he walked northwards the following morning, veering as his rifle caused the compass' primitive needle to wander. He found water once, slurping it greedily in spite of its bitter, brackish taste. He saved his own bottled water. He found a dead ox around midday and chased the scavengers away long enough to slash several hunks of meat from its flank. He ate them raw, grimly aware that his chance for a fire had died with his suit.

He stumbled on into the hot afternoon sun, still heading north. He realized by midafternoon that he'd gotten himself in serious trouble. He felt feverish in the blistering sun, then chilled. His stomach surged and he lost control of his bowels. He fell to his knees, vomiting up the half-digested gobbets of meat. He lay, moaning and holding his stomach as it surged in knots and cramps. Twice he attempted to press on, and twice he collapsed on the ground, folded around the agony in his gut. He blacked out several times, aware that each time he awakened the sun had visibly moved further in the sky. The pain in his gut grew worse each time he awoke.

He began to hallucinate, imagining himself as a little boy, wrestling for the school prize and his clan's honor. Benno sat in the stands, the proud parent, looking very dignified except for Kit's ax, which stuck out of his head.

"You've got to win," Benno told him, "got to save us all."

Ward adjusted his tights and looked around. His opponent entered the ring. Seladra grinned at him, then went into a wrestler's crouch.

Ward looked at his father, who still hadn't noticed the ax. "But, Dad," he cried in a little boy's voice, "I love her."

"I know, son," Benno said, smiling sadly, "but you can't let that stop you."

Seladra jumped on him. She seemed to be everywhere, pinning his arms and legs as he thrashed and kicked. Her face appeared close to his for a moment. He punched her and heard her cry out and roll away. They stood panting, about a meter apart. A laser appeared in her hand.

"I'm sorry, Ward," she said.

A finger tapped his shoulder. Ward looked back. Benno, his brains leaking out of his skull, handed him Kit's ax.

"You got to do it, boy," Benno said. "It's the only thing that will save the family." Ward whirled and struck with the ax, hitting Seladra again and again until his senses faded.

He thought he awoke into another dream. He lay, swaddled and bound, in the back of a cargo van. Mona peered down at him, her right eye puffy with a classic shiner.

"Where am I?" he asked.

The maybe-Mona looked down at him smiled. "Well, look who's awake," the phantasm said. "'Bout time, too." She glanced around. "You're inside a cargo van on your way back to Complein. Dr. Silman will meet us there."

"What happened?" His throat was dry and parched. He licked his lips. They felt cracked and split. The sour taste of vomit lay heavy on them. He almost retched again.

"We were hoping you could tell us," Mona answered. "We found you lying in the sand, curled up and crying your father's name. When we tried to lift you up, you attacked me." She brought her hand to her swollen eye. "Clocked me good, too."

She looked towards the front of the car. "We were lucky Carlo had his suit on. You went after him with that old rifle. He had to blast it to get it away from you. He also used his armor to hold you long enough to get restraints on you."

"I see," Ward answered. "It's too bad you're all hallucinations. I could use a drink." Mona shook her head in slow negation. "I'm sorry, Ward," Mona said, "but until we find out what's wrong with you, we don't dare."

Ward relaxed into his bindings. "That's okay, I didn't think you could."

Mona poured some water from a bottle into a cup and dabbed the end of a clean shop cloth in the water. She held the cloth to Ward's lips, wetting them. He sucked greedily on the cloth, trying to draw every molecule into his parched body.

The water went a long way to convince him of her existence.

"How'd you find me?" he asked scratchily, once the worst of his thirst had been slaked.

Mona looked across the van at him. "Judith," she said flatly.

"I don't understand," Ward replied.

Mona frowned. "We couldn't figure out how an abduction team had gotten inside the compound, snatched you, shut off the alarms, and escaped. There wasn't any evidence to speak of and a lot of what we did find didn't make any sense." She raised her hand, palm up, as though pointing to someone. "The kitten thought that perhaps you'd gone to meet someone and had turned off the alarm yourself."

She laughed. "We couldn't figure out why you'd go without taking your laser, unless it was to meet someone you'd feel safe with. Judith pointed out that under the circumstances you must have been decoyed by a woman." She looked sour. "Stal told me where he was going the night he got killed. I knew you'd gone to see that tramp." Her lips thinned as she looked down at him. "Wasn't hard to figure out the rest." She almost smiled again. "You know, Judith's a lot smarter than she looks. I thought she kept her brains between her legs."

Theisiger stepped back from the driver's console. He looked rested and fit, though a little worn. "Mona's being too modest," Carlo said. "She deserves much of the credit."

Ward looked a question at her. She shrugged.

"She took a job with Wing as a scullery maid. It was too far down the food chain to be noticed. One day they sent her to wash cars. One was Seladra's—"

"Bitch!" Mona interrupted.

Theisiger smiled and continued. "Anyway, she checked the locator presets on her vehicle, then went through the direction finders and transponder frequencies. She copied those down and transmitted 'em to me. We've been running 'em down ever since."

"That led us to the Freemen," Carlo said. "Nice chaps. I'd like to send them a little diphtheria for Christmas. Anyway, one old broad thought we worked for somebody else. She told us you'd stolen the suit and that her husbands had gone after you. She begged us not to kill her or the men, then curtly informed us we owed her money for your care and feeding as well as for the use of her granddaughter. The change in her manner was bizarre."

Carlo turned to check on his autopilot. Mona picked up the story.

"We followed your trail to that abandoned suit. We knew you'd been in it recently from the thermal residue. We figured you hadn't gotten far. Carlo started a circular search pattern while I used high-altitude imaging and a computer scanner to find your trail. It was a simple matter from there."

"How'd you know I wasn't dead?" Ward asked.

"Easy," Mona replied, "there were still Wings alive in Skywing."

"We have to go back!" Ward suddenly said, struggling against his restraints.

"Why?" Mona asked, alarmed. "I hope you're not having another seizure."

"That suit brought me through a lot," he replied. "I

can't just abandon it." Mona got a dermal patch out of the medical kit and slapped it on Ward's sunburnt skin.

His voice began to wander as the drug took effect. "B'sides, 'twas better than who had it deserved . . ." He drifted away.

"Okay, Ward," she said to his sleeping form. She turned and banged on the partition that separated the driver from the cargo space.

"Carlo," she called, "we have to go back."

Chapter 12

Satterjee sat nervously in the anteroom beneath Theisiger's office. He stood and gaped as Ward entered. "Mona told me a little, but I had no idea!" Ward appeared to Satterjee as if he'd camped out in a vegetable slicer.

Ward's hands, face, and ears shone with the whitish glisten of spray-on skin used to keep burns moist and protected. Satterjee knew it was expensive on New Hope and as a result doctors usually doled it out sparingly. The thick layer on Ward told Satterjee just how seriously he'd been burned.

Ward also wore a pad on his neck, a brace on his knee, and had a plastic shunt jutting from his forearm. He looked wan and tired but alert as he took Satterjee's measure.

"How is he?" Satterjee asked the doctor.

"Well," Silman replied, "he's got second and third degree burns, dehydration, sun poisoning, anemia, malnutrition, a strained knee, a minor secondary infection, and a raging case of muta-form contamination. Other than that, I'd say he's fine."

Satterjee furrowed his brows. The effect looked comical with his bald head. "Muta-forms?" he asked. "How'd he manage that?"

"*I*," Ward interjected dryly, "ate or drank something that contained local cultures. I'll be taking my lunch out of a needle until Silman here gets my intestines under control." Ward pursed his lips in irritation. "I'd appreciate it if you didn't talk over me like I was a coffee table," he concluded petulantly.

"Sorry," Satterjee and Silman replied together. Satterjee jumped to fill the awkward pause that followed. "Mona called me up here, Ward. She said it was important."

"Yes," he replied. He turned to the physician. "Doc, if you'll excuse us." Carlo followed Silman to the door and locked it. Ward turned to look at the banker. Satterjee looked at Ward's eyes. They held no human feeling or compassion.

"Is that loan still available?" Ward asked.

Satterjee felt his heart skip a beat. "Yeah, sure. How much do you want?"

"The whole thing," Ward replied. "You said I could get as much as I needed. Do you stand by that?"

Satterjee silently nodded.

"Good," Ward said, "I want five hundred thousand by the first of next week. The same again by the week after that. I'll send you requisitions from then on until Wing is no more. Can you do it?"

Satterjee nodded slowly, taken aback at the sheer size of Ward's demand. "Do you think you'll really need that much?"

"No," Ward replied, "probably not. I want to see just how deep your friends' pockets are." He smiled thinly. "Besides, when'll be the next time I get an interest-free loan?"

Satterjee took out a notepad. "How do you want the funds distributed?"

"You'd better take that up with my chief of staff," Ward answered, cocking his finger at Theisiger.

Carlo looked as startled as Satterjee felt.

"Chief of staff?" Carlo said. "What gives, Ward?"

"I need your expertise," Ward explained. "I'm willing to pay you for it. Draw yourself a salary. Be generous."

"Ward," Carlo argued, shaking his head, "this isn't necessary."

"Yes, it is," Ward answered. "I'm going to be hiring every freelance suit and mercenary with PBA in West Hills, and maybe the continent as well. I'll also be recalling Tuchman retainers to the flag. They won't respect you if they don't think you're getting paid what you're worth."

Carlo didn't look happy, but he acceded with a single dip of his chin.

"You know," Satterjee mused, "my backers might be able to help with the troops. I know they've got some good men on retainer. Would you like them?"

Ward made a point of considering it. "Hmm, I'll tell you what. Have them come down to the Hardesty place the day after tomorrow. Carlo and I'll take a look at them."

"Hardesty?" Satterjee looked puzzled. "What's up with them?"

"Our next stop," Carlo interjected.

"I don't get it," Satterjee replied.

"Come with us," Ward answered, "you will."

The three left together for Ward's ground car. Satterjee saw that Benno's old logo had been crossed out in favor of a Wing symbol. Ward had in turn obliterated that.

"What are you going to use for your clan sign, Ward?" Satterjee asked as they buckled themselves in. Carlo brought the ground car up smoothly, adjusting the outputs to perfectly balance the vehicle.

"My token will be the amoeba," Ward replied coolly.

"The what?" answered Satterjee, revolted.

"The amoeba," repeated Ward, "is a survivor. It engulfs its enemies and I owe my life to one."

"You can't be serious!" Satterjee snapped. Ward shrugged and looked away. The trip to the border continued in silence.

When they arrived, Satterjee's opinion of the Hardesty camp exactly mirrored Ward's when he had first seen it. "What a dump!"

Ward made a wry face. "It doesn't look any better on the ground."

Hardesty met them as they landed at the edge of the dueling field. "So you're back agin'. What do ya want now?"

Satterjee made a face as though he could smell the men, even though the breeze came over his shoulder and into Hardesty's face.

Ward wasted no time. "I want to buy you out."

Hardesty looked stunned. "Wha'cha mean 'buy me out'? You always said we din't had no right ta' be here."

"That's right," Ward replied, "you don't."

Hardesty looked confused. A thin, hatchet-faced woman came up the path and stood beside him.

"I need the ground for a project I'm pursuing. I'm willing to pay for it," Ward pressed.

"Ah don' get it." Hardesty set his jaw stubbornly.

Ward tried a different tack. "Look, I'll give you fifty thousand for what you're claiming here."

Hardesty didn't bat an eye. "Where are we 'sposed ta' go?" he asked. Satterjee thought he heard a bit of whine building in the man's voice.

Ward looked around. "You stay right here. When we're done, I'll sell you the plot back."

Satterjee saw the woman's face light up as comprehension dawned. "Take it!" she hissed in Hardesty's ear.

Hardesty looked at her. "What?"

"If they buy our land, they'll admit our claim!" she said triumphantly to Hardesty. "They can't buy it without admitten' we can sell it!" She looked hard at Ward. "We get clear title?"

"Yes," he replied.

"Do it!" she told Hardesty.

He looked confused. "How much you gonna' want for

the land when we wanna buy it back?" he asked in a thick voice.

"Twenty-five thousand," Ward answered instantly. "You'll end up with your own place and a twenty-five thousand grubstake." Ward looked out over the depressing steading. "Where would you say the limits of your claim are?"

Hardesty licked his lips. Satterjee could almost see the wheels spinning in his mind as he tried to decide on how greedy to get.

The woman beat him to the punch. "Ten klicks along the creek, and three on either side."

Ward grinned harshly. "Why not five?"

"Wing's gonna love that," Satterjee muttered under his breath. "Half the dirt he's selling belongs to them."

The woman jabbed Hardesty in the ribs. "Damn you, do it!" Hardesty, caught between Ward, the woman, and his confusion, held his hands up. Everyone took that for agreement.

"Satterjee," Ward asked, "will you draw up the contract? The lady and Carlo will witness, I think."

Satterjee simply altered a boilerplate contract, bending the terms to language the woman and Hardesty could understand. All parties seemed acceptably satisfied with the results, with the exception of Hardesty. Satterjee thought he still looked far behind the learning curve as he penned his X.

"It's done!" Ward said triumphantly. He turned to Carlo. "Will you take Satterjee back to Complein so he can start working on the money? Also, Mona should be finished posting the ads on the network. You can pick her up in Complein." He carefully rubbed his hands together. "We've got a lot of work to do."

Satterjee shuttled out to the steading on a daily basis, checking in with Ward and getting his orders for disbursements. He was amazed at the speed with which

Ward turned his new home into a fortress on the Wing border.

A group of combat engineers, former Tuchman retainers, were among the first to join up. Ward compelled them to accept a mercenary contract, stipulating lavish pay and benefits. The engineers seemed nonplussed at first, arguing that they wanted only two things: a safe place to lay their heads and a shot at Wing. Many of Benno's former retainers seemed irritated that Ward expected to pay them to do what they were itching to do anyway.

The opposite was true of the mercenaries called to Ward's banner. Many were hard professionals, drawn to the cause by money, the chance for booty, or for the action. A few seemed little more than armed bandits, eager for the opportunity for some organized looting. Theisiger screened the applicants with a practiced eye, running them through their paces on the dueling field while he separated the wheat from the chaff.

Ward hadn't noticed Lupe Vargas until two days after Theisiger had enrolled him. Ward pulled his old friend aside and said, "Do your folks know you're here, Lupe?"

"They know," Lupe said. "They aren't thrilled about it, if that's what you mean; but they know a Vargas pays his debts. You backed us when we needed help."

Ward squeezed his friend's shoulder. "Don't be a hero," he said. "We're going to need farmers after this business is over, too. But I'm glad you're around, buddy."

The support staff, under Mona's care and Judith's surprisingly capable help, flourished under the rain of money. Mona focused her attention on the "hard" items: maintenance, administration, pay, and facilities. Judith lent her considerable talents to managing the "soft" issues: the consumables—food, medicine, ammunition, and laundry. Egg sent half of his technicians to Mona as a forward service facility for the troops' PBA. He kept the rest with him in Complein in a second echelon maintenance area and safehouse.

A few weeks after Ward first brought him to the Hardesty place, Satterjee sat in his office, amazed at the manifest that spooled out of his printer. He read it twice, certain it was a misprint or wish list. He tapped Mona's number into his computer and waited for the machine to route the call. Her wan face appeared in his screen.

"What can I do for you?" she said tiredly.

"I got your latest requisition," he replied. "Is this right? *Ten* more loads of plastiform and concrete? Two training simulators and a portable ground control station. I also see you want two loads of fresh vegetables daily. What is going on up there?"

She yawned. "Sorry," she apologized, "we haven't' gotten much sleep up here. The plastiform is to expand the bunker line. We're still getting recruits up here and Ward doesn't want anyone sleeping unprotected. The simulators'll help with troop evaluations and the ground control unit'll help manage the ground car traffic here. It's starting to get backed up."

She shrugged. "I don't know about the food, that's not my department. You need to ask the kitten about that."

Satterjee furrowed his brow. "The kitten?"

"Judith," Mona answered, her tone waspish. "Ward's bed-buddy. She's good with logistics, too." She looked away for a moment. "Who'd have guessed?"

"All right," Satterjee said, "I'll see you get the stuff. By the way, did some people arrive this morning?"

"If you mean the mercs," Mona answered, "Ward put them into the landing cycle. He's gone up to the training area to meet them."

"I see," Satterjec answered. "Tell Ward that they are very gifted people. I'm sure he'll put them to good use."

"I'm sure," Mona answered. Satterjee heard a buzz through the communications unit. "I have to go," Mona said, "I've got another call." She abruptly cut the circuit.

"That was rude," Satterjee said to the blank screen.

Back at the Hardesty place, Ward looked up from where he and Theisiger were comparing notes on the latest applicants. A long, sleek ground car flashed overhead and settled in for a landing turn. Theisiger looked at Ward. "Is this something of yours?"

"No," Ward answered as he closed his armor's faceplate, "I've never seen it before."

They exchanged bemused looks as a central hatch opened and a ramp slid to the ground. Troops in battle suits filed off the transport.

Ward looked at Carlo. "What the hell kind of armor is that?"

Theisiger looked as though he'd swallowed a live toad. "That, my friend, is a Mark Three Hegemony Enforcement suit." He took a deep breath. "The HES Three is used by the Terrans."

"Well, that's interesting," Ward said. "They look strange. What's that weapons configuration?"

Theisiger looked unhappy. "They're heavier than most colonial suits," he answered, "and pack a bigger punch. Those big wrist modules carry either twinned lasers or a laser/coil gun combination. The other arm has a powerknife and three-shot rocket launcher. The big, bulky shoulder rigs are backpack rocket launchers while those two assholes over there have portable sensor suites. Very tough."

Ward and Carlo exchanged a glance. "They're loaded for bear," Carlo said quietly.

The Terrans organized themselves into six teams of two behind their leader, forming a security wedge as they walked towards Ward and Theisiger. Ward tensed as Carlo moved a step to his right. The troop leader ignored their skittishness.

"You are Ward Tuchman?" the leader asked.

"Yes," Ward replied, "who wants to know?"

"We spoke earlier," the leader answered, "my name's Parkhurst."

"Are you from Earth?" Ward asked.

Parkhurst shrugged. "We're from Satterjee." He rotated his helmet to the right and removed it. The man had brown curly hair, brown eyes, and his smooth, unlined face was neither handsome nor ugly. He could have been black, or white, or Asian, or Maori, all depending on the light.

Ward gestured to Carlo. "This is Carlo Theisiger. He's in charge of the combat troops. He'll be your boss."

Parkhurst turned his attention to Theisiger. Ward watched them exchange brief, calculating looks.

"You're an emigré, aren't you?" Parkhurst said. "North American Standard genetic template?"

"Yeah," Carlo replied shortly. "I'm from Earth."

Ward stepped between them. "What kind of terms do you want for your people? The standard contract?"

"No need," Parkhurst replied, "we've already been paid."

"I see," answered Theisiger in a cool voice.

"I think you'll fit in just fine," Ward interjected quickly, looking at Carlo. "What do you think?"

Theisiger glanced at him, his expression one of quiet disapproval. "You're the boss," he said after a moment.

Ward turned his attention back to Parkhurst, who'd watched their byplay carefully. No expression crossed his face.

Carlo smiled thinly. "You can have bunker South Three. It hasn't quite finished curing yet, but I'm sure you'll manage."

"Thanks," Parkhurst said, "I'm sure that will do fine." He gestured to the troops behind him. "My people need practice. Do you have any live targets we can work over?"

Ward and Carlo traded glances. "Umm, we're still

working that out," Ward answered. "I'm planning to season the units against live opponents. My support staff is collecting all the grievances that Wing has inflicted on my clan. As long as we're agenting Tuchman people who are seeking redress, we stay legal. We can kill as many as we want within those bounds.There should be plenty for everybody."

Parkhurst licked his lips, neither pleased nor displeased at the news.

Ward looked towards the camp. "Park your transport in the motor pool, then see Judith at the supply bunker. She'll arrange your billeting." He grinned. "She'll be easy to recognize. She's the only one not wearing paramilitary kit."

"Fine," Parkhurst said. He turned and stumped away towards the transport. The troops withdrew to the craft. Carlo waited for the ramp to retract before he turned to Ward. "I don't like this," he said.

Ward raised an eyebrow.

"They're here for their own reasons, not ours," Carlo stressed. "We went to a lot of time and trouble to make sure everyone signed contracts. We agreed that we wanted *everybody* to be taking our nickel." He tipped his head toward the cluster following Mona. "I don't like having that many heavily armed men I don't own sitting right in the middle of the compound."

"I agree," Ward said.

Carlo looked puzzled. "Then why'd you take them?"

Ward grinned. "This way I can keep track of them. I don't have to worry about what they might be up to if they're working for me."

Carlo made a face. "I wouldn't be too sure."

Ward grinned. "Then let's keep them busy until we figure out what their game is, okay?"

Carlo dug at the ground with the toe of his boot. "You do realize the time may come when we'll have to do something about them?"

"Yeah," Ward answered, "I know. But for now, I can use their firepower."

Theisiger spread his palms, acceding to Ward's argument. "Okay," he said, "but I don't have to like it."

"Between us boys," Ward said conspiratorially, "I don't like it much either. Thirteen crack troopers is too good to pass up, though. Whatever their motives."

"Okay," Carlo said with a grin and mock salute, "we'll commit them as soon as we can."

"Tell them, they'd better keep it clean. Other than that, the more Wings they kill now, the fewer we'll have to fight later. That goes for all our fighters. I won't pay bounty for questionable kills."

"I'll tell 'em," Carlo replied. "We're hitting our first targets tonight."

Seven days later, a *very* irritated Samuel Denison cooled his heels outside the temporary shelter that served as Ward's new office. Judith sat with him on the bench in the sun. Denison thought she looked quiet and demure as she typed into her pocket computer. She wore a colorful red and blue skirt and simple blouse, a marked contrast to the green and gray kits everyone else in the compound seemed to wear. She hummed happily as she typed away.

Denison paced back and forth, grumbling that Ward appeared to be keeping him waiting deliberately. He'd just about made up his mind to barge through the shelter's curved door when it opened of its own accord.

Ward walked out, accompanied by a woman in her early thirties. "Don't worry, ma'am," he said. "If Wing really did kill your son's dog, and there were witnesses, we'll send some people over to take care of it."

"I'd really appreciate that," she answered. "They done a lot of bad stuff. I'm glad your people have taken up for us." Denison made a rude noise. She gave him a hard look as she left.

Samuel's control slipped a notch as he looked at Ward. "Is that what you're playing at, then? Kill anything Wing, on any pretense?"

"Basically, yes," Ward replied.

Denison was taken aback. "I didn't expect such a forthright answer. We need to talk."

Ward gestured to his office. "Watch your head."

Samuel cocked his thumb over his shoulder, indicating the woman. "Was that for my benefit, or are you really going to dispatch a team to kill people over a dog?"

"It's real," Ward answered. "*Any* provocation for *any* reason, past or present, invites retaliation."

"Well," Denison answered, "I've had to deal with the results of your little war here. Do you realize that your people have killed forty-some Wings in the last week? Forty some families have lost someone they cared about."

Ward looked bored at the recitation.

"Don't you care?" Denison snapped.

"No," Ward replied bluntly, "I don't." He abruptly sat on the bench. Mona, still typing, moved gracefully to make room for him. "The body count, incidently, is fifty-two dead, nineteen wounded, as of four o'clock today." A ghost of a smile played about his lips. "I should know, I'm the one paying bounty."

Denison shook his head. "Ward, have a heart, would you? Stop this before more people get killed."

"Why?" Ward asked. "If you and your precious Council had offered me justice after the attack on LaPort, none of this would be happening. Now I have to do it my way."

"No, you don't," Denison argued. "You've got the upper hand. You've got better people, better leadership, and the advantage of numbers. You don't have to *do* anything."

Ward stretched his neck. Denison heard vertebrae snap

and pop. "The funny thing about momentum," Ward continued, "is that if you don't use it, you lose it."

Denison pressed his case. "Wing's in bad shape. They've lost a lot of people and morale's plummeted. You can afford to back off a bit." He took a deep breath. "Wing's asked to meet you on neutral ground to try and settle this. Why haven't you accepted?"

"I've been on neutral turf with Wing before," Ward answered dryly, "I can't say I liked it." He held up his hands for emphasis. The spray-skin had faded, leaving behind pink new flesh. "I got burned. If Wing wants to talk to me, they come here."

"I know about your conditions," Denison replied. "Wing's been to see me."

"And?" asked Ward.

"He asked me to guarantee his safety." Denison met Ward's eyes. "I wasn't certain I could do that."

"I see," Ward replied.

"Damn it, Ward!" Denison leaned on the desk. "You've got to realize the Council is watching this. They're pissed already with Wing for their high-handed attack on LaPort. You're rising quickly on their shit list, too. Call off this mindless vendetta."

"Oh, it isn't mindless. Not with the planning that goes on around here." He looked at Denison. "Are you telling me that the Council's going to be after me for getting back what's mine?"

Denison dodged the question. "You are going to have to work with them in the future. You have a tough row to hoe, and they can help you with it. Don't burn that bridge."

Ward laughed. "Nice use of clichés. What do you suggest?"

Denison exhaled loudly. "Guarantee Wing's safety. Meet with him. Try to arrange a settlement. Appease the Council."

"All right," Ward said slowly, his expression troubled.

"But the bastard comes to me alone. No bodyguards, no backups, no nurses. Nothing. Those are my terms."

Denison stepped back. "All right, then. I'll pass that along." Ward stepped around the desk towards the door. "If Wing thinks this is some kind of ploy to buy time," he declared, "tell him I won't wait long."

"You won't have to," Denison replied grimly. "He's waiting for my call."

"How convenient," Ward said sarcastically. "Is there anything else I can do for you?"

"Yes," Denison said. "I heard about your separate peace with Complein. Did you really intend to grant independence?"

Ward shrugged. "It seemed the expedient thing to do." His expression grew accusing. "They told me you began enforcing the old customs agreements. Was that for my benefit?"

Denison shrugged. "Basically, yes. I wanted to track what you were doing. I knew you had to fence your wins somewhere. I also heard Wing was trying to take advantage of the situation by importing a lot of stuff into Complein."

"And?" Ward asked.

Denison shrugged again. "And nothing. Wing bought half the damn city, but they didn't bring in anything interesting."

Ward looked bored. "Is there anything else I can do for you?"

"Yeah," Denison said, "stop this."

Ward looked away. "Mona will see you to your ground car. Have a nice day."

He stood and walked into his office as Denison ground his teeth.

Judith looked up at him. "I'm sorry, Mr. Denison." She smiled sweetly. "Would you like some tea?"

"No," he said tiredly, discarding a half-dozen angry responses, "I want peace."

Ward waited for her to escort Denison away before he buzzed Carlo.

The duelist's voice answered at once. "Yeah, Ward, what can I do for you?"

"Do we have any operations planned for tonight?" Ward asked.

"Only three," Carlo replied. "Targets are getting thin on the ground." He smiled."Parkhurst is hitting a warehouse containing items taken from your house. Tuchman Three is taking down a Wing retainer who supplied troops that looted LaPort, and the Manza sisters are challenging some outriders accused of a rape."

"Cancel them," ordered Ward.

"Why?" Theisiger replied. "Is something up?"

"I don't know," Ward answered honestly. "I just had a rather strange conversation with Denison. I'm expecting a visit from Skywing." He made a face. "Every time I meet a Wing, something bad happens afterwards."

"Sounds reasonable," Carlo answered. "You'd be surprised how often these hunches play out." Ward heard papers shuffle. "We aren't doing anything that can't wait another day. I'll attach the Manzas to Tuch Three. That, together with Parkhurst's people, will give us two squads just in case." Carlo looked at his watch. "We'll go ahead and send them out, then have them hunker down till we need 'em."

"Fine," Ward approved, "do it. I'll be in my room if you need me. I need a nap."

"That's a good idea," Carlo said. "You haven't been sleeping well. Are you still having nightmares?"

"Yeah," Ward answered, "they get pretty intense."

"I'll let you know when Wing gets here," Carlo told him. "Go lie down."

"Yes, mother," he replied as he set the comm-link down. He walked to the shelter he shared with Judith. Garibaldi, alert and ready in his battle armor, stood guard outside. Ward smiled as he slipped inside. He quickly stripped and crawled under the covers. He was exhausted, but sleep evaded him as his mind churned. He closed his eyes against the light.

He looked up as he caught the scent of lavender and rose.

"Carlo sent me," Judith said quietly.

The buzz of a comm-link, seemingly next to his ear, awoke him from his deep slumber. He reached across Judith's still form before it buzzed again.

"Yeah?" he said as he rubbed his bleary eyes.

"Look alive," Carlo said. "Parkhurst's techs detected an inbound vehicle they think is Wing. It should be here in another twenty minutes."

Ward looked at his watch. Six hours gone in the blink of an eye. "Those guys are good," he commented. "What does Parkhurst call them?"

"Scouts," Carlo replied dryly. "What do you want me to do with Wing when he gets here?"

"Have him come in blindfolded," he told Theisiger. "Tell him no helpers, no guards, nothing. Not even a cane. I won't have him spying, and I won't risk having him take me out."

Theisiger replied, "I'll pass that along as soon as he calls for landing instructions." Judith awakened, stretching gracefully. She opened her mouth to speak as Carlo's voice again came across the comm-link.

"Okay, boss," he said, "consider it done."

"Fine," Ward answered. "Has Egg had any luck with those chips Parkhurst's scout gave us to link radios?"

"Yeah," Carlo said. "It's an E-PROM. It behaves as advertised, interfacing their system to ours. Egg says it has an extra pin, one that really doesn't belong."

"What's it do?" Ward asked.

"Egg doesn't know," replied Carlo. "He thinks it lets the chip access the core system. He wants to clip it off before he puts them in the suits."

"Fine," Ward affirmed. "Call me when Wing comes into the landing cycle."

"Roger," Theisiger said as he closed the circuit.

Judith looked at him pensively. "Spying really isn't the reason you don't want Wing to have any help, is it?" she asked.

Ward seemed a little taken aback. "No, not really," he said.

"It looks to me more like deliberate humiliation," she pressed. "He's old. He can barely walk. Is there really any need to do this?"

Ward turned away, troubled by the exchange. "I didn't realize you'd become my conscience," he said a little waspishly.

"Somebody has to," she retorted.

He whirled to face her. "Is that what you think?"

She looked away, refusing to meet his eyes. "The more I know you, the more like Marble you seem."

He jerked back, stung. "What's that supposed to mean?"

"You are so bound up in your revenge that you're forgetting to be a person," she said sadly. "Wing'll be humiliated enough coming to you hat in hand. Do you really need to take all his dignity?"

"You couldn't possibly understand."

She lifted her chin. "Do you think you have the monopoly on getting hurt?" She looked away.

Ward slid out of the bed. "I have to get ready. I don't have time for an argument."

He was still toweling his hair dry when the comm-link buzzed again. Judith spoke softly into it a moment, then handed it to him. "It's for you. It's Carlo."

"Yeah?" he said into the transceiver's grille.

"One Wing vehicle on final approach," Carlo informed him. "They're going to comply with your stipulations, but they aren't happy."

"Tough," he said. "I'm on my way."

He met Carlo and one of Parkhurst's spook troops on the edge of the landing area just as the lights of Wing's limousine came into view. The sensor tech raised a hand-held scanner.

"I'm reading two people—one in front and one in back. No armor and no weapon signatures." He turned to Ward. "He's clean."

"I'd give my eyeteeth for a scanner that accurate," Carlo mumbled.

The tech smiled. "Sorry. It's not for sale."

The car landed. Ward tensed as a single door hissed open. Skywing sat in the rear seat, looking shrunken and shriveled. A colored cloth had been bound over his eyes.

"Well," Wing said irritably, "can I have my man help me, or do you expect me to get out by myself?"

Ward looked at Theisiger.

"Don't help him," Carlo warned. "You don't know what he might have hidden."

"Good point," Ward answered sotto voce. He spoke louder, to Wing: "He can help you. But you're on your own once you're on your feet."

"Mighty kind of you," Wing replied dryly. The chauffeur exited and extended his hands so Wing could grab them. The frail old man wheezed and sputtered as the retainer helped him to his feet. He seemed to have some trouble orienting himself.

"I'm over here," Ward said as the Wing of Skywing aimed himself forty-five degrees off the mark. Ward watched the old man stumble as he tried to find Ward. He walked with a hesitant shamble, his knees trembling as they tried to support his weight. He took several careful steps, then almost fell as his shoe caught a small irregularity in the landing pad.

Wing almost fell again as he closed to within a couple of steps of Ward. Ward could hear his breath wheezing in his chest as he hunched over, trying to force his weak legs to bear him just a little further. Ward felt a bit ashamed. *Am I becoming Marble?* he said to himself. *Or Nuys?* He looked at his companions. Carlo had pursed his lips and was staring at his feet.

Ward reached his hand out to Wing, catching him on the shoulder as he almost fell. Skywing placed his dry, leathery hand over Ward's. Ward placed Wing's hand on his shoulder and helped him to the office.

Wing wheezed and stumbled even on that smooth surface. Ward's slow pace seemed too fast for the older man. Wing didn't appear strong enough to hold himself up, and the pressure of his bent body constricted his lungs. He was panting heavily by the time they reached the door to the temporary shelter. Ward helped him over the sill and to a chair.

"You can take the blindfold off, now," Ward said as he sat. Wing rubbed his eyes and glanced around. He didn't seem especially impressed with Ward's spartan camp desk and folding chairs. Ward waited for Wing's breathing to settle.

The old man made a sour face. "Have I jumped through enough hoops to satisfy you, young man?"

"We'll see," Ward answered.

"I've accepted *this*," Wing said as he held up the blindfold, "in order to stop things before they get worse."

"Talk to me," Ward replied.

Wing sighed. "Here's my offer. You stop this and we call it even." He met Ward's eyes. Ward saw the quiet loathing behind his opponent's cool gaze. "In exchange, I give you my granddaughter, Seladra, to be your wife and to violate at your leisure. I'll even make you my heir, appointing you to lead the clan on my death."

"Why all this?" Ward asked.

"I've led Wing since the beginning." Skywing sighed. "Built it with my own hands. I don't want to see that all go to waste. The only way I can stop you from destroying Clan Wing is to give it to you. So, that's what I'm doing." He slumped in his seat.

"Not good enough," Ward replied, frost in his voice.

Wing looked up. "All right then, I'll abdicate in your favor *if* you wed Seladra. You'll control both Wing and Tuch."

"Still not enough," Ward repeated.

Wing looked puzzled. "What more is there?"

Ward stood and leaned over the camp desk, his expression one of cold fury.

"The only way"—he ground each syllable out slowly, as though tasting each word—"the butchers of LaPort can save themselves is to flee the district. Everybody. Men, women, children. Everyone. Whomever buys the real property has two choices: either assume Tuchman retainership or continue the feud."

"That will mean the extinction of my clan!" Wing protested.

"Yes," Ward snapped, "that was something that you tried to visit on Tuchman, as I recall. You, however, did not give my father the option of walking away."

Wing rubbed his eyes with the heels of his hands. "There's no other way?" he asked tiredly.

"I want Wing gone," Ward said, his voice cold. "One way or the other, I'll get my way."

"I see." Wing slumped in his seat. "May we have a truce while we consider?"

"No," Ward answered.

"Then I guess we have nothing left to discuss. You'll have our answer very soon." Wing made as if to stand, then held out the blindfold. "Do you plan to humiliate me more or can I leave?"

"Just go," Ward said.

Theisiger jerked the door open, apparently fearing the worst. Ward looked up and saw his worried expression.

"He refused to deal?" Carlo asked.

"He offered me a peace that would leave him his honor," Ward answered simply. "I turned him down."

Carlo sucked air in between his teeth. "I'll call an alert for tonight."

Ward looked up, his expression troubled. "I think that would be a very good idea."

Chapter 13

Ward, dressed in full armor, stood behind Parkhurst's scouts as they plotted the positions of the approaching Wing forces. They carried their own battle helmets under their arms as they briefed a pair of Mona's technicians on the finer points of their sensor consoles.

"What's the count?" Ward asked.

The scout made a wry face. "A hundred and forty, give or take a few. They look to be wearing every scrap of armor and loose jump pack they could beg, borrow, or steal."

Ward looked at the screen. "What are those big blips behind the main wave?"

"Armored ground crawlers," the scout replied, "carrying artillery and secondary troops. They'll try to hammer us while the assault force is still maneuvering."

Ward looked at his status board. "We've got forty-five here, and two dozen hidden with Parkhurst. Will seventy be enough?"

The scout shrugged. "Well, all things being equal, they'll need about three to one to win. They've got us about two to one, and that doesn't count the camp, the unarmored troops, or us." He grinned. "Their morale is pretty screwed. I don't think they can do it. It ought to be a cakewalk."

Ward's heart pounded in spite of the scout's encouraging projection. "Still, so many," he whispered. He looked at the scout. "How long until they get here?"

"Fifteen minutes local time, twenty-two standard Terran," the Terran said, "give or take."

Ward looked at the screen again. "I have to go. Can I get this on my HUD?"

The scout nodded. "Yeah, your suit should handle the data." He thought a moment. "Give me a long count so I can check the system."

Ward closed his helmet and switched his radio to the Terran's frequency. He counted slowly until the scout raised one hand.

"Okay," he said, "you should have it." He took a bridging cable and ran it from his screen to the communications port. "I'm running it through our channel. It'll remain encrypted, but anyone with our augmentation chips'll be able to read it. How's that?"

"Great!" Ward said. "Will you be joining the festivities?"

The scouts looked at each other. "We'll be joining our own unit."

Ward looked concerned. "You plan to cross the enemy lines?"

"Don't worry," the first scout said. "We've snuck in and out of places you could never imagine." His partner gave him a hard look.

Ward went up the stairs toward Carlo and his waiting troops. Theisiger stood ready, his helmet dangling from a shoulder clip. Ward turned to him. "The scouts rigged the control board into my suit. Check their special frequency. You should have data." He thought his voice sounded nervous and high-pitched. Carlo gripped him by the shoulder.

"Don't worry, Ward," Carlo replied, "you know how to fight. You've been on raids, and you've survived some serious shit. This ain't nothing." Ward thought he heard hesitation in Carlo's voice.

"Aren't you nervous?" Ward asked.

"Yeah, this ain't like a fight or raid," he replied,

contradicting himself. "In battles, the shit is flyin' in all directions. You can die any way, any time. Raidin' and fightin' are a lot cleaner." He smiled broadly. "I'm told that in battles, you usually forget your fear and just do your job."

"What do you mean 'I'm told'?" Ward demanded. "Haven't you ever been in a real battle?"

"Not like this." Theisiger swore softy as he tapped into Ward's data channel. "Not this big." He grinned. "All you're going to hear is me hyperventilating." He checked his display. "We have to shift some dispositions. Remember your clock facings: twelve o'clock points directly towards Wing. We need to move the Second Squad Tuchman to cover the ten to two area behind Mercs One and Two. The mercenary squads' seam is right where the center of their force'll hit us. We'll need to backstop that." He shook his head. "I didn't think they'd go at us headon."

"What about the Tuchman side?" Ward asked. "Tuch One will be the only squad to cover everything from two to ten o'clock. You've got three of our four squads pointed in one direction!"

"No," Carlo answered patiently. "We've got good fields of fire from Bunkers One and Four." Two squares on the Star of David bunker formation pulsed as he spoke. "We've also got two teams of unarmored troops hiding under thermal blankets. They've got indirect fire weapons and Piats to cover the dead space."

Ward heard him exhale loudly. "If they hit us dead on," Carlo continued, "they'll run into three squads' concentrated fire. Our mercs will probably be pinned down or committed early. Tuch Two will be on an inside lane. They can float around and go where the fire is heaviest. If Wing slops around the edge of the mercenaries, they'll be able hold them until we can move other forces."

Ward knew the battle plan. He was just making Carlo

go over it one more time because he was nervous. "What about Parkhurst's people and Tuchman Three?"

Carlo mimed the plan with his hands. "We'll wait for the Wings to commit, then bring Parkhurst's people around directly behind them. We'll launch 'em into Wing's rear, catching them between us. It's a hammer and anvil move."

"What if they have a rear guard?" Ward asked.

"Probably they will," Theisiger answered. "But it won't be their best troops. Those'll be up front." He thought a moment. "Consider it this way: Wing will have swept that area on the advance. All the action will be behind the people facing to the rear. We move quickly enough and quietly enough, we'll be able to take them in the train while they're lookin' at the pretty fireworks ahead of them."

He shrugged. "Even if they are alert, I don't think they'll be enough to stop us. If they do, then we execute a pincers with us and Parkhurst attacking at once. It'll work if we don't lose our heads."

"Okay," Ward said, "we know what we're doing. The only thing left to do now is fight."

Carlo seemed like he wanted to say more.

"What's wrong?" Ward asked.

Theisiger looked distinctly uncomfortable. "I don't want you close to the line. You have to stay alive to lead your people, not to get yourself killed."

"Maybe that works on Earth, but here, Tuchmans lead from the front. This is not negotiable."

"Please, Ward," Carlo urged, "meet me halfway on this." Ward set his jaw.

Mona's voice cut across all communication channels. "Inbound enemy PBA. Estimated strength between one hundred thirty and one hundred fifty. Estimated time of arrival three minutes. All support personnel to defensive positions. Good luck."

Carlo thumbed his override, clearing the channel.

"Wing has split into five groups. Three groups are forward while two are holding back. The left-hand forward numbers thirty. They're moving fast towards the nine o'clock position. The other two are overlapped and heading to twelve o'clock high. It looks like a single envelopment tactic coupled with a down-the-throat. The back two groups are stopped and fanned . . ."

The whistle of incoming rockets drowned him out. He and Ward leapt for cover, sheltering in the stairwell above the command bunker. Ward heard several coil guns rip and saw lasers flash as the defenders fired on the falling projectiles. The arching brilliant blue-green streams looked like fireworks in the night.

A few rounds detonated, but most passed through unharmed and burst over the defenders' heads. Airfoils hummed and buzzed, tearing away overhead cover and mowing down the few troops who were in the open.

Ward heard the first screams of the wounded. He blocked them out and concentrated on the closing Wing forces. Carlo bounded away in the lull between salvos.

Ward heard the distant *thum-thum* of the rocket launchers and the higher bark of short-range mortars. A moment later the second salvo tore the air above the defenders, wounding more of Ward's troops.

The front rank of Tuchman fighters engaged, pouring swaths of fire into the Wings. He stared in awe as thirty coil guns ripped the night apart with their flickering fire. The Wings scattered, leaving the dead strewn across the field. Their neat, even lines shattered as they dove for cover. The first airfoils sang and buzzed overhead as the Wings began to return fire.

Ward waited for the fire to slacken before he jumped up and bolted for the nearest slit trench. A deep *pom-pom* joined the noise of the other ordnance. He saw two orange globes arching lazily towards his lines.

"Air burst! Air burst! Get down!" a voice screamed over the radio. Ward dove for cover as the first globe burst. The expanding fuel-air mixture engulfed the trench in front of him in a hellish explosion. The second, a near-miss, hammered him into the ground as it detonated. A sheet of flame passed over him. He stumbled into the scorched trench, almost tripping over an unarmored body. He peered down at the charred figure a moment before he saw the diagnostic probe clenched in its burned fingers.

A suited warrior scrambled by. "Get out of there, you asshole," she yelled at Ward, "can't you see they've got us registered?"

Ward looked up as another globe emerged from the Wing lines. He scrambled out of the trench and across the torn earth, stumbling after the retainer. They collapsed together in the Tuch Two bunker just as the globe exploded in the trench behind them.

A heavy mortar shell hit directly overhead as Ward picked himself up out of the dirt. Thin plumes of dust trickled down from overhead. "Nice dive, asshole," somebody commented dryly.

"I'd be a little more respectful if I were you," Ward heard a familiar voice say. "That's the man who signs our paychecks." He turned and saw a heavily appliquéd and camouflaged partial suit with a squad leader's emblem on it. The troop opened his faceplate.

Ward recognized him as one of Dr. Silman's guards. "How's it goin', Dave?"

The former guard chief shrugged. "Sometimes it rains, sometimes it pours."

The rockets hit a moment later, sounding like firecrackers after the roar of the mortars.

He heard Carlo's voice on the command circuit. "Mona, baby, are you out there?"

"Yeah," she responded, her voice tight and strained, "call me 'baby' again and your wife'll be sleeping with a soprano."

"I've got some goobers in a ravine about two hundred

meters out," Carlo answered, sounding chipper. "Do you have anything for them?"

"Hold on," she replied. "Stand by for daisy cutters."

Dave gestured for Ward to join him. They stepped together up onto the firing step and looked out the bunker's slits. "You're going to want to see this," the squad leader said. Ward saw a ripple of yellow and red flickers through the trees. The noise of the detonations reached him a moment later, the individual explosions blended together by the trees and terrain into a rumbling roar.

"Command-detonated mines, twenty-four total," Mona reported a moment later.

"That'll hurt 'em," Carlo commented.

Ward set his radio to scan the units' channels.

The bunker channel drew his attention. "Bunker Four to Command. Tallyho. I've got six . . . correction, eight coming up out of the ravine."

Ward heard the pounding as the heavy machine gun in the bunker opened up on the troops. The ancient Browning chopped down four before the rest could scamper back under cover.

Dave stood with his head cocked, listening to another channel. Ward scanned the frequencies, trying to find the communication. Dave muttered something and began to fan his troops out along the trench line that formed their primary defensive work. Men and women spaced themselves out along the outer face of the trench, coil guns and lasers extended, looking for targets.

Ward looked at him. "What's going on?"

"Parkhurst's men say that the Wings are readying to jump off."

Ward fought down the flash of fear that ran through him. "Is there anything I can do here?"

Dave turned to him, his face impossible to read behind his faceplate. "I lost my number two man. You can fill in." He pointed towards a trench.

"Thanks." Ward trotted out of the bunker. He turned his head to look back when a mortar struck the overhead cover. A shaped charge cut through the center of the bunker and incinerated Dave where he stood, slagging his armor and weapons. The blast hurled Ward into the trench's outer wall. He slumped to the ground, momentarily stunned. He started to get to his knees when another armored figure slammed into him, pinning him to the ground.

"What the hell?" he demanded.

"Popcorn rounds! Stay down!" his benefactor shouted. They crawled around the first dog-leg in the zigzagging trench and listened to the sound of explosive cored ring penetrators cracking, sending their hypervelocity airfoils winging at random intervals. A boost-pack's fuel cell exploded. Ward felt the compression wave through his suit as the trench directed the blast. Ward glanced up at the fireball rising over the center of Tuchman Two squad.

"What the hell was that?" he yelled to his companion.

"A bunker buster. Very bad." The trooper scrambled away.

"Ward!" Theisiger called, sounding almost frantic. "Are you all right?"

Ward keyed his radio. "I'm just a little singed. The squad leader was killed in the bunker." His mind recoiled from the horror of the burning suits. "I'm taking over Tuch Two."

"All right," Carlo said. "Switch to the platoon circuit and wait for orders. Check the survivors. Make sure they're ready."

"Got it," Ward replied. He skipped along the trench, checking the remainder of the squad. The center point was still too hot with flying ammo to cross over. He picked a name at random from the left side survivors and assigned her as his vice-leader.

The trench, herringboned and dotted with fighting positions, girdled the third of the compound that directly faced the Wing estates. Carlo had wanted the trench to completely ring the base to provide a means of moving troops without exposing them needlessly. It, like so many other things at the site, hadn't been completed before the attack.

The heavy machine gun in Bunker One fired, throwing tracer sabot slugs at the enemy. The base's solitary mortar pit opened up a moment later, hurling rounds from the single, obsolete 120-millimeter clip-fed mortar. Ward admired the mortar crew's bravery as they served their weapon without protective armor. They fired three rounds, dropping one directly on top of Wing's main line, before the enemy opened up with rockets and their own mortars. The crew ducked back underneath their overhanging shelter as the first rounds whistled in.

Wing counterbattery fire completely masked the pit in a wall of explosions. Ward saw, in the intervals between shells, that the pit's retaining wall had failed. The mortar pit looked like a large crater set in the midst of a field of smaller holes. Ward saw a hand bravely waving from the shelter, announcing to the world that someone had survived the hail.

A single late-falling shell detonated in the exact center of the pit a moment later. The explosion blanked Ward's optics as the mortar's ammunition went up in a giant secondary explosion.

A hiss-crackle on the circuit announced an incoming message. "Stand by," Mona's voice called out, "here they come."

Ward stepped up on the firing platform as the largest of the forward three Wing groups emerged from cover. They hopped and ran forward in pairs, one covering another's movements until they lost discipline, melting into a liquid surge of advancing firepower.

Wing's other two forward elements attempted to give covering fire. Ward watched the wink and flash of coil guns ripping off streams of rounds at the defenders. Part of the center group slopped towards Ward's right. They masked their fellows' supporting fire almost immediately. Ward saw several Wings fall as they were hit by friendly fire.

Then all hell broke loose. The mercenary squads in front of Ward opened, firing long bursts as they cut down advancing Wing troops in a bloody scythe of ring penetrators. The advance stalled as the main assault scampered for cover and began to return fire. The beleaguered right-hand side collapsed as Wing fired on Wing.

The mortar rounds fell with greater intensity as the Wing crews fed clip after clip into their tubes. Rockets continued to work their havoc as well, spraying the area with their lethal payloads but inflicting little practical damage on Ward's forces. Protected as they were by berms and trench barriers, the mercenaries blazed back, heaping fire upon fire on the exposed Wing forces. Trees fell, cut through by the relentless tungsten rings. Rocks shattered under the impact of massed lasers, exploding like bombs. The Wing detachment on the left tried to withdraw, only to discover that, as on the right side, their only covered route led through the massed fire of their supporting forces.

Left with no option, they crawled forward towards their objective, a small knoll on Ward's nine o'clock position. The Wings shed blood for every meter they gained, but they slowly made their way towards the high ground. The broken bodies and shattered armor left a clear trail linking them to the main effort. Ward's squad flexed and stretched along the trench, keeping them under fire.

The first Wings went to cover behind the knoll, safe for the moment from the squads' fire. Ward quickly switched to the command channel. "Mona, what do you have for target number, uhh, four . . . the nine o'clock knoll?"

She paused. "That's target reference point six, not four. I've got high explosive and daisy cutters."

"Do it!" Ward ordered.

Mona didn't answer. A second later mines placed in the dead spaces behind the knoll began to detonate. Ward heard the rippling blasts and saw the flashes as the linear shaped charges cut knee-high across the open ground.

"Damn," Ward cried. "That was impressive. I think you got 'em!"

"Nope," she answered, "I'm getting micro-vibrations from the seismic sensors. There's still a few down there."

Chuff! Chuff! Chuff! Ward whipped his head around and saw a barrage of small rockets hitting the front line. Ripple after ripple struck the outer berm. Ward saw dozens of flashes along the ravine. "Rocket launchers!" he screamed into his radio. "Get down!"

This was where Ward's preparations paid for themselves. Despite the massed Wing fire, the concrete bunkers and firing pits with overhead cover permitted the Tuchman defenders to hold in place. There were casualties, sure, when a series of mortar rounds brought the roof down on a foxhole or a lucky shot through a firing slit penetrated a faceplate. Ward cringed every time his AI reported that another of his people showed no vital signs.

But the Wings, attaching across open terrain, were losing four or five for every Tuchman who fell.

Ward popped his head out of the trench to check his troops' fire and almost had it taken off by a bursting rocket. He tried to clear his ringing head as he checked the fight on his HUD. He saw a single large graphic emerge from the Wing line and cross the open area towards Bunker Four. He heard fire from the defensive position intensify and the bunker chief's voice on the circuit. "We need help! We got a bomb-car comin' for us!"

Ward risked peeking out over the trench. He saw a single ground car arch out of the Wing line and aim for bunker Four, pursued by several hot streams of coil gun fire. The bunker's gunners shifted targets and began shredding the incoming car. It burst into flames.

Newton's laws held sway. The debris from the car continued on its trajectory and plowed into the face of the bunker. Six barrels of liquid explosive spilled out of the cargo box and rolled across the ground. Ward closed his eyes as the first detonated.

The shock wave flattened many of the defenders. Ward glanced over the top of the trench as Bunker Four's debris rained down. He saw a gaping hole where the bunker had been, a lost tooth in the perimeter's defensive array. Ward heard the radio come alive with a babble of confused voices as the AI scanned across the general frequency.

Another salvo of mortar rounds whistled in, sounding subtly different to Ward's ear. He looked up and saw the first shell burst in midair. Smoke canisters spewed from the bursting shells and plummeted to the ground.

"Go to infrared," Ward commanded as he overrode his AI and manually reset his suit optics.

"I don't see anything," a young voice wailed. "My IR's blanked, too!" Ward heard the panic building and was at a complete loss about what to do. His own vision faded to within a few meters as the smoke blanked both his infrared and vision enhancement systems.

"Here they come!" a voice yelled. Fearful voices filled the Tuch Two channel. "What's going on?" they demanded. "Why can't I see?"

Theisiger's voice cracked like a whip across the chatter. "Listen up! The smoke has special chemicals to screw up infrared. You can use your lidar to guesstimate direction and range while it clears." He paused. "Try not to breathe it without filters. It'll kill you."

Ward checked his heads-up display. Three lines of red dots skimmed the ground, closing on the compound. Fire poured from the mercenaries' line as the shelling eased. Ward doubted they could see their targets any better than Tuchman Two, but that wasn't stopping them from probing with brief coil gun blasts. Screams through the smoke indicated that some shots hit. A few of Ward's troops began to return fire.

"Merc One to Tuch Two," an urgent voice appealed in Ward's ear. "Give us a break! You're puttin' your shots all over us!"

"Cease fire," Ward yelled. "Tuch Two—cease fire!"

Tuch Two tapered off guiltily.

The Wings closed a few meters closer, only to be met by an increasing hail of airfoils and deadly lasers as the IR-masking smoke bled away. Ward saw the meadowed surface now looked like the surface of the moon. Ward saw brief movements highlighted by his AI as it tracked the activities of individual Wings. Individuals from the mercenaries' line began to fall back to the squad bunkers to secure fresh coil gun cassettes. It seemed apparent to Ward that, the mortars and smoke notwithstanding, the Wing advance was dying on the vine. The mercenaries, well under cover and lavishly supported with airfoils, were chopping the assault parties to dogmeat between the lines. Wing's secondary troops added their indirect fire, trying to drive the Tuch forces under cover again. This time the defenders' blood was up. A trooper fell here and there, victims of the mortar fire, but the fire into the Wing lines continued undiminished.

Ward realized they'd reached a tactical stalemate. Wing could neither advance nor withdraw, yet had found adequate cover from Ward's direct-fire weapons. Not for the first time, he wished he'd paid more attention to indirect weapon systems. The mines had been their best option, but Mona had already used most of those that they had had time to install.

He tried to find Carlo on the net to find out what he planned to do when he saw a thin line of blue dots drifting towards the rear of the Wing forces. The symbols wandered close enough for the master IFF interrogator to return a signal. The dots began to resolve themselves into Parkhurst's troops and Tuch Three.

The Wing forces attempted another surge, backed by feverishly firing rockets and mortars. Parkhurst timed his fire to coincide perfectly with the climax of the Wing attack. Just as the two Wing lines rose to advance, Parkhurst opened up on the Wing rear guard and the secondary troops' armored personnel carriers. Reddish-gold blooms of fire shattered the horizon, throwing bodies and mortar equipment high in the air. The lines of Wings hesitated, caught by the devastation behind them. In that moment, airfoils and lasers scythed them front and back. The Wings stood up to the brutal fire longer than Ward expected. He joined his fire to that of the others in the squad, aware only of the overwhelming fatigue that washed over him. He poured stream after stream into the flagging armored troops in the hinterland. Through it all, the world grew gray and still, his awareness reduced to a pinprick as he selected target after target, sometimes alone, sometimes in concert with several others. The Wings, caught between Parkhurst's hammer and the anvil of the camp, began to surrender. The first several to attempt it were cut down. Then Theisiger's voice was there, intruding into all nets, ordering that prisoners be taken.

Ward stood up in his colorless world, gray smoke from faded flames swirling over the gray torn ground, as he searched for another enemy. His heart pounded in his chest, overriding all other sounds. Then a distant clatter and crash intruded itself into his awareness.

Sound and color returned in a rush. The radio chattered to life as Tuchman warriors babbled, cried, and cheered into the ether. The flames licked, red and yellow, from the destroyed bunker, the battered APCs, and the shot-torn earth. And everywhere he looked, he saw the dead.

He panted, trying to draw oxygen into his body. A flurry of shots and explosions broke out on the far right. He whirled and scrambled up the side of the trench, trying to see what was going on.

"A group broke through Tuch One!" a panicked voice said. "Maybe ten or twelve—headed onto Tuchman lands."

Carlo's voice cut across the wild report as his AI switched to the higher priority command channel. "Ward?"

"Yeah," he replied.

"We got most of them. One small group made it through our lines. Take your squad and the mercs and pursue. All you need is to bring them to ground. We'll take 'em down as soon as we get organized."

Ward called his survivors to him. The mercenaries, already drifting back, were quickly rounded up to begin pursuit. Ward boosted after the Wings with his people, attempting to run them to ground.

Ward was so intent upon pursuit that he didn't recognize the terrain they crossed. It was only when he passed the burned and rusted hulk of a crashed ground car that he realized he'd run his quarry almost all the way to Benno's manor house. The leading Wings, distantly visible, entered into a stone hut at the top of the hill. He had to look twice before he recognized the steading as Stallart's. He felt a lump in his throat.

He turned towards his closest troops, halted their chase. "Just a little more and they're ours."

The mercenary to his left took careful aim with his coil gun. He fired a tightly controlled burst that dropped one of the trailing Wings within a few meters of the hut's doors. The rest of the fugitives scampered inside.

The mercenary took a long look at the house and turned to Ward. "Screw that. I can see the damn quartz in that cottage from here. My laser ain't gonna work for shit against that and I'm out of coilers and jump-juice. I ain't goin' nowhere."

Ward heard other mercenaries agree as they approached. One armored troop set down on the ground. Ward heard the mercenaries' fans whirring as they tried to drag oxygen into their suits. He looked at his HUD and saw blue dots scattered out over several kilometers. He had barely more troops than Wing at the moment.

"All right," he said reluctantly, "first we ring them, then we put up sentries, *then* we rest. Understand?"

They began to reorganize into coherent squads. Ward chafed at the delay as they sorted themselves out and took off for their perimeter sectors.

He heard a ground car hiss overhead. He looked up to see it heel steeply on its side as a jumpy Tuchman shot at it.

"Hold up!" Carlo's voice bellowed over all circuits. "We're friendly!" Ward ran to the car as it landed. Theisiger bounced out, his helmet hanging from its strap. He was grinning from ear to ear. "That's the first time I've been thankful for lousy accuracy." He laughed.

"How did it go?" Ward asked.

Carlo grinned again. "It looks like we killed about sixty and wounded about the same. We think about two dozen got away, most in singles or in pairs." He pointed with his chin upslope. "Except for this lot."

"We're scattered across several kilometers, and dog tired," Ward said, looking at the troops lounging nearby. "I told 'em to rest."

"Good plan," Theisiger said. "I've got coil gun magazines in the car. If you'll have some people unload them, we can use the vehicle to round up your lost sheep."

He paused. "Parkhurst and his people should be here in about twenty minutes. Once they get here, you can stand squads down for refit. Mona should be here with chow in a bit."

"Mona?" Ward asked. "Why not Judith?"

"Your little friend," Carlo said dryly, "caught an airfoil in the buttocks while diving for cover. Apparently she lashed up with one of Mona's unarmored squads."

Ward looked concerned. "Is she going to be all right?"

Carlo laughed. "Silman put five stitches in her right cheek and gave her a thick pillow. She'll be fine. He said to congratulate you on your find, by the way."

"Thanks." Ward took a deep breath. "How many did we lose?"

Carlo's light mood evaporated. "We had twelve killed. Half were in Bunker Four when it went. Ten wounded, not including Judith."

"Damn it," Ward swore, "they'll pay for that!"

Carlo scratched his cheek. "I think they already did. Their losses were five times ours."

"It hurts, Carlo," Ward admitted as he took off his helmet. "I didn't mind killing Wings when I started this. I even enjoyed it. But it was just me I was risking. Nobody else."

"What about Mona?"

"No," he answered, "she was doing it for her own reasons." He looked at his feet. "But now, my decisions are getting *my* people killed. Six Tuchman people died in that bunker because of me." Ward looked at his hands. "I feel dirty. There's a creek down there. I'm going to wash."

Carlo looked gravely at him. "If you're going to bathe, Ward, then you'd better let your people go as well."

Ward nodded absently as he walked down the slope to the creek bank. He'd barely had time to immerse himself when he heard other splashes and a bonfire blazed up in the shallow valley. When he had finished,

Ward looked over to the fire. He stood up and saw they'd placed it near the point where Stallart had held off the Wing squad so long ago. Ward felt a lump grow in his throat.

He stepped out of the creek. Theisiger, wearing a fresh set of coveralls, held out a towel.

"Where did all this come from?" Ward asked.

"I'm glad to see you took your own sweet time," Carlo replied dryly." Mona's been here about ten minutes. She brought fresh clothes, towels, and a big pot of stew. Tuch Two is still scattered all over the countryside, but Merc One and Tuch One are intact. I've got them resting while Merc Two and Tuch Three watch the hut." He pointed through the trees. "Parkhurst, et al., are over there by themselves."

Ward looked up as a four-seat ground car swept overhead. "Who the hell could that be?" He had only just slid into a coverall and booties when a Tuchman retainer led Denison to him.

"I see you came dressed for the party," Ward said dryly as he saw Denison's full PBA. "And you brought guards, too. Do you think you'll need 'em?"

Denison shrugged. "Tawn, my guard chief, gets irate when I step into unpoliced firefights without an escort. It violates her sense of propriety."

"What brings you down this way?" Ward asked.

"I heard your little war going on and thought I'd come down and observe," Denison answered lightly.

Ward tousled his hair dry. "Just don't interfere."

"I have no intention of making this situation any worse," Denison answered grimly, "but I would like to have the opportunity to negotiate an honorable settlement."

"There's nothing to settle. Wing started this and now Tuchman is going to finish it. You may stay or you may leave. I don't care which. Just don't interfere."

He turned to Carlo. "I think most of the chasers have

had a chance to rest. It's time to have them suit back up."

"What do you have in mind?" Denison asked.

Ward scratched his ear. "I'm going to lead the final assault myself, with Carlo here, and Parkhurst's squad."

"Are those your super-troops?" Denison asked. He noticed that the man beside Ward didn't seem especially happy with the news.

"Terrans," Theisiger corrected, making the word into an obscenity.

Denison's eyebrow shot up. "Hegemony?"

"What other kind is there?" Theisiger looked pained.

"Why are you using *them*?" Denison then asked Ward.

"Well," Ward answered, "their battle suits are better than ours, on average, and their training seems better." He smiled grimly. "They obey orders, for one thing. I noticed during the fight that they stay organized and act in concert. Our people go at it one-on-one, three shooting at one target while another enemy gets off scot free. We fight battles like we fight duels, confused and with every man for himself. We got lucky this time 'cause we had a better cause."

He rubbed his head again with the towel. "Here's how I figure it. If we do an assault with our people, it'll turn into a bums' rush. A lot of us'll die before we take 'em out."

He draped the towel around his neck. "Parkhurst's people'll do it as a unified advance. They'll get across to the house and get the door kicked in with a minimum of fuss. Wing is demoralized, cowed. We can take them out with only a few casualties."

Theisiger tugged his lip a moment. "That makes sense," he admitted. "Well, Ward, you're becoming a leader."

Ward looked grim. "If I have to lose people," he added, "I'd rather they were strangers."

Carlo looked offended. "Trying to cut your overhead?"

"No," Ward answered, "I don't have to face their families if they get killed." He turned away. "I'm going to go talk to Parkhurst and tell him the plan." He walked away.

Theisiger glanced at Ward's departing back. "That boy will make a fine Clan Chief."

Denison nodded and removed his helmet. "*If* he outgrows this penchant for bloodshed." He extended his hand to Carlo. "By the way, my name's Sam Denison."

"Carlo Theisiger," the duelist replied. They shook hands.

Ward heard their low voices as he broke through the trees. Parkhurst's group had sequestered itself a bit away from the main group. Ward saw eight or nine troops relaxing. Several were spooning helpings from a steaming stew pot.

Parkhurst intercepted him before he got too close. "Can I help you?" the Terran said.

"Yeah," Ward answered. He was just about to tell the mercenary leader about the assault plan when he saw light glitter off the Terran's shoulder. Ward glanced around and saw all of the Terrans wore skin-tight black-and-white bodysuits.

"What's that?" Ward asked, pointing at the suit.

Parkhurst casually plucked at his shoulder. "This? It's an Earth-made synthetic undersuit. We wear them underneath our armor."

"What's it do?" Ward pressed.

Parkhurst seemed a bit irritated by the question. "It works like a thermal suit. It wicks away heat and sweat. It cuts down on skin abrasion, makes a better sensor contact, and has a male/female relief tube. Is there anything else?"

"Yeah," Ward asked. "I'd like to get one. Where'd you buy them?"

"Complein," Parkhurst answered, just a little too quickly.

Ward sniffed the pot. "That smells good." He stepped around Parkhurst and walked towards the Terrans, who clustered around the hot food, plates in hand, as they waited their turn. Parkhurst grumbled something Ward didn't hear and followed him.

Ward peered into the gloom. "Where'd you guys put the plates?" he asked.

"Over there," a squadee replied, pointing to a white blob in the dark. Ward fumbled with the package. A man in an undersuit stepped over. A glowing cigarette coal marked his presence.

"Here, mac, let me give you some light." He bent down and ignited his lighter.

"Thanks," Ward said politely as he reached inside the packing box and retrieved a plate. He glanced up. His jaw fell.

The suits weren't black and white. They were *blue* and white. Wing Blue.

"Well," Ward said, hoping he sounded casual. He was literally surrounded by Terrans. "I'll get the rest of my people ready."

He turned and started to walk back the way he'd come.

"Hey!" cried a Tuchman retainer twenty feet back in the darkness. "They're wearing *Wing* colors! Where'd they get those?"

Ward spun and knocked the lighter from the hand of the man holding it. In the sudden darkness he dived to the left. His fingers recoiled from the hot pan. He fumbled for the handle, ignoring the pain as the wire loop burned into his palm.

The Terrans had gotten the Wing suits by looting the Wing starship that had disappeared. That was the only place Terran gear in Wing colors could have come from. These were the people who'd caused the Wings to almost destroy the Tuchmans—and who were now helping destroy the Wings.

And the Hegemony they served would be the only winner.

Ward heard a voice close by. "He's over there!" Ward hurled the pot at the voice and was rewarded by a scream as scalding hot stew and metal hit a Terran. Ward turned and took flight for his equipment.

"That tears it," he heard Parkhurst say. "Get your gear on."

Ward pounded into the clearing and nearly got shot by Denison's guards for his trouble.

"What the hell is wrong with you?" Theisiger demanded as he stepped in front of the guard's raised coil gun.

"It's Parkhurst," Ward panted. "He's turned on us!"

"Shit, I knew it!" Theisiger said. He sprinted for his armor as Ward opened the carapace to his. Ward slipped inside, clothes and all.

He breathed a sigh of relief. He recalled that prior to his jaunt with the Freemen he could barely fit inside naked, much less clothed. He closed the catches and stood. His arms twitched and jerked as the fabric brushed the sensors. He slapped his helmet on as Theisiger stood up.

"This is Carlo," Ward heard on his suit all-call. "Parkhurst's men are on the rampage. Anybody in armor who can, follow my transponder to the field." He turned to Ward. "Most of our people are out of position. This may be tough. At least the Terrans're out of rockets." Carlo looked at Denison. "Are you in?"

Ward turned towards the field as a pair of Terrans burst through the underbrush, followed by two more. Theisiger whirled into action, moving faster than Ward believed possible. He blurred in Ward's infrared as he jumped between them. Both Terrans turned inward. Their fire discipline was too good to shoot their fellows.

Carlo used the seconds gleaned from their hesitation to whip to the right and hose one with his coil gun. He precisely tapped each knee with a long stream, then cut through the Terran's faceplate, all in a matter of seconds.

The second trooper paused long enough for Ward to leap forward. He waited the few moments needed for an AI solution, then poured fire into the Terran's flank, literally blowing him away. Ward heard a clatter over his right shoulder. He whipped his head around and saw Denison's guard team engage the remaining pair. Denison remained aloof, his own coil gun raised.

Ward stared at him. Denison pointed the weapon towards Ward and fired. Ward looked down, expecting to be hit. He heard instead a body tumble behind him. He turned and saw the Terran falling away, his faceplate pierced by a half-dozen airfoils. Ward stared at Denison.

"Never," Sam said quietly, "leave an enemy behind you."

Ward tried to push his heart out of his throat enough to answer, then looked at Carlo. Theisiger had whipped his coil gun around and used it to place precise bursts into each of the corpses, double-tapping them for security. Denison's guards ranged the second pair, trading shots as the Terrans withdrew to avoid being flanked. Ward watched Tawn take one in the legs with a high deflection shot, then chew through the carapace as the Terran fell. Denison tipped his head towards the fight. "Your friend is good," he said.

"Yeah," Ward answered, "I didn't realize how good."

Denison nodded. "Tawn's no slouch, either."

Denison's guard seemed to realize Theisiger waited, poised to move to the remaining Terran's flank. She stepped to one side, maneuvering Parkhurst's man towards Carlo. The Terran raised his coil gun. Tawn thwarted him with deft shots that spoiled the Earther's aim and caused him to sidestep. Carlo sighted carefully and fired a single shot. The Terran froze, then slowly crumpled. Ward saw the single hole in the Terran's faceplate as the body rolled onto its side.

"Damn," Tawn said, "that was *good*."

Theisiger and Tawn shared a look then sprinted towards the sound of coilers ripsawing in the middle-distance. The two guards were already several steps ahead. Ward fell in behind them, noticing for the first time the screams and shouts as Parkhurst's remaining squadees tore into the mercenaries and retainers.

Ward's little group burst Parkhurst's bivouac site, only to find them gone.

Denison turned to Carlo. A stream of incoming fire heralded a single Terran, backstepping away from the clearing. "Enough already." Denison raised his coil gun. Theisiger nodded and followed suit, quickly joined by the two guards and Ward. They fired as one, cutting the Terran down.

More screams and shouts ripped the night, followed by the chatter of coil guns. They sprinted towards the sounds of combat, clearing the stream in boost-assisted leaps and running flat out for the main site. They passed a trail of bodies, some armored, some not. Many of the dead wore little more than towels.

"Bastards," Ward swore grimly. Lasers and coil guns fired close ahead. Ward burst into the clearing just as a pair of Parkhurst's troops cut down another retainer. Five other bodies lay around the clearing, three killed in the process of getting into their armor.

He shouted and keyed his coiler, pouring a stream of rings into one Terran. Carlo quickly joined him, adding his own fire. The Terrans broke, fleeing through the trees. Ward took up the pursuit, then almost had his neck broken as Carlo planted his feet and held him back. "No!" the duelist yelled in his ear. "You go after them and you're asking to be ambushed. Follow me!" He took off at an angle to the Terrans, firing his boost-pack to augment his sprinting speed. Ward followed. They crashed through the brush, startling the Terrans who lurked, watching their back trail.

They reacted a moment faster, shattering the tree next to Ward as he dove for cover.

"Denison," Carlo yelled, "are you out there?"

"Yeah," he answered, "what can I do you for you?"

Carlo cranked off a laser shot, his blue-green beam slicing through the night. He ducked as another volley of rings cut close overhead.

"Did you see where I shot?" he called to Denison.

"Yeah," Sam returned.

"I've got two hiding there!" Carlo yelled.

"We got 'em!" Sam answered.

"Aren't you worried about them hearing you?" Ward asked as he climbed up on his haunches to squeeze off a few shots.

"What does it matter?" Carlo answered. "They know where we are as soon as we fire and they know where Denison is. What's the big secret?"

Denison's trio opened up from an oblique. The pressure on the Terrans became too intense and they broke. The massed fire brought one down. Tawn stepped over and coolly shot the writhing Terran through the faceplate.

They resumed the chase, pursuing the remaining troops into a tree line.

"Look," shouted Ward, "there's Parkhurst!" He pointed to a small copse where the Terran leader and his two surviving troops stood over three Tuchman bodies. Ward glanced around and saw that most of his retainers were still out of range.

"The supply vehicle is through those trees. They can escape if they make that!" Theisiger shouted.

"I'm not sure that they want to escape," Denison said as he stepped over to them. He pointed as Parkhurst moved tangent to his escape route. A single mercenary burst from hiding and fled, unarmored, through the trees. Ward Denison, Carlo, and the guards watched as the Terran cut the mercenary down.

"That's enough!" Ward said, stalking toward Parkhurst.

The Terran saw him coming. He turned. "You've only got me five to four," he sallied. "You'll have to do better than that." He held up a box. "Not that it matters."

Ward continued to stump towards him, his weapons rising as he drew a bead. Parkhurst pointed the box at Ward and pressed a button. Nothing happened. He looked at the box a moment, pointed it again, and mashed the button.

"If that's related to those chips you gave us, we already clipped the pins," Ward warned him.

Parkhurst tossed the box over his shoulder. "Well, that was inconvenient." He stepped into a fighting crouch. "Who's going to fight me first?"

Theisiger stepped forward. "Me!"

"No, Carlo," Ward replied grimly, "I don't plan to give him the pleasure." He turned to the small group and saw the Tuchman retainers trickling in. "Execute him." Five coil guns rose and spoke as one. When they were silent, Parkhurst lay still. Ward turned to the remaining Terrans and pointed. The coilers spoke again. Carlo walked amongst the fallen, placing a single laser bolt into each as insurance.

Ward stood for long time, looking at the dead. "Sam, this must end." Denison thought Ward looked sad in the predawn light. Ward looked up at him. "Wing did what they did, but they were led to it. The Terrans, the Hegemony, set Wing up. They set us up, too." He pointed to a dead, still smoking, Terran. "All this time, we've been fighting each other, and *they* were the real enemy." He shook his head. "Seladra had the right of it. She figured it out, but I wouldn't listen." He looked abruptly at Stallart's cottage. "Wing's still up there, still trapped."

He looked at Denison. "I think a truce is in order. Will you help?"

"Yes," Denison said at once, "and the sooner the better."

Ward laid down and began to open his armor.

Denison looked down at him. "Have you lost some weight?"

"Yeah," Ward answered, "diet by trauma. I don't recommend it. It involves Freemen."

Denison looked confused. "Are you ready?"

Ward adjusted his coverall. "I think so."

They walked together towards Stallart's cottage. Ward passed the shattered cistern, the burned-out barn, and the path he and Denison had once walked down together. The memories threatened to overwhelm him.

Tuchman retainers and mercenaries drifted in the wake of the little procession. Ward saw Mona attach herself to his flank, her eyes hard. Ward glanced down at her and saw she didn't appear to be armed. He breathed a silent sigh of relief.

They stepped up to the cottage as the first rays of the morning sun peeked over the horizon.

"Ho, Wing," Ward called out formally. "I've come to parlay. I'm not armed. Denison's agreed to mediate. Come out and we'll talk."

He waited several minutes before the door opened a crack, then wider. Seladra stepped out first, her hair askew and her helmet under one arm. She looked wild and desperate. "You'll guarantee our safety?" she asked Ward.

"I'll guarantee it," Denison injected.

She looked first at Ward, then at Sam. "All right," she said heavily. She led the thin procession out of Stallart's house. Several had been injured and were visibly suffering. Ward felt Mona stiffen beside him. He ignored her, fixing his gaze on Seladra.

"You were right," he said, "it *was* the Hegemony. They

set us against each other, like animals, and watched us fight. I only found the proof tonight." He grinned wryly. "I'm sure you heard the aftermath."

She looked up, her eyes full of pain. "It's too late. Tuchman is gone, killed by us. Wing is gone, killed by you. Neither of us is in fit shape to do anything against anyone."

"That's true," he replied, "neither of us by ourselves. But together, if we unite, we can rebuild." He looked at Denison. "I understand now."

Seladra stared hard at Ward. "I don't. What are you saying?"

Ward shrugged heavily. "I'm saying that to unify the clans, we go back to plan A. We get married."

Seladra looked stunned. "After all that's happened?"

"Yes," Ward answered, "the last time we were, umm, together, you told me about your duty. It took precedence over everything else. I see mine clearly now. The Hegemony *is* a threat. My duty to the Centauri colonies is to rebuild my clan." He gave her a thoughtful look. "*Our* clan."

Seladra quirked the corner of her mouth up in what might charitably have been called a smile. "Well, I suppose . . ."

"*No!*" Mona shouted. She stormed forward into the space between Ward and Seladra. Denison, startled, recoiled away. She stabbed a finger at Ward. "It's not that easy. You can't just smooth over murder, not like that!" She stabbed her finger at the mound next to the house. "That's where we buried my husband!"

Selandra held her hands out. "Please, Ward," she said imploringly.

Mona turned her gaze to Seladra, who recoiled from the naked hate. Mona snarled, an almost animal noise, "And as for you . . ."

She lifted her shirt. Ward saw the black HEAP pistol tucked into her waistband. He jumped, knowing he was already too late. She whipped the gun out and fired it into Seladra at point-blank range.

"Nooo!" Ward and Seladra screamed together as the shaped charge burst against her midriff. The plasma lanced through her, cutting her almost in half. She crumpled silently to the ground. The crowd stood stunned. Ward fell to his knees. "No," he wailed.

Mona held the smoking pistol up and walked over to the grave. She dropped the pistol amongst the flowers that were just unfolding as they were kissed by the first morning light.

"That was for my husband," she said in a voice like ashes.